W0013723

OMNIBUS:

Fast One
Seven Slayers

-BY-

Paul Cain

RESURRECTIONARY PRESS
2006

***

Resurrectionary Press LLC

http://www.resurrectionarypress.com

***

***

Resurrectionary Press says:

"From hell's hot I stabbeth thee."

Fast One

(1933)

Chapter One

KELLS WALKED NORTH on Spring. At Fifth he turned west, walked two blocks, turned into a small cigar store. He nodded to the squat bald man behind the counter and went on through the ground-glass-paneled door into a large and bare back room.

The man sitting at a wide desk stood up, said, "Hello," heartily, went to another door and opened it, said: "Walk right in."

Kells went into a very small room, partitioned off from the other by ground-glass-paneled walls. He sat down on a worn davenport against one wall, leaned back, folded his hands over his stomach, and looked at Jack Rose.

Rose sat behind a round green-topped table, his elbows on the table, his long chin propped upon one hand. He was a dark, almost too handsome young man who had started life as Jake Rosencrancz, of Brooklyn and Queens. He said: "Did you ever hear the story about the three bears?"

Kells nodded. He sat regarding Rose gravely and nodded his head slowly up and down.

Rose was smiling. "I thought you'd have heard that one." He moved the fingers of one hand down to his ear and pulled violently at the lobe. "Now you tell one. Tell me the one about why you've got such a load on Kiosque in the fourth race."

Kells smiled faintly, dreamily. He said: "You don't think

I'd have an inside that you'd overlooked, do you, Jakie?" He got up, stretched extravagantly and walked across the room to inspect a large map of Los Angeles County on the far wall.

Rose didn't change his position, he sat staring vacantly at the davenport. "I can throw it to Bolero."

Kells strolled back, stood beside the table. He looked at a small watch on the inside of his left wrist, said: "You might get a wire to the track, Jakie, but you couldn't reach your Eastern connections in time." He smiled with gentle irony. "Anyway, you've got the smartest book on the Coast—the smartest book west of the Mississippi, by God! You wouldn't want to take any chances with that big Beverly Hills clientele, would you?"

He turned and walked back to the davenport, sank wearily down and again folded his hands over his stomach. "What's it all about? I pick two juicy winners in a row and you squawk. What the hell do you care how many I pick?—the Syndicate's out, not you."

He slid sideways on the davenport until his head reached the armrest, pulled one long leg up to plant his foot on the seat and sprawled the other across the floor. He intently regarded a noisily spinning electric fan on a shelf in one corner. "You didn't get me out in this heat to talk about horses."

Rose wore a lightweight black felt hat. He pushed it back over his high bronzed forehead, took a cigarette out of a thin case on the table and lighted it. He said: "I'm going to reopen the Joanna D.—Doc Haardt and I are going to run it together—his boat, my bankroll."

Kells said: "Uh huh." He stared steadily at the electric fan, without movement or change of expression.

Rose cleared his throat, went on: "The Joanna used to be the only gambling barge on the Coast, but Fay moved in with the Eaglet, and then Max Hesse promoted a two-hundred-and-fifty-foot yacht and took the play away from both of them." Rose paused to remove a fleck of cigarette paper from his lower lip. "About three months ago, Fay and Doc got together and chased Hesse. According to the story, one of the players left a box of candy on the Monte Carlo—that's Hesse's boat—and along about two in the morning it exploded. No one was hurt much, but it threw an awful scare into the customers and something was said about it being a bigger and better box next time, so Hesse took a powder up the coast. But maybe you've heard all this before."

Kells looked at the fan, smiled slowly. He said: "Well—I heard it a little differently."

"You would." Rose mashed his cigarette out, went on: "Everything was okay for a couple weeks. The Joanna and Fay's boat were anchored about four miles apart, and their launches were running to the same wharf; but they both had men at the gangways frisking everyone who went aboard—that wasn't so good for business. Then somebody got past the protection on the Joanna and left another ticker. It damn near blew her in two; they beached, finally got into dry dock."

Kells said: "Uh huh."

"Tonight she goes out." Rose took another cigarette from the thin case and rolled it gently between his hand and the green baize of the table.

Kells said: "What am I supposed to do about it?"

Rose pulled the loose tobacco out of one end of the cigaret, licked the paper. "Have you got a match?"

Kells shook his head slowly.

Rose said: "Tell Fay to lay off."

Kells laughed—a long, high-pitched, sarcastic laugh. "Ask him to lay off."

"Run your own errands, Jakie," Kells swung up to sit, facing Rose. "For a young fella that's supposed to be bright," he said, "you have some pretty dumb ideas."

"You're a friend of Fay's."

"Sure," Kells nodded elaborately. "Sure, I'm everybody's friend. I'm the guy they write the pal songs about." He stood up. "Is that all, Jakie?"

Rose said: "Come on out to the Joanna tonight."

Kells grinned. "Cut it out. You know damn well I'd never buck a house. I'm not a gambler, anyway—I'm a playboy. Stop by the hotel sometime and look at my cups."

"I mean come and look the layout over." Rose stood up and smiled carefully. "I've put in five new wheels and–"

"I've seen a wheel," Kells said. "Make mine strawberry." He turned, started toward the door.

Rose said: "I'll give you a five-percent cut."

Kells stopped, turned slowly, and came back to the table. "Cut on what?"

"The whole take, from now on."

"What for?"

"Showing three or four times a week.... Restoring confidence."

Kells was watching him steadily. "Whose confidence, in what?"

"Aw, nuts. Let's stop this god-damned foolishness and do some business." Rose sat down, found a paper of matches and lighted his limp cigarette. "You're supposed to be a good friend of Fay's. Whether you are or not is none of my business. The point is that everyone thinks you are, and if you show on the boat once in a while it will look like everything is under control, like Fay and I have made a deal; see?"

Kells nodded. "Why don't you make a deal?"

"I've been trying to reach Fay for a week." Rose tugged at the lobe of his ear. "Hell! This coast is big enough for all of us; but he won't see it. He's sore. He thinks everybody's trying to frame him."

"Everybody probably is." Kells put one hand on the table and leaned over to smile down at Rose. "Now I'll tell you one, Jakie. You'd like to have me on the Joanna because I look like the highest-powered protection at this end of the country. You'd like to carry that eighteen-carat reputation of mine around with you so you could wave it and scare all the bad little boys away."

Rose said: "All right, all right."

The phone on the table buzzed. Rose picked up the receiver, said "Yes" three times into the mouthpiece, then "All right, dear," hung up.

Kells went on: "Listen, Jakie. I don't want any part of it. I always got along pretty well by myself, and I'll keep on getting along pretty well by myself. Anyway, I wouldn't show in a deal with Doc Haardt if he was sleeping with the mayor—I hate his guts, and I'd pine away if I didn't think he hated mine."

Rose made a meaningless gesture.

Kells had straightened up. He was examining the nail of his index-finger. "I came out here a few months ago with two grand and I've given it a pretty good ride. I've got a nice little joint at the Ambassador, with a built-in bar; I've got a swell bunch of telephone numbers and several thousand friends in the bank. It's a lot more fun guessing the name of a pony than guessing what the name of the next stranger I'm supposed to have shot will be. I'm having a lot of fun. I don't want any part of anything."

Rose stood up. "Okay."

Kells said: "So long, Jakie." He turned and went through the door, out through the large room, through the cigar store to the street. He walked up to Seventh and got into a cab. When they passed the big clock on the Dyas corner it was twenty minutes past three.

* * * * *

THE DESK CLERK gave Kells several letters, and a message: Mr. Dave Perry called at 2:35, and again at 3:25. Asked that you call him or come to his home. Important.

Kells went to his room and put in a call to Perry. He mixed a drink and read the letters while a telephone operator called him twice to say the line was busy. When she called again, he said, "Let it go," went down and got into another cab. He told the driver: "Corner of Cherokee and Hollywood Boulevard."

Perry lived in a kind of penthouse on top of the Virginia Apartments. Kells climbed the narrow stair to the roof, knocked at the unsheathed fire door; he knocked again, then turned the knob, pushed the door open.

The room filled with crashing sound. Kells dropped on one knee, just inside, slammed the door shut. A strip of sunlight came in through two tall windows and yellowed the rug. Doc Haardt was lying on his back, half in, half out of the strip of sun. There was a round bluish mark on one side of his-throat, and, as Kells watched, it grew larger, red.

Ruth Perry sat on a low couch against one wall and looked at Haardt's body. A door slammed some place toward the back of the house. Kells got up and turned the key in the door through which he had entered, crossed quickly and stood above the body.

Haardt had been a big loose-joweled Dutchman with a mouthful of gold. His dead face looked as if he were about to drawl: "Well... I'll tell you ..." A small automatic lay on the floor near his feet.

Ruth Perry stood up and started to scream. Kells put one hand on the back of her neck, the other over her mouth. She took a step forward, put her arms around his body. She looked up at him and he took his hand away from her mouth.

"Darling! I thought he was going to get you." She spoke very rapidly. Her face was twisted with fear. "He was here an hour. He made Dave call you...."

Kells patted her cheek. "Who, baby?"

"I don't know." She was coming around. "A nance. A little guy with glasses."

Kells inclined his head toward Haardt's body, asked: "What about Doc?"

"He came up about two-thirty.... Said he had to see you and didn't want to go to the hotel. Dave called you and left word. Then about an hour ago that little son of a bitch walked in and told us all to sit down on the floor...."

Someone pounded heavily on the door.

They tiptoed across to a small, curtained archway that led to the dining room. Just inside the archway Dave Perry lay on his stomach.

Ruth Perry said: "The little guy slugged Dave when he made a pass for the phone, after he called you. He came to, a while ago, and the little guy let him have it again. What a boy!"

Someone pounded on the door again and the sound of loud voices came through faintly.

Kells said: "I'm a cinch for this one if they find me here. That's what the plant was for." He nodded toward the door. "Can they get around to the kitchen?"

"Not unless they go down and come up the fire escape. That's the way our boy friend went."

"I'll go the other way." Kells went swiftly to Haardt's body, knelt and pick up the automatic. "I'll take this along to make your story good. Stick to it, except the calls to me and the reason Doc was here."

Ruth Perry nodded. Her eyes were shiny with excitement.

Kells said: "I'll see what I can get on the pansy—and try to talk a little sense to the telephone girl at the hotel and the cab driver that hauled me here."

The pounding on the door was almost continuous. Someone put a heavy shoulder to it, the hinges creaked.

Kells started toward the bedroom, then turned and came back. She tilted her mouth up to him and he kissed her. "Don't let this lug husband of yours talk," he said—jerked his head down at Dave Perry—"and maybe you'd better go into a swoon to alibi not answering the door. Let 'em bust it in."

"My God, Gerry! I'm too excited to faint."

Kells kissed her again, lightly. He brought one arm up stiffly, swiftly from his side; the palm down, the fist loosely clinched. His knuckles smacked sharply against her chin. He caught her body in his arms, went into the living room and laid her gently on the floor. Then he took out his handkerchief, carefully wiped the little automatic, and put it on the floor midway between Haardt, Perry and Ruth Perry.

He went into the bedroom and into the adjoining bathroom. He raised the window and squeezed through to a narrow ledge. He was screened from the street by part of the building next door, and from the alley by a tree that spread over the back yard of the apartment house. A few feet along the ledge he felt with his foot for a steel rung, found it, swung down to the next, across a short space to the sill of an open corridor-window of the next-door building.

He walked down the corridor, down several flights of stairs and out a rear door of the building. Down a kind of alley he went through a wooden gate into a bungalow court and through to Whitley and walked north.

* * * * *

CULLEN'S HOUSE WAS on the northeastern slope of Whitley Heights, a little way off Cahuenga. He answered the fourth ring, stood in the doorway blinking at Kells. "Well, stranger. Long time no see."

Cullen was a heavily built man of about forty-five. He had a round pale face, a blue chin and blue-black hair. He was naked except for a pair of yellow silk pajama-trousers; a full-rigged ship was elaborately tattooed across his wide chest.

Kells said: "H'are ya, Willie," went past Cullen into the room. He sat down in a deep leather chair, took off his Panama hat and ran his fingers through red, faintly graying hair.

Cullen went into the kitchen and came back with tall glasses, a bowl of ice and a squat bottle.

Kells said: "Well, Willie–"

Cullen held up his hand. "Wait. Don't tell me. Make me guess." He closed his eyes, went through the motions of mystic communion, then opened his eyes, sat down and poured two drinks. "You're in another jam," he said.

Kells twisted his mouth into a wholly mirthless smile, nodded. "You're a genius, Willie." He' sipped his drink, leaned back.

Cullen sat down.

Kells said: "You know Max Hesse pretty well. You've been out to his house in Flintridge."

"Sure."

"Do you know what Dave Perry looks like?"

"No."

Kells put his glass down. "A little patent-leather, pop-eyed guy with a waxed mustache. Wears gray silk shirts with tricky brocaded stripes. Used to run a string of trucks down from Frisco—had some kind of warehouse connection up there. Stood a bad rap on some forged Liberty Bonds about a year ago and went broke beating it. Married Grant Fay's sister when he was on top."

"I've seen her," Cullen said. "Nice dish."

"You've never seen Dave at Hesse's?"

Cullen shook his head. "I don't think so."

"All right. It wouldn't mean a hell of a lot, anyway." Kells picked up his glass, drained it, stood up. "I want to use the phone."

He dialed a number printed in large letters on the cover of the telephone book, asked for the Reporters' Room. When the connection was made, he asked for Shep Beery, spoke evenly into the instrument: "Listen, Shep, this is Gerry. In a little while you'll probably have some news for me.... Yeah.... Call Granite six five one six.... And Shep—who copped in the fourth race at Juana?... Thanks, Shep. Got the number?... OK."

Cullen was pouring drinks. "If all this is as bad as you're making it look—you have a very trusting nature," he observed.

Kells was dialing another number. He said, over his shoulder: "I win twenty-four hundred on Kiosque."

"That's fine."

"Perry shot Doc Haardt to death about four o'clock."

"That's fine. Where were you?" Cullen was stirring his drink.

Kells jiggled the hook up and down. "Goddamn telephones," he said. He dialed the number again, then turned his head to smile at Cullen. "I was here."

The telephone clicked. Kells turned to it, asked: "Is Number Four on duty?" There was a momentary wait, then: "Hello, Stella? This is Mister Kells... Listen, Stella, there weren't any calls for me between two and four today.... I know it's on the record, baby, but I want it off. Will you see what you can do about it?... Right away?... That's fine. And Stella, the number I called about three-thirty—the one where the line was busy... Yes. That was Granite six five one six.... Got it? ... All right, kid, I'll tell you all about it later. 'Bye."

Cullen said: "As I was saying—you have a very trusting nature."

Kells was riffling the pages of a small blue address book. "One more," he said, mostly to himself. He spun the dial again. "Hello—Yellow? Ambassador stand, please.... Hello. Is Fifty-eight in?... That's the little bald-headed Mick, isn't it?... No, no: Mick.... Sure... Send him to two eight nine Iris Circle when he gets in.... Two... eight... nine ... That's in Hollywood; off Cahuenga...."

They sat for several minutes without speaking. Kells sipped at his drink and stared out of the window. Then he said: "I'm not putting on an act for you, Willie. I don't know how to tell it; it doesn't make much sense, yet." He smiled lazily at Cullen. "Are you good at riddles?"

"Terrible."

The phone rang. Cullen got up to answer it. Kells said: "Maybe that's the answer." Cullen called him to the phone. He said, "Yes, Shep," and was silent a little while. Then he said, "Thanks," hung up and went back to the deep leather chair. "I guess maybe we can't play it the way I'd figured," he said.

"There's a tag out for me." Cullen said slowly, sarcastically: "My pal! They'll trace the phony call that your girl friend Stella's handling, or get to the cab driver before he gets to you. We'll have a couple carloads of law here in about fifteen minutes."

"That's all right, Willie. You can talk to 'em."

Cullen grinned mirthlessly. "I haven't spoken to a copper for four years."

Kells straightened in his chair. "Listen. Doc went to Perry's to see me.... What for? I was with Jack Rose being propositioned to come in with him and Doc, on the Joanna. They're evidently figuring Fay or Hesse to make things tough and wanted me for a flash." He looked at his watch. Cullen was stirring ice into another drink.

Kells went on, swiftly: "When I open the door at Perry's, somebody lets Doc have it and goes out through the kitchen. Maybe. The back door slammed but it might have been the draft when I opened the front door. Dave is cold with an egg over his ear and Ruth Perry says that a little queen with glasses shot Doc and sapped Dave when he spoke out of turn...."

Cullen said: "You're not making this up as you go along, are you?"

Kells paid no attention to Cullen's interruption. "The rod is on the floor. I tell Ruth to stick to her story... Cullen raised one eyebrow, smiled faintly with his lips. Kells said: "She will," went on: "... and try to keep Dave quiet while I figure an alibi, try to find out what it's all about. I smack her to make it look good and then I get the bright idea that if I leave the gun there they'll hold both of them, no matter what story they tell. They'd have to hold somebody; Doc had a lot of friends downtown."

Kells finished his drink, picked up his hat and put it on. "I figured Ruth to office Dave that I was working on it and that he might keep his mouth shut if he wasn't in on the plant." Cullen sighed heavily.

Kells said: "He was. Shep tells me that Dave says I had an argument with Doc, shot him, and clipped Dave when he tried to stop me. Shep can't get a line on Ruth's story, but I'll lay six, two, and even that she's still telling the one about the little guy." He stood up. "They're both being held incommunicado. And here's one for the book: Reilly made the pinch. Now what the hell was Reilly doing out here if it wasn't tipped?"

Cullen said: "It's a set-up. It was the girl." Kells shook his head slowly. "Dave knows it and is trying to cover for her," Cullen went on. "She told you a fast one about the little guy and I'll bet she's telling the same story as Dave right now."

"Wrong."

Cullen laughed. "If you didn't think it was possible you wouldn't look that way."

"You're crazy. If she wanted to frame me she wouldn't've put on that act. She wouldn't've..."

"Oh, yes, she would. She'd let you go and put the finger on you from a distance." Cullen scratched his side, under the arm, yawned.

Kells said: "What about Dave?"

"Maybe Doc socked Dave."

"She'd cheer."

"Maybe." Cullen got up and walked to a window. "Maybe she cheered and squeezed the heater at the same time. That's been done, you know."

Kells shook his head. "I don't see it," he said. "There are too many other angles."

"You wouldn't see it." Cullen turned from the window, grinned. "You don't know anything about feminine psychology–"

Kells said: "I invented it."

Cullen spread his mouth into a wide thin line, nodded ponderously. "Sure," he said, "there are a lot of boys sitting up in Quentin counting their fingers who invented it too." He walked to the stair and back. "Anyway, you had a pretty good hunch when you left Exhibit A on the floor."

"I'm superstitious. I haven't carried a gun for over a year," Kells smiled a little.

Cullen said: "Another angle—she's Fay's sister."

"That's swell, but it doesn't mean anything."

"It might." Cullen yawned again extravagantly, scratched his arms.

Kells asked: "Yen?"

"Uh huh. I was about to cook up a couple loads when you busted in with all this heavy drama." Cullen jerked his head toward the stair. "Eileen is upstairs."

Kells said: "I thought the last cure took."

"Sure. It took." Cullen smiled sleepily. "Like the other nine. I'm down to two, three pipes each other day."

They looked at one another expressionlessly for a little while.

A car chugged up the short curving slope below the front door, stopped. Kells turned and went into the semidarkness of the kitchen. A buzzer whirred. Cullen went to the front door, opened it, said: "Come in." A little Irishman in the uniform of a cab driver came into the room and took off his hat. Cullen went back to the chair and sat down with his back to the room, picked up his drink.

The phone rang.

Kells came out of the kitchen and answered it. He stood for a while staring vacantly at the cab driver, then said, "Thanks, kid," hung up, put his hand in his pocket and took out a small neatly folded sheaf of bills. "When you brought me here from the hotel about four o'clock," he said, "I forgot to tip you." He peeled off two bills and held them toward the driver.

The little man came forward, took the bills and examined them. One was a hundred, the other a fifty. "Do I have to tell it in court?" he asked.

Kells smiled, shook his head. "You probably won't have to tell it anywhere."

The driver said: "Thank you very much, sir." He went to the door and put on his hat.

Kells said: "Wait a minute." He spoke to Cullen: "Can I use your heap, Willie?"

Cullen nodded without enthusiasm, without turning his head.

Kells turned to the driver. "All right, Paddy. You'd better stall for an hour or so. Then if anyone asks you anything, you can tell 'em you picked me up here—on this last trip—and hauled me down to Malibu. No house number—just the gas station, or something."

The driver said, "Right," went out.

"Our high-pressure police department finally got around to Stella." Kells went back to his chair, sat down on the edge of it and grinned cheerfully at Cullen. "How much cash have you got, Willie?" Cullen gazed tragically at the ceiling.

"It was too late to catch the bank," Kells went on, "and it's a cinch I can't get within a mile of it in the morning. They'll have it loaded."

"I get a break. I've only got about thirty dollars."

Kells laughed. "You'd better keep that for cigarets. I've got to square this thing pronto and it'll probably take better than change—or maybe I'll take a little trip." He got up, walked across the room and studied his long white face in a mirror. He leaned forward, rubbed two fingers of one hand lightly over his chin. "I wonder if I'd like Mexico."

Cullen didn't say anything.

Kells turned from the mirror. "I guess I'll have to take a chance on reaching Rose and picking up my twenty-four Cs."

Cullen said: "That'll be a lot of fun."

* * * * *

THE FIRST STREET lights and electric signs were being turned on when Kells parked on Fourth Street between Broadway and Hill. He walked up Hill to Fifth, turned into a corner building, climbed stairs to the third floor and walked down the corridor to a window on the Fifth Street side. He stood there for several minutes intently watching the passersby on the sidewalk across the street. Then he went back to the car.

As he pressed the starter, a young chubby-faced patrolman came across the street and put one foot on the running board, one hand on top of the door. "Don't you know you can't park here between four and six?" he said.

Kells glanced at his watch. It was five thirty-five. He said: "No. I'm a stranger here."

"Let's see your driver's license."

Kells smiled, said evenly: "I haven't got it with me."

The patrolman shook his head sadly. "Where you from?" he asked.

"San Francisco."

"You're in the big city now, buddy." The patrolman sneered at Kells, the car, the sky. He seemed lost in thought for a half-minute, then he said: "All right. Now you know."

Kells drove up Fourth to the top of the hill. His eyes were half closed and there was an almost tender expression on his face. He swore softly, continuously, obscenely. His anger had worn itself out by the time he had parked the car on Grand and walked down the steep hill to the rear entrance of the Biltmore. He got off the elevator at the ninth floor, walked past the questioning stare of the woman at the key desk, down a long hall, knocked at the door of Suite 9D.

Rose opened the door. He stood silently, motionlessly for perhaps five seconds, then he ran his tongue over his lower lip and said: "Come in."

Kells went into the room.

A husky, pale-eyed young man was straddling a small chair, his elbows on the back of it, his chin between his hands. His sand-colored hair was carefully combed down over one side of his forehead. His mouth hung a little open and he breathed through it regularly, audibly.

Rose said: "This is Mister O'Donnell of Kansas City... Mister Kells."

The young man stood up, still straddling the chair, held out a pink hand. "Glad t' know you."

Kells shook his hand cursorily, said: "I stopped by for my dough."

"Sure." Rose went to a cabinet and took out a bottle of whiskey and three glasses. "Why didn't you pick it up at the store?"

Kells walked across the room and sat down on the arm of a big, heavily upholstered chair. O'Donnell was in his shirtsleeves. O'Donnell's coat was lying across a table, back and a little to one side of Kells.

Kells said: "I want it in cash,"

Rose put the bottle and glasses down on a wide central table.

"I haven't got any cash here," he said, "we'll have to go over to the store." He went toward the telephone on a desk against one wall. "I'll order some White Rock."

Kells said: "No."

Rose stopped, turned—he was smiling. O'Donnell unstraddled the chair and sauntered in Kells's general direction. His pale eyes were fixed blankly on Kells's stomach. Kells stood up very straight, took two long swift sidewise steps and grabbed O'Donnell's coat. The automatic in a shoulder holster which had been under the coat clattered to the floor. O'Donnell dived for it and Kells stamped hard on his fingers, brought his right knee up hard into O'Donnell's face. O'Donnell grunted, lost his balance and fell over backward; he rolled back and forth silently, holding both hands over his nose.

Rose was standing by the central table, holding the whiskey bottle by the neck. He was still smiling as if that expression had hardened, congealed on his face.

Kells stooped and scooped up the gun.

There was a wide double door at one side of the room, leading to a bedroom, and beyond, directly across the bedroom, there was another door leading to a bath. It opened and a very blonde woman stuck her head out. She called: "What's the matter, Jack?"

Kells could see her reflected indistinctly in one of the

mirrors of the wide double door. He and O'Donnell were out of her line of vision.

Rose said: "Nothing, honey." He tipped the bottle, poured a drink.

"Is Lou here yet?" She raised her voice above the sound of water running in the tub.

"No."

The blonde woman closed the door. O'Donnell sat up and took out a handkerchief and held it over his nose.

Kells said: "Now..."

Rose shook his head slowly. "I've got about a hundred an' ten."

Kells rubbed the corner of one of his eyes with his middle finger. He said: "All right, Jakie. I want you to call the shop, and I want you to say 'Hello, Frank?'—and if it isn't Frank I want you to wait till Frank comes to the phone, and then I want you to say 'Bring three thousand dollars over to the hotel right away.' Then I want you to hang up."

Rose picked up the glass and drank. "There isn't more than four hundred dollars at the store," he said. "It's all down on the Joanna —for the opening."

Kells looked at him thoughtfully for a little while. "All right. Get your hat."

Rose hesitated a moment, looked down at O'Donnell, then walked over to a chair near the bedroom door and picked up his hat.

Kells said: "Now, Jakie, back into the bedroom." Kells transferred the automatic to his left hand, took hold the back of O'Donnell's collar with his right, said, "Pardon me, Mister O'Donnell."

He dragged O'Donnell across the floor to the bedroom door—keeping Rose in front of him—across the bedroom floor to the bathroom. He opened the bathroom door, jerked O'Donnell to his feet and shoved him inside. The blonde woman in the tub screamed once. Then Kells took the key from the inside of the door, slammed the door, cutting the sound of her second scream to a thin cry, locked it.

Rose was standing at the foot of one of the twin beds. The dark skin was drawn very tightly over his jaw muscles. He looked very sick.

Kells put the key in his pocket. He grinned, said: "Come on."

They walked together to the outer door of the suite. Kells lifted one point of his vest, stuck the automatic inside the waistband of his trousers. He let his belt out a notch or so until the gun nestled as comfortably and as securely as possible beneath his ribs, then pulled the point of his vest down over the butt. It made only a slight bulge against the narrowness of his waist.

He said: "Jakie, have you any idea how fast I can get it out and how well I can use it?"

Rose didn't say anything. He ran the fingers of one hand down over the left side of his face and looked at the floor.

Kells went on: "I've been framed for one caper today and I don't intend to be framed for another. The next one'll be bona fide—and I'd just as soon it'd be you, and I'd just as soon it'd be in the lobby of the Biltmore as any place else." He opened the door and switched out the light. "Let's go."

They went down in the elevator, out through the Galleria to Fifth Street and up the south side of the street to Grand, walked up the steep hill to the car.

Kells said: "You'd better drive, Jake. I haven't got a license."

Rose said he didn't have a license either.

* * * * *

ROSE DROVE. They went up Grand to Tenth, over Tenth to Main. When they turned into Main, headed south, Kells twisted around in the seat until he was almost facing

Rose. Kells's hands were lying idly in his lap. He said: "Who shot Doc?"

Rose turned his head for a second, smiled a little. "President Roosevelt."

Kells licked his lips. "Who shot Doc, Jakie?"

Rose kept his eyes straight ahead. He turned his long chin a fraction of an inch towards Kells, spoke gently, barely moving his mouth: "Perry and the DA and all the papers say you did. That's good enough for me."

Kells chuckled. He said: "Step on it. Your chum from Kansas City won't stay kicked up forever." He watched the needle of the speedometer quiver from twenty-five to thirty-five. "That'll do."

They went out Main to Slauson, east to Truck Boulevard, south.

Kells said: "You're a swell driver, Jakie—you should've stayed in the hack racket back in Brooklyn." He looked at the slowly darkening sky, went on, as if to himself: "There must be a very tricky inside on this play. The rake-off on all the boats together wouldn't be worth all his finaygling—shootings and pineapples and what have you." He turned slowly, soft-eyed toward Rose. "What's it all about?"

Rose was silent. He twisted his lips up at the corners. As they neared the P & O wharf where the Joanna motor launches tied up, Kells said: "You look a lot more comfortable now that you're getting near the home grounds. But remember, Jakie—one word out of turn, one wrong move, and you get it right in the belly. I'm just dippy enough to do it. I get mad when a goose tries to run out on me."

They left the car in a parking station, walked down the wharf. It was too early for customers. A few crap and blackjack dealers, waiters, one floor man whom Kells knew slightly were lounging about the small waiting room, waiting for the first boat to leave. They all stopped talking when Kells and Rose went into the waiting room.

The floor man said, "Hello, boss," to Rose, nodded to Kells.

Rose said: "Let's go."

The man who owned the launches came out of his little office. He said: "Mickey ain't here yet. He makes the first trip."

Rose looked away from him, said: "Take us out yourself." The man nodded doubtfully, locked the office door and went out toward the small float where the four boats that ran to the Joanna were tied up. The dealers and waiters got up and followed him. The floor man lagged behind. He acted as if he wanted to talk to Rose.

Kells took Rose's arm. "Let's go over here a minute, first," he said.

They crossed the wharf to where one of the Eaglet launches was moored at the foot of a short gangway. A big red-faced man was working on the engine.

Kells called to him: "Has Fay gone aboard yet?"

The man straightened up, nodded. "He went out about six o'clock."

Kells said: "You go out and tell Fay that Kells sent you. Tell him I'm going aboard the Joanna to collect some money. Tell him to send some of the boys with you, and you come back and circle around the Joanna until I hail you to pick me up. Got it?"

The red-faced man said: "Yes, sir—but we're expecting quite a crowd tonight—and one of the boats is out of commission...."

Kells said: "That's all right—one boat can handle the crowd. This is important." He grinned at Rose: "Isn't it, Jakie?"

Rose smiled with his mouth: his eyes were very cold and far-away.

The red-faced man said: "All right, Mister Kells." He spun the crank, and when the engine was running he put the big aluminum cover over it, cast off the lines and went to the wheel.

Kells and Rose went across the wharf and down onto the float and aboard the Joanna launch. A helper cast off the lines and the launch stood out through the narrows, down the bay.

Darkness came over the water swiftly.

They rounded the breakwater, headed toward a distant twinkling light. One of the dealers talked in a low voice to the man at the wheel; two of the waiters chattered to each other in Italian. The others were silent.

In the thirty-five or forty minutes that it took to clime up to the Joanna, the wind freshened and the launch slid up and down over the long smooth swells. The lights of the Joanna came out of the darkness through thin ribbons of fog.

Kells walked up the gangway a step behind and a little to the left of Rose. Several seamen and hangers-on stood at the rail, stared at them. They crossed the cabaret that had been built across the upper deck, went down a wide red-carpeted stairway to the principal gambling room. It ran the width and nearly the length of the ship. Dozens of green-covered tables lined the sides: Blackjack, chuck-a-luck, faro, roulette, craps. Two dealers were removing the canvas covers from one of the big roulette tables.

They turned at the bottom of the stairs and went aft to a white ath-warship bulkhead. There were three doors in the bulkhead; the middle one was ajar. They went in.

Swanstrom sat in a tilted swivel chair at a large roll-top desk. Swanstrom had been Doc Haardt's house manager; he was a very fat man with big brown eyes, a slow and eager smile. A black-and-white kitten was curled up on his lap.

The swivel chair creaked as he swung heavily forward and stood up. He put the kitten on the desk, said—:

"How are ya, Jack?"

Rose nodded abstractedly, cleared his throat. "This is Mister Kells.... Mister Swanstrom."

Swanstrom opened his mouth. He held out his hand toward Kells and looked at the door. Kells had stopped just inside the door; he half turned and closed it, pressed the little brass knob and the spring lock clicked. He stood looking at Rose, Swanstrom, the room.

There was a blue-shaded drop light hanging from the center of the overhead and another over the desk. There was a big old-fashioned safe against one wall, and beside it there was a short ladder leading up to a narrow shoulder-height platform that ran across all the forward bulkhead—the one through which they had entered. The bulkhead above the platform was lined with sheet iron and there was a two-inch slit running across it at about the height of a medium sized man's eyes. There were two .30-30 rifles on the platform, leaning against the bulkhead. There was another narrow door back of the desk.

Rose went to the desk and sat down, took a gray leather key case out of his pocket and unlocked one of the desk drawers. He slid the drawer open and took out a cigar box and opened it, took out a sheaf of hundred-dollar notes, slid the rubber band off onto two fingers and counted out twenty-four. He put the rest back in the box, the box back in the drawer, locked it. He counted the money again and held it out toward Kells. "Now, if you'll give me a receipt..." he said.

Kells took the money and tucked it into his inside breast pocket, said: "Sure. Write it out." His face was hard and expressionless.

Rose scribbled a few words on a piece of paper and went to the desk and leaned over and signed it.

Swanstrom was still standing in the middle of the room looking self-consciously at Kells, a meaningless smile curving his mouth. He said: "Well, I guess I better go up and see if everything's ready for the first load." Kells said: "We'll all go."

There was silence for a moment and then a new thin voice lisped: "Please lock your hands together back of your neck." Kells slowly turned his head and looked at the narrow white door behind the desk. It had been opened about three inches and the slim blue barrel of a heavy-caliber revolver was stuck through the opening. As he watched, the door swung open a little farther and he saw a little dark man standing in the dimness of the passageway. The little man was leaning against the side of the passageway and holding the revolver pointed at Kells's chest and smiling through thick-lensed glasses. Kells put his hands back of his neck.

Rose came around the desk and took the automatic out of Kells's belt, held it by the barrel and swung it swiftly back and then forward at Kells's head. Kells moved his hand enough to take most of the butt of the automatic on his knuckles, and bent his knees and grabbed Rose's arm. Then he fell backwards, pulled Rose down with him.

The little man came into the room quickly and kicked the side of Kells's head very hard. Kells relaxed his grip on Rose and Rose stood up, brushed himself off and went over and kicked Kells very carefully, drawing his foot back and aiming, and then kicking very accurately and hard.

The kitten jumped off the desk and went to Kells's bloody head and sniffed delicately. Kells could feel the kitten's warm breath. Then everything got dark and he couldn't feel anything any more.

Chapter Two

THERE WAS VERY dim yellow light coming from somewhere. There were voices. One was O'Donnell's voice but it was from too far off to make out the words. Then the voices went away.

Kells moved his shoulder an inch at a time and turned his head slowly. It felt as if it might fall in several pieces. He closed his eyes. The yellow light was coming through a partially-opened door at the other end of a long dark storeroom. Kells could dimly see cases piled along the sides. He could see a man pitting on one of the cases, silhouetted against the pale light.

The man stood up and came over and looked down at him. Kells closed his eyes and lay very still and the man walked back and sat down and put his elbows on his knees, his chin in his hands. There was thin jazz music coming from somewhere above; the man tapped his foot, in time.

Kells watched him for a long time; then the man got up and came over again and lighted a match and held it down near his face. He went away through the door and closed it behind him. In the moment that the door was open Kells saw that the room was very big, and rounded at the end opposite the door—following the line of the ship's stern. There were hundreds of cases piled along the sides. Then the door closed and it was dark.

Kells got up slowly, holding his head between his hands,

took out a handkerchief and tried to wipe some of the dried blood from his face. He went swiftly to the door, found it locked. He leaned against the bulkhead, and sharp buzzing hammers pounded inside his skull.

In a little while he heard the man coming back. He stood flat against the bulkhead just inside the door, and when the man came in Kells slid one arm around his neck and pulled it tight with his other hand. The man's curse was cut to a faint gurgle; they fell down and rolled across the deck. Kells kept his arm pressed tightly against the man's throat and after a time he stopped struggling, went limp. Kells lay panting beside him for a few minutes without releasing his hold and then, when he was sure that the man was unconscious, got up. He stooped and fumbled in the man's pockets, found a box of matches and a small woven-leather blackjack.

He went swiftly to the door, through to a narrow L-shaped room where unused chairs, stools, tables were stored. There was a hatchway with a steep-sloped stair leading down to another compartment. Kells went quietly down.

There was a paper-shaded light over the flat desk; there were two bunks. A man in overalls was snoring in one. There was a watertight door in one bulkhead and Kells went through it to a dark passageway that led forward along the ship's side. About thirty feet along the passageway he stepped on something soft, yielding; he lighted a match and held it down to the drained face of the little man who had said "Please lock your hands together back of your neck." There was a dark stain high on the front of his shirt; the heavy blue revolver was gripped in his outstretched hand. He was breathing.

Kells pried the revolver out of the little man's hand and stood up. He balanced the revolver across his fingers and a kind of soft insanity came into his eyes. He shook out the match and went back along the dark passageway, through the compartment where the overalled man was sleeping, up to the L-shaped storeroom. In the far end of the L there was another narrow door. Kells swung it open softly.

Swanstrom was sitting at the desk with his back to the door. Another man, a spare thin-haired consumptive-looking man was sitting on a chair on the platform, one of the 30-30's across his knees. He looked at Kells and he looked at the big blue revolver in Kells's hand and he put the .30-30 down on the platform.

Swanstrom swung around and opened his mouth, and then he smiled as if he were very tired.

Kells said: "Twenty-four hundred, and goddamned quick."

The thin moan of saxophones came down to them from somewhere above.

Swanstrom inclined his head toward the desk. He said, still with the tired smile: "I ain't got a key."

The lock of the other door clicked and the door opened and Rose and O'Donnell came in. They stood still for perhaps five seconds; O'Donnell was almost behind Rose. He closed the door and then he reached for the light-switch on the bulkhead. Kells squeezed the big Colt; O'Donnell fell forward to his hands and knees, shook his head slowly from side to side, sank down and forward onto his face.

Most of Kells's face was dark with dried blood. His eyes were glazed, insane. He said: "Anybody else?"

He swayed. He moved slowly toward Rose. Swanstrom was staring at O'Donnell; Swanstrom stood up, and in the same instant someone knocked heavily on the door, the knob rattled. Someone shouted outside. Kells moved toward Rose. His cold eyes and the slim blue barrel of the revolver were focused on Rise's belt buckle.

Rose licked his full lower lip, and sweat glistened on his dark forehead. He put one hand into his inside pocket and took out the folded sheaf of hundred-dollar notes, held them towards Kells.

Kells took them, nodded. He grinned, and the grin was a terrible thing on his bloody face. He backed slowly, carefully to the door through which he had entered, said, "First man through gets one in the guts," backed out and closed the door.

He went swiftly to the hatchway, down. The man who had been asleep had gone. Kells went through the passageway to the little man, lighted a match and saw that he was conscious.

His eyes were open behind the thick glasses and he smiled up at the flare of the match, kicked viciously at Kells's knee.

Kells said: "Now, now—Garbo."

He gripped the little man by the collar and dragged him along the passageway. There was sudden faint light at the after end and he waited until a shadow came into the light, shot at it once, twice. The sound was like thunder in the narrow space.

They went on laboriously, Kells dragging the little man, the little man cursing him softly, savagely. The after end of the passageway was dark now. Kells sucked in breath sharply. There was acrid smoke in the darkness—something more than the smell of black powder. It was like burning wood. Kells pressed his body against the bulkhead, risked another match.

A little way ahead there was a large rectangular port—a coaling port—in the ship's side, another on the inboard side of the passageway. The match flickered out and Kells edged forward, felt in the darkness for the big iron clamps. They were stiff from disuse but he strained and tugged until all but one were unscrewed, laid back. The last he hammered with the butt of the revolver until it gave; thrust all his weight against the plate. It creaked, swung slowly outward.

The sea was black, oily. The fog had thinned a little and the ship rolled lazily on a long even ground swell. Far to the left, Kells could see yellow sky over Long Beach, and to the right a distant winking light that might be the Eaglet. There was no sign of the launch.

Then he heard shouting and the sound of people running on the deck above him. He waited, listened, looked at the sea. The black water reddened; Kells leaned far out of the port and saw a long tongue of flame astern. As he watched, the water and the sky brightened. All the after quarter of the ship was afire.

When he again looked forward, a launch had rounded the bow, was idling about two hundred yards off.

Kells stuck the revolver in his belt, untied and kicked off his shoes. Then he took out the revolver, fired twice into the red darkness. By the mounting glow from astern he thought he saw a white hand, raised; the launch swung toward him in a wide circle.

He put the sheaf of crisp bills into his hip pocket, buttoned the flap. He took off his coat and threw it and the revolver into the sea. He picked the little man up in his arms, said, "Pull yourself together, baby—we're going bye-bye," got him somehow through the port, dropped him. Then he stood on the lower edge of the port, took a deep breath, dived. There was darkness and the shock of cold water.

He came to the surface a few yards from the little man, reached him in two long strokes and hooked one hand under his armpit. The shock had revived him—he struggled feebly.

Kells grunted, "Take it easy," and swam toward the launch.

The red-faced man whom Kells had talked to on the wharf leaned over the gunwale; together they hoisted the little man aboard. Then the red-faced man helped Kells. He had been alone in the launch. He went to the wheel.

Kells took off his trousers and wrung them out. He said: "How come you're alone?"

The red-faced man put his wheel hard over, spat high into the wind. "Fay said for you to go something yourself," he said. "I went back to the wharf and then I got to worrying, so I come out by myself."

Kells squatted beside the little man, looked back at the Joanna. Her after third was an up-and-down pillar of flame.

"Looks like a fire to me," he said. He looked down at the white, drawn face. "You've been playing with matches."

The little man smiled.

"It's a fire, sure enough." The red-faced man touched the-throttle. Then he added: "There ain't much of a crowd. They'll all have a lifeboat apiece." He chuckled to himself. "You're pretty wet—where do you want to go?"

Kells said: "Eaglet." He put on his pants.

* * * * *

FAY SAT IN a big chair behind a desk. He was a very big, powerfully muscled man with straight black hair, a straight nose, empty ice-gray eyes.

There was a woman. She sat on one side of the desk with a large glass in her hand. She was very drunk—but in a masculine way.

Kells stood across from Fay. His expression was not pleasant. He said: "What's it all about? Were you trying to get me killed?"

Fay said: "Why not?"

The woman giggled softly.

Fay turned his head without changing his blank expression, looked at the little man who had been carried into the cabin, laid on a couch. "Who's your boy friend?"

The woman said: "Nemo Kastner of KC—little Nemo, the chorus boy's delight."

Kells looked at the woman. She was blonde—but darkly, warmly. Her mouth was very red without a great deal of rouge, and her eyes were shadowed and deep. She was a tall woman with very interesting curves.

Fay said: "This is Miss Granquist."

Kells nodded shortly. He took a bottle and a glass from the desk, went to the little man.

Fay got up and went to one of the ports. He looked out at the Joanna, spur of fire against the horizon. "Beautiful!" he said—"beautiful!" Then he turned and went over to where Kells knelt over little Kastner.

Kells held a glass of whiskey to Kastner's mouth. Kastner drank as if he wanted it very much.

Kells looked up at Fay. He dipped his head toward Kastner, said: "This is the young fella who rubbed Doc."

Fay twisted his mouth to a slow sneer. His eyes dulled. He said: "You shot Doc, you son of a bitch—and tried to hang it on Ruth."

Kells stood up slowly.

Kastner laughed quietly, carefully, as though it hurt his chest. "God almighty!" he said—"what a bunch of suckers." His lisp was soft, slight.

Kells and Fay stood looking at one another for a little while. Then the woman said: "You'd better get a doctor for his nibs," She was sitting with her elbows on the desk, holding her face tightly between her hands.

Kastner shook his head. He laughed again as though moved by some secret, uncontrollable mirth. There was a little blood on his mouth.

Kells said: "You want a drink." He poured more whiskey into the glass and sat down beside Kastner.

"What a bunch of suckers!" Kastner looked at the glass

of whiskey. He looked at and through Kells. "Rose called Eddie O'Donnell and me after you left him this afternoon. He said Dave Perry had called while you were there—told him that Doc was at the joint in Hollywood waiting for you...."

Kells held the glass to Kastner's mouth. He drank, closed his eyes for a moment, went on: "Perry knew Rose was going to have Doc bumped—an' he knew Rose wanted to frame it for you. Only he'd figured on doing it on the boat. It looked like a good play."

Kells said: "Why me?"

Kastner coughed and held one hand very tightly against his chest. "Rose thinks you're a wrong guy to be on somebody else's shoe—an' he wanted to tie it up to Fay."

Kastner's dark, near-sighted eyes wandered for a moment to Fay. "Rose figures on airing everybody he ain't sure of—he's got a list. That's why he sent for Eddie an' me. He wants to move in on the whole town—him and Dave Perry and Reilly."

Kastner stopped, closed his eyes. Then he went on with his eyes closed: "Doc was in their way—and besides, Rose wanted the boat for himself."

Kells poured more whiskey into the glass. He said: "The Joanna came out tonight; how did they get the load?"

Kastner said: "She came out last night, an' they worked all night transferring cargo from a couple schooners—twelve hundred cases. The play was to run it in, three cases to a launch, each trip. They've got a swell federal connection at the wharf—the point was to get it by the cutters."

Kastner coughed again. "That's about all."

Fay went back to the desk, sat down. Kells held the glass of whiskey toward Kastner but Kastner shook his head. Kells drank a little of it.

Kastner went on listlessly: "Eddie an' me went to Perry's an' I busted in and waited for you. Doc was scared. That's the reason he'd wanted to see you: he had some kind of an in on what Rose was going to do an' wanted help. He was scared pea green."

Kells grinned at Fay.

Kastner twisted on the couch. Suddenly he spoke very rapidly, as if he wanted to say a great many things all at once: "Eddie waited down on the street to give me a buzz on the downstairs bell when you started up. Rose had called Reilly an' he was all set with three men to make the pinch—two in front an' one in the, alley."

Kells asked: "How come you sapped Dave?"

"He was putting on an act for the girl so she wouldn't think he was in on it. He got too realistic."

Kells looked at Fay, spoke to Kastner: "I thought Reilly was Lee Fenner's man."

"He was. He was Fenner's best spot in the Police Department until Rose started selling him big ideas." Kastner's little face was growing very white.

Kells said: "There'll be a doctor here in a minute—I sent the launch ashore for one." Then he walked to a port and looked out at the paling sky. He spoke without turning: "Reilly's the Lou that Rose and O'Donnell were waiting for at the hotel...."

"And he's the Lou they were waiting for on the boat—so they could let you have it resisting arrest—make it legal."

Kells went over to the desk. Fay was abstractedly playing with a small penknife; the woman still sat with her face between her hands.

Kells turned his head toward Kastner, asked very casually: "Who popped you?"

Kastner smiled a little. He said: "I don't remember."

The woman laughed. She put her hands on the table and threw her head back and laughed very loudly. Kastner looked at her and there was something inexpressibly cold and savage in his eyes.

Kells bent over the desk and took up a pen and wrote a few words on a piece of paper. He took the paper and the pen over to Kastner, said: "It'll make things a lot simpler if you sign this."

The little man glanced at the paper and his eyes were suddenly dull, empty. He said: "Nuts." He grinned at Kells, and then his face tightened and he died.

* * * * *

KELLS AND FAY sat at a table in Fay's apartment in Long Beach. The woman, Granquist, was asleep in a big chair. It was about eight-thirty, and outside it was gray and hot.

Kells said: "That's the way it'll have to be. None of us is worth a nickel as a witness."

Fay sipped his coffee and sat still for a little while; then he got up and went to the telephone and called Long Distance. He asked for a number in Los Angeles, waited a while, said: "Hello. This is Grant Fay. I want to talk to Fenner...." There was a pause and then he said: "Wake him up."

He waited a little while and then he said: "Hello, Lee.... There's a friend of mine here with an idea..."

Fay gestured and Kells got up and went to the phone. He said: "This is Kells.... Reilly's double-crossing you. He and Jack Rose aim to take over the town. They're importing a lot of boys from the East, and you're on the wrong side of their list...."

There was a long silence during which Kells held the receiver to his ear and grinned at Fay. Then he said: "My idea is that you reach Ruth Perry right away. She's incommunicado but you can beat that. Tell her there isn't any use trying to protect Dave any longer for Haardt's murder. Tell her that I said so.... Then see that she gets bail. When Dave finds out she's confessed, he'll have a lot of things to tell you.... Sure—he's guilty as hell."

Kells hung up and went back to the table. He said: "That oughta be that." He sat down and poured himself another cup of coffee and inclined his head toward Granquist.

Fay said: "She came out to the boat last night and said she'd been here a week or so from Detroit. She says she's got a million dollars' worth of information that she wants to peddle for five grand. She says it'll crack the administration wide open and that we can call our own shots next election."

Kells laughed quietly.

Fay went on expressionlessly: "I told her I wasn't in politics and wasn't in the market for her stuff, but she thought I was kidding her. She soaked up a couple bottles of Scotch and finally got down to twenty-five hundred. A few more slugs and she'd probably sell for a dollar ninety-eight. She said she needs new shoes."

Fay's Negro houseboy came in from the kitchen and cleared away the breakfast things.

Kells stood up. He said: "I'm going to take a nap while the wheels of justice make a couple turns." He went to the bedroom door, turned and spoke to the boy: "Call me in two hours." He went into the bedroom.

* * * * *

WHEN THE HOUSEBOY woke Kells, Fay had gone. Kells asked the boy to make some more coffee, shook Granquist awake.

"How about some Java?"

She said: "Sure."

They sat at the table and drank a great deal of coffee. Kells sent the boy out for a paper. RUTH PERRY CONFESSES HUSBAND SHOT HAARDT was spread across the front page.

Kells said: "Ain't nature wonderful!" He got up and put on a suit-coat Fay had given him. "I'm going to town."

Granquist said: "Me too. Can I ride with you?"

They went down and got into a cab and went to the parking station near the P & O wharf where Kells had left Cullen's car.

It was very hot, driving into Los Angeles. Kells took off his coat and drove in his shirtsleeves. His face was battered and Fay's shoes hurt his feet and he wanted very much to get into a bathtub and then get into bed.

He said: "Did you come out with Kastner and O'Donnell?"

Granquist looked at him out of the corners of her eyes, smiled sleepily. She said: "Uh huh."

"You O'Donnell's girl?"

"My God, no! I just came along for the ride." She slid down into the corner of the seat and closed her eyes.

Kells said: "Do you think O'Donnell shot Kastner?"

He looked at her. She nodded with her eyes closed.

He parked the car off Eighth Street and they went into a side entrance of the hotel, up the service stairway to Kells's room. He said: "I'll have to go downtown for questioning this afternoon—if they don't pick me up before. I want to have four or five hot baths and a little shut-eye first."

He went into the bathroom and turned on the water, took off his clothes and put on a long dark-green robe. When he came out, Granquist had curled up on the divan, was asleep. She had taken off her hat—awry honey-colored hair curved over her face and throat.

The telephone buzzed while Kells was in the tub. It buzzed again after he'd got out. He answered it, stared vacantly out the window and said: "All right—put her on." Then he said: "Hello, Ruth.... Swell.... No, I've got to go out right away and I won't be back until tonight. I'll try to give you a ring then.... Sure.... Okay, baby—'bye."

Granquist stirred in sleep, threw one arm above her head, sighed. Her eyelids fluttered. Kells stood there for a while looking at her.

* * * * *

AT ONE-THIRTY, Kells got out of a cab and went into the Sixth Street entrance of the Hayward Hotel. In the elevator he said: "Four." Around two turns, down a short corridor, he knocked at a heavy old-fashioned door.

A voice yelled: "Come in."

There were three men in the small room. One sat at a typewriter near the window. He had a leathery good-natured face and he spoke evenly into the telephone beside him: "Sure.... Sure...."

The other two were playing cooncan on a suit-box balanced on their laps. One of them put down his hand, put the suit-box carefully on the floor, stood up. Kells said: "Fenner."

The man at the telephone put one hand over the mouthpiece, turned his head to call through an open door behind him: "A gent to see you, Lee."

The man who had stood up walked to the door and nodded at someone in the next room and turned to Kells. "In here."

Kells went past him into the room and closed the door behind him.

That room was larger. Fenner, a slight, silver-haired man of about fifty, was lying on a bed in his trousers and undershirt. There was an electric light on the wall behind the bed. Fenner put down the paper he had been reading and swung up to sit facing Kells. He said, "Sit down," and picked up his shoes and put them on. Then he went over and raised the blind on one of the windows that looked out on Spring Street. He said:

"Well, Kells—is it hot enough for you?"

Kells nodded, said sarcastically: "You're harder to see than De Mille. I called your hotel and they made me get a Congressional Okay and make out a couple dozen affidavits before they gave me this number." He jerked his head toward the little room through which he had entered. "What's it all about?" Fenner sat down in a big chair and smiled sleepily. He took a crumpled package of Home Runs out of his pocket, extracted a cigarette and lighted it. "About a year ago," he said, "a man named Dickinson—a newspaperman—came out here with a bright idea and a little capital, and started a scandal sheet called the Coaster." Fenner inhaled his cigarette deeply, blew a soft gray cone of smoke toward the ceiling. "He ran it into the ground on the blackmail side and got into a couple libel jams...."

Kells said: "I remember."

Fenner went on: "I got postponements on the libel cases and I got the injunction raised. Now it's the Coast Guardian; A Political Weekly for Thinking People. Dickinson is still the editor and publisher, and"—he smiled thinly—"I'm the silent partner. The first number comes out next week—no sale, we give it away."

Kells said: "The city campaign ought to start rolling along about next week...."

Fenner slapped his knee in mock surprise. "By George! That's a coincidence." He sat grinning contentedly at Kells. Then his face hardened a little and a faint, fanatical twinkle came into his eyes. He spoke, and it was as if he had said the same thing many times before: "I'm a wording boss, Mister Kells. I gave this city the squarest deal it ever had. They beat my men at the polls last time but by God they didn't beat me—and next election day I'm going to take the city back."

Kells said: "I doubt it." He smiled a little to take the edge off his words, went on: "What did you get from Perry?"

"Nothing." Fenner yawned. "I got to his wife right after you called and gave her your message and arranged for her bail. She's witness number one for the State. It took me a little longer to beat the incommunicado on Perry, and when I saw him and told him she had confessed, he closed up like a clam."

Kells took off his hat and rubbed his scalp violently with his fingers. "It must have taken a lot of pressure to make a yellow bastard like him pipe down."

Fenner said: "Who killed Haardt?"

"Perry'll do for a while, won't he?" Kells put on his hat.

"Are you sure you're in the clear?"

"Yes." Kells stood up. "You've got enough to work on. Lieutenant Reilly, who was your best in the force, is in a play with Jack Rose to take over the town and open it up over your head. Dave Perry was in on it. They want it all—and they figure that you and I and a few more of the boys are in their way."

He walked over to the window and looked down at the swarming traffic on Spring Street. "Doc Haardt was in their way—figure it out for yourself."

Fenner said: "You act like you know what you're talking about."

"I do."

Fenner went on musingly: "One of the advantages of a reform administration is that you can blame it for everything. Maybe opening up the town for a few weeks isn't such a bad idea."

"But it's nice to know about it when you're supposed to be the boss...." Kells smiled. "And it won't be so hot when it gets so wide open that a few of Reilly and Rose's imports from the East come up here and shove a machine gun down your throat."

Fenner said: "No."

"Me—I'm going to scram," Kells went on. "I came out

here to play, and by God if I can't play here I'll go back to Broadway. My fighting days are over."

Fenner stared quizzically at Kells's bruised, battered face, smiled. "You'd better stick around," he said, "I like you."

"That's fine." Kells went to a table and poured himself a glass of water from a big decanter. "No—I'm going down to the station and see if they want to ask me any questions, and then I'm going home and pack. I've got reservations on the Chief: six o'clock."

Fenner stood up. "That's too bad," he said. "I have a hunch that you and I would be a big help to one another."

He held out his hand. Kells shook it, turned and went to the door. Then he turned again, slowly. "One other thing," he said. "There's a gal out here—name's Granquist—came out with a couple of Rose's boys; claims to have a million dollars' worth of lowdown on the administration. I can't use it. Maybe you can get together."

Fenner said: "Fine. How much does she want?"

Kells hesitated a bare moment. "Fifteen grand."

Fenner whistled. "It must be good," he said. "Send her out to my hotel. Send her out tonight—I'll throw a party for her."

"She'll go for that. A lush." Kells smiled and went out the door and closed it behind him.

* * * * *

HE WENT INTO the Police Station, into the Reporters' Room to the right of the entrance. Shep Beery looked up over his paper and said: "My God! What happened to your face?"

They were alone in the room. Kells looked with interest at the smudged pencil drawings on the walls, sat down. "I got it caught in a revolving door," he said. "Does anyone around here want to talk to me?"

"I do, for one." Beery put the paper down and leaned across the desk. He was a stoop-shouldered gangling man with a sharp sad face, a shock of colorless hair. "What's the inside on all this, Gerry?"

"All what?"

Beery spread the paper, pointed to headlines: PERRY INDICTED FOR HAARDT MURDER; WIFE CONFESSES. Beery's finger moved across the page: GAMBLING BARGE BURNS; 200 NARROWLY ESCAPE DEATH WHEN JOANNA D SINKS.

Kells laughed. "Probably just newspaper stories."

"No fooling, Gerry, give me a lead." Beery was intensely serious.

Kells asked: "You or your sheet?"

"That's up to you."

Kells trailed a long white finger over his discolored right eye. "If you read your paper a little more carefully," he said, "you'll find where an unidentified man was found dead near a wharf at San Pedro." He put his elbows on the desk, leaned close to Beery. "That's Nemo Kastner of Kansas City. He shot Doc Haardt on Jack Rose's order and helped frame it for me. He was shot by O'Donnell, his running mate, when they had an argument over the cut for Haardt's kill. He set fire to the ship–"

"... And swam four miles with a lungful of lead." Beery had been thumbing through the papers; pointed to the item.

"Uh huh."

"Who shot O'Donnell?"

Kells said: "You're too god-damned curious. Maybe it was Rose. Is he going to live?"

"Sure."

"That's swell." Kells took a deep breath.

"Now that's for you," he said, "Perry'll have to take the

fall for Doc's murder for the time being; he was in on it plenty, anyway. Kastner's dead and I couldn't prove any of it without getting myself jammed up again. If anything happens to me you can use your own judgment, but until something happens that is all under your hat. Right?"

Beery nodded.

Kells stood up, said: "Now let's go upstairs and see if the captain can think of any hard ones."

They went out of the room into the corridor, upstairs. Captain Larson was a huge watery-eyed Swede with a bulbous, thread-veined nose.

Beery said: "This is Kells.... He thought you might want to talk to him."

The captain shook his head slowly. He looked out the window and took a great square of linen out of his pocket and blew his nose. "No—I don't think so," he said slowly. "Cullen and the cab driver say you was at Cullen's house yesterday afternoon when Haardt was shot."

He looked up at Kells and his big mouth slit across his face to show yellow uneven teeth. "Was you?"

Kells smiled faintly, nodded.

"That's good enough for me." The captain blew his nose again noisily, folded the handkerchief carefully and put it in his pocket. "Perry's the only one who says you killed Doc. Lieutenant Reilly thinks you did but we can't run this department on thinks.... I think Perry's guilty as hell."

They all nodded sagely.

Kells said: "So long, Captain." He and Beery started out of the room.

The captain spoke again as Kells went through the door: "Where was you last night?"

Kells turned. "I was drunk. I don't remember." His eyes glittered with amusement.

The big man looked at him and his face wrinkled slowly to a grin. "Me too," he said. He slapped his thigh and laughed—a terrific crashing guffaw. His laughter followed Kells and Beery down the stairs, through the corridor, echoing and re-echoing.

Beery said: "See you in church."

Kells went out into the sunlight, walked down First to Broadway, up Broadway to his bank.

The teller told him he had a balance of five thousand, one hundred and thirty dollars. He asked that the account be transferred to a New York bank, then changed his mind.

"I'll take it in cash."

The teller gave him five thousand-dollar notes, a hundred, a twenty and a ten-dollar bill. Kells took the sheaf of twenty-four new hundred-dollar bills out of his pocket and exchanged twenty of them for two more thousand-dollar notes. He folded the seven thousand-dollar notes and put them in a black pin-seal cardcase, put the case in his inside breast pocket. He put the five hundreds and the smaller bills in his trouser pocket and went out and got into a cab.

He said "Ambassador" and looked at his watch. It was two-forty; he had three hours and twenty minutes to get home and pack and make the Chief.

* * * * *

"GERRY." GRANQUIST CALLED to him as he crossed the lobby.

He waited until she had crossed to him, smiled ingenuously. "Gerry in the hay, baby," he said gently. "Mister Kells in public."

She laughed softly—a metallic softness.

Kells asked: "Did you get my note?"

"Uh huh." She spoke rapidly, huskily. "I woke up right after you left, I guess. Your phone's been raising bloody hell. I'm going home and get some sleep...."

She held out a closed, black-gloved hand; Kells took his key.

He said: "Come on back upstairs—I've found a swell spot for your stuff."

"Oh—yeah?" Her face brightened.

They went to the elevator, up to Kells's room. Granquist sat in a steel-gray leather chair with her back to the windows, and Kells walked up and down.

"Lee Fenner has been the boss of this town for about six years," he said. "The reform element moved in last election, but Fenner's kept things pretty well under control—he has beautiful connections all the way to Washington...."

He paused while Granquist took out tobacco and papers, started to roll a cigarette.

"You wanted to sell your stuff to Fay for five grand," he went on. "If it's as good as you think it is we can get fifteen from Fenner.... That's ten for you and five for me"—he smiled a little—"as your agent...."

Granquist said: "I was drunk when I talked to Fay. Fifteen's chicken-feed. If you want to help me handle this the way it should be handled we can get fifty."

"You have big ideas, baby. Let's keep this practical."

Granquist lighted her cigaret, said: "How would you like to buy me a drink?"

Kells went into the dressing room and took two bottles of whiskey out of a drawer. He tore off the tissue-paper wrappings and went back into the room and put them on a table.

"One for you and one for me." He took a cork-screw out of his pocket.

The phone buzzed.

Kells went to the phone, and Granquist got up and took off her gloves and began opening the bottles.

Kells said: "Hello.... Yes—fine, Stella.... Who?... Not Kuhn, Stella—maybe it's Cullen.... Yeah.... Put him on...."

He waited a moment, said: "Hello, Willie... Sure...."He laughed quietly. "No, your car's all right. I'll send one of the boys in the garage out with it, or bring it out myself if I have time.... I'm taking a powder.... The Chief: six o'clock.... Uh huh, they're too tough out here for me. I'm going back to Times Square where it's quiet.... Okay, Willie. Thanks, luck—all that... G'bye."

He hung up, went to the table and picked up one of the opened bottles. He said: "Do you want a glass or a funnel?"

Granquist took the other bottle and sat down, jerked her head toward the phone. "Was that on the square—you're going?"

"Certainly."

"You're a sap." She tilted the bottle to her mouth, gurgled.

Kells went to a little table against one wall, took two glasses from a tray and went back and put them on the center table. He poured one of them half full. "No, darling—I'm a very bright fella." He drank. "I'm going to get myself a lot of air while I can. The combination's too strong. I'm not ambitious.

"You're a sap."

Kells went to a closet and took out two traveling bags, a large suitcase. He took the drawers out of a small wardrobe trunk, put them on chairs.

"You'd run out on a chance to split fifty grand?" She was elaborately incredulous.

Kells started taking things out of the closets, putting them in the trunk. "Your information is worth more to Fenner—than anyone else," he said. "If it's worth that much he'll probably pay it. You can send me mine...."

"No, god-damn it! You stay here and help me swing this or you don't get a nickel."

Kells stopped packing, turned wide eyes toward

Granquist. "Listen, baby," he said slowly, "I've got a nickel. I'm getting along swell legitimately. You take your bottle and your extortion racket, and screw...."

Granquist laughed. She got up and went to Kells and put her arms around his body. She didn't say anything, just looked at him and laughed.

The wide, wild look went out of his eyes slowly. He smiled. He said: "What makes you think it's worth that much?"

Then he put her arms away gently and went to the table and poured two drinks.

Chapter Three

AT ABOUT six-forty Kells dropped Granquist at her apartment house on the corner of Wilcox and Yucca.

"Meet you in an hour at the Derby."

She said: "Oke—adios."

Kells drove up Wilcox to Cahuenga, up Cahuenga to Iris, turned up the short curving slope to Cullen's house. The garage doors were open, he drove the car in and then went up and rang the bell. No one answered. He went back down and closed the garage doors and walked down to Cahuenga, down Cahuenga to Franklin.

He stood on the corner a little while and then went into a delicatessen and called a Hempstead number. The line was busy, he waited a few minutes, called again, said: "Hello, Ruth.... Swell... Listen: I'm going to be very busy tonight—I've got about a half-hour.... You come out and walk up to Las Palmas, and if you're, sure you're not tailed come up Las Palmas to Franklin.... If you're not absolutely sure take a walk or something.... I'll give you a ring late.... Yeah...."

He went out and walked over Franklin to Las Palmas. He walked back and forth between Las Palmas and Highland for ten minutes and then walked down the west side of Las Palmas to Hollywood Boulevard. He didn't see anything of Ruth Perry.

He went on down Las Palmas to Sunset, east to Vine and

up Vine to the Brown Derby.

Granquist was in a booth, far back, on the left.

She said: "I ordered oysters."

Kells sat down. "That's fine." He nodded to an acquaintance at a nearby table.

"A couple minutes after you left me," she said, "a guy came into my place and asked the girl at the desk who I was. She said 'Who wants to know?' and he said he had seen me come in and thought I was an old friend of his..."

"And..."

"And I haven't got any old friends."

"What'd he look like?" Kells was reading the menu.

"The girl isn't very bright. All she could remember was that he had on a gray suit and a gray cap."

Kells said: "That's a pipe—it was one of the Barrymores."

"No." Granquist shook her head very seriously. "It might've been a copper who tailed us from your hotel, or it might've been one of–"

Kells interrupted her suddenly: "Did you leave the stuff in your apartment?"

"Certainly not."

Kells said: "Anyway—we've got to do whatever's to be done with it tonight. I'm getting the noon train tomorrow."

"We're getting the noon train."

Kells smiled, looked at her a little while. He said: "When you can watch a lady eat oysters and still think she's swell—that's love."

He ordered the rest of the dinner.

Granquist carried a smart black bag. She opened it and took out a big silver flask, poured drinks under the table.

The dinner was very good.

After a while, Granquist said with sudden and exaggerated seriousness: "I haven't told you the story of my life!"

Kells was drinking his coffee, watching the door. He turned to her slowly, said slowly: "No—but I've heard one."

"All right. You tell me."

"I was born of rich but honest parents...."

"You can skip that."

He grinned at her. "I came back from France," he said,—"with a set of medals, a beautiful case of shell shock and a morphine habit you could hang your hat on."

He gestured with his hands. "All gone."

"Even the medals?"

He nodded. "The State kept them as souvenirs of my first trial."

Granquist poured two drinks.

"I happened to be too close to a couple of front-page kills," Kells went on. "There was a lot of dumb sleuthing and a lot of dumb talk. It got so, finally, when the New York police couldn't figure a shooting any other way, I was it."

Granquist was silent, smiling.

"They got tired trying to hang them on me after the first three but the whisper went on. It got to be known as the Kells Inside...."

"And at heart you're just a big, sympathetic boy who wouldn't hurt a fly."

"Uh, huh." He nodded his head slowly, emphatically. His face was expressionless.

"Me—I'm Napoleon." Granquist took a powder puff out of the bag and rubbed it over her nose.

Kells beckoned a waiter, paid the check. "And beyond the Alps lies Italy. Let's go." It was raining a little.

Kells held Granquist close to him. "The Knickerbocker is just around the corner on Ivar," he said—"but I'm going to put you in a cab and I want you to go down to Western Avenue and get out and walk until you're sure you're not being followed. Then get another cab and come to the Knickerbocker—I'll be in ten-sixteen."

The doorman held a big umbrella for them and they walked across the wet sidewalk and Granquist got into a cab. Kells stood in the thin rain until the cab had turned the corner down Hollywood Boulevard, then he went back into the restaurant.

Ruth Perry was sitting in the corner booth behind the cashier's desk. She didn't say anything. Kells sat down. There was a newspaper on the table and he turned it around, glanced at the headlines, said: "What do you think about the European situation?"

"Who was that?" Ruth Perry inclined her head slightly toward the door.

Kells put his elbows on the table and rubbed his eyes with his fingers. "None of your business, darling." He looked up at her and smiled. "Now keep your pants on. I stand to make a ten-or fifteen-thousand-dollar lick tonight, and that one"—he gestured with his head toward the door—"is a very important part of the play."

Ruth Perry leaned back and looked at the ceiling and laughed a little bit. Presently she said: "What are you going to do about Dave?"

"What do you want me to do?"

"I'm not going to go on the stand and lay myself open to a perjury rap."

Kells shook his head. "You won't have to, baby. The trial won't come up for a month or so and we can spring Dave before that"—he smiled with his mouth—"if you want to."

They were silent for a little while.

Then Kells said: "I've got to go now—call you around twelve."

He got up and went out into the rain. He walked up to the corner of Vine and Hollywood Boulevard and went into the drugstore and bought some aspirin, took two five-grain tablets and then went out and crossed the Boulevard and walked up Vine Street about a hundred yards. Then he crossed the street and walked back down to the parking station next to the Post Office. He stood on the sidewalk watching people across the street for a little while, then went swiftly back through the parking station and down the ramp to the garage under the Knickerbocker Hotel.

* * * * *

HE GOT OUT of the elevator on the tenth floor and knocked at the door of ten-sixteen. Fenner opened the door.

Fenner said: "Well, Mister Kells—you didn't catch your train." He smiled and bowed Kells in.

They sat in the big living room and Fenner poured drinks. He poured three drinks and leaned back and asked: "Where's the little lady?"

"She'll be up in a few minutes."

Someone came out of the bathroom and through the bedroom. Fenner got up and introduced the dark medium-sized man that came in. "This is Bob Jeffers—God's gift to Womanhood... Mister Kells."

Kells stood up and shook hands with Jeffers. He was a motion-picture star who had had a brief and spectacular career; had been on the way out for nearly a year. He was drunk. He said: "It is a great pleasure to meet a real gunman, Mister Kells."

Kells glanced at Fenner and Fenner shook his head slightly, smiled apologetically. Kells sat down and sipped his whiskey.

Jeffers said: "I'm going up and get Lola." He took up his glass and went unsteadily out of the room, through the hallway, out the outer door.

"You mustn't mind Jeffers."

Kells said: "Sure." Then he leaned back in his chair and stared vacantly at Fenner. "Have you got twenty-five grand in cash?"

Fenner looked at him very intently. Then he smiled slowly and shook his head. "No," he said. "Why?"

"Can you get it—tonight?"

"Well—possibly. I–"

Kells interrupted, spoke rapidly. "I've talked to the lady. She's got enough on Bellmann to run him out of politics—out of the state, by God! You're getting first crack at it because I have a hunch he isn't sitting so pretty financially. It's the keys to the city for you—it's in black and white—an' it's a bargain."

"You seem to have a more than casual interest in this..."

Kells nodded. "Uh, huh," he said, smiled. "I'm the fiscal agent."

Fenner stood up and walked up and down the room, his hands clasped behind him, a lecture-platform expression on his face.

"You forget, Kells, that the Common People—the voters—are not fully informed of Mister Bellmann's connections, his power in the present administration."

"That's what your Coast Guardian's for."

Fenner stopped in front of Kells. "Just what form does this, uh—incriminating information take?"

Kells shook his head, slowly. "You'll have to take my word for that," he said. He leaned forward and put his empty glass on the table.

The doorbell rang. Fenner went out into the hall, followed Granquist back into the room. Kells got up and introduced her to Fenner, and Fenner took her coat into the bedroom and then came back and poured drinks for all of them.

"Mister Kells has raised the ante to twenty-five thousand," he said. He smiled boyishly at Granquist.

She took her drink and sat down. She raised the glass to her mouth. "Hey, hey." They all drank.

Granquist took a sack of Durham, papers out of her bag, rolled a cigarette.

Fenner said: "Of course I can't enter into a proposition involving so much money without knowing definitely what I'm getting."

"You put twenty-five thousand dollars in cash on the line and you get enough to put the election on ice." Kells got up and went over to one of the windows. He turned, went on very earnestly: "And it's a hell of a long ways from that now."

Fenner pursed his lips, smiled a little. "Well—now..."

"And it's got to be done tonight."

Granquist got up and put her empty glass on the table.

Fenner said: "Help yourself, help yourself."

She filled the two glasses on the table with whiskey and ice and White Rock. She said: "Do you let strangers use your bathroom?"

Fenner took her through the hallway to the bedroom and turned on the light in the bath, came back and sat down and picked up the telephone, asked for a Mister Dillon. When the connection was made, he said: "I want you to bring up the yellow sealed envelope that's in the safe.... Yes, please—and bring it yourself." He hung up and turned to Kells. "All right," he said, "I'll play."

Kells sat down and crossed his legs. He studied the glistening toe of his left shoe, said: "It's going to sound like a fairy tale," looked up at Fenner. "Bellmann's a very smart guy. If he wasn't he wouldn't be where he is."

Fenner nodded impatiently.

Kells said: "The smarter they are, the sappier the frame they'll go for. Bellmann spent weekend before last at Jack Rose's cabin at Big Bear." He leaned forward and took his glass from the table. "Rose has been trying to get a feeler to him for a long time, has tried to reach him through his own friends. A few weeks ago Rose took a big place on the lake not far from Bellmann's, invited Hugg and MacAlmon—Mac is very close to Bellmann—up for the fishing, or what have you? They all dropped in on Bellmann in a spirit of neighborliness, and he decided he'd been wrong about Rose all these years. Next day he returned the call. When Hugg and Mac came to the city they left Rose and Bellmann like that"—he held up two slim fingers pressed close together.

Granquist came in, sat down. Kells turned his head in her direction. Without letting his eyes focus directly on her, he said: "That's where baby comes in."

Fenner lighted a cigaret, coughed out smoke.

"She came out with friends of Rose from KC," Kells went on. "Bellmann met her at Rose's and took her big. That was Rose's cue. He threw a party—one of those intimate, quiet little affairs—Rose and a showgirl, Bellmann and"—he smiled faintly at Granquist—"this one. They all got stiff—I don't mean drunk, I mean stiff. And what do you suppose happened?"

He paused, grinned happily at Fenner. "Miss Granquist had her little camera along, took a lot of snapshots." He turned his grin toward Granquist. "Miss Dipso Granquist stayed sober enough to snap her little camera."

Fenner got up and took Granquist's empty glass, filled it. He looked very serious.

Kells went on: "Of course it all came back to Rose in the morning. He asked about the pictures and she gave him a couple of rolls of film she'd stuck in the camera during the night, clicked with the lens shut, blanks. She discovered that the lens wasn't open when she gave them to him, they had one of those morning-after laughs about it. Bellmann had a dark green hangover; he didn't even remember about the pictures until a day or so later and then he wrote Miss Granquist a couple of hot letters with casual postscripts:

'How did the snapshots turn out, darling?' cracks like that."

Kells got up, stretched. "You see, it gets better as it goes along."

"What are the pictures like?" Fenner was standing near Granquist, his little pointed chin thrust toward Kells.

"Don't be silly. They're right out of the pocket of one of those frogs that work along the Rue de Rivoli." Kells ran his fingers through his hair. "That's not the point though. It's not what they are, it's who they're of: Mister John R. Bellmann, the big boss of the reform administration, the Woman's Club politician—at the house and in the intimate company of Jack Rose, gambler, Crown Prince of the Western Underworld and a couple of, well—questionable ladies."

"And exactly what am I buying?"

"The negatives and one set of prints. My word that you're getting all the negatives and that there are no other prints. The letters—and certain information as to what Bellmann and Rose talked about before they went under...."

The doorbell rang.

Fenner said: "That'll be Dillon." He went out into the hallway and came back with a sandy-haired, spectacled man. Both of them were holding their hands above their shoulders in the conventional gesture of surprise. Two men whom Kells had never seen before came in behind them. One, the most striking, was rather fat and his small head stuck out of a stiff collar, his tie was knotted to stick straight out, stiffly from the opening in his collar. He held a short blunt revolver in his hand.

* * * * *

THE FAT MAN said: "Go see if the tall one has got anything in his pockets."

The other man went to Kells. He was a gray-faced nondescript young man in a tightly belted raincoat. He went through Kells's pockets very carefully and when he had finished, said: "Sit down."

Dillon shifted his weight from one foot to the other and the fat man, who was almost directly behind him, raised the revolver and brought the muzzle down hard on the back of his head. Dillon grunted and his knees gave away and he slumped down softly to the floor.

The fat man giggled quietly, nervously. He said: 'That's one down. Every little bit helps,"

Kells sat down on the divan and leaned back and crossed his legs.

The fat man said: "Put your hands up, Skinny." Kells shook his head slightly.

The young man in the raincoat leaned forward and slapped Kells across the mouth. Kells looked up at him and his face was very sad, his eyes were sleepy. He said: "That's too bad."

Fenner turned his head, spoke over his shoulder to the fat man: "What do you want?"

"I don't want you. Go sit down in that chair by the window."

Fenner crossed the room, sat down.

The fat man said: "Reach back of you and pull the shades shut."

Granquist said sarcastically: "Now pull up a chair for yourself, Chub." She leaned forward toward the table. "Ain't you going to have a drink?"

Kells said: "Don't say 'ain't,' sweet."

The fat man sat down in the chair nearest the door. His elbows were on the arms of the chair and he held the revolver loosely on his lap, said: "I want a bunch of pictures that you tried to peddle to Bellmann, girlie."

"Don't call me girlie, you son of a bitch!"

Kells looked at Granquist, shook his head sadly. "That's something you forgot to tell me about," he said.

"I want all the pictures," the fat man repeated, "an' I want two letters—quick."

Granquist was staring at the fat man. She turned slowly to Kells. "That's a lie, Gerry. I didn't crack to Bellmann."

Fenner stood up. "I won't stand for this," he said. He thrust his hands in his pockets and took a step forward.

"Sit down." The fat man moved the revolver slightly until it focused on Fenner's stomach.

Fenner stood still.

Kells said: "Does the fella who sent you know that if anything happens to me the whole inside gets a swell spread in the morning papers?"

The fat man smiled.

"The inside on Haardt and the barge and Perry, and the Sunday-school picnic at Big Bear?" Kells went on.

Granquist was watching him intently.

"I made that arrangement this afternoon." Kells leaned side-wise slowly and put his empty glass on an end table.

The fat man looked at Fenner and Kells, and then he looked at Granquist, and at the bag tucked into the chair beside her. He said: "That's a dandy. Let's have a look at it, girlie."

Granquist stood up in one swift and precise movement. She moved to the window so swiftly that the fat man had only time to stand up and take one step toward her before she had moved the drape aside with her shoulder, crashed the bag through the window.

Glass tinkled on the sill.

Kells stood up in the same instant and brought his right fist up from the divan in a long arc to the side of the gray-faced young man's jaw. The young man spun half around and Kells swung his right fist again to the same place. The young man fell half on the divan, half on the floor.

The fat man moved toward Kells, stopped in the center of the floor.

Granquist yelled: "Smack him, Gerry...."

Kells stood with his feet wide apart. He grinned at the fat man.

Fenner was standing near Granquist at the window. His eyes were wide and he tried to say something but the words stuck in his throat.

The fat man backed toward the door. "I ain't got orders to shoot," he said, "but I sure will if you press me." He backed out into the semidarkness of the hallway and then the outer door slammed.

Granquist ran across the room, stopped a moment in the doorway, turned her head toward Kells. She said, "I'll get the bag," and she spoke so rapidly, so breathlessly, that the words were all run together into one word. She went into the darkness.

Kells turned to Fenner. "Give her a hand."

He bent over the young man, took a small automatic out of his raincoat pocket and handed it to Fenner. "Hurry up—I've got to telephone—I'll be right down."

Fenner took the automatic dazedly. He looked at the man on the floor and at Kells, and then he came suddenly to life. "It's in the court," he said excitedly. "I can get out there from the third floor."

"Maybe the bag was a stall. Don't let her get out of your sight." Kells sat down at the telephone.

Fenner hurried out of the room.

Kells waited until he heard the outer door slam, then got up and went to Dillon. He knelt and drew a long yellow envelope from Dillon's inside breast pocket. It was heavily sealed. He tore off the end and looked inside. Then, smiling blankly, he tucked it into his pocket.

He went to the broken window, raised it carefully and leaned out over the wet darkness of the court for a moment.

He went into the kitchen and stood on the stove, looked through the high ventilating window across the narrow air-shaft to the window of an adjoining apartment. Then he went into the bedroom and got his hat and Granquist's coat and went out of the apartment, across the corridor to the elevator.

On the way down, he spoke to the elevator boy: "It is still raining?"

"Yes, sir. It looks like it was going to rain all night."

Kells said: "I wouldn't be surprised."

The night clerk came out of the telephone operator's compartment.

Kells leaned on the desk. "Your Mister Dillon is in ten-six-teen. He had an accident. There's another man in there whom Fenner will file charges against. Have the house dick hold him till Fenner gets back."

He started to go, paused, said over his shoulder: "Maybe you'll find another one trying to get in or out of the court. Probably not."

He went out and walked up Ivar to Yucca, west on Yucca the short block to Cahuenga. The rain had become a gentle mist for the moment; it was warm, and occasional thunder drummed over the hills to the north. He went into an apartment house on the corner and asked the night man if Mister Beery was in.

"He went out about ten minutes ago." The night man thought he might be in the drugstore across the street.

Beery was crouched over a cup of coffee at the soda fountain. Kells sat down beside him and ordered a glass of water, washed down two aspirin tablets. He said: "If you want to come along with me, you might get some more material for your memoirs."

Beery put a dime on the counter and they went out, over to Wilcox. They went into the Wilcox entrance of the Lido, upstairs to the fourth floor and around through a long corridor to number four thirty-two.

Granquist opened the door. Her face was so drained of color that her mouth looked dark and bloody in contrast to her skin. Her mouth was slightly open and her eyes were wide, burning. She held her arms stiffly at her sides.

There was a man lying on his face, half in, half out of the bathroom. His arms were doubled up under his body.

Beery walked past Granquist, slowly across the room to a table. He turned his head slowly as he walked, kept his eyes on the man on the floor. He took off his hat and put it on the table.

Kells closed the door quietly and stood with his back against it.

Granquist stared at him without change of expression.

Beery glanced at them.

Kells smiled a little. He said: "This isn't what I meant, Shep—maybe it's better."

Beery went to the man on the floor, squatted and turned the head sidewise.

Granquist swallowed. She said: "Gerry, I didn't do it. I didn't do it."

Beery spoke softly, without looking up: "Bellmann."

* * * * *

KELLS LOCKED THE door. He looked at the floor, then he went to the table and reached under it with his foot, kicked an automatic out into the light.

Granquist walked unsteadily to a chair, sat down and stared vacantly at Beery bending over the body. She said in a hollow, monotonous voice: "He was like that when I came in. I stopped downstairs and then I came up in the elevator and he was like that when I came in—just a minute ago."

Kells didn't look at her. He took out a handkerchief and picked up the automatic and held it to his nose. He held it carefully by the handkerchief and snapped the magazine out of the grip, said: "Two."

Beery stood up.

Kells laughed suddenly. He threw back his head and roared with laughter. He sat down and put the automatic on the table, wiped his eyes with the handkerchief.

"It's beautiful!" he said brokenly.

Granquist stared at Kells and then she leaned back in the chair and her eyes were very frightened. She said: "I didn't do it," over and over again.

Kells's laughter finally wore itself out. He wiped his eyes with the handkerchief and then he looked up at Beery. "Well," he said, "why the hell don't you get on the phone? You've got the scoop of the season."

He leaned back and smiled at the ceiling, improvised headlines: "Boss Bellmann Bumped Off By Beauty. Pillar of Church Meets Maker. Politician—let's see—Politician Plugged as Prowler by Light Lady." He stood up and crossed quickly to Beery, emphasized his words with a long white finger against Beery's chest. "Here's a pip! Reformer Foiled in Rape. Killer says: 'I shot to save my honor, the priceless inheritance of American womanhood.'"

Beery went to the telephone. He said: "We've been a Bellmann paper—I'll have to talk to the Old Man."

"You god-damned idiot! No paper can afford to soft-pedal a thing like this. Can't you see that without an editorial OK?"

Beery nodded in a faraway way, dialed a number. He asked for a Mister Crane; when Crane had answered, said: "This is Beery. Bellmann has been shot by a jane, in her apartment, in Hollywood... Uh huh—very dead."

He grinned up at Kells, listened to an evident explosion at the other end of the line. "We'll have to give it everything, Mister Crane," he went on. "It's open and shut—there isn't any out.... OK Switch me to Thompson—I'll give it to him."

Granquist got up and went unsteadily to the door. She put her hand on the knob and then seemed to remember that the door was locked. She looked at the key but didn't touch it. She turned and went into the dinette, took a nearly empty bottle out of the cupboard and came back and sat down.

Beery asked: "What's your name, sister?"

Granquist was trying to get the cork out of the bottle. She didn't say anything or look up.

Kells said: "Granquist." He looked at her for a moment, then went over to the window, turned his head, slightly toward Beery: "Miss Granquist."

Beery said, "Hello, Tom," spoke into the telephone in a low even monotone.

Kells turned from the window, crossed slowly to Granquist. He sat down on the arm of her chair and took the bottle out of her hand and took out the cork. He got up and went into the dinette, poured the whiskey into a glass and brought it back to her, sat down again on the arm of the chair. "Don't take it so big, baby," he said very softly and quietly. "You've got a perfect case. The jury'll give you roses and a vote of thanks on the 'for honor' angle—and it's the swellest thing that could happen for Fenner's machine—it's the difference between Bellmann's administration and a brand-new one..."

"I didn't do it, Gerry." She looked up at him and her eyes were dull, hurt. "I didn't do it! I left the snaps and stuff in the office downstairs when I went out—the bag was a gag...."

Kells said: "I knew they weren't in the bag—you left it in the chair when you went into the bathroom."

She nodded. She wasn't listening to him. She had things to say. "I ran back here when I left Fenner's. I picked up the stuff at the office—had to wait till the manager got the combination to the safe out of his apartment. Then I came up here to wait for you."

She drank, put the glass on the floor. She turned, inclined her head toward Bellmann. "He was like that. He must have come here for the pictures—he'd been through my things...."

Kells said: "Never mind, baby—it's a set up...."

"I didn't do it!" She beat her fist on the arm of the chair. Her eyes were suddenly wild.

Kells stood up.

Beery finished his report, hung up the receiver. He said: "Now I better call the station."

"Wait a minute." Kells looked down at Granquist and his face was white, hard. "Listen!" he emphasized the word with one violent finger. "You be nice. You play this the way I say and you'll be out in a month—maybe I can even get you out on bail...."

He turned abruptly and went to the door, turned the key. "Or"—he jerked his head toward the door, looked at the little watch on the inside of his wrist—"there's a Frisco bus out Cahuenga in about six minutes. You can make it—and ruin your case."

Outside, sultry thunder rumbled and rain whipped against the windows. Kells slid a note off the sheaf in his breast pocket, went over and handed it to her. It was a thousand dollar note.

She looked at it dully, slowly stood up. Then she stuffed the note into the pocket of her suit and went quickly to the chair where Kells had thrown her coat.

Kells said: "Give me the pictures."

Beery was staring open-mouthed at Kells. "Gerry, you can't do this," he said. "I told Tommy we had the girl–"

"She escaped."

Granquist put on her coat. She looked at Kells and her eyes were soft, wet. She went to him and took a heavy manila envelope out of her pocket, handed it to him. She stood a moment looking up at him and then she turned and went to the door, put her hand on the knob and turned it, then took her hand away from the knob and held it up to her face. She stood like that a little while and then she said. "All right," very low.

She said, "All right," again, very low and distinctly, and turned from the door and went back to the big chair and sat down.

Kells said: "Okay, Shep."

* * * * *

ABOUT TEN MINUTES later Beery got up and let Captain Hayes of the Hollywood Division in. There were two plain-clothes men and an assistant coroner with him.

The assistant coroner examined Bellmann's body, looked up in a little while: "Instantaneous—two wounds, probably thirty-two caliber—one touched the heart." He stood up. "Dead about twenty minutes."

Hayes picked up the gun from where Kells had replaced it under the table, examined it, wrapped it carefully.

Kells smiled at him. "Old school—along with silencers and dictaphones. Nowadays they wear gloves." Hayes said: "What's your name?"

Beery said: "Oh, I'm sorry—I thought you knew each other. This is Gerry Kells... Captain Hayes."

"What were you doing here?" Hayes was a heavily built man with bright brown eyes. He spoke very rapidly.

"Shep and I came up to call on my girl friend here"—Kells indicated Granquist who was still sitting with her coat on, staring at them all in turn, expressionlessly. "We found it just the way you see it."

Hayes glanced at Beery, who nodded. Hayes spoke to Granquist. "Is that right, miss?"

She looked up at him blankly for a moment, then nodded slowly. "That'll be about all, I guess." Hayes looked at Kells. "You still at the Ambassador?"

"You can always reach me through Shep."

Hayes said: "Come on, miss."

Granquist got up and went into the dressing room and packed a few things in a small traveling bag.

One of the plain-clothes men opened the door, let two ambulance men in. They put Bellmann's body on a stretcher and carried it out.

Kells leaned against the doorframe of the dressing room, watched Granquist. "I'll be down in the morning with an attorney," he said. "In the meantime, keep quiet."

She nodded vaguely and closed the bag, came out of the dressing-room. She said: "Let's go."

The manager of the apartment house was in the corridor with one of the Filipino bellboys, a reporter from the Journal and a guest. The manager was wringing his hands. "I can't understand it—no one heard the shots."

One of the plain-clothes men looked superiorly at the manager, said: "The thunder covered the shots."

They all went down the corridor except Beery and Kells and the manager. The manager went to the door, smiled weakly at Kells. "I'll close up Miss Granquist's apartment."

Kells said: "Never mind—I'll bring the key down."

The manager was doubtful.

Kells looked very stern, whispered: "Special investigator." He and Beery went back into the apartment.

Beery called his paper again with additional information: "Captain Hayes made the arrest.... And don't forget: the Chronicle is always first with the latest...." He hung up, lighted a new cigarette from the butt of another. "From now on," he said, "I'm going to follow you around and phone in the story of my life, from day to day."

Kells asked: "Are they giving it an extra?"

"Sure. It's on the presses now—be on the streets in a little while."

"That's dandy."

Kells went into the kitchen, switched on the light. He looked out the kitchen window and then he went to a tall cupboard—the kind of cupboard where brooms are kept in a modern apartment—opened the door.

Fenner came out, blinking in the bright light. He said: "I would have had"—he swallowed—"would have had to come out in another minute. I nearly smothered."

"That's too bad."

Beery stood in the doorway. He said: "For the love of–"

Fenner went past Beery into the living room, sat down. He was breathing hard.

Kells strolled in behind him and sat down across the room, facing him.

Fenner took out a handkerchief and dabbed at his mouth and forehead. He said: "I followed her as you suggested—and when she went in through the lobby, I came up the side stair intending to meet her up here."

Kells smiled gently, nodded.

"I didn't want to be seen following her through the lobby, you know."

"No."

Beery was still standing in the kitchen doorway, staring bewilderedly at Fenner.

"I knocked but she hadn't come up yet," Fenner went on, "so I opened the door—it was unlocked—and came in."

Kells said: "The door was unlocked?"

Fenner nodded. "In a few minutes I heard her coming up the hall and she was talking to a man. I went into the kitchen, of course, and she and Bellmann came in. They were arguing about something. Bellmann went into the bathroom I think, and then I heard the two shots during one of the peals of thunder. I didn't know what to do—and then when I was about to come out and see what had happened, you knocked at the door."

Fenner paused, took a long breath. "I didn't know it was you, of course, so I hid in the cupboard."

Kells said: "Oh."

"I thought it would be better if I didn't get mixed up in a thing of this kind, in any way."

Kells said, "Oh," again. Then he looked up at Beery, said: "Sit down, Shep—I want to tell you a story."

Beery sat down near the door.

Kells stretched one long leg over the arm of his chair, made himself comfortable. "This afternoon I told Mister Fenner"—he inclined his head toward Fenner in one slow emphatic movement—"that I knew a gal who had some very hot political info that she wanted to sell."

Beery nodded almost imperceptibly.

"He was interested and asked me to send her to his hotel tonight. I had a talk with her, and the stuff sounded so good that I got interested too—took her to Fenner's myself."

Fenner was extremely uncomfortable. He looked at Kells and dabbed at his forehead; his lips were bent into a faint forced smile.

"We offered the information—information of great political value—to Mister Fenner at a very fair price," Kells went on. "He agreed to it and called the manager of his hotel and asked him to bring up an envelope containing a large amount in cash."

Kells turned his eyes slowly from Beery to Fenner. "When the manager came in a couple of benders came in with him. They'd been waiting in the next apartment, listening across the airshaft to find out what they had to heist—it was supposed to look like Rose's stick-up—or Bellmann's...."

Fenner stood up.

Kells said: "But it was Mister Fenner's. Mister Fenner wanted to eat his cake and have crumbs in his bed, too."

Fenner took two steps forward. His eyes were flashing. He said: "That's a lie, sir—a tissue of falsehood!"

Kells spoke very softly, enunciating each word carefully, distinctly: "Sit down, you dirty son of a bitch."

Fenner straightened, glared at Kells. He half turned toward the door.

Kells got up and took three slow steps, then two swiftly, crashed his fist into Fenner's face. There was a sickening crackly noise and Fenner fell down very hard.

Kells jerked him up and pushed him back into the chair. Kells's face was worried, solicitous. He said very slow—almost whispered: "Sit still."

Then he went back to his chair and sat down, went on: "One of the boys sapped the manager. They fanned me and made a pass for Granquist's handbag. She tossed it out the window, smacked one of them and the other one went after the bag. Granquist faked going after the bag too and I sent Fenner after her, figuring that the stuff wasn't in the bag and that she'd come back here and that the three of us would get together here for another little talk."

Fenner was pressing himself back into the corner of the chair. He was holding his hands to his bloody face and moaning a little.

"When I sent Fenner after Granquist," Kells went on, "I gave him a gun—one of the boy's. He was so excited about getting to the bag, or keeping G in sight that he forgot to frisk the manager for his big dough...."

Kells took the yellow envelope out of his pocket. "So I got it." He leaned forward, pressed the edges of the envelope and a little packet of cigar coupons fell out on the floor.

"Almost enough to get a package of razor blades."

Beery grinned.

Kells said: "Granquist headed over here, so Fenner knew

that the bag had been a stall, followed her. When she came in past the office he ducked up the side way and, figuring that she had come right up, knocked at her door."

Beery said: "How did he know which apartment was hers?"

"He had us tailed from my hotel early this evening. His man got her number from the mail-boxes in the lobby, gave it to him before we got to his place tonight."

Beery nodded.

Kells said: "Am I boring you?"

"Yes. Bore me some more."

"Bellmann had come up here after some things he wanted—some very personal things that he couldn't trust anyone else to get. He probably paid his way into the apartment—I'll have to check up on that—and didn't find what he was looking for, and when Fenner knocked he thought it was either Granquist, who he wanted to talk to anyway, or whoever let him in."

Kells took a deep breath. "He opened the door, and..." Kells paused, got up and went to Fenner, looked down at the little twisted man and smiled. "Mister Fenner knows a good thing when he sees it—he jockeyed Bellmann into a good spot and shot him through the heart." Fenner mumbled something through his hands. "He waited for a nice roll of off-stage thunder and murdered him."

Beery said: "That's certainly swell. And I haven't got any more job than a rabbit." He stood up, stared disconsolately at Kells. "My God! Bellmann killed by the boss of the opposition—the most perfect political break that could happen, for my paper—and I turn in an innocent girl, swing it exactly the other way politically. My God!"

Beery sat down and reached for the telephone. Kells said: "Wait a minute."

Beery held up his right hand, the forefinger pointed, brought it down emphatically towards Kells. "Nuts!"

Kells said: "Wait a minute, Shep." His voice was very gentle. His mouth was curved in a smile and his eyes were very hot and intent. Beery sat still.

Fenner got up. Holding a darkening handkerchief to his face, tottered toward the door.

Kells went past him to the door, locked it. He said: "Both you bastards pipe down and sit still till I finish." He shoved Fenner back into the chair. "As I was about to say: you were a little late, you heard Granquist outside the door, wiped off the rod—if you didn't, I did—put in under the table and ducked into the cupboard."

Beery said slowly: "What do you mean: you wiped it off?"

Kells didn't answer. He squatted in front of Fenner, said: "Listen, you—what do you think I put on that act for—ribbed Granquist into taking the fall? Because she can beat it." His elbows were on his knees. He pointed his finger forcibly at Fenner, sighted across it. "You couldn't. You couldn't get to first base...."

Fenner's face was a bruised, fearful mask. He stared blankly at Kells.

"A few days ago—yesterday—all I wanted was to be let alone," Kells went on. "I wasn't. I was getting along fine—quietly—legitimately—and Rose and you and the rest of these—gave me action."

He stood up. "All right—I'm beginning to like it." He walked once to the window, back, bent over Fenner. "I'm taking over your organization. Do you hear me? I'm going to run this town for a while—ride hell out of it."

He glanced at Beery, smiled. Then he turned again to Fenner, spoke quietly: "I was going East tomorrow. Now you're going. You're going to turn everything over to me and take a nice long trip—or they're going to break your goddamned neck with a rope."

Kells went to the small desk, sat down. He found a pen,

scribbled on a piece of Lido stationery. "And just to make it 'legal, and in black and white', as the big business men say—you're going to sign this—and Mister Beery is going to witness it."

Beery said: "You can't get away with a–"

"No?" Kells paused, glanced over his shoulder at Beery. "I'll get away with it big, young fella. And stop worrying about your job—you've got a swell job with me. How would you like to be chief of police?"

He went on writing, then stopped suddenly, turned to Fenner. "I've got a better idea," he said. "You'll stay here where I can hold a book on you. You stay here and in your same spot—only you can't go to the toilet without my okay," He got up and stood in the center of the room and jerked his head toward the desk. "There it is. Get down on it—quick."

Fenner said, "Certainly not," thickly.

Kells looked at the floor, said: "Call Hayes, Shep."

Beery reached for the telephone.

Fenner didn't look at him. He held his hands tightly over his face for a moment, mumbled, "My God!"—then he got up and went unsteadily to the desk, sat down. He stooped over the piece of paper, read it carefully.

Kells said: "If Granquist beats the case—and she will—and you don't talk out of turn, I'll tear it up in a month or so."

Fenner picked up the pen, shakily signed.

Kells looked at Beery, and Beery got up and went over and read the paper. He said: "This is a confession. Does it make me an accessory?"

Kells said: "It isn't dated."

Beery signed and folded the paper and handed it to Kells.

Kells glanced at it, turned to Fenner. "Now I want you to call your Coast Guardian man, Dickinson, and any other key men you can get in touch with, and tell them to be at your joint at the Knickerbocker in a half-hour."

Fenner went into the bathroom, washed his face. He came back in a little while and sat down at the telephone.

Kells held the folded paper out to Beery. "You're going downtown anyway, Shep," he said. "Stick this in the safe at your office—I'll be down in the morning and take it to the bank."

Beery said: "Do I look that simple? I've got a wife and family."

Kells put the folded paper in his own pocket.

"Anyway, I'm not going downtown. I'm coming along," Beery picked up his hat. Kells nodded abstractedly, glanced at his watch; it was twenty-two minutes past ten. Outside, there was a long ragged buzz of faraway thunder and the telephone clicked as Fenner dialed a number.

Chapter Four

FIVE MEN SAT in Fenner's apartment at the Knickerbocker.

Fenner sat at one end of the divan. Hanline, Fenner's secretary, sat beside him, then Abe Gowdy, Fenner's principal contact man with the liberal element. They hadn't been able to reach Dickinson.

Gowdy swung the vote of practically every gambler, grafter, bootlegger and so on in the county, except the few independents who tried to get along without protection. He was a bald, paunchy man with big white bulbs of flesh under his eyes, a loose pale mouth. He wore dark, quiet clothes; didn't drink.

Hanline was a curly-haired, thin-nosed Jew. He drank a great deal.

He and Beery and Kells all drank a great deal.

Kells got up and walked to one of the windows. He said: "Try him again."

Fenner reached wearily for the phone, asked for a Fitzroy number, listened a little while and hung up.

Kells turned, came back and stopped near Fenner, looked first at Gowdy, then Hanline.

"Gentlemen," he said. "Lee"—he indicated Fenner with a fond pat on the shoulder—"Lee and I have entered into a partnership." He paused, picked up a small glass full of whiskey and cracked ice, drank most of it.

"We all know," he went on, "that things haven't been so good the last three or four years—and we know that unless some very radical changes are made in the city government things won't get any better." Hanline nodded slightly.

"Lee and I have talked things over and decided to join forces." Kells put down the glass.

Gowdy said: "What do you mean: 'join forces,' Mister Kells?"

Kells cleared his throat, glanced at Beery. "You boys have the organization," he said. "You, Gowdy—and Frank Jensen, and O'Malley—and Lee here. My contribution is very important political information, which I'll handle in my own way and at my own time—and a lot of friends in the East who are going to be on their way out here tomorrow."

Hanline looked puzzled. Gowdy glanced expressionlessly at Fenner.

"Bellmann's dead," Kells went on—"and the circumstances of his murder can be of great advantage to us if they're handled in exactly the right way. But that, alone, isn't going to swing an, election. We've got the personal following of all the administration to beat—and we've got Rose's outfit to beat...."

Hanline asked: "Rose?"

Kells poured himself another drink. "Rose has built up a muscle organization of his own in the last few months—and a week or so ago he threw in with Bellmann."

Hanline and Gowdy glanced at one another, at Fenner.

Kells said: "There it is." He sat down.

Fenner got up and went into the bedroom. He came back presently, said: "It's a good proposition, Abe. Mister Kells wants to put the heat on Rose–"

Kells interrupted: "I want to reach Dickinson tonight and see if we can't get the first number of the Guardian on the streets by morning. There are certain angles on the

Bellmann thing that the other papers won't touch."

Hanline said: "Maybe he's at Ansel's—but they won't answer the phone there after ten."

"Who's Ansel?"

Hanline started to answer but Gowdy interrupted him: "Did you know Rose was backing Ansel?" Gowdy was looking at Fenner.

Fenner shook his head, spoke to Kells: "Ansel runs a couple crap games down on Santa Monica Boulevard—Dickinson plays there quite a bit."

Kells said: "So Dickie is a gambler?"

Hanline laughed. "I'll bet he's made a hundred thousand dollars with the dirt racket in the last year," he said. "And I'll bet he hasn't got a dollar and a quarter."

Kells smiled at Fenner. "You ought to take better care of your hired men," he said. Then he got up, finished his drink and put on his hat. "I'll go over and see if I can find him." Beery said: "I'll come along." Kells shook his head slightly.

Hanline stood up, stretched, said: "It's the second or third building on the south side of the street, west of Gardner—used to be a scene painter's warehouse or something like that—upstairs."

"Thanks." Kells asked Fenner: "Dickinson's the guy that was typewriting at the place downtown?"

Fenner nodded.

Hanline said: "If you don't mind, I'm going back downstairs and get some sleep. I was out pretty late last night."

"Sure." Kells glanced at Gowdy.

Kells and Hanline went out, down the elevator. Hanline got off at the fifth floor. Kells stopped at the desk, asked for the house detective. The clerk pointed out a heavy, dull-eyed man who sat reading a paper near the door. Kells went over to him, said: "You needn't hold the man Fenner was going to file charges against."

The house detective put down his paper. He said: "Hell, he was gone when I got upstairs. There wasn't nobody there but Mister Dillon."

Kells said: "Oh." He scratched the back of his head. "How's Dillon?"

"He'll be all right." Kells went out and got into a cab.

* * * * *

ANSEL'S TURNED OUT to be a dark, three-story business block set flush with the sidewalk. There were big For Rent signs in the plate-glass windows and there was a dark stairway at one side.

Kells told the cab driver to wait, went upstairs.

Someone opened a small window in a big heavily timbered door, surveyed him dispassionately.

Kells said: "I want to see Ansel."

"He ain't here."

"I'm a friend of Dickinson's—I want to see him."

The window closed and the door swung slowly open; Kells went into a small room littered with newspapers and cigarette butts. The man who had looked at him through the window patted his pockets methodically, silently.

Another man, a very dark-skinned Italian or Greek, sat in a worn wicker chair tilted back against one wall.

He said: "Your friend Dickinson—he is very drunk."

Kells said, "So am I," and then the other man finished feeling his pockets, went to another heavy door, opened it.

Kells went into a very big room. It was dark except for two clots of bright light at the far end. He walked slowly back through the darkness, and the hum of voices grew louder, broke up into words: "Eight.... Point is eight, a three-way... Get your bets down, men.... Throws five—point is eight.... Throws eleven, a field point, men.... Throws four—another fielder. Get 'em in the field, boys.... Five... Seven, out. Next man. Who likes this lucky shooter?..."

Each of the two tables was lined two deep with men. One powerful green-shaded light hung over each table. The dice man's voice droned on: "Get down on him, boys.... Ten—the hard way.... Five.... Ten—the winner—All right, boys, he's coming out. Chuck it in...."

Kells saw Dickinson. He was standing at one end of one of the tables. He was swaying back and forth a little and his eyes were half closed; he held a thick sheaf of bills in his left hand.

"Seven—the winner...."

Dickinson leaned forward and put his forefinger unsteadily down beside a stack of bills on the line. The change man reached over, counted it and put a like amount beside it.

"Drag fifty, Dick," he said. "Hundred-dollar limit."

Dickinson said thickly:—"Bet it all."

The change man smiled patiently, picked up a fifty-dollar bill and tossed it on the table nearer Dickinson.

A small, pimpled old man at the end of the table caught the dice as they were thrown to him, put them into the black leather box, breathed into it devoutly, rolled.

Kells elbowed closer to the table.

"Eleven—the winner...."

Dickinson stared disgustedly at the change man as a hundred dollars in tens and twenties was counted out, lain down beside his line bet. The change man said: "Drag a C, Dick."

"Bet it!" Dickinson said angrily.

Kells looked at the change man. He said: "Can you raise the limit if I cover it behind the line?"

The man glanced at a tall well-dressed youth behind him for confirmation, nodded.

Kells took a wad of bills out of his trouser pocket and put two hundred-dollar bills—down behind the line. Dickinson looked up, and his bleary, heavy-lidded eyes came gradually to focus on Kells.

He said, "Hello there," very heartily. Then he looked as if he were trying hard to remember, said: "Kells! How are ya, boy?"

At mention of Kells's name it became very quiet for a moment.

Kells said: "I'm fine."

The little pimpled man rolled.

The dice man said: "Six—an easy one.... He will or he won't.... Nine pays the field.... Six—right...."

The change man picked up Kells's two hundred-dollar bills, tossed them down beside Dickinson's bet.

Dickinson grinned. He said: "Bet it."

Kells took a thousand-dollar note from his breast pocket, put it down behind the line.

Dickinson said: "Better lay off—I'm right...."

"Get down on the bill." Kells smiled faintly, narrowly.

"Damned if I won't." Dickinson counted his money on the table and the money in his hand: "Four hundred, six, eight, nine, a thousand, thousand one hundred an' thirty. Tap me."

The tall young man said: "Hurry up, gentlemen—you're holding up the game."

Several men wandered over from the other table. The little man holding the dice box said:

"Jesus! I don't want..."

Kells was counting out the additional hundred and thirty dollars.

Dickinson said: "Roll."

"Eleven—the winner."

The change man picked up Kells's money, cut off a twenty for the house, threw the rest down in front of Dickinson.

The little man raked in the few dollars he had won for himself, walked away.

The dice man picked up the box.

Kells said: "Got enough?"

"Hell, no! I'll bet it all on my own roll." Dickinson held out his hand for the box.

"Make it snappy, boys." The tall young man frowned, nodded briefly at Kells.

Dickinson was checking up on the amount. He said: "Two thousand, two hundred and forty..."

Kells put three thousand-dollar notes behind the line. The dice man threw a dozen or more glittering red dice on the table; Dickinson carefully picked out two.

"Get down your bets, men.... A new shooter.... We take big ones and little ones.... Come, don't-come, hard way, and in the field.... Bet 'em either way...."

Dickinson was shaking the box gently, tenderly, near his ear. He rolled.

"Three—that's a bad one...."

Kells picked up his three notes; the change man raked up the bills in front of Dickinson, counted them into a stack, cut off one and handed the rest to Kells.

"Next man.... Get down on the next lucky shooter, boys...."

Kells folded the bills and stuck them into his pocket.

Dickinson looked at the-tall young man, said: "Let me take five hundred, Les."

The young man looked at him with soft unseeing eyes, turned and walked away. Kells gestured with his head and went over to a round green-covered table out of the circle of light. Dickinson followed him, they sat down.

Kells said: "Can you get the paper out by tomorrow morning?"

Dickinson was fumbling through his pockets, brought out a dark brown pint bottle. He took out the cork, held the bottle toward Kells. "Wha' for?"

Kells shook his head but Dickinson shoved the bottle

into his hands. Kells took a drink, handed it back.

"Bellmann was fogged tonight and I want to give it a big spread."

"The hell you say!" Dickinson stared blankly at Kells. "Well, wha'd'y know about that!" Then he seemed to remember Kells's question. "Sure."

Kells said: "Let's go."

"Wait a minute. Let's have another drink."

They drank.

Dickinson said: "Listen. Wha'dy' think happened tonight? Somebody called me up an' offered me ten grand, cold turkey, to ditch Lee."

"Ditch him, how?"

"I don't know. They said all I had to do was gum up the works some way so that the paper wouldn't come out. They said I'd get five in cash in the mail tomorrow, an' the rest after the primaries."

"What did you say?"

"I said, 'Listen, sister, Lee Fenner's been a damned good friend to me.' I said–"

Kells said: "Sister?"

"Yeah. It was a broad."

They got up and went through the semidarkness to the little room, out and downstairs to the street. It was raining very hard. Dickinson said he had a car; Kells paid off the cab and they went into the vacant lot alongside the building.

Dickinson's car was a Ford coupe; he finally found his keys and opened the door. Then a bright spotlight was switched on in a car at the curb. There was a sharp choked roar and something bit into Kells's leg, into his side. Dickinson stumbled, fell down on his knees on the running board; his face and the upper part of his body sagged forward to the floor of the car. He lay still.

* * * * *

KELLS LAY DOWN in the mud beside the car and drew-up his knees and he could taste blood in his mouth. His teeth were sunk savagely, deeply into his lower lip, and there were jagged wires of pain in his brain, jagged wires in his side.

He knew that it had been a shotgun, and he lay in the mud with rain whipping his face, wondered if Dickinson was dead, waited for the gun to cough again.

Then the spotlight went out and Kells could hear the car being shifted, into gear; he twisted his head a little and saw it pass through the light near the corner—a Cadillac.

He crawled up onto the running board of the Ford and shook Dickinson a little, and then he slowly, painfully, pushed Dickinson up into the car—slowly.

He pressed the knob that unlocked the opposite door and limped around the car and crawled into the driver's seat. He could feel blood on his side; blood pounded through his head, his eyes. He pried the keys out of Dickinson's hand and started the motor. Dickinson was an inert heap beside him. He groaned, coughed in a curious dry way.

Kells said: "All right, boy. We'll fix it up in a minute." Dickinson coughed again in the curious way that was like a laugh. He tried to sit up, fell forward and-his head banged against the windshield. Kells pulled him back into the seat and drove out of the lot, turned east on Santa Monica. Dickinson tried to say something, groped with one hand in the side pocket. He finally gave it up, managed to gasp: "Gun—here."

Kells said. "Sit still."

They went down Santa Monica Boulevard very fast, turned north on La Brea. Kells stopped halfway up the block and felt in Dickinson's pocket for the bottle, but it had been broken, the pocket was full of wet glass.

They went up La Brea to Franklin, over Franklin to

Cahuenga, up Cahuenga and Irish to Cullen's house.

Kells's side and leg had become numb. He got out of the car as quickly as he could, limped up the steps. Cullen answered the first ring, stood in the doorway looking elaborately disgusted, said: "Again?"

Kells said: "Give me a hand, Willie. Hurry up." He started back down the steps.

"No! God damn you and your jams!"

Kells turned and stared at Cullen expressionlessly, and then he went on down the steps. Cullen followed him, muttering; they got Dickinson out of the car, carried him up into the house.

Cullen was breathing heavily. He asked: "Why the hell don't you take him to the Receiving Hospital?"

"I've been mixed up in five shootings in the last thirty-two hours." Kells went to the telephone, grinned over his shoulder at Cullen. "It's like old times—one more and they'll hang me on principle."

"Haven't you got any other friends? This place was lousy with coppers yesterday."

"Wha's the matter, darling?"

Kells and Cullen turned, looked at the stairway. Eileen, Coin's girl, was standing halfway down. She swayed back and forth, put her hand unsteadily on the banister. She was very drunk. She was naked.

She drawled: "Hello, Gerry."

Cullen said: "Go back upstairs and put on your clothes, slut!" He said it very loudly.

Kells laughed, said: "Call Doc Janis—will you, Willie?" He limped to the door, looked down at his torn, muddy, bloodstained clothes. "And loan me a coat. Willie—or I'll get wet."

* * * * *

A BLACK TOURING car with the side curtains drawn was parked in the reserved space in front of the Knickerbocker. Kells had been about to park across the street; he slowed down, blinked at it. The engine was running and there was a man at the wheel. It was a Cadillac.

He stepped on the throttle, careened around the corner, parked in front of the library. He jumped out and took the revolver out of the side pocket, slipped it into the pocket of Cullen's big coat; he turned up the deep Collar and hurried painfully back across the street, down an alley to a service entrance of the hotel.

The boy in the elevator said: "Well, I guess I was right—I guess it's going to rain all night."

Kells said: "Uh huh."

"Tch tch tch." The boy shook his head sadly.

"Has Mister Fenner had any visitors since I left?"

"No, sir—I don't think so. Not many people in and out tonight. There was three gentlemen went up to nine little while ago. They was drunk, I guess." He slid the door open. "Ten, sir."

Kells said: "Thank you."

He listened at the door of ten-sixteen, heard no sound, rang the bell and stood close to the wall with the revolver in his hand. The inner hallway was narrow—the door would have to be opened at least halfway before he could be seen.

It opened almost at once, slowly. A yellow-white face took form in the darkness, and Kells stepped in to the doorway. He held the revolver belly-high in front of him. The yellow-white face faded backwards as Kells went in until it was the black outline of a man's head against orange light of the living room, until it was the figure of a short Latin standing with his back against the wall at one side of the door, his arms stretched out.

Beyond him, Fenner and Beery kneeled on the floor, their faces to the wall. On the other side of the room O'Donnell stood with a great blue automatic leveled at Kells's chest. O'Donnell was bareheaded and a white bulge of gauze and cotton plastered across his scalp. His mouth was open and he breathed through it slowly, audibly. Except for the sharp sound of his breathing, it was entirely still.

Kells said: "I'll bet I can shoot faster than you, Adenoids." O'Donnell didn't say anything. His pale eyes glittered in a sick face and the big automatic was glistening and steady in his fat pink hand.

Fenner leaned forward, put his head against the wall. Beery turned slowly and looked at Kells. The Mexican was motionless, bright-eyed.

Then Beery said, "Look out!" and something dull and terrible crashed against the back of Kells's head, there was dull and terrible blackness. It was filled with thunder and smothering blue, something hot and alive pulsed in Kells's hand. He fell.

* * * * *

THERE WAS LIGHT that hurt his eyes very much, even when they were closed. Someone was throwing water in his face. He said: "Stop that, damn it—you're getting me wet!" Beery said: "Sh—easy."

Kells opened his eyes a little. "The place is backwards."

"This is the one next door, one across the airshaft where Fenner's stick-up men were stashed. Fenner had the key." Beery spoke very quietly.

"God! My head. How did I get in here?"

Beery said: "Papa carried you." He stood up and went to the door for a minute, came back and sat down. "And what a piece of business! You were out on your feet—absolutely cold—squeezed that iron, one, two, three, four, five, six—like that. One in the wall about six inches above my head, five in baby-face."

"That was O'Donnell." Kells closed his eyes and moved his head a little. Beery nodded. "Who hit me?"

"Rose."

Kells looked interested. "What with—a piano?"

"A vase...."

"Vahze."

Beery said: "A vase—a big one out of the bedroom. I don't think he had a gun."

"Would you mind beginning at the beginning?" Kells closed his eyes again.

"After you left, Fenner and Gowdy sat there like a couple bumps on a log, afraid to crack in front of me."

Kells nodded carefully, held his head in his hands.

"After a while, Gowdy got bored and went home—he lives around the corner. I was sucking up a lot of red-eye, having a swell time. Then about five minutes before you got here the bell rang and Fenner went to the door, backed in with Rose and O'Donnell and the spiggoty. O'Donnell and the spick was snowed to the eyes. Rose said, 'What did Kells get from that gal that bumped Bellmann, and where is it?' Fenner went into a nose dive—he was scared wet, anyway. They made us get down on the floor–"

Kells laughed, said: "You looked like a couple communicants."

"—and Rose frisked both of us and started tearing up the Furniture. Some way or other I got the idea that whether he found what he was looking for or not, we weren't going to tell about it afterwards."

Beery paused, lighted a cigaret, went on quietly: "Rose was sore as hell, and O'Donnell and the greaser were leaking C out of their ears. The greaser kept fingering a shiv in his belt—you know: the old noiseless ear-to-ear trick."

Kells said: "Maybe. They popped Dickinson and me outside Ansel's. If they're that far in the open maybe they'd want to get Fenner too."

"And Beery—the innocent bystander...."

"I doubt it, Shep. I don't think Rose would have come along if it was a kill."

"Well, anyway—he'd got around to the bedroom when you rang. He switched out the light and waited in there in the dark. You came in and went into your Wild West act with baby-face, and Rose came behind you and took a bead on your skull with the vase—vahze. Then he and the greaser scrammed—quick."

Kells reached suddenly into his inside pocket, then took his hand out, sighed. "Didn't he fan me?"

"No. I grabbed O'Donnell's gun when he fell—anyway, I think Rose was too scared to think about that." Kells said: "Go on."

Beery looked immensely, superior. "Well, the old rapid-fire Beery brain got to work. I figured that you had to be out of there quick and I remembered what you'd said about this place next door. Fenner was about to go into his fit—I got the key from him and talked about thirty seconds' worth of sense, and carried you in here—and the gun." He nodded at the revolver on the couch beside Kells.

"Where's Fenner now?"

"Over at the Station filing murder charges against Rose and the greaser."

Kells said: "That's swell."

"The house dick and a bunch of coppers and a lot of neighbors who had heard the barrage got here at about the same time. It was the fastest police action I've ever seen; must have been one of the radio cars. I listened through the airshaft. Fenner had pulled himself together, told a beautiful story about Rose and O'Donnell and the Mex crashing in, O'Donnell getting it in an argument with Rose."

Beery mashed out his cigarette. "He's telling it over at headquarters now—or maybe he's on his way back. You've been out about a half-hour."

Kells sat up unsteadily, said: "Give me a drink of water." He bent over and very carefully rolled up his trouser leg, examined his injured leg.

A little later there was a tap at the door and Beery opened it, let Fenner in.

Fenner looked very tired. He said: "How are you, Gerry?"

"I'm fine, Lee—how are you?" Kells grinned.

"Terrible—terrible! I can't stand this kind of thing." Fenner sat down.

"Maybe you'd better take a trip, after all." Kells smiled faintly, picked up the revolver. "Things are going to be more in the open from now on, I guess—I'll have to carry a gun." He looked down at the revolver.

"By God, I'll get a permit for a change," he said: "Can you fix that up?"

Fenner nodded wearily. "I guess so."

"And Lee, we made a deal tonight—I mean early—the twenty-five grand, you know. I'm going to handle the stuff, of course; but in the interests of my client, Miss Granquist, I'll have to consummate the sale."

Fenner looked at the floor.

"A check'll be all right."

Fenner nodded. "I'll go in and make it out," he said. "Then I'll have to say goodnight—I'm all in."

"That'll be all right."

Fenner went out and closed the door.

Kells sat looking at the door for a moment and then he said: "Shep—you're the new editor of the Coast Guardian. How do you like that?"

"Lousy. I don't carry enough insurance."

"You'll be all right. A hundred a week and all the advertising you can sell on the side."

"When do I start?"

"Right now. I parked Dickinson up at Bill Cullen's. I'll

drop you there and you can get the details from him—if he's conscious. I'll turn the, uh—data over to you...."

Beery rubbed his eyes, yawned. He smiled a little and said: "Oh well, what the hell. I guess I'm beginning to like it."

Kells looked at his wrist. "The bastards smashed my watch—what time is it?"

"Twelve-two."

Kells picked up the telephone and called a Hempstead number. He said: "Hello, baby... Sure... Have you got any ham and eggs?... Have you got some absorbent cotton and bandages and iodine?... That's fine, I'll be up in about ten minutes... I've been on a party."

* * * * *

DOCTOR JANIS LOOKED wiser than any one man could possibly be. His head was as round and white and bare as a cue ball; his nose was a long bony hook and his eyes were pale, immensely shrewd.

He jabbed forceps gently into Kells's leg, said: "Hurt?"

Kells stuck out his lips, shook his head slightly. "No. Not very much."

"You're a damned liar!" Janis straightened, glared.

Bright sun beat through the wide east windows; the old instrument case against one white wall glistened. Kells was half lying on a small operating table. He stared at the bright point of sunlight on the wall, tried not to think about the leg.

"God deliver me from a sadistic doctor," he said.

Janis grinned, bent again over the leg, probed deeper. "That Was a dandy." He held a tiny twisted chunk of lead up in the forceps' point, exhibited it proudly. "Now you know how a rabbit feels."

"Now I know how it feels to be a mother. You're as proud

of a few shot as a good doctor would be of triplets."

Janis chuckled, jabbed again with the forceps.

At a little after eight-thirty, Kells left Janis's office in the Harding Building. It had rained all night; the air was sharp, clear. He limped across Hollywood Boulevard to a small jewelry store, left his watch to be repaired and asked that they send it to him at the hotel as soon as possible. He went out and bought a paper and got a cab, said, "Ambassador," leaned back and spread the paper. Then he sat up very straight.

A headline read: WOMAN IN BELLMANN KILLING ESCAPES.

He glanced out the window at a tangle of traffic as the cab curved into Vine Street; then leaned back again slowly, read the story:

> Early this morning, Miss S. Granquist, alleged by police to be the self-confessed slayer of John R. Bellmann, prominent philanthropist and reformer, was "kidnapped" from Detectives Breen and Rail after the car in which they were taking her from the Hollywood Police Station to the County Jail had been forced to the curb near Temple Street and Coronado, crashed into a fire plug. Officer Breen was slightly injured, removed to the Receiving Hospital. Rail described the "abductors" as, "eight or nine heavily armed and desperate men in a cream-colored coupe." He neglected to explain how "eight or nine" men and a woman got away in a coupe. Our motor-car manufacturers would be interested in how that was done. It is opportune that another example of the inefficiency of our police department occurs almost on the eve of the municipal primaries. The voters....

Kells folded the paper, knocked on the glass and told the driver to make it fast. They cut over Melrose to Normandie, out of the heavy traffic, over Normandie to Wilshire Boulevard and into the big parking circle of the Ambassador.

Kells told the driver to wait, hurried up to his room and changed clothes. He called the desk, was told that Mister Beery had called twice, called Beery back at the Hay ward Hotel downtown. The room line was busy. He took a long drink and went back down and got into the cab. It took twenty-five minutes to get through the traffic on lower Seventh Street to the Hayward. Fenner opened the door of the small outer room on the fourth floor; they went through to the larger bedroom. Kells said: "You're down early, Lee."

Fenner glanced at the rolled newspaper in Kells's hand, nodded, smiled wanly.

"Where's Beery?" Kells took off his hat and coat. Fenner sat down on the bed. "He went over to the print shop about an hour ago. He ought to be back pretty soon." Kells sat down carefully. Fenner asked: "How's the leg?"

"Doc Janis picked eleven shot out of it like plucking petals off a daisy. It came out odd—he loves me." Kells unrolled, unfolded the paper, looked over it at Fenner. "Do you know anything about this?"

"I do not." Fenner said it very quietly, very emphatically.

"What do you think?"

"Rose."

Kells stared at Fenner steadily. He moved his fingers on the arm of the chair as though running scales. He said: "What for?"

"She's crossed him up all the way—he's the kind of a crazy guy that would take a long chance to get even."

Kells sat staring blankly at Fenner for perhaps a minute. Then he said slowly: "I want you to call Gowdy—everybody you can reach who might have a line on it...."

Fenner got up and went to the phone. He called several numbers, spoke softly, quietly.

After a little while the other door opened and someone came through the outer room. It was Beery. He said: "We can't get it on the newsstands before noon."

"That'll be all right." Kells was still sitting deep in the big chair. Fenner was at the telephone. Beery took off his coat and hat, flopped down on the bed.

"Maybe I can get a couple hours' snooze," he said.

Fenner hung up the receiver and looked at Kells. "You might pick up something at the Bronx, out on Central Avenue. It's a nigger cabaret run by a man named Sheedy. Rose is supposed to be a partner—he was seen there last night."

"Who's Sheedy?"

Beery said: "A big dinge—used to be in pictures...."

"You know him?"

"A little."

"Get on the phone and see if you can locate him. He wouldn't be at his joint this time of day."

Beery sighed, sat up. "The law's looking for Rose too, Gerry," he said. "You're not going to get anything out of any of these boys."

Kells half smiled, inclined his head toward the phone. Then he stood up.

"If that son of a bitch got her—which is a long shot"—he looked sideways at Fenner—"he'll give her everything in the book. I got her into it—and by God! I'll get her out if I have to turn the rap back on Lee and let the whole play slide." He turned, went to one of the windows. "And if Rose did get her and lets her have it. I'll spread his guts from here to Caliente."

Beery got up and went to the phone. "You're getting plenty dramatic about a gal you turned up yourself," he said.

Kells turned from the window and looked at Beery, and his eyes were cold, his mouth was partly open, faintly smiling.

He said: "Right."

* * * * *

SHEEDY COULDN'T be located.

Fenner got Officer Rail on the phone and Kells talked to him. Rail said he couldn't identify any of the men who had taken Granquist; he thought one of them was crippled, wore a steel brace on his leg. He wasn't sure.

Kells called Rose's place on Fifth Street; there was no answer. He called the Biltmore, was told that Rose hadn't been in for two days; Mrs. Rose was out of town.

Beery napped for an hour. Kells and Fenner sat in the outer room; Fenner read a detective-story magazine and Kells sat deep in a big chair, stared out the window. Hanline stopped in for a minute. He said he'd speak to one of the bellboys downstairs, send up a bottle.

At a little after ten-thirty the phone rang. Fenner answered it, called Kells.

A man's high-pitched voice said: "I have been authorized to offer you fifteen thousand dollars for the whole issue of the Guardian, together with the plates and all data used in its make-up."

Kells said, "I don't know what you're talking about," hung up.

He told Fenner to hurry down to the switchboard, try to trace the call; waited for the phone to ring again. It did almost immediately. The man's voice said: "It will be very much to your advantage to talk business, Mister Kells."

"Who's your authority?"

"The Bellmann estate."

Kells said: "If you know where Miss Granquist is and can produce her within the next half-hour, I'll talk to you."

There was a long silence at the other end of the line. Then the man said: "Wait a minute." After a little while a woman's voice said: "Gerry! For God's sake get me out of this!..." The voice trailed off as if she had been dragged away from the phone. The man's voice said: "Well?" Fenner came in, nodded to Kells. Kells said: "Okay. Bring her here." He hung up. The phone rang again but he didn't answer. He sat grinning at Fenner. Fenner said excitedly: "West Adams—about a block west of Figueroa."

"That wasn't even a good imitation of the baby." Kells stood up. "But maybe they'll come here and try to do business on that angle. That'll be swell."

"But we'd better get out there, hadn't we?"

Kells said: "What for? They haven't got her or they wouldn't take a chance faking her voice. They'll be here—and I'll lay ten to one they don't know any more about where Rose and the kid are than we do."

Kells went back to his chair by the window. "I told Shep to plant some men at the print shop in case there's trouble there. Did he?" Fenner nodded.

There was a knock at the door; Fenner said, "Come in," and a boy came in with a bottle of whiskey and three tall glasses of ice on a tray. He put the tray on a table; Fenner gave him some change and he went out and closed the door.

At twenty minutes after eleven a Mister Woodward was announced. Fenner went into the bedroom, closed the door.

Woodward turned out to be a small yellow-haired man, wearing tortoise-shell glasses; about thirty-five. He sat down at Kells's invitation, declined a drink.

He said: "Of course we couldn't bring Miss Granquist here. She's being sought by the police and that would be too dangerous. She'll be turned over to you, together with a certified check for fifteen thousand dollars, as soon as the issue of the Guardian, the plates and the copy are turned over to us."

Kells said: "What the hell kind of a cheap outfit are you? The stuff's worth that much simply as state's evidence—let alone its political value to your people."

"I know—I know." Woodward bobbed his head up and down. "The fact of the matter is, Mister Kells—my people are up against it for cash. They'll know how to show their appreciation in other ways, however."

"What other ways?"

"Certain political concessions after election—uh—you know." Woodward glanced nervously at his watch. "And it is imperative that you make a decision quickly."

Kells said: "I'm not in politics. I want the dough. Lay fifty thousand on the line and show me Miss Granquist"—he looked at his watch, smiled—"and it is imperative that you make a decision quickly."

Woodward stood up. "Very well, Mister Kells," he said. His voice had risen in pitch to the near-falsetto of the telephone conversation. "What you ask is impossible. I'll say good-day."

He started toward the door and Kells said: "Hold on a minute." The big automatic that had been O'Donnell's glittered dully in his hand. "Sit down."

Woodward's blue eyes were wide behind his glasses. He went back toward the chair.

Kells said: "No. Over by the phone."

Woodward smiled weakly, sat down at the telephone stand.

"Now you'd better call up your parties and tell them everything's all right—that we made a deal."

Woodward was looking at the rug. He pursed his lips, shook his head slowly.

"There's a direct line in the other room," Kells wept on, "if you'd rather not make it through the switchboard."

Woodward didn't move except to shake his head slowly; he stared at the floor, smiled a little.

"Hurry up." Kells stood up.

Then the phone in the bedroom rang; Kells could faintly hear Beery say "Hello." It was quiet for a moment and then the bedroom door opened and Fenner stood in the doorway looking back at Beery.

Beery said: "You sure?... Just the press and the forms.... All out?... All right, I'll be right over." The receiver clicked and Beery came into the doorway. He glanced at Woodward, grinned crookedly at Kells.

"They blew up the joint," he said. "But nearly all the stuff was out. A hand press and a couple of linotypes were cracked up and one guy's got a piece of iron in his shoulder, but they discovered it in time and got everybody else and the sheets out. The originals are in the safe."

He struck an attitude, declaimed: "The first issue of The Coast Guardian; A Political Weekly for Thinking People, is on the stands."

Kells turned slowly, sat down. He looked steadily at Woodward for a while and then he said: "As representative of the Bellmann estate"—he paused, coughed gently—"do you think you're strong enough to beat charges of coercion, conspiracy to defeat justice, dynamiting, abduction—a few more that any half-smart attorney can figure out?"

Woodward kept his eyes down. "That was a stall about the girl. We haven't got her, and we don't know where Rose is...."

"So Rose has got her?"

Woodward looked up, spoke hesitantly: "I don't know."

"If you've got any ideas, now's a swell time to spill

them."

Woodward glanced at Beery, Fenner, back to Kells. "My people don't want to have anything to do with Rose," he said. "He's wanted for murder and if he's caught he'll get the works." He smiled again, went on slowly: "He called up this morning and said you shot O'Donnell—said he could prove it...."

Fenner laughed quietly.

Kells said: "Where did he call from?"

Woodward shook his head. "Don't know."

Beery had gone back into the bedroom. He came into the doorway again, pulling on his coat. "I'll be back in about an hour, Gerry," he said. He poured himself a short drink, swallowed it and went out making faces.

Kells asked Woodward: "Where can I find you?"

Woodward hesitated a moment. "I've got an office in the Dell Building—the number's in the book."

"You can go."

Woodward got up and said: "Good-day, sir." He nodded at Fenner, went out.

Kells took Fenner's twenty-five-thousand-dollar check out of his inside coat pocket. He unfolded it and looked at it for a minute and then he said: "Let's go over to the bank and have this certified."

They went out together.

Chapter Five

KELLS SLEPT MOST of the afternoon. Doctor Janis stopped by at seven. The leg was pretty stiff.

Janis said. "You ought to stay in a couple days, anyway. You're damned lucky it was the edge of the fan got you—Dickinson got the middle...."

Kells asked: "How is he?"

"He'll be all right. He's too tough."

Janis put on his coat and hat and went to the door. "You had a break," he said—"don't press it." He went out.

Kells telephoned Fenner. There had been several steers on Rose—all of them bad. Sheedy hadn't been located. The Mexican who had been with Rose was probably Abalos, from Frisco. He lived at a small hotel on Main street which was being watched. Reilly was being tailed.

Beery came up about eight. "Everything's lovely," he said. "All the evening papers carried the Guardian stuff—I'm the fair-haired boy at the Chronicle." He put down his glass. "You want me to keep the Chronicle job too, don't you?"

Kells said: "Sure."

Beery stooped over the low table and mixed himself a drink. "I'm going to the fights. Swell card."

"So am I."

Beery squinted over his shoulder. "You'd better stay in the hay," he said.

Kells swung up, sat on the edge of the bed. "Got your ducats?"

"Yeah. I was going to take the wife."

"Sure—we'll take her. Call up and see if you can get three together, close." Kells limped into the bathroom, turned on the shower.

Beery sat tinkling ice against the sides of his glass. When Kells turned off the shower Beery yelled: "The old lady don't want to go anyway."

Kells stood in the bathroom door, grinning.

Beery looked up at him and then down at his glass. "I guess she don't like you very well." He picked up the phone and asked for a Hollywood number.

Kells disappeared into the bathroom again, and when he came out Beery smiled happily, said: "Okay. She'd rather go to a picture show."

* * * * *

THE SEATS WERE fifth row, ringside—two seats off the aisle. The second preliminary was in its last round when Kells and Beery squeezed past a very fat man in the aisle seat, sat down.

The preliminary ended in a draw and the lights flared on. Kells nodded to several acquaintances, and Beery leaned forward, talked to a friend of his in the row ahead. He introduced the man to Kells: Brand, feature sports writer for an Eastern syndicate.

Kells had been looking at his program, asked: "What's the price on Gilroy?"

"The boys were offering three to two before dinner—very little business. I'll lay two to one on Shane."

Gilroy was a New York Negro, a heavyweight who had been at the top of his class for a while. Too much living, and racial discrimination—too few fights—had softened him.

The dopesters said he'd lost everything he ever had, was on the skids. Shane was a tough kid from Texas. He was reputed to have a right-hand punch that more than made up for his lack of experience.

Kells remembered Gilroy—from Harlem—had known him well, liked him. He said: "I'll take five hundred of that."

Brand looked at him very seriously, nodded.

Beery looked disgusted. He leaned toward Kells, muttered: "For God's sake, Gerry, they're grooming Shane for a title shot. Do you think they're going to let an unpopular boogie like Gilroy get anywhere?"

Kells said: "He used to be very good—he can't have gone as bad as they say in a year. I've only seen Shane once and I thought he was lousy...."

"He won, didn't he?"

"Uh huh."

Beery was looking at Kells sideways with wide hard eyes.

The man sitting with Brand turned around and drawled: "You don't happen to have any more Gilroy money, do you?"

"Sure."

The man said: "I'll give you eighteen hundred for a grand."

Kells nodded.

Beery looked like he was going to fall off his chair. He muttered expletives under his breath.

A man crawled into the ring, followed by two Filipinos with their seconds. The house lights dimmed.

"Ladies and gentlemen... Six rounds ... In this corner—Johnny Sanga ... a hundred an' thirty-four..."

Kells said: "I'll be back in a minute." He got up and squeezed out past the fat man.

At the head of the corridor that led to the dressing

rooms a uniformed policeman said: "You can't go any farther, buddy."

Kells looked at him coldly. "I'm Mister Olympic—I own this place." He twisted a bill around his finger, stepped close and shoved it into the copper's hand, went on.

Gilroy was sitting on the edge of a rubbing table while a squat heavily sweatered youth taped his hands. A florid be-jeweled Greek sat in a chair tilted back against the wall, smoking a short green cigar. He stood up when Kells opened the door, said: "You can't come in here, mister."

Gilroy looked up and his face split in a huge grin. "Well Ah'll be switch—Mistah Kells!" He got up and came towards Kells, held out his half-taped hand.

Kells smiled, shook hands. "H'are ya, Lonny?"

Gilroy's grin was enormous. He said: "Sit down—sit down."

Kells shook his head, leaned against the table. He glanced at the Greek and at the boy who had resumed taping the big Negro's hand. He looked at Gilroy, said: "You win?"

"Shuah—shuah." Gilroy's grin was a shade less easy. "Shuah, Ah win."

Kells kept looking at him. Gilroy looked at the Greek, then back at Kells. He shook his head slightly. "How long you been out hyah, Mistah Kells?"

Kells didn't answer. He stared at Gilroy vacantly. The Greek looked at Gilroy and then glanced icily at Kells, went out of the room. The squat youth kept on taping Gilroy's hand mechanically.

Gilroy said: "No. Ah don't win." He said it very softly.

"How much are you getting?"

Gilroy's face had become very serious. "Nothin'," he said. "Not a nickel."

Kells rubbed the back of one hand with the palm of the other.

Gilroy went on: "Not a nickel—but Ah get plenty if Ah

don't throw it...."

"What are you talking about?"

The boy finished one hand. Gilroy flexed it, looked at the floor.

"They've put the feah o' God in me, Mistah Kells. If Ah win, Ah don't go home tonight—maybe."

Kells turned to face him squarely, said: "You mean you're going to take a dive for nothing.

"If that's the way you want to put it—yes, sah."

The boy started on the other hand. Gilroy went on: "Ah been gettin' letters an' phone calls an' warnin's for a week...."

"Who from?"

"Don't know." Gilroy shook his head slowly.

Kells glanced at his watch. He said: "Do you figure you owe me anything, Lonny?"

Gilroy looked at him, and his eyes were big, liquid. "Shuah," he said—"shuah—Ah remembah."

"This is my town, now. I want you to go in and win, if you can. I'll have a load of protection here by the time you get in the ring—you can stick with me afterwards." Kells looked at him very intently. "This is important."

Gilroy was entirely still—for a moment. He stared at his hands. Then he nodded slowly without looking up.

Kells said: "I'll be back here afterwards!"

He went out of the room, closed the door. He found a telephone, called Fenner. Fenner wasn't in, he had the call switched to Hanline's room; when Hanline answered, Kells told-him to send the two best muscle men he could locate to the entrance of Section R, Olympic Arena, quickly. Hanline said: "Sure—what's it all about?" Kells said: "Nothing. What's the use of having an organization if I don't use it?"

On the way back to his seat Kells saw Fay. They walked together to an archway through which they could see the ring. The Filipinos were locked in a slow and measured dance; the electric indicator above the ring read: ROUND FIVE.

Kells asked: "Who's interested in Shane?"

Fay shrugged. "His mother, I suppose..."

"Is this so-called syndicate building him up?"

"Sure."

Kells pointed a finger, jabbed it at Fay's chest. "And—who the hell is the syndicate?"

Fay said: "Rose—and whoever his backers are."

Kells looked at the ring. "Your guess is as good as mine. Get down on Gilroy." He walked away with an extravagantly mysterious and meaningful look over his shoulder.

Back in his seat Kells tapped Brand's shoulder. "If you gentlemen would like to get out from under," he said, "you can copper those bets now."

Brand turned to Kells's wide smile. His drawling friend was engrossed in the last waltz of the Filipinos.

"I have information..." Kells widened his smile.

Brand shook his head, matched his smile, said: "No—Shane's good enough for me."

"That's what I thought. That's the reason I made the offer."

Beery was yelling at one of the Filipinos. He glanced at Kells without expression, shouted at the ring: "Ask him what he's doing after the show."

The last preliminary was declared a draw. The semi-wind-up came up: six rounds—a couple of dark smart flyweights, one on his way to a championship. It was a pretty good fight but it was the favorite's all the way.

The main event followed almost immediately. The announcer climbed into the ring—the referee, Shane, Gilroy, a knot of seconds. Shane got a big hand. Gilroy got a pretty good reception too—the black belt was well represented and Gilroy was well liked. The disk was tossed for corners, taping was examined and the referee's instructions passed.

"Ladies and gentlemen... Ten rounds ... In this corner—Arthur Shane—the Texas Cyclone... Two hundred an' eight pounds ... In this corner—Lou Gilroy ... A hundred ninety-six...."

The announcer and seconds scrambled out of the ring. Gilroy and Shane touched gloves, turned toward their corners. At the gong Shane whirled, almost ran across the ring. Gilroy looked faintly surprised, waited, calmly ducked Shane's wild right hook. They exchanged short jabs to the body and Shane straightened a long one to Gilroy's jaw.

Shane's hair was so blond it was almost white. It stuck straight up in a high pompadour above his-round pink face, flopped back and forth as he moved his head. He was thick, looked more than his two hundred and eight pounds. Gilroy had put on fat in the year since Kells had seen him in action, but it looked hard. His rich chocolate-brown body still sloped to a narrow waist, straight well-muscled legs. He looked pretty good.

Shane came in fast again; Gilroy backed against the ropes, came out and under Shane's right—they clinched. The referee stepped between them, and Gilroy clipped Shane's chin as he sidled away. They exchanged short jabs to the head and body, fell into another clinch. Gilroy brought both hands up hard to Shane's body. Shane danced away, came in fast again and snapped Gilroy's head back with a long right. They were stalling, waiting for the other to lead at the bell. The round was even.

The second and third rounds were slow—the second Shane's by a shade, the third even.

Shane came out fast in the fourth, grazed Gilroy's jaw with the long right, drove his left hard into Gilroy's stomach. Gilroy straightened up and his mouth was open; Shane stepped a little to one side, took Gilroy's weak counter on his shoulder and hooked his right to Gilroy's unprotected jaw. There was a snap and Gilroy sank down on his knees.

The crowd roared. Several people stood up.

Gilroy took a count of eight, got up grinning broadly. He ducked Shane's wild uppercut, stepped inside and pounded Shane's body, but his punches lacked steam. The muscles of his face were taut, his eyes big—he had been hurt. They clinched. The round was Shane's.

Gilroy held on during the first part of the fifth, but snapped out of it in time to smack Shane around considerably before the bell. Shane was tiring a little. It should have been Gilroy's round but was declared even.

The sixth and seventh were Gilroy's by a small margin. He seemed to have recovered all his speed; Shane brought the fight to him, made a good show of rushing but it didn't mean much. Gilroy took everything Shane had to give—fought deliberately, hard, well.

The rounds stood two apiece, three even. Kells watched Shane between the seventh and eighth, decided that whatever the fix had been, he wasn't in on it. He looked worried, but it didn't look like the kind of worry one would feel at being double-crossed. His backers had evidently let him believe that he would win or lose fairly. As a matter of fact it hadn't been bribery or a frameup, strictly speaking—they'd simply scared Gilroy and it had almost worked.

Brand turned around, smiled uncomfortably.

Kells whispered to Beery: "The eighth does it." He looked at Gilroy. Gilroy was lying back, breathing deeply. He raised his head and stared intently at the faces around the ring. Kells tried to catch his eye but the seconds were crawling out of the ring, the gong sounded.

Shane rushed again and Gilroy stood very still, blocked Shane's haymaker and swung his left in a long loop to Shane's head. Shane fell as if he had been hit with an axe. Gilroy looked down at him wonderingly for a second, shuffled to a neutral corner. Everyone stood up. The referee was counting but he couldn't be heard above the roar; his arm moved up and down and his lips moved.

Shane sat up, got unsteadily to his feet. Gilroy came in and put out his two hands and pushed him. Gilroy was smiling self-consciously. Shane was all right; he shook his head and went after Gilroy, and Gilroy curled him on the side of the head, jabbed straight left to his face. Shane stepped in close and swung his right in a wide up-and-down circle, hit Gilroy a good ten inches below the belt, hard.

Gilroy folded up slowly. He held his hands over the middle of his body and bent his knees slowly. His face was twisted with pain. He stumbled forward and straightened up a little and then fell down on his side and drew his knees up.

Shane was leaning against; the ropes and his breathing was sharply audible in the momentary silence.

Then the ring filled with people; Gilroy was carried to his corner. The announcer was shouting vainly for silence. One of Shane's seconds held the ropes apart for him; he stared dazedly at the crowd, ducked through the ropes, into the tunnel that led to the dressing rooms.

"Gilroy—on a foul." The announcer made himself faintly heard.

Brand's friend turned around and grinned wryly at Kells, shook his head sadly. "The son of a bitch," he said—"the dirty son of a bitch."

* * * * *

AT THE ENTRANCE to Section R, Kells almost ran into the fat man who had stuck him up at Fenner's. His tie was sticking out of his high stiff collar at the same cocky angle, his small head was covered by a big, violently plaid cap.

He stared at Kells's shoes, said: "Hanline sent us." He jerked his head at a fairly tall middle-aged man who looked like a prosperous insurance salesman. "This is Denny Faber."

Kells laughed.

The fat one grinned good-naturedly. "I sure slipped up the other night," he said—"the gal cramped my style." He glanced at Beery, looked back at Kells's shoes, went on: "My name is Borg."

Kells introduced Beery. Then the four of them went through the crowd to the dressing rooms.

There were a dozen or more men—mostly Negroes—in the corridor outside Gilroy's room. Kells shouldered through, opened the door. The florid Greek was standing just inside, smiling happily. He poked a finger at Kells.

"I told you we would win—I told you," he said. He turned, frowned at Beery and Borg—Faber had waited outside.

Kells said: "These gentlemen are friends of mine."

They came in behind him.

Gilroy was lying naked on the rubbing table. His face was covered with little beads of sweat. He turned his head, said: "Hello, Mistah Kells."

Kells went over to him. "How do you feel?"

"Ah'm all right. The Doc here says it's jus' a scratch"—he grinned with all his face—"jus' a scratch."

The doctor nodded.

Kells turned to Borg, said: "Get a cab and wait outside the little gate, down at the end...." He gestured with his hand.

"We got a car." Borg started toward the door.

"That's fine—we'll be out in a few minutes."

Gilroy sat up slowly, picked up a towel and wiped his face. He said:

"How about a showah, Doc?"

The doctor said it would be all right. He was putting on his coat. Kells took a roll of bills out of his pocket, slipped one off and gave it to the doctor.

Beery was standing near the door. He jerked his head and Kells went over to him. Beery asked quietly: "Brand gave you a check?"

Kells nodded.

"The other guy paid off in cash?"

"Yes."

"Gimme. You run a chance of getting into plenty of excitement tonight. I'm going home—I'd better take care of the bankroll."

"I've got Fenner's check too and somewhere around ten grand soft." Kells smiled, shook his head. "Every time I sock something in a bank something happens so I can't get to it. Something's liable to happen to you...."

"Or you."

"Uh huh—so I'll keep the geetus." Kells went back and sat down on the table.

The Greek began a long and vivid account of why Gilroy was the "coming champion."

"I tell you, Mister Kells—your name is Kells, ain't it?—Lonny is better than Johnson in his flower—in his flower...."

Beery said: "I'll call you in the morning." He and the doctor went out together.

Gilroy came out of the shower, dressed. On the way to the car, Kells asked: "Do you know Sheedy?"

"Vince Sheedy? Shuah." Gilroy stayed close to Kells, watched the people they passed, carefully. "His place is right aroun' the co'nah from my hotel."

"Let's go there and celebrate. I want to meet him."

Borg and Faber were sitting in a big closed car outside the little gate. Beery was in the tonneau.

Kells said: "I thought you were going home."

"Oh, what the hell—I'd just as well come along and see the fireworks—if any." Beery sighed.

Kells and Gilroy got in beside him. Kells leaned forward,

spoke to Borg: "Gilroy, here, has had some scare letters. We're going to take care of him for a few days."

Borg said: "Sure."

Gilroy told them how to get to Sheedy's place. Kells watched through the rear window but couldn't spot anyone following them. Traffic was heavy. They went down Sixteenth to Central Avenue, turned south.

The rear entrance to Sheedy's Bronx Club was tricky. They left the car in a parking station, went down a narrow passageway between two-buildings. Gilroy knocked at a door in the side of the passageway; it was opened and they went downstairs, through a large kitchen, into a short hallway.

Gilroy said: "There's a front way in, but this is the best because we want a private room"—he looked at Kells for confirmation—"don't we?"

Kells nodded.

Gilroy tried one of the doors in the hallway. It was locked. He tried another, opened it and switched on the light.

The room was small. There was a round table with a red-and-white tablecloth in the middle of the room and there were six or seven chairs and a couch. Gilroy pressed a button near the door.

Borg and Faber sat down and Kells stretched out on the couch. Beery studied the photographs—mostly clipped from "Art Models" magazines—on the walls.

A waiter came and Gilroy told him to get Sheedy.

Sheedy turned out to be a very tall, very yellow skeleton. Dinner clothes hung from his high, pointed shoulders as though the least wind would whip them out like a flat black sail. He nodded to Beery. He said: "I am very happy to meet you, Mister Kells." His accent was very precise. Kells guessed that if the name meant anything special to him he was a remarkable actor.

Gilroy asked: "Was you at the fight, Vince?"

"Yes ... I lost." Sheedy smiled easily.

Gilroy giggled. "Hot dawg! 'At serves you right—nex' time you know bettah."

Sheedy raised his brows, nodded sadly.

"Hash us up a load of champagne–" Gilroy made a large gesture. "An' send some gals back to sing us a song."

Sheedy said: "Right away, Lonny"—bowed himself out. He was back in about a minute, asked Kells to come into the hallway. "Some fellows just came in"—he inclined his head toward the front of the place—"asked if Lonny was here. I said no."

"Who are they?"

"Man named Arnie Taylor—a Negro—and three white boys. I don't know them."

Kells said: "Who's Taylor?"

Sheedy shook his head. "I don't think he's a—particular friend of Lonny's."

"Where's Rose?" Kells spoke very softly, quickly.

Sheedy looked surprised. Then he smiled slowly. "I'm afraid you've got some wrong ideas."

Kells waited; Sheedy went on: "I haven't the slightest idea."

Kells looked at him sleepily, silently.

Sheedy said: "He was here last night—I haven't seen him since."

"Thanks." Kells turned to go back into the room.

Sheedy caught his shoulder. "Rose and I do a little business together," he said—"that's all." He was smiling slightly, looking very straight at Kells.

Kells said: "Liquor business?"

Sheedy shook his head.

"White stuff?"

Sheedy didn't say anything.

Kells looked at the door to the cabaret, said: "Tell Taylor Lonny's back here."

Sheedy said: "I'm under one indictment here, Mister Kells. If there's any trouble and it gets loud I'll lose my license."

"It won't get loud."

The door to the cabaret opened and a very light-colored Negro with straight blue-black hair came into the hallway. There was a white man behind him, and the white man took a stubby revolver out of his coat pocket.

The Negro said: "Sorry, Vince."

Sheedy put his hands up.

Kells clicked a button-switch on the wall with his elbow but the lights in the hallway stayed on.

The white man stayed at the end of the hallway about ten feet away from them. He was short, with a broad bland childlike face. He held the revolver close to his stomach, pointed indiscriminately at Kells and Sheedy.

Taylor came up to them, felt Kells for a gun.

Sheedy started to speak, and then the room door opened and Gilroy stood outlined against darkness.

He asked: "Wha's the mattah with the lights?"

Taylor turned his head, jerked an automatic put of his belt, swung it toward Gilroy. Kells slammed his open left hand down hard on Taylor's arm and then he got his other arm around Taylor's neck and hugged him back close to the walls so that Taylor was between him and the short white man.

The white man turned swiftly and disappeared through the door to the cabaret, Sheedy after him. Then Borg came out past Gilroy and clubbed his gun, tapped Taylor back of the ear. Taylor went limp and Kells let him slide down awkwardly to the floor.

Gilroy said: "Well, fo' goodness' sake!"

* * * * *

THEY TURNED OFF Whittier Boulevard and drove a long way along a well-paved road. The road ran between fields; there were a few dark houses and occasionally a light at an intersection.

Kells sat on the left side of the tonneau and Borg sat on the right side and Taylor was between them. Gilroy and Faber were in front. Gilroy had insisted on coming. Beery had gone home.

Kells said: "Where is Rose?"

Taylor made a resigned gesture with one hand. "I tell you, Mister Kells—I don' know," he said. "If I knew–"

Borg swung his fist around into Taylor's face.

Taylor whimpered and put his arms up over his face. He tried to slide farther down in the seat, and Borg put his arm around his shoulders and held him erect.

"Where's Rose?" Kells pursued relentlessly.

"I don' know, Mister Kells.... I swear to God I don' know...." Taylor spoke into the cloth of his coat sleeve; the words were broken, sounded far away.

Borg pulled Taylor's arm down from his face very gently, held his two hands in his lap with one of his hands, swung his fist again.

Taylor struggled and freed one of his hands and put it over his bloody face. "I tell you I got orders that was supposed to come from Rose," he panted—"but they were over the phone ... I don't know where they was from...."

They rode in silence for a little while, except for the sound of Taylor's sobbing breath. Then they turned into a dirt road, darker, winding.

Kells said: "Where's Rose?"

Taylor sobbed, mumbled unintelligibly.

Gilroy turned around and looked at Taylor with hurt, softly animal eyes. Then he looked at Kells, and Kells nodded. There was a little light from a covered globe on the dashboard. Gilroy kept looking at Kells until he nodded again and then Gilroy tapped Faber's arm; the car stopped, the headlights were switched off.

Kells took the big automatic out of a shoulder holster. He opened the door and put one foot out on the running board, and then he spoke over his shoulder to Borg: "Bring him out here. We don't want to mess up the car."

Taylor screamed and Borg clapped his hand over his mouth—then Taylor was suddenly silent, limp. His eyes were wide and white and his lips moved.

Borg said, "Come on—come on," and then he saw that Taylor couldn't move and he put his arms around him and half shoved, half lifted him out of the door of the car. Taylor couldn't straighten his legs. He put one foot on the running board and his knees gave away and he fell down in the road.

Gilroy got out on the other side, said: "Ah'm goin' to walk up the road a piece." His voice trembled. He went into the darkness.

Taylor was moaning, threshing around in the dust.

Kells squatted beside him. Then he straightened up and spoke to Faber: "Pull up about thirty feet."

Faber looked surprised. He let the clutch in and the car moved forward a little way.

Kells squatted beside Taylor in the darkness again, waited. He held the automatic in his two hands, between his legs. The dim red glow of the taillight was around them.

Taylor rolled over on his back and tried to sit up. Kells helped-him, held one hand on his shoulder. Taylor's eyes were bulging; he looked blindly at the redness of the taillight, blindly at Kells—then he said very evenly, quietly: "He's in Pedro—Keystone Hotel...." Fear had worn itself out, had taken his strength and left him, curiously, entirely calm. He no longer trembled and his voice was even, low. Only his eyes were wide, staring.

Kells called to Borg and they helped Taylor back to the

car. They picked up Gilroy a little way ahead. He stared questioningly at Taylor, Kells.

Kells said: "He's all right."

They headed back toward town.

* * * * *

THE NIGHT CLERK at the Keystone in San Pedro remembered the gentlemen: the dark, good-looking Mister Gorman and the small and Latin Mister Ribera. They had checked in early yesterday morning, without baggage. They had made several long-distance calls to Los Angeles during the day, sent several wires. They had left about seven-thirty in the evening; no forwarding address.

It was a quarter after one. Kells checked his watch with the clock in the lobby, thanked the clerk and went out to the car. He got in and sat beside Borg, grunted: "No luck."

They had taken Gilroy home—Faber had stayed with him.

Borg asked: "Where to?"

Kells sat a little while silently staring at nothing. He finally said: "Drive down toward Long Beach."

Borg started the car and they went down the dark street slowly. The fog was very thick; street lights were vague yellow blobs in the darkness.

Kells tapped Borg's knee suddenly. "Have you ever been out to Fay's boat?"

Borg hadn't. "I ain't much of a gambler," he said. "I went out to the Joanna D. once, before it burned up—with a broad."

"Do you remember how to get to the P & O wharf?"

Borg said he thought so. They turned into the main highway south. After about a half-hour, they turned off into what turned out to be a blind street. They tried the next one and had just about decided they were wrong again when Borg saw the big white P & O on the warehouse that ran out on the wharf. They parked the car and walked out to the waiting room.

Kells asked the man in the office if the big red-faced man who ran one of the launches to the Eaglet was around.

The man looked at his watch. "You mean Bernie, I guess," he said. "He oughta be on his way back with a load."

They sat down and waited.

* * * * *

BERNIE LAUGHED. He said: "You ain't as wet as you were the last time I saw you."

Kells shook his head. They walked together to the end of the wharf.

Kells asked: "You know Jack Rose when you see him?"

"Sure."

"When did you see him last?"

Bernie tipped his cap back, scratched his nose. "Night before last," he said, "when you and him went out to the Joanna."

"If you were wanted for murder in LA and wanted to get out of the country for a while how would you do it?"

"I don't know." Bernie spat into the black water alongside the wharf. "I suppose I'd make a pass at Mexico."

"If you were going by car you wouldn't be coming through Pedro."

"No."

"But if you were going by boat?"

Bernie said: "Hell, if I was going by boat I wouldn't go all the way to Mexico. I'd go out and dig in on China Point."

Kells sat down on a pile. "I've heard of it," he said. "What's it all about?"

"That's God's country." Bernie grinned, stared through the sheets of mist at the lights of the bay. "That's the rum runners' paradise. All the boys in the racket along the coast hang out there. They come in from mother ships—and the tender crews.... I'll bet there's a million dollars' worth of stuff on the island. They steal it from each other to keep themselves entertained...."

"How long since you were there?"

"Couple years—but I hear about it. They got a swell knockdown drag-out cafe there now—the Red Barn."

Kells said: "It isn't outside federal jurisdiction."

"No. A cutter goes out and circles the island every month or so. But they pay off plenty—nobody ever bothers 'em."

"That's very interesting," Kells stood up. "How would Rose get out there?"

Bernie shook his head. "A dozen ways. He'd probably get one of the boys who used to run players to the Joanna to take him out. It's a two-hour trip in a fast boat."

They walked back toward the waiting room.

Kells said: "It's an awfully long chance. Do you suppose you could get a line on it from any of your friends?"

"I don't think so. I know a couple fellas who worked for Rose and Haardt, but with Rose wanted they wouldn't open up."

Bernie took out a knife and a plug of tobacco, whittled himself a fresh chew.

Kells said: "Try."

"Okay."

They went into the waiting room and Bernie went into the telephone booth.

Borg had found a funny paper. He looked up at Kells, said, "I'll bet the guys that get up these things make a pile of jack—huh?"

Kells said they probably did.

Borg sighed. "I always wanted to be a cartoonist," he said.

Bernie came out of the booth in a little while. "There's

a man named Carver got a string of U Drive pleasure boats down at Long Beach," he said. "He says a couple men and a woman hired one about eight-thirty and ain't come back yet. One of 'em sounds like Rose. The other was a little guy; and the woman, he don't know about—she was bundled up."

Kells smiled as if he meant it, said: "Come on."

"We wouldn't get out there till daylight in my boat. Maybe I can borrow the Comet—I'll go see."

Bernie went out, came back in a few minutes shaking his head.

"He wants fifty dollars till ten in the morning," he said. "That's too damn much."

Kells took a sheaf of bills out of his pocket, peeled off two.

"Give him whatever he wants out of this," he said. "And does he want a deposit?"

"No." Bernie started for the door. "He keeps my boat for security."

Kells and Borg followed him out, across the wharf, across a rickety foot bridge and down to a wide float.

Bernie gave the man who was waiting there one of the bills, said: "I'll pick up the change when I come back."

The man asked: "Don't you want me to come along?"

Bernie glanced at Kells.

Kells said: "Thanks—no. We'll get along."

The Comet was a trim thirty-foot craft; mahogany and steel and glistening brass. She looked very fast.

Bernie switched on the running lights and started the engine. The man cast off the lines; Bernie spun the wheel over and they swung in a wide curve away from the float and out through the narrows to the cut that led to the outer bay.

The fog was broken to long trailing shreds. The swell was long, fairly easy.

Bernie snapped on the binnacle light. "I hope I ain't forgot the course," he said. "I think it'll clear up when we get out a ways—but I'm usually wrong about fog."

Borg said, "That's dandy," with dripping sarcasm.

Kells went down into the little cabin, lay down on one of the bunks and watched the red and green and yellow buoy lights slide swiftly by the portholes. After a while they rounded the breakwater and there weren't any more lights to watch.

* * * * *

KELLS WAS AWAKENED by Bernie whispering: "We made it in an hour and fifty minutes." Then Bernie went outside.

It was very dark. Borg was lying in the other bunk, groaning faintly.

Kells said: "What the hell's the matter?"

Borg didn't answer.

"You aren't sick!" Kells was emphatically incredulous.

It was quiet for a minute and then Borg said slowly: "Who's the best judge of that—me or you?"

Kells got up and went outside. Bernie had doused the running lights; there was a thin glow from the binnacle—and darkness. The fog felt like a wet sheet.

Bernie said: "There's a big cruiser tied up on the other wharf. I coasted by close—I don't think there's anybody aboard."

"Any other boats?"

"I couldn't see any." Bernie switched off the binnacle light. "There's another little cove on the other side of the island, but nobody uses it."

Kells said: "We're not tied up, are we?"

"Sure."

Kells looked at Bernie admiringly. "You're a wonder. It

didn't even wake me up."

Bernie chuckled. "You're damn' right I'm a wonder." They climbed up on the wharf, crossed quietly. The cruiser was big, luxurious, evidently deserted—Bernie couldn't make out the name. Except for a few rowboats and the Comet, it was the only boat at the wharf. Kells said: "Well—I guess I'm wrong again." They walked up the wharf, and Bernie found a path and they walked along the bottom of a shallow gully, up to the left across a kind of ridge.

The fog was so heavy they didn't see the light until they were about twenty feet from it. Then they went forward silently and a big ramshackle shed took form in the gray darkness. The light came from a square window on the second floor.

Bernie said: "This used to be a cattle shelter—they've built onto it. I guess it's the place they call the Red Barn."

They found a door and Kells knocked twice. There was no answer so he turned the knob, pushed the door open.

There was a kerosene lamp at one end of a short bar. The room was long, windowless; the ceiling sloped to a high peak at one end. There was a stairway leading up to a balcony of rough timbers, and there was an open door on the balcony leading into a lighted room.

At first Kells thought the downstairs room was deserted; then by the flickering uncertain light of the lamp he saw a man asleep at one of the half dozen or so tables. There was another man lying on a cot against one wall. He rolled over and said, "Wha'd' you want?" sleepily. Kells didn't answer—the man looked at him blearily for a moment and then grunted and rolled back with his face to the wall.

A man came out on the balcony and stood with his hands on the railing, silently staring down at them. He was of medium height, appeared in the inadequate light to be dark, swarthy.

Kells said: "How are chances of buying a drink?" The

man suddenly stepped out of the doorway so that a little more light fell on Kells's upturned face. Then he threw back his head and laughed noiselessly. His shoulders shook and his face was twisted with mirth, but there was no sound.

Bernie looked at Kells. Kells turned and glanced at the man on the cot, looked up at the swarthy man again. The man stopped laughing, looked down and spoke in a hoarse whisper:

"Sure. Come up."

He turned, disappeared into the room. Kells said, "Wait," to Bernie. He went up the stairs two at a time, into the room.

It was a fairly large room, square. There were a few rather good rugs on the floor, a flat-topped desk near the far wall, several chairs. There were two big lamps—the kind that have to be pumped up, hiss when lighted.

The man closed the door behind him, went to the desk and sat down. He waved his hand at a chair but Kells shook his head slightly, stood still.

The man's face was familiar. It was deeply lined and the eyes were very far apart, very dark. His mouth was full and red, and his hair was very short, black.

Kells asked: "Where do I remember you from?"

The man shook his head. "You don't." There was some sort of curious impediment in his speech. Then he smiled. "I'm Crotti."

Kells pulled a chair closer to the desk. He said: "I'll still buy a drink."

Crotti opened a drawer and took out a squat square bottle, a glass. He pushed them across the desk, said: "Help yourself."

Kells poured himself a drink, sat down.

He knew Crotti very well by reputation, had once had him pointed out in a theater crowd in New York. A big-timer, he had started as a minor gangster in Detroit, become in the space of three or four years a national figure. A flair for color, a certain genius for organization, good political connections had kept him alive, out of jail and at the top. The press had boomed him as a symbol: the Crime Magnate—in New York he was supposed to be the power behind the dope ring, organized prostitution and gambling, the beer business—everything that was good for copy.

Crotti said: "This is a miracle." His voice was very thin, throaty.

Kells remembered that he had heard something of an operation affecting the vocal cords, that Crotti always spoke in this curious confidential manner.

He asked: "What's a miracle?"

Crotti leaned back in his chair. "In the morning," he said, "your hotel was to be called, an invitation was to be extended to you to visit me—out here."

He opened a box of cigars on the desk, offered them to Kells, carefully selected one.

"And here you are."

Kells didn't answer.

Crotti clipped and lighted his cigar, leaned back again. "What do you think of that?"

Kells said: "What do you want?"

"Since you anticipated my invitation may I ask what you want?"

Kells sipped his drink, shrugged. "I came out for a drink of good whiskey," he said.

He looked around the room. There were two closed doors on his right, a window on his left. In front of him, behind Crotti, there was another large square window—the one he had seen from the outside. He finished his drink, put the glass on the desk.

"I'm looking for a fella named Jack Rose," he said. "Ever hear of him?"

Crotti nodded.

"Know where he is?"

"No." Crotti smiled, shook his head.

They were both silent for a minute. Crotti puffed comfortably at his cigar and Kells waited.

Crotti cleared his throat finally, said: "You've done very well."

Kells waited.

"You've helped eliminate a lot of small fry: Haardt, Perry, O'Donnell—you've run Rose out of town and you have the Fenner and Bellmann factions pretty well in hand. You can write your own ticket..."

"You make it sound swell." Kells poured himself a drink. "What about it?"

"I'm going to cut you in."

Kells widened his eyes extravagantly. "What do you mean—cut me in?"

"I'm going to clean up all the loose ends and turn the whole business over to you..."

Kells said: "My, my—isn't that dandy!" He put the full glass down on the desk. "What the hell are you talking about?"

Crotti flicked the ashes from his cigar, leaned forward.

"Listen," he said. "Things are pretty hot back East. I've been running a couple ships up here with stuff from Mexico for a year. Now, I'm going to move all my interests here, the whole layout. I'm going to take over the coast."

"And? ..."

"And you're in."

Kells said: "I'm out."

Crotti leaned back again, studied the gray tip of his cigar. He smiled slowly. "I think you're in," he said.

* * * * *

KELLS TOOK A little tin box of aspirin out of his

pocket, put two tablets on his tongue and washed them down with whiskey.

"You seem to have kept pretty well in touch with things out here."

Crotti said: "Yes. I sent an operative out a few weeks ago to look things over—a very clever girl...." He took the cigar out of his mouth. "Name's Granquist."

Kells sat very still. He looked at Crotti and then he grinned slowly, broadly.

Crotti grinned back. "Am I right in assuming that you were looking for Rose because you thought he had something to do with Miss Granquist's—uh—escape?"

Kells didn't answer.

Crotti stood up. "I always take care of my people," he said as pompously as his squeaky voice would permit. He went to one of the doors, swung it open. The inner room was dark.

Crotti called: "Hey—Swede."

There was no answer. Crotti went into the room; Kells could hear him whispering, evidently trying to wake someone up.

He unbuttoned his coat, shifted the shoulder holster. Crotti reappeared in the doorway, and Granquist was behind him. Crotti went back to his chair, sat down.

Granquist stood in the doorway, swaying. Her eyes were heavy with sleep and she stared drunkenly about the room, finally focused on Kells. She sneered as if it were difficult for her to control her facial muscles, put one hand on the doorframe to steady herself.

She said thickly: "Hello—bastard."

Kells looked away from her, spoke to Crotti. "Nice quiet girl. Just the kind you want to take home and introduce to your folks."

Crotti laughed soundlessly.

Granquist staggered forward, stood swaying above

Kells. "Bastard framed me," she mumbled—"tried t' tag me f' murder...."

She put one hand out tentatively as if she were about to catch a fly, slapped Kells very hard across the face.

Crotti stood up suddenly.

Kells reached out and pushed Granquist away gently, said: "Don't be effeminate."

Crotti came around the desk and took Granquist by the shoulders, pressed her down into a chair. She was swearing brokenly, incoherently; she put her hands up to her face, sobbed. Crotti said: "Be quiet." He turned to Kells with a deprecating smile. "I'm sorry."

Kells didn't say anything.

It was quiet for a little while except for Granquist's strangled, occasional sobs. Crotti sat down on the edge of the desk.

Kells was staring thoughtfully at Granquist. Finally he turned to Crotti, said: "I played the Bellmann business against this one"—he jerked his head at Granquist—"because it was good sense, and because I knew I could clear her if it got warm. Then when she got away I figured Rose had her and went into the panic. I've been leaping all over Southern California with a big hero act while she's been sitting on her lead over here with an armful of bottles...."

He sighed, shook his head. "When I'm right, I'm wrong." Then he went on as if thinking aloud: "Rose and Abalos and a woman—probably Rose's wife—hired a boat at Long Beach tonight and didn't come back."

Crotti glanced at Granquist. "Rose had an interest in one of the big booze boats," he said—"the Santa Maria. She was lying about sixty miles off the coast a couple days ago. He probably headed out there."

He puffed hard at his cigar, put it down on an ashtray, leaned forward.

"Now about my proposition..." he said. "You've started

a good thing but you can't finish it by yourself. I've got the finest organization in the country and I'm going to put it at your disposal so that you can do this thing the way it should be done—to the limit. LA county is big enough for everybody–"

Kells interrupted: "I think I've heard that someplace before."

Crotti paid no attention to the interruption, went on: "—for everybody—but things have got to be under a single head. This thing of everybody cutting everybody else's throat is bad business—small-town stuff."

Kells nodded very seriously.

"We can have things working like a charm in a couple weeks if we go at it right," Crotti went on excitedly. "Organization is the thing. We'll organize gambling, the bootleggers, the city and state and federal police—everything."

He stood up, his eyes glittering with enthusiasm. "We can jerk five million dollars a year out of this territory—five million dollars."

Kells whistled.

Granquist had put her hands down. She was sitting deep in the chair, glaring at Kells. Crotti picked up his cigar and walked up and down, puffing out great clouds of blue-gray smoke.

"Why, right this minute," he said, "I've got a hundred and fifteen thousand dollars' worth of French crystal cocaine on one of my boats—a hundred and fifteen thousand dollars' worth, wholesale. All it needs is protected landing and distribution to a dozen organized dealers."

Kells nodded, pouring himself another drink.

Crotti sat down at the desk, took out a handkerchief and wiped his face.

"And you're the man for it," he said. "My money's on you...."

Kells said. "That's fine," smiled appreciatively.

"Your split is twenty per cent of everything." Crotti crushed his cigar out, leaned back and regarded Kells benignly. "Everything—the whole take."

Kells was watching Crotti. He moved his eyes without moving his head, looked at Granquist. "That ought to pay for a lot of telephone calls," he said.

"Then it's a deal."

"No."

Crotti looked as if he'd found a cockroach in his soup. He said incredulously: "You mean it isn't enough?"

"Too much."

"Then why not?"

Kells said: "Because I don't like it. Because I never worked for anybody in my life and I'm too old to start. Because I don't like the racket, anyway—I was aced in. It's full of tinhorns and two-bit politicians and double-crossers—the whole damned business gives me a severe pain in the backside." He paused, glanced at Granquist.

"Rose and Fenner both tried to frame me," he went on. "That made me mad and I fought back. I was lucky—I took advantage of a couple breaks and got myself into a spot where I could have some fun."

He stood up. "Now you want to spoil my fun."

Crotti stood up, too. He shook his head. "No," he said. "I want to show you how to make it pay."

Kells said: "I'm sorry. It's a swell proposition but I'm not the man for it—I guess I'm not commercially inclined. It's not my game...."

Crotti shrugged elaborately. "All right."

Kells said: "Now, if you'll ask the man behind me to put his rod away I'll be going."

Crotti's lips were pressed close together, curved up at the corners. He turned and looked into the big window behind him—the man who stood just inside the doorway through which they had entered was reflected against outer darkness.

Crotti nodded to the man and at the same moment Granquist stood up, screamed. Kells stepped into line between Crotti and the door, whirled in the same second—the big automatic was in his hand, belching flame.

The man had evidently been afraid of hitting Crotti, was two slugs late. He looked immensely surprised, crashed down sideways in the doorway. Crotti was standing with his back to the window, the same curved grimace on his face. There were pounding steps on the stair. Kells stepped over the man in the doorway, ran smack into another—the man who had been asleep on the cot—at the top of the stair. The man grabbed him around the waist before he could use the gun; he raised it, felt the barrel-sight rip across the man's face. There were several more men in the big room below, two on the stairs, coming up.

He planted one foot in the angle of the floor and wall, shoved hard; locked together, they balanced precariously for a moment, fell. They hit the two men about halfway down, tangled to a twisted mass of threshing arms, legs. The banister creaked, gave way. Kells felt the collar of his coat grabbed, was jerked under and down. He struck out with the gun, squeezed it. The gun roared and he heard someone yell and then something hit the center of his forehead and there was darkness.

Chapter Six

THE FOG WAS wet on Kells's face. He opened his eyes and looked up into the grayness, rolled over on his side slowly, looked into thick, unbroken grayness. He held his hand in front of him at arm's length and it was a shapeless mass of darker gray. He sat up and leaden weights fell in his skull like the mechanism that opens and closes the eyes of dolls. He lay down again and turned his head slowly, held his watch close. It was a little after six, full daylight, but the fog made it night.

Then he heard someone coming, the crunch of feet on gravel. He reached for the gun, found the empty holster, noticed suddenly with a sharp sensation in the pit of his stomach that his coat was gone.

Someone squatted beside him, spoke: "How d'you feel?" It was Borg. Kells could see the thick outline of his head and shoulders.

Kells said: "Terrible. Where the hell's my coat?"

"God! Me saving his life an' he wants his coat!" Borg giggled softly.

"What happened?"

"Everything." Borg sighed, sat down in the gravel with his mouth close to Kells's ear. "After you an' the navigator went ashore I went on the wharf and laid down for a while. Then in a couple minutes somebody came out an' I thought it was you till I seen there was four of them. I ducked behind some ropes and stuff that was laying there and they came out and saw the boat an' jawed awhile in some spick language. Then they lit out for some place an' I got up and tailed them and run into the navigator."

There was the sound of a shot suddenly, some place below and to Kells's left.

Borg said: "That's him now—what a boy!"

Kells sat up.

Borg went on: "He was carrying on about smelling trouble up at some kind of barn an' he wanted a gun. I wouldn't give him mine, so he said he was going back to the boat an' bust open a locker or something where he thought there was one. He–"

There was another shot.

Kells said: "What the hell's that all about?" He jerked his head toward the sound, immediately wished he hadn't.

"That's him—he's all right. Wait'll I tell you...." Borg shifted his position a little, went on: "I went on up the path an' I'll be damned if that navigator didn't catch up with me, an' he had the dirtiest-looking shotgun I ever saw. When we got to the house, he said. 'You go in the front way an' I'll go in the back,' so I waited for him to get around to the back—an' about that time there was two shots inside."

Kells lay down again on his stomach. Borg twisted around lay beside him.

"I went in and you was doing a cartwheel downstairs with three or four guys on your neck. There was another guy there an' he made a pass at me and I shot him right between the eyes...."

Borg leaned close to Kells, tapped his own head between the eyes with a stubby forefinger.

Kells said: "Hurry up."

"I'm hurrying. They was tearing hell out of you an' I was trying to pick one of 'em off when the navigator came in the back way and started waving that shotgun around. He yelled so much they had to see him. Then another guy came out on the balcony and I took a shot at him, but I guess I missed—he ducked back in the upstairs room."

Borg sighed, shook his head. There was another shot below, then two more, close together.

"Well—I got off to one side to give the navigator a chance," Borg went on, "but he had a better idea—he came over on my side and we jockeyed around till I could get a hold of you, and then we backed out the front—me dragging you, and the navigator telling the boys what a swell lot of hash they'd make if he let go with that meat grinder. When we got outside I drug you a little to one side–"

Kells interrupted: "Didn't I have my coat?"

"Hell, no! You was lucky to have pants the way those guys was working you over. We tried to carry you between us but we couldn't make any headway that way—it was so dark and foggy we kept falling down. So the navigator fanned tail for the boat and I drug you through a lot of brush and we got up here after a while. A half a dozen more guys went by on the way to the house—the island's lousy with 'em. If it hadn't been for the fog..."

Kells asked: "Bernie's at the boat, now?"

"Sure—and a swell spot. The fog's not quite so heavy down there and he can pick 'em off as soon as they show at the head of the wharf. Only I thought he'd shove off before this...."

"He's waiting for us, sap." Kells rose to his knees.

"Oh yeah? Maybe you can figure out a way for us to get there."

Kells asked: "Which direction should the side of the cove be?"

"I haven't the slightest."

Kells got shakily to his feet, rubbed his head, started down a shale bank to his left. He said: "Come on—we'll have to take a chance."

Borg got up and they went down the bank to a shallow draw. An occasional shot sounded on the far side of a low ridge to their right. The fog wasn't quite so thick at the bottom of the draw; they went on, came out in a little while-on to a narrow beach. There was a jagged spit of rock running out across the sand from one side of the draw. The fog was thinning.

They waited for the next shot; then Kells, calculating direction from the sound, said, "Come on"—they ran out along the rocks to the edge of the water.

Kells kicked off his shoes, waded in; Borg followed. The fog was heavy over the water—they swam blindly in the direction—Kells figured the Comet to be.

After a little while the end of the wharf took form ahead, a bit to the right. They circled toward it, came up to the bow of the big cruiser. They swam around the cruiser, under the wharf and up to the Comet's stern.

Kells grabbed the gunwale, pulled himself up a little way and called to Bernie. Bernie was creftiched in the forward end of the cockpit, behind the raised forward deck. He whirled and swung the gun toward Kells, and then he grinned broadly, put down the gun, crawled over and helped Kells climb aboard. He muttered, "Good huntin'," went back and picked up the gun; Kells helped Borg.

Borg was winded—he lay at full length on the deck, gasping for breath. Kells started toward Bernie, and then his bad leg gave way, he fell down, crawled the rest of the way.

He said: "Get the engine started—I'll take that for a minute."

Bernie gave him the gun and a handful of shells, went down to the engine. Kells called to Borg, told him to work his way to the after line, cut it. There was a shot at the head of the wharf, a piece of wood was torn from the edge of the cowling, fell in splinters.

Borg rolled over slowly, got to his knees. He was still panting. He looked reproachfully at Kells, fumbled in his pocket and took out a small jackknife, started worming his way aft.

The engine went over with a roar.

There was an answering roar of shots from the shore.

Bernie came galloping up to the wheel. Kells glanced back at Borg, saw him sawing at the stern line; he took a bead on the bow line, pulled the trigger. The line frayed; Kells aimed again, gave it the other barrel.

Bernie said: "That's enough—I can part it now...." He slid the clutch in, threw the wheel over.

Kells was hastily reloading. He glanced back at Borg, saw the stern line fall, saw Borg sink down exhausted, so flat that he was safe.

The bow line snapped. They skipped in a fast shallow arc toward the head of the wharf. There was a rattle of gunfire. Kells pushed the shotgun across the cowling, sighted. Two puffs of smoke grew over an overturned dinghy on the beach; he swung the barrel toward the smoke, pulled the trigger.

Then they straightened out, headed through the mouth of the cove toward the open sea. Bernie kicked the throttle. A few desultory shots popped behind them.

Kells put down the gun, sat down on the deck and rolled up his wet trouser leg. The leg wasn't very nice to look at—Doc Janis's dressing was hanging by a thin strip of adhesive tape. Kells called Borg.

Borg got up slowly. He came forward, squatted beside Kells.

Bernie yelled: "There's some peroxide and stuff in the for'd locker on the port side—I busted it open."

Borg went into the cabin.

Kells fished in his trouser pockets, brought out a wad of

wet bills and some silver, spread it out on the deck beside him. There was a thousand-dollar note and the eight hundreds which Brand's friend had paid off with after the fights. There was another wad of fifty- and hundred-dollar and smaller bills. Fenner's twenty-five-thousand-dollar check, Brand's for a thousand, and around eight thousand in cash had been in the coat. And Fenner's confession.

Kells looked up; Bernie was looking at him, grinned. "Wet as usual," he said. "You better take off your clothes an' get in a bunk."

Kells said: "Step on it. I've got to call up a friend of mine."

He picked up several of the wet bills, folded them, put a half dollar inside the fold to give them weight, slid them across the deck to Bernie.

"That ought to cover damages on the boat, too," he said.

Borg came out of the cabin with absorbent cotton and adhesive and peroxide.

Kells picked up some more bills, rolled them into a ball and shoved them into Borg's free hand, said: "Try to buy yourself a yacht with that..." He counted what was left.

Borg poured peroxide on the leg.

Kells said: "I came out to California with two grand." He shoved the bills into a heap. There was a little pile of silver left. He counted it with his finger.

"Now I've got two—and seventy cents." He picked up the silver, held it in his palm, smiled at Borg. "Velvet."

Bernie shouted: "I hope I remember the way back!"

Kells said; "Don't let that worry you," stared forward into the fog.

* * * * *

THERE WAS A small zebra galloping up and down the

footboard. He was striped red white blue like a barber pole; his ears were tasseled, flopped back and forth awkwardly. Then he faded into a bright mist; the room tipped over to darkness. Kells yelled...

Then it was raining outside. Gray....

After a while Kells opened his eyes and looked up at Borg, said: "Hello, baby," softly.

Borg giggled. He said: "Don't be sentimental."

Doc Janis same over and stared bleakly down over Borg's shoulder. He said: "By God! I never saw such a tough egg."

Kells blinked at him, closed his eyes. He heard Janis talking to Borg as if from a great distance: "Give him all the whiskey he wants, but no more of this. Understand?"

Kells wondered idly what this was. He mumbled, "Gimme drink a water," fell asleep.

When he awoke he lay with his eyes closed listening to rain beat against the windows.

He said, "What time is it?" opened his eyes.

Borg and Shep Beery were playing cards on a table in the center of the room. Beery said: "That's twice I've ruined my hand waiting for three hundred pinochle." He got up and came over to the bed, grinned down at Kells.

"What do you care—you're not going any place."

Kells looked past Beery at Borg, looked around the room. He said: "What the hell is this?"

Borg was shuffling the cards. There was a bridge lamp beside the table and the light fell squarely on his fat, pale face. He shook his head sadly without looking up.

"Slug-nutty."

Beery sat down on the edge of the bed, whispered confidentially: "This is the Palace, Gerry—you're the Prince of Wales.

"I'm Mary, Queen of Snots." Borg looked up, smiled complacently.

Kells closed his eyes, said: "Give me a drink."

Beery reached over and took a tumbler, a big bottle from a stand beside the bed, poured a drink; Kells sat up slowly, carefully.

Beery handed him the glass. "You've been out like a light for a few days. We didn't figure the hotel was a good spot right now so we moved you over here. It's the Miramar, on Franklin."

Kells held the glass with both shaking hands, tipped it, drank deeply.

Borg got up, came over and leaned on the foot of the bed.

"Where do you remember to?" he asked.—Kells handed the empty glass to Beery, lay down. "When we got back from the island, I phoned Fenner—and had Bernie get a bottle...."

"Four bottles.... And you sucked up three of 'em. I had to practically clip you to get a swallow. You said your leg hurt an' you wanted to get drunk...."

Kells said: "Sure, I remember...."

"You did."

Beery chuckled. "Uh huh," he said. "You did."

"Then when we got you to the hotel," Borg went on, "an" into bed, you started having the screaming heebies and the Doc give you a shot in the arm—so you got worse...." Kells smiled faintly. His eyes were closed. "The Doc was running around in circles wringing his hands because he thought the leg was going to gangrene or something. You started roaring for more M, and then when I left you alone for a minute you got up an' promoted a tube of hyoscine someplace, an' a needle..." Borg paused, straightening up and finished disgustedly: "An' I'll be god-damned if you didn't shoot the whole bloody tube!"

Beery said: "Then you began to get really violent—tried to do a hundred an' eight out the window, wanted to walk across the ceiling—things like that. We smuggled you out of the hotel and brought you over here." Kells said: "Give me a drink, Shep." He sat up again slowly, took the glass. "How many days?"

Beery said: "Four."

Kells drank, laughed, "four bottles—four days.... Four's my lucky number..." He squinted at Borg. "Once I bet four yards on a four-to-one shot in the fourth race on the Fourth of July..." He handed the glass to Beery, sank back on the pillow. "Horse ran fourth."

Borg snorted, turned and went into the bathroom. Kells looked around the room again. "Nice joint," he said. "How much am I paying for it?"

"I don't know." Beery lighted a cigarette. "Fenner has some kind of lien or mortgage or something on the building—he said he'd take care of the details."

"It was his suggestion—bringing me here?"

Beery nodded.

"Where is he?"

"Long gone. When you told him Crotti had his confession he scrammed. I got him on the phone just before he checked out of the Knickerbocker and he said he'd call over here and fix it for the apartment—said he'd get in touch with you later."

Kells smiled. "All the big boys... It's simply a process of elimination. Fenner and Rose gone—Bellmann dead. Now if we can only angle Crotti into committing suicide..." He paused, glanced at Borg coming back from the bath. "Did Fat, here, tell you all about the island sequence?"

Borg said: "Sure I told him—all I knew."

"Crotti propositioned me to come in with him on a big play to organize the whole coast," Kells went on. "Will you please tell me why these bastards keep dealing me in, and then figure that if I'm not for 'em I'm against 'em? First Rose—but that was an out-and-out frame; then Fenner thought he and I'd make a great team. Now, Crotti—and the funny part of that one is I think he was on the level about it."

Beery said: "It must be the way you wear your clothes."

"Sure. It's just your natural charm." Borg made a wry face, went back to the table and began laying out solitaire.

"Of course Crotti's got the right idea about organization." Kells rubbed his eyes—with his knuckles. "But the fun in an organization is being head man."

Beery said: "The other night at Fenners when you were putting on that act for Gowdy, you said you had some friends on the way out here. Was that a gag?"

"Certainly. I wanted to impress Gowdy with my importance to his outfit. You can get my torpedo friends in the East into a telephone booth."

"Well—if Crotti says war"—Beery got up and went over to one of the rain-swept windows—"we're sitting pretty...."

"Uh huh." Borg looked at Kells. "In a pig's eye. We three, an' whatever strong-arm strength Gowdy swings—and that doesn't amount to a hell of a lot...."

"And against us...." Beery turned from the window, stuck his hands deep in his pockets. "There's all Crotti's mob—and that's supposed to be the best in the country. There's Rose, with his syndicate behind him, and all the loogans he's imported from back East. There's the Bellmann outfit. They weren't very efficient when they blew up the print shop the other day, but you can't figure from that–"

"And by God!—most of them are in uniform," Borg interrupted.

Beery smiled faintly, nodded. "Uh huh—we're in a swell spot."

Kells was staring at the ceiling. He said: "Now's a good time to get out."

Beery looked at Borg; Borg took a toothpick out of his vest pocket, stuck it in his mouth and went back to his solitaire.

"I didn't mean that," Beery said. "Only, what are we going to do?"

"Get out." Kells's eyes were fixed blankly on the ceiling. "I've been pretty lucky up to now. Partly because everybody that's been against me has figured that the inside would get a big press spread if anything serious happened to me."

He looked at Beery. "Through you—spread through you, I mean. That doesn't make it very safe for you."

Beery was looking at the floor.

"The luck's beginning to run out," Kells went on. "I dropped all the dough I'd made since I've been out here, on the island, because I was dumb enough to get heroic about that bitch Granquist—and she was Crotti's plant all the time...."

Beery said: "You didn't tell me about that."

"I'm telling you now. She was sent out here by Crotti to look things over—start the organization ball rolling."

"Well, well. Damned clever, these Swedes." Beery sat down at the table.

No one said anything for a minute. Beery watched Borg play solitaire. Kells's eyes wandered again to the ceiling.

"You're absolutely right," he finally said. "We'd better take a sneak while we're all in one piece."

Beery stood up and poured himself a drink. He waved the glass at Kells. He said: "We've gone too far—an' it's too much fun. We can still smack the Bellmann administration down—and anyway, these rats don't know whether we're strong or not. You'll be up and around in a couple days—we can count on a hand from Fay, if we need it...."

Borg was staring at the cards. He said, "Sure," without looking up.

"No." Kells shook his head slowly. "It's too tough. You boys have been a great help, but–"

"Shut up! You can crawl out if you want to, but I'll

stick—I'm having a swell time." Beery grinned down at Kells, gulped his drink.

Borg looked up, said, "Sure," quietly. He stood up.

Kells laughed. He glanced at the bottle on the bedstand, said: "Draw three, Shep."

* * * * *

THEY HAD DINNER sent up from Musso & Frank's, on the Boulevard.

Doctor Janis stopped by about nine o'clock.

"Two days," he said—"two more days at least. Then you can go out for a little while, if you take it easy—on crutches."

Kells was sweating; his eyes burned and he yawned a great deal. He said: "Maybe I'd better have one more load in the arm, Doc—to sort of taper off on."

"You'll taper off on whiskey and milk, young fella—and like it." The doctor put two small yellow capsules on the stand. "If you get too jumpy you can take these before you go to sleep."

Janis and Beery went out together; Beery was going home. Borg played solitaire for a while and Kells sat up in bed, tried to read the papers.

Borg said: "Denny Faber is still trailing around with Gilroy."

"You can call him off—Gilroy ought to be okay by now."

At eleven Borg stood up, stretched, said: "I'm going byebye." He went into the bedroom—Kells was on the wall bed in the living room. Borg came back in his underwear, got Kells a glass of water, made a pass at tucking him in.

"If you want anything," he said, "just yell and fire a few shots and throw your shoe through the window. I'm a very light sleeper."

Kells said he would.

Borg went back into the bedroom and Kells turned out the lights, tried to sleep. He heard the bell in the big church on Sunset Boulevard strike twelve. Rain drummed against the windows, and the wind was blowing.

Sometime around one he got up, hobbled into the bath. He scrubbed his teeth and got back to the bed by using a chair for support, hopping slowly on one foot. He took the capsules Janis had left, washed them down with whiskey and water. He slept after a while—heavily, dreamlessly.

When he awoke he lay rigid for a little while listening to rain beating against the windows. Then a voice whispered close to his ear: "Wake up—darling."

Kells lay very still, turned his eyes toward the darkness.

Granquist said: "Wake up—darling."

Kells moved his head until he could see the silhouette of her crouched body against the pale reflected light of the wall.

She spoke rapidly, breathlessly: "Are you all right, darling—can you walk? We've got to get out of here right away..."

He smiled a little and raised his head a little and said: "Will you please go away?"

She sank to her knees beside the bed and tried to take his head in her arms.

"Please," she said. "We've got to go quickly. Please...."

Kells put her arms away and sat up and pulled the pillows up behind him. "How the hell did you get in?"

"I put on act for the night man—told him I wanted to surprise you. He came up and let me in with the passkey..."

"Go on—surprise me."

"Gerry," Granquist's eyes were big in the faint light; drops of rain glistened on her small dark hat, her dark close-fitting coat—"I've been in an awfully bad spot since you shot up Crotti's camp. I got away this afternoon when

Fenner came out to do business about his confession—Crotti didn't know anything about it but he let Fenner think he did ..."

"What do you mean, Crotti didn't know about it?" Kells put his hand on her wrist.

"I got to your coat first—I've got Fenner's confession and his certified check for twenty-five thou—and your cash...."

She clicked open a small handbag, took out a handful of crumpled papers and currency, dropped it on the bed. He looked down at it a little while and then he let his head fall back again against the pillow, bent it slightly sideways.

He said: "You're a strange gal." He put his hand on her wrist again, held it tightly.

She tried to speak. She got up and walked to the window and then back, sat down on the edge of the bed.

Kells asked: "Why do we have to leave here?"

"Because you haven't Fenner's protection any longer—he thinks Crotti has this"—she nodded at the stuff on the bed. "The whole layout is against you now—Crotti, Rose, Fenner, the Bellmann people...."

Kells switched on the lamp beside the bed, unfolded and smoothed out the sheet of Lido stationery with Fenner's shakily signed confession.

"We have this," he said. "Fenner hasn't played ball—I can stick it into him and break it off. And we've got around thirty-five grand. We're in a swell spot to play both ends against the middle."

"No, Gerry." Her voice was harsh, strained. "Please, no, Gerry—let's go away, quick. I'm scared...."

Kells was silent a while, looking at her abstractedly.

Then he said: "The middle against both ends, by God!" He put out one arm and cupped his hand against the back of Granquist's neck and pulled her to him.

* * * * *

IN THE MORNING the sun came out warm, bright.

At about nine-thirty Borg came out of the bedroom in trousers and a green silk undershirt. Granquist had had things sent up from the commissary, was preparing breakfast in the kitchen. Borg leaned against the side of the door and looked at her and then he smiled blankly at Kells, said: "Well, well."

"From now on"—Kells bent his head a little to one side—"Fenner's on the other team."

Borg went to the table and sat down. "I still like your side," he said—"an' I want to pitch."

"You're not very bright. See if you can get Faber on the phone—tell him to come up here."

Borg reached for the phone, dialed a number.

Granquist brought breakfast in on a big tray. There was orange juice and an omelette and toast and coffee.

Borg finally got Faber and talked to him a little while, and then he looked up Woodward's number in the Dell Building, downtown, dialed it, took the phone to Kells.

Kells said, "Hello," asked for Woodward, and then he said: "This is Kells. If you come out to the Miramar Apartments on Franklin and Cherokee, in Hollywood, I think we might do a little business." He hung up, smiled at Granquist.

"You'll have to duck while he's here, baby," he said. "He's the undercover legal representative for the Bellmann administration and you're still number one suspect for Bellmann's shooting—you'll have to lay low till we hang it on Fenner and make it stick."

She nodded.

After a little while someone knocked at the door; Borg got up and let Beery in. Beery threw his hat on a chair, stared with bright, surprised eyes at Granquist, said: "Well—it's a small world."

She smiled. "Coffee?"

Beery nodded and Granquist went out into the kitchen.

Kells said: "Fenner went out to see Crotti yesterday."

Beery sat down, smiled down his nose.

"Now we don't have to worry about kicking any of our crowd in the tail," Kells went on, "because we haven't got any."

Beery raised his brows, said: "Crowd?"

"Uh huh—crowd."

Beery glanced around the room, back to Kells. "Since this joint was Fenner's suggestion," he said, "wouldn't it be a swell time to move?"

Kells shook his head slowly. "What for? Any of 'em can find me if they want me—and they'll all be wanting to before long. This is as good a spot as any...."

Granquist came in with coffee and toast on a small tray, Beery stood up, bowed, took the tray and sat down.

Kells said: "I'm going to turn on the heat—Shep—only this time I'm going to make it pay. It's been for fun up to now—now it's for dough."

Borg was playing solitaire at the table. He looked up, said, "Hooray," dryly.

"The lady"—Kells inclined his head toward Granquist—"picked up all the stuff I lost at Crotti's. Fenner thinks Crotti's got his confession, but I've got it—and Fenner's going to find out about that. So is Woodward, who ought to be willing to give his eye teeth—and the mayor's eye teeth—for it. He's on his way up here now."

Beery lighted a cigarette.

"They can both buy it," Kells went on, "and for plenty."

He turned to Borg. "See if you can get Hanline at the Knickerbocker."

Borg picked up the phone, dialed a number. After a moment he got up and handed the phone to Kells.

Kells said: "Hello—Hanline?... Tell that boss of yours

that I've got the stuff he's dealing with Crotti about. Tell him that in the next two hours I'm going to sell it to the best offer. He'll know what I mean... Tell him that the bidding starts at fifty grand, and that he'd better be damned quick...."

Kells hung up, grinned at Beery. "Now watch things happen," he said.

Beery was looking at Granquist. "Where does Miss G get off if you peddle Fenner's confession back to him? It's the one thing that leaves her in the clear."

Kells moved his grin to Granquist. "We've figured that out," he said.

The house-phone rang: Borg answered it, said, "Send him up," hung up. He said, "Faber," over his shoulder, went to the door.

Granquist looked questioningly at Kells. Kells shook his head. "Borg's running mate—I'll give you twelve guesses where I'm going to send him."

Faber came in, said hello to Kells and Beery, half nodded to Granquist, sat down. Kells said: "Drink?"

"Sure."

Kells looked at Granquist and she got up and went into the kitchen, came back with a bottle and a glass and handed them to Faber. He poured himself a drink.

Kells said: "Fenner isn't your boss any longer—how do you like that?"

Faber glanced at Borg, tipped the glass to his mouth, took it down when it was empty, said: "I like that fine."

"I want you to go to the Villa Dora out on Harper"—Kells looked up at Borg—"your car's still here, isn't it?" Borg said: "Yeah."

"Take the car," Kells went on, "and hang on the front of that place until you see three big pigskin keesters go in and find out which apartment they go to. I don't know who'll have 'em, but there'll be three—and they'll probably come up in a closed Chrysler."

Faber said: "Uh huh." He picked up the bottle and poured himself another drink. He looked at Beery, then at the rest of them quickly. "Anybody else?"

Beery nodded; Granquist went out and got another glass.

Kells said: "Call here pronto—but I mean pronto. Spot a phone and call here the minute you connect. We'll be over right away and pick you up."

Faber nodded, drank. He put down his glass and stood up. "Villa Dora—that's below Sunset Boulevard, isn't it?"

Beery said: "Yes—between Sunset and Fountain."

Kells was looking out the window. "They'll probably come in between two this afternoon and nine tonight. You'd better get something to eat before you go out."

Faber said: "Okay." He put on his hat and said, "So long," and went out.

Beery smiled at Kells. "Are you going mysterious on me?"

"Those three cases are full of cocaine"—Kells was looking at Granquist—"according to my steer. A hundred and fifteen thousand dollars' worth—and there's a hundred and fifteen thousand dollars in cash waiting for them some place in the Villa Dora. It's Crotti's stuff and I have a hunch Max Hesse is on the buying end. I don't want the junk—I want the dough."

Beery stood up. He said: "Gerry—you're losing your mind. When you buck Crotti you're bucking a machine. They'll have a dozen guns trained on that deal—every angle figured–"

Granquist interrupted: "He's right. Gerry—you can't...."

"What do you think about it?" Kells was staring morosely at Borg.

Borg put a black ten on a red Jack. "It'd be a nice lick,"

he said.

Kells put his leg down carefully, stood up. He held out his arm to Beery. "Give me a hand to the donnaker, Shep," he said.

Beery helped him across the room.

When Kells came back, Borg said: "The Doc called. He says he's sending over some crutches for you—an' for you to keep off that leg."

Beery helped Kells back to the big chair. He sat down and put his leg up on the other chair, muttered: "I don't want any crutches."

Then he turned his head to smile at Granquist. "Isn't it about time you brought us all a drink, baby?"

Granquist got up and went into the kitchen.

Kells asked: "What time is it?"

Beery was standing beside Kells's chair. He glanced at his watch, held it down for Kells to see: eleven-five.

* * * * *

AT ELEVEN-TWENTY Woodward was announced. Granquist went into the bedroom and closed the door, and Borg let Woodward in.

Woodward's eyes were excited behind his wide-rimmed tortoise-shell glasses. He bowed nervously to Beery and Borg, sat down in the chair near Kells at Kells's invitation.

"How would you like to buy the originals of all the dirt on Bellmann.?" Kells began.

Woodward smiled faintly. "We've discussed that before Mister Kells," he said. "I'm afraid it's too late to do anything about it now—your Coast Guardian has published several of the pictures and the story...."

Kells said: "You can doctor the negatives and claim they're forgeries—and I can give you additional information with which you can prove the whole thing was a conspiracy to blackmail Bellmann."

Woodward pursed his lips. He glanced at Beery, said: "Don't you think we might discuss this alone, Mister Kells?"

Kells shook his head shortly.

"In addition to all that," he went on "—the pictures and the information—I can give you"—he paused, leaned forward slightly—"absolute proof that Lee Fenner shot Bellmann."

Woodward's eyes widened a little. He leaned back in his chair and wet his lips, stared at Kells as if he weren't quite sure he had heard correctly.

"Lee Fenner killed Bellmann," Kells repeated slowly. He took a crumpled piece of paper out of the breast pocket of his dressing gown, straightened it out and tossed it on Woodward's lap.

Woodward picked it up and held it close to his face, put his hand up and adjusted his glasses. He put the paper back on the arm of Kells's chair in a little while, cleared his throat, said: "Who is Beery, who witnessed Fenner's signature with you?"

Kells inclined his head toward Beery, who was sitting at the table watching Borg's solitaire.

Woodward said: "How much do you want?"

"Plenty." Kells picked up the piece of paper, held it by a corner. He grinned at Beery. "It's lousy theater," he said. "The 'incriminating confession'"—he said it very melodramatically. "All we need is the 'Old Homestead,' some papier-mache snow and a couple of bloodhounds."

"And you ought to have a black mustache." Beery looked up, smiled.

Woodward said: "As I told you—my, uh—people are pressed for cash."

"I don't give a damn how pressed they are. They can do business with me now—big business—and get their lousy administration out of the hole, or they can start packing to move out of City Hall. This is the last call...."

Woodward started to speak and then the phone rang. Borg answered it, put his hand over the transmitter, nodded to Kells. Then he got up and brought the phone over.

Kells said: "Hello.... Wait a minute—I want you to meet a friend of mine."

He spoke to Woodward: "In case you're figuring this for a plant I want you to talk to this guy. You'd know Fenner's voice, wouldn't you?"

Woodward nodded. He took the phone from Kells, hesitantly said: "Hello."

Kells reached over and took the phone back. He smiled at Woodward, said: "Hello, Lee... That was Mister Woodward, a big buyer from downtown... Uh huh ... Now don't get excited, Lee—we haven't made a deal yet ... Why don't you come on over?... Yes—and bring plenty of cash—it starts at fifty grand... Okay, make it snappy."

He hung up, stared vacantly at Woodward's tie.

"Now I'm not going to argue with you," he said. "You heard what I told Fenner. You'd better get going—first here, first served."

Woodward stood up. "I'll see what I can do," he said. He put on his hat, nodded to Beery and Borg and started toward the door.

Kells said: "And don't get ideas. If you come back here with the law and try to hang a 'conspiracy to defeat justice' rap on me I'll swear that the whole god-damned thing is a lie—and so will my gentlemen friends." He jerked his head at Beery and Borg.

Woodward had turned to listen. He nodded, turned again and went out and closed the door.

Kells said: "This is going to be a lot of fun even if it doesn't work."

"You said something about being all washed up with the

fun angle..." Beery got up and poured himself a drink. "You said something about being out for the dough."

"Watch it work." Kells leaned back in the chair and closed his eyes.

* * * * *

FENNER PUT THIRTY thousand-dollar notes on the arm of Kells's chair. Kells took the piece of crumpled paper out of his breast pocket and handed it to Fenner, and Fenner unfolded it and looked at it and then took a cigarette lighter out of his pocket and touched the flame to a corner of the paper.

Kells said: "Now get out of here while you're all together." He said it very quietly.

They were alone in the room.

Fenner said: "What could I do, Gerry? I had to go to Crotti when you told me he had this." He put the last charred corner of paper in an ash-tray. "It took me a couple of days to get to him—I was damned near crazy...."

"Right." Kells moved his head slowly up and down and his expression was not pleasant. "You were plenty crazy when you offered Crotti my scalp."

Fenner stood up. He didn't say anything, just stood there looking out the window for a minute—then he turned and started toward the door.

"I'll give you a tip, Lee," Kells's voice was low; he stared with hard cold eyes at Fenner. "Take it on the lam—quick." Fenner opened his mouth and then he closed it, swallowed. He said: "Why—what do you mean?"

Kells didn't answer; he stared at Fenner coldly. Fenner stood there a little while and then he turned and went out. Borg and Granquist came out of the kitchen.

Kells said: "Thirty. I wonder if we'll do as well with Woodward. These guys don't seem to take me seriously when I talk about fifty thousand. Maybe it's the depression."

At a few minutes after one, Woodward telephoned. The crutches that Janis had called about had been delivered and Kells was practising walking with them. He put them down, sat down at the table and took the phone from Borg. He said, "Hello," and then listened with an occasional affirmative grunt. After a minute or so he said,' "All right—make it fast," hung up.

He grinned at Granquist. "Twenty more. Up to now it's been a swell day's work. If we get it...."

Borg said: "Do you mind letting me in on how the hell you're going to sell this thing to Woodward when you've already sold it to Fenner?"

Kells took two more pieces of creased crumpled paper from his pocket, tossed them on the table in front of Borg.

Borg looked at the two, smiled slowly. "How about making them up in gross lots?" he said.

Kells inclined his head toward Granquist. "The baby's work. She used to be in the business—she went over to the Lido early this morning and snagged the letterheads."

Granquist was sitting in the big chair by the window. Kells picked up the two pieces of paper and put them back in his pocket, got up and hobbled over to her, sat down on the arm of the chair.

"You're awfully quiet, baby," he said. "What's the matter?"

She looked up at him—and her eyes were frightened.

"I want to go—I want us to go," she said huskily. "Something awful's going to happen...."

Kells put his arm around her head, pulled it close against his chest.

"If we get the twenty from Woodward," he said very quietly—"and the big stuff from Crotti, it'll make almost two hundred grand–"

"We've got enough," she broke in. "Let's go, Gerry—please."

He sat without moving or speaking for a little while,

staring out the window at the brightness of the sun. Then he got up and went back to the table and took up the phone and asked the operator to get him the Sante Fe ticket office.

When the connection had been made, he said: "I want to make reservations on the Chief, tomorrow evening—a drawing room—two...."

Granquist had turned. She said: "Tonight, Gerry."

Kells smiled at her a little. He shook his head and said: "Yes... Kells, Miramar Apartments in Hollywood—send them out."

Then he hung up and reached across the table for the bottle and glasses, poured drinks. He raised his glass.

"Here's to Crime—and the Chief tomorrow night."

There was a knock at the outer door and Granquist went into the bedroom; Borg got up and let Woodward in.

Woodward was very nervous. He put two neat sheafs of thousand- and five-hundred-dollar notes on the table, said: "There you are, sir."

Kells tossed one of the forged confessions across the table and slid one of the thousand-dollar notes out of the sheaf, examined it carefully.

Woodward said: "And the other things—the pictures and things?..."

"They're downtown. I'll call Beery to turn them over to you—at the Hayward."

Woodward nodded. He went over to the window and adjusted his glasses, peered closely at the paper. He turned to say something and then there was a sharp sound and glass tinkled on the floor. Woodward stood with his mouth open a little while, then his legs buckled under him slowly and he fell down and stretched one arm out and took hold the bottom of one of the drapes. He rolled his head once, back and forth, and his glasses came off and stuck out at an angle from the side of his head. His eyes were open, staring.

Chapter Seven

KELLS SAID: "Well...."

Borg was half standing. He moved his arm and very deliberately put the cards down on the table, then straightened, moved toward Woodward's body.

Kells said: "Don't go near the window."

Granquist came into the bedroom door and stood with one hand up to her face, staring at Woodward.

Borg said: "It must have been from that joint." He pointed through the window to the tall apartment house halfway down the block.

Kells said gently: "Bring me my clothes." Granquist didn't move, stood staring at Woodward blankly. Kells stood up. He said: "Bring me my clothes." Borg went swiftly to the bedroom door, past Granquist into the bedroom, coming back almost immediately with a tangled mass of clothes under his arm. He held a short blunt revolver in one hand down straight at his side.

Granquist went to a chair against one wall and picked up her coat and put it on. She went to the table and stood with both hands on the table, leaning forward a little.

Kells sat down and took his clothes from Borg, one piece at a time, put them on. The phone rang.

Kells picked it up, said: "Hello.... Shep—we're shoving off. Woodward's just been shot—through the window, from the roof of the place next door.... Uh hum. Maybe some of Crotti's boys tailed Fenner—your guess is as good as mine.... Call me in a half-hour at the Ambassador. If I'm not there I'll be in jail—or on a slab.... Hell! No. Let 'em find him.... 'Bye."

He hung up, finished dressing rapidly, got up and limped to one side of the big window and pulled the cord that closed the drapes. Woodward's hand was clenched on the bottom of one of the drapes and it moved a little as the drape closed. The paper had fallen, lay a little way from his other hand.

Kells stood looking down at Woodward a minute, then went to the table and picked up the two thin stacks of money, put them in his pocket.

Borg had gone back into the bedroom. He came into the doorway and he had put on his shirt and coat, he went to a mirror near the outer door and carefully put on his hat. Granquist picked up the crutches. Kells shook his head, said: "My leg feels swell." They went out into the corridor.

There was a man standing near the elevators but he paid no attention to them, entered one of the elevators while they were still halfway down the hall.

They waited a minute or so, got into the same elevator when it came back up. It was automatic—Kells pushed the sub-basement button. He said: "Maybe...?"

Borg watched the sixth floor go by through the little wire-glass window. "The basement is as good a hunch as any," he said. "There's a garage with a driveway out onto Cherokee. Maybe we can promote a car—or if we can get down to Highland, to the cab stand...."

"Why didn't you call a cab?" Granquist was leaning back in a corner of the elevator.

Kells looked at her vacantly, as if he had not heard. "Maybe this is a lot of apcray," he said—"maybe we're a cinch. But if that was Crotti"—he gestured with his head up toward the apartment—"he'll have a dozen beads on the place." The elevator stopped and they went into a dark corridor, down to a door to the garage. There was a tall man with a very small mustache asleep in a big car near the archway that led out into Cherokee. He woke up when Borg stepped on the running board.

Borg asked: "How're chances of renting a car?" The man rubbed his eyes, climbed out and stood between Kells and Borg. He said: "Sure. I got a Buick an' I got a Chrysler."

"Are either of them closed?" Kells leaned on Granquist's shoulder, winked at Borg meaninglessly. The man said: "Yeah—the Buick."

He went toward a Car five down the line from the one he had been sleeping in.

Kells said: "That'll do. How much deposit do you want?"

"You want a driver?"

"No." Borg opened one rear door of the car and helped Granquist in.

The man said: "No deposit if you live here. It's two an' a quarter an hour."

"Maybe we'll be out all night—you'd better take this." Kells gave the man two bills, got in through the front door carefully. He put his leg out straight under the dashboard.

Borg went around to the other side and squeezed in behind the wheel. He pressed the starter and the man reached in and pulled the choke and the engine roared; Borg scowled at the man and pushed the choke back in. They swung in a wide circle out through the archway into the sunlight.

Kells turned and spoke sharply to Granquist: "Lie down on the seat."

She muttered something unintelligible and lay down on her side across the back seat.

They turned swiftly down Cherokee and a spurt of flame came out of a parked, close curtained limousine to meet them, lead thudded, bit into the side of the car. Borg stepped on the throttle, they plunged forward, past.

Kells looked back at Granquist. She was lying with her eyes tightly closed and her face was very white. He put one arm back toward her and she rose suddenly to her knees, put her hands on his shoulder.

He smiled. "We're all right, baby," he said softly. "They build these cars in Detroit—that's machine-gun country."

Borg was crouched over the wheel. He spoke out of the side of his mouth: "Are they coming?"

Kells was looking back, shook his head. "They're turning around—they were parked the wrong way." Granquist slid back to the seat.

They turned west on Yucca to Highland, jogged up Highland to Franklin, turned west on Franklin. They stopped between Sycamore and La Brea a little while and watched through the glass oval in the back of the car; the limousine had evidently been lost.

Borg got out and looked at the side of the car.

"It must have jammed," he said. "Four little holes, and a nick on one of the headlights. One of 'em missed the carburetor by about an inch—that was a break."

Kells said: "Let's go over and see how Faber is making out."

Borg climbed back into the car and they went on up Franklin to La Brea and down La Brea to Fountain. At the corner of Fountain and Harper they parked under a big pepper tree.

Kells turned around and spoke to Granquist: "You take the car—you can drive it, can't you?—and go down to the Ambassador and wait for us." He reached into his pocket, fished out a key. "Go up to my room and pack all the stuff that isn't already packed. Call up the Santa Fe and tell 'em to send the reservations there. If we get everything cleaned up tonight we'll drive down to San Bernardino and lay low tomorrow and get the Chief out of there tomorrow night."

Kells and Borg got out of the car and Granquist climbed over into the front seat. She said, "Be careful," without looking at Kells. She shifted gears and let the clutch in a little way and the car moved ahead.

Kells said: "Beery'll be calling in a little while. Tell him to come up to the hotel as soon as he can."

Granquist nodded without turning and the car moved ahead swiftly.

Kells and Borg crossed to the west side of Harper and walked slowly up toward Sunset Boulevard. Kells's limp was pronounced.

Borg asked: "How is it?" He bobbed his head at Kells's leg.

"All right."

They went slowly and without speaking up Harper, and a little way below the Villa Dora, Faber stuck his head out of Borg's car. They went over to it and Kells got into the tonneau and sat down; Borg stood outside, leaned on the front door.

Faber said: "Nothing yet."

Kells sat for several minutes staring absently at a long scratch on the back of the front seat. Then he said: "Let's go in and see what we can find." He leaned forward.

Faber lifted the flap of the right side pocket, slipped a black Luger out onto the seat beside him. He turned and looked at Kells and nodded at the gun. Kells reached over and took the gun and stuck it into the waistband of his trousers, pulled the point of his vest down over it.

"We're going in to try to find a hundred and fifteen grand in cash," he said. "I don't know who's got it—we'll have to try the mailboxes and see if we can get a lead."

Borg said: "We probably won't."

Kells opened the door and started to get out.

"Why don't you wait here and I'll see if I can find anything?" Borg took a light-colored cigar out of his outer breast pocket and bit off the end.

Kells looked at him a moment sleepily, nodded, sat down.

Borg went up the street and disappeared into the Villa Dora. He was back in a few minutes with a soiled envelope on which he had scrawled the names of the occupants.

Kells took it, looked at it, asked: "Are you sure this is all?"

"Yeah." Borg nodded. "It's a big joint, but I guess the apartments are big too—there are only twelve mailboxes."

Kells studied the names. Then he said: "MacAlmon—that's Bellmann's silksock ward heeler. I thought he lived in Beverly Hills." He stared at the envelope. "That'd be a tricky piece of business—if MacAlmon was go-between on the white stuff. I can figure his tie-up with Max Hesse—if Hesse is really the buyer—but how the hell would Crotti get to him?"

Faber looked interested at the mention of Crotti's name. He said: "Maybe this would be more fun for me if I knew what it was all about."

Borg said: "Crotti's delivering a load of C, and the hundred and fifteen we want to locate is what somebody up there"—he jerked his head toward the apartment house—"has got to pay for it with."

"Oh." Faber turned to Kells. "Count me out—I don't want any part of Crotti."

Kells smiled slowly. He said: "Okay."

Faber started to get out of the car and then he looked at Kells's hands; Kells had slipped the Luger out of his waistband, was holding it loosely on his lap.

Borg said: "Aw, for God's sake, cut it out." He looked from Kells to Faber.

Kells was smiling faintly at Faber. He said very seriously:

“Your cut on this lick is ten grand. You’ve got one coming now—an’ you can have it, but you’ll have to stick around until this is over.” He put his hand into his pocket and slid out a roll of bills, pulled one off and held it toward Faber.

Faber looked at it a little while, then he grinned sourly, said: “Well—if I’ve got to stay I might as well work.” He took the bill, folded it carefully and put it into his watch pocket. “Deal me in—ten grand’ll buy a lot of flowers.”

“Me—I want to be cremated.” Borg was staring soberly into space. “No flowers, but plenty of music.” He glanced at Kells. “You know—Wagner.”

Kells said: “Let’s go and see if Mister MacAlmon is in.”

He and Faber got out of the car and they all went up the street and into the Villa Dora.

* * * * *

MISTER MACALMON WAS in. He stood in the middle of his high-ceilinged living room with his hands in the air.

Kells said: “I’m sorry about this. I haven’t anything against you or Hesse—if Hesse is in with you? But I’ve got plenty against Crotti and plenty against your whole bloody combination. I’ve been double-crossed to death. I’m goddamned tired of it—an’ I need the dough.”

MacAlmon was almost as tall as Kells. His thick brown hair was combed straight back from a high narrow forehead, and his eyes were dark, sharp.

He said: “This is plain robbery. How far do you think you’re going to get with it?”

“Don’t be silly.” Kells looked at the stack of currency on the table. “I’ll have the federal narcotic squad on their way out here in two minutes—and I’ll see that you’re here when they get here. Then all they’ll have to do is wait for the stuff to come in. When you’re pinched on a dope deal that's this big, see who you can get to listen to a squawk about money."

Borg was leaning against the outer door spinning the blunt revolver around his forefinger. Faber had waited outside.

Kells went to the telephone on a low round table, picked it up. "I've never called 'copper' on anybody in my life," he said. "But here it is...." He spun the dial.

MacAlmon put his hand down. He said: "Wait a minute." He sat down in a big chair and leaned forward and put his elbows on his knees. He looked at Kells and his face was flushed and he tried very hard to smile. "Wait a minute."

Kells said into the telephone: "Information—what's the number of the Federal Building?" He waited a moment, said, "Thank you," pressed the receiver down with his thumb.

MacAlmon said: "How would you like to make twenty-five more?" He inclined his head toward the money on the table.

"This is enough." Kells shook his head. "All I want is a fair price for the time I've put in. This is it."

MacAlmon leaned back in the chair. "The stuff that's being-delivered here this afternoon is worth exactly twice what's being paid for it, to me—my people," he said. "I don't care who gets the money—if you'll hold off until the transfer has been made and the stuff is in my possession I'll give you a twenty-five grand bonus."

Kells said: "No."

Someone knocked at the door.

Borg pressed his lips together and let his eyelids droop, shook his head sadly. He held the blunt, black revolver loosely in his hand and looked at Kells.

Kells framed the word, "Faber," with his lips. Borg kept on shaking his head. Kells took the Luger out of his belt and crossed the room and stood close to the wall; he nodded slightly to Borg.

Crotti and two other men came in. One of the men was carrying a big pigskin kitbag; one carried two. Crotti looked at MacAlmon and then he turned his head and looked at Borg. He hadn't seen Kells. The man with one bag put it down on the floor, straightened. Borg closed the door. Kells said: "Hello."

The man who had been carrying one bag took one step sideways. At the same time he jerked an automatic out of a shoulder holster, sank to one knee and swung the automatic up toward Borg. Borg's gun roared twice.

Crotti had taken two or three steps forward. His head was turned toward Kells and his black wide-set eyes were big, his thick red mouth hung a little open.

The man with two bags still stood just inside the door. His small face was entirely expressionless; he bent his knees slowly and put down the bags. The other man looked up at Borg and his face was soft and childlike and surprised; then he toppled over on his side.

MacAlmon was standing up. Kells moved toward Crotti. Borg was staring at Crotti: he moved suddenly forward, very swiftly for a fat man, and took the revolver barrel in his left hand and swung the gun back and brought it down hard on the back of Crotti's head. Crotti was still looking at Kells. His eyes went dull and he fell down very hard.

The man with two bags had turned and put his hand on the doorknob. Kells said, "Hey," and the man turned and stood with his back against the door.

Kells went to the door swiftly and reached past the man and turned the key in the lock and took it out and put it in his pocket. He went back to the table and put down the Luger, scooped the money up and stuffed it into his pockets. He glanced at MacAlmon, indicated the three kitbags with his eyes.

"Now you've got it. What are you going to do with it?"

MacAlmon was staring down at Crotti. Borg was watching the man at the door. Kells said: "We're off!"

Borg went to the man at the door and patted his pockets, felt under his arms.

They went out through the kitchen, out through the service entrance into the hall. They heard someone pounding at the front door as they went out. They went down the hall, down the back stairs and out a side door to a small patio. At the street side of the patio Borg stood on a bench and looked over the wall. He shook his head and stepped down, said: "Faber's gone."

Kells said: "Maybe we can get through to the next street."

They went to the other end of the patio and through a gate to a kind of alleyway that led down to Fountain. They went down the alleyway and turned west on Fountain. They went into a drugstore on the corner and Kells drank a Coca-Cola while Borg called a cab.

While they were waiting for the cab Kells bought some aspirin, swallowed two tablets.

Borg said: "That's just a habit. That junk don't do you no good."

Kells nodded absently.

In a little while the cab came along.

* * * * *

KELLS AND GRANQUIST and Beery, and Borg sat in Kells's room at the Ambassador.

"Here's the laugh of the season..." Beery tilted his chair back against the wall. "The apartment at the Miramar was in Fenner's name. We had the maid service cut out—none of the help ever saw you there..."

Kells finished his drink, put the glass on a table.

Beery went on like a headline: "Fenner is being sought for

questioning in connection with the Woodward murder."

Borg chuckled.

"And there's a warrant out, for him for Bellmann's shooting on the strength of the confession they found on Woodward." Beery tilted his chair forward, reached for his glass. "The Woodward one is being blurbed as 'The Through the Window Murder.'"

Kells asked: "Who found the body?"

"Some glass from the window fell down into the driveway and somebody went up to find out who was carrying on."

Granquist said: "There must be something there they can trace to us." She didn't look very happy.

Kells glanced at her, grinned at Beery. "Miss Pollyanna G will now recite–"

She interrupted him: "Let's go, Gerry—please..." She stood up.

Kells said: "Buy us all a drink, baby."

He went on to Beery: "They'll probably trace us through Doc Janis—or telephone calls—or something."

Beery shook his head. "They'll be tickled to death to hang the whole thing on Fenner."

"Do you think they'll be so tickled they'll drop the case against me entirely?" Granquist turned from the table, came toward them with three tall glasses between her hands.

Kells said: "Shep and I will find out about that in about a half hour."

"And we'll find out what happened at MacAlmon's after you left." Beery stood up and took his drink from Granquist.

Someone knocked at the door.

Granquist froze, with a glass held out toward Borg; Beery opened the door and a porter came in.

He smiled, nodded to Kells. "You want your luggage to go down sir?"

Kells said: "Yes. The trunk's to go on the Chief tomorrow

night. Put the other stuff where we can load it into a car."

The porter said: "Yes, sir." He tilted the trunk and dragged it out through the door. Beery went back and sat down.

Borg had taken his drink from Granquist. He said: "What I want to know is how the hell am I going to get my automobile."

Kells turned from the desk. "Will you please stop wailing about that wreck?" he said. He held out a singly folded sheaf of bills and Borg reached up and took it.

Kells went back to his chair, sat down and tossed another sheaf of bills in Beery's lap.

Beery looked down at it a moment, and then he picked it up and stuck it in his pocket, said: "Thanks, Gerry."

Granquist gave Kells one of the tall glasses. "Stirrup cup."

They all drank.

The porter came back into the room and loaded himself down with hand luggage, went out.

Kells said: "We're all in a swell spot. The baby here"—he nodded toward Granquist—"is still wanted for Bellmann's murder—maybe. Shep and I have got to go down and okay our signatures on Fenner's confession—and maybe they'll want to talk to me about Woodward, or what happened at MacAlmon's, and if there's been any squawk from MacAlmon's they'll be looking for Fat." He grinned at Borg.

Beery took a long envelope out of his inside coat pocket, turned it over several times on his lap. "If this doesn't square any beef they can figure," he said, "I'm a watchmaker."

The porter came back into the room for the last of the hand luggage. They all finished their drinks and went out to the elevator, down to the cab stand.

They took two cabs. Kells and Beery got into the first one; Granquist and Borg got into another, and all the hand luggage was put in with them. Kells told the driver of the second cab to keep about a half-block behind them when they stopped downtown.

Then he went back to the other cab and got in with Beery and said: "Police Station."

* * * * *

BEERY SIGNED THE affidavit and pushed it across the desk to Kells.

Captain Larson blew his nose. He said: "You understand you both will be witnesses for the state when we get Fenner?"

Kells nodded.

"An' this Granquist girl—she's a material witness too." The captain widened his watery blue eyes at Beery, leaned far back in his swivel chair.

Kells read the affidavit carefully, signed.

Larson said: "What do you know about the Woodward business?"

"Nothing." Kells put his elbow on the desk, his chin in his hand, stared at Larson expressionlessly. "I lost Fenner's confession shortly after it was signed—before I could use it. Woodward evidently got hold of it someway and was trying to peddle it back to Fenner."

"If Fenner was in his place at the Miramar when Woodward was shot, how come he left the confession there?" Larson was looking out the window, spoke as if to himself.

Kells shook his head slowly.

Larson said: "I suppose you know you're tied up with all this enough for me to hold you." He said it very quietly, kept looking out the window.

Kells smiled a little, was silent.

Beery leaned across the desk. "Fenner killed Bellmann,"

he said. "That's a swell break for the administration. It'd be even, a better break if all the dirt on Bellmann that the Coast Guardian published was proven to be fake—wouldn't it?"

Larson turned from the window. He took a big handkerchief out of his pocket, blew his nose violently, nodded.

Beery took the long envelope out of his pocket and put it on the desk and shoved it slowly across to Larson.

"Here are the originals of the photographs and a couple of letters. You can burn 'em up and then challenge the Coast Guardian people to produce—or you can have 'em doctored so they'll look like phoneys."

Larson looked down at the envelope. He asked: "Who are the Coast Guardian people?"

Kells smiled, said: "Me—I'm them."

Larson slit the envelope, glanced at its contents. Then he put the envelope in the top drawer of his desk and stood up; Kells and Beery stood up, too. Larson reached across the desk and shook hands with them. They went out of the office, downstairs.

Kells said: "It looks like MacAlmon hasn't squawked—maybe he got away with the junk after all."

They passed the Reporters' Room and Beery said: "Wait a minute—maybe I can find out." He went in and telephoned and came out, shook his head. "Nothing yet."

Their cab was across the street. Kells looked up First Street to where the second cab had been parked on the other side of Hill Street. It had gone. He stood there a moment looking up First, then he said, "Come on," and crossed the street, asked the driver: "What happened to the other cab?"

The driver shook his head. "I don't know. It was there a minute ago an' then I looked up an' it was gone."

Kells got into the cab, stared through the open door at

Beery. His face was hard and white. "We were going to an auto-rental joint over on Los Angeles Street and hire a car and driver to take us down to San Bernardino. But she didn't know the address—they couldn't have gone over there."

Beery said: "Maybe they were in a 'no parking' zone and had to go around the block."

A short gray-haired man came out on the steps of the Police Station and called across to Beery: "Telephone, Shep—says it's important."

Beery ran across the street and Kells got out of the cab and followed as fast as he could. That wasn't very fast; his leg was hurting pretty badly. When he went into the Reporters' Room, Beery was standing at a telephone, jiggling the hook up and down savagely, yelling at the operator to trace the call. Then he said: "All right—hurry it—this is the Police Station," hung up and looked at Kells.

The man who had called Beery to the phone glanced at them and then got up and went out into the hall.

They looked at one another silently for a moment and Beery sat down on one of the little desks. He said: "They've got her."

"Who?"

"I don't know—Crotti and MacAlmon I guess. You're supposed to do business with MacAlmon...."

"What do you mean, business?" Kells was standing by one of the windows, his mouth curved in a hard and mirthless grin.

"They want their hundred and fifteen, and they want it quick. I don't know who I talked to—I couldn't place the voice. He said the price goes up twenty-five grand a day—and they'll send you one of her teeth every day, just to remind you...."

Kells laughed. He looked out the window and laughed without moving his head, and the sound was cold and dry and rattling. He said: "To hell with it. Where did those saps get the idea she means that much to me? All she's given me is a lot of grief—I don't want any part of her." Beery sat staring at Kells with a very faint smile on his lips. "I'm in the clear—I've got mine. I'm going." Kells went unsteadily toward the door, and then he turned and held out his hand. Beery stood up and took his hand and shook it gravely.

Kells said: "Why, goddamn it, Shep—she's double-crossed me a half dozen times. How do I know this isn't another one of those Scandinavian gags? She was Crotti's gal in the first place...."

Beery nodded slowly. He said: "Sure."

Kells turned again toward the door. He took two or three steps and then he turned again and limped wearily over to one of the desks, sat down. He sat there a little while staring into space.

Then he said: "See if you can get MacAlmon, Shep."

Beery smiled, picked up the phone.

* * * * *

THERE WERE SIX men in MacAlmon's big living room at the Villa Dora. Crotti sat sidewise at a desk against one wall, leaned with one elbow on the big pink blotter that covered the desk. His thick red lower lip was thrust out, curved up at the corners in a fixed and meaningless smile.

There were two men sitting in straight-backed chairs on the other side of the room. One was Max Hesse. He was fat, ruddy-cheeked, blond; his suit looked as if it might have been cut out of a horse blanket. The other man was dark and slight. He fidgeted a great deal. He had been introduced simply as Carl. Kells sat in one of the big armchairs near the central table and Beery sat on the edge of the table.

MacAlmon paced from the door to the table, back again. Kells said: "Certainly not. You haven't got Granquist here—I haven't got the dough. Turn her over to me in the open and without any finaygling and you can send anyone you want to a spot I'll give them, with an order from me. They can call you with an okay when they get the money. Then-we'll walk." Crotti moved his fixed smile from MacAlmon to Kells. He said: "You are very careful." The soft slurred impediment in his speech made it sound like a whisper.

Kells nodded without speaking, without looking at him. Hesse laughed, a high dry cackle.

MacAlmon glanced at Crotti, then stopped his pacing, spoke to Kells: "She is here." He raised his eyes to the balcony that ran across half one side of the room. He called: "Shorty."

One of the three doors on the balcony opened and a squat over-dressed Filipino came out and leaned on the balustrade. He tipped his bright green velours hat to the back of his head, stared coldly, expressionlessly at MacAlmon. MacAlmon said: "Bring her down." The Filipino went back into the room and then came into the doorway with Granquist.

Her hair was loose, hung in straw-colored and angular disorder over her shoulders. Her eyes were wide, unseeing. A white silk handkerchief had been stuffed into her mouth, and her hands were knotted behind her back.

Kells said: "Take that god-damned gag out of her mouth." He spoke almost without moving his lips.

Beery stood up.

"I am very sorry." Crotti spoke sidewise to Kells. "She raised a lot of hell...." He nodded to the Filipino.

The Filipino reached up delicately and flicked the handkerchief out of her mouth by one corner. She caught her breath sharply; her eyes rolled up whitely for a second then she closed them and swayed sideways with one hip against the balustrade.

Kells stood up slowly.

Crotti said: "Sit down."

Granquist opened her eyes and turned her head slowly and looked down at Kells. She opened her mouth a little and tried to speak. Then the Filipino took her arm and guided her down the stair, to a low chair between Kells and Crotti. She sank down into it, and the Filipino took a little knife out of his pocket and reached behind her and cut the twisted cord that held her hands. She leaned back and put her hands up to her face.

MacAlmon walked to the door and back. Crotti asked: "How do you feel, sister?" Granquist didn't move or show in any way that she had heard.

Kells sat down in the big chair, and Beery sat down again on the edge of the table.

Kells took a thin black card case out of his pocket and removed a card and spoke over his shoulder, to Beery: "Got a pencil?"

MacAlmon had come back from the door and was standing near Kells. He took a silver pencil out of his vest pocket, handed it to him. Hesse got up and went out into the kitchen and came back with a glass of water and put it down on the arm of Granquist's chair. He tapped her shoulder, smiled down at her. She took her hands away from her face a moment and stared blankly up at him, then she put her hands back over her eyes.

"How many men have you got outside?" Kells glanced at Crotti. Crotti wasn't smiling any more. His wide-set eyes were very serious.

He said: "Two—one car." He took a dark green cigar out of his breast pocket, bit off the end, lighted it.

Kells was watching him, smiling faintly. Crotti looked up from lighting his cigar, nodded slowly, emphatically.

Hesse said: "I've got just my chauffeur—he is waiting...." Kells put the card down on the arm of his chair, scribbled something on it. He said: "You can send Carl, here"—he jerked his head toward the slight nervous man—"and whoever's outside after the dough. Berry will go along and tell 'em where to go." He was looking at Carl. "When you're paid off, Beery will call us here and you can okay it for your boss." He nodded at Crotti.

Crotti was smiling again. He said: "All right."

Carl got up and came over to pick up the card. Beery was at the telephone; he made a note of the number.

Kells went on: "Maybe the spick had better go along too." The Filipino looked at him coldly. Crotti shook his head.

Kells grinned, shrugged.

He said: "I'll see you later, Shep." Beery nodded and put on his hat, went to the door with Carl.

They went out.

Kells called to Berry as he was closing the door: "Tell that cab driver to sit on it—we'll be out in a little while."

MacAlmon went to a wall switch, snapped on several more lights. Then he went over and lay down on a wide divan under the big front windows. The drapes were tightly drawn.

Kells glanced at the tall clock in one corner. It was seven-fifty.

Hesse had taken MacAlmon's place at pacing up and down the floor.

Kells got up and limped to Granquist's chair, sat down on one arm of it and leaned close to her with his arm on her shoulder.

She whispered, "Gerry—I'm so sorry," without looking at him.

"Shut up, baby." He smiled down at her and pushed her hands gently down from her face.

"How's your leg?"

He said: "Swell." He patted his leg gingerly with one hand.

She moved her head over against his side. "It happened

so damned quick," she said—"I mean quickly. They pulled up alongside of us and two of them got into the cab and stuck a rod into the driver and me and we came out here. Borg jumped out as soon as he saw them and ran down First Street—the car they came up in went after him...."

Kells said: "He got away—he was waiting for us at the corner below the station. He's got the hundred and fifteen down at a little hotel on Melrose. That's where Shep's taking Crotti's boys...."

Granquist sighed, whispered: "That's a lot of money." Kells shook his head slowly. "That's the first really illegitimate pass we've made—maybe we didn't deserve it." He rubbed his forehead hard. "What happened to the cab with our stuff in it?"

"It's out in the driveway. They sapped the driver—he's upstairs sleeping it off."

They were silent a little while and then Kells said: "We forgot to send back the car we rented from the Miramar—remind me to do that as soon as we can."

"Uh huh." Granquist's voice was muffled. Kells got up and went into the kitchen. He tried the back door, but it was locked and there was no key in it. When he came back Crotti had straightened around at the desk, was bent over it reading a paper.

Kells asked: "How's the fella my fat friend popped this afternoon?"

Crotti turned his head, nodded. "He's all right." The phone rang and Kells answered it. MacAlmon swung up to sit on the edge of the divan. Crotti turned slowly in his chair toward Kells. Hesse stopped near the door. The Filipino was tilted back in a chair near the stairway—that led up to the balcony and the room upstairs; his hat was pulled down over his eyes and he did not move.

Kells said, "Yes, Shep," into the telephone. He listened a little while and his face was cold and hard, his eyes were heavy. Then he said, "All right," and hung up the receiver.

He spoke, more to Granquist than to any of the rest of them: "Borg's gone."

Granquist leaned forward slowly. Hesse said: "Who's Borg?"

"The guy who's got your money." Kells smiled slowly at Hesse. Then he glanced at the Filipino and there was a black automatic in the Filipino's hand. He was still tilted back against the wall and his hat almost covered his eyes.

Crotti stood up. He moved a little toward Kells and then stood very straight and stared at Kells and the muscles of his deeply lined white face twitched a little. He shook his head almost imperceptibly at the Filipino.

He said slowly: "No—I will do it myself, Shorty." He put his hand to his side under the arm, under his coat, and took out a curiously shaped German revolver. He held it down straight at his side for a moment and then raised it toward Kells. He raised it as if he would like to be raising it very slowly and deliberately, but couldn't; he raised it very swiftly.

Kells's shoulders were hunched together a little. His chin was in and he looked at Crotti's feet and his eyes were almost closed. Granquist stood up and her face was dead white, her hands were clawed in front of her body. She made no sound.

Then there was a sharp crashing roar. It beat twice, filled the room with dull sound.

Kells still stood with his shoulders a little together, his eyes almost closed.

Crotti swayed once to the left. His expression was querulous, worried; the revolver fell from his hand, clattered on the floor. One of his legs gave way slowly and he slipped down on one knee, fell slowly heavily forward on his face.

Kells turned his head swiftly, looked up. Borg was grinning down at him from the balcony; the short blunt blue revolver was lisping smoke in his hand. The Filipino was bent over, holding his wrist between his hand and knees. He whirled slowly on one foot—his hat had fallen off and his broad flat face was twisted with pain.

Borg said: "By God! Just like they do in the movies." Hesse was at the door.

Borg swung the revolver around toward him, said: "Wait a minute."

MacAlmon hadn't moved. He was still sitting on the edge of the divan, staring at Crotti. Kells said: "Let's go."

* * * * *

THEY STOPPED AT a drugstore near Sixth and Normandie. Borg pulled up ahead of them in the other cab, and he and the driver transferred Kells's luggage to the one cab.

Kells said to the driver: "You can call up and report where this cab is if you want to." He gestured toward the second cab. "The driver is out at the joint we just left—Apartment L."

Borg said: "Maybe. They're probably all out of there by now."

"They wouldn't take the driver."

"They might—he could testify against 'em." Kells and the driver went into the drugstore to telephone.

Kells called Beery at home, said: "Swell, Shep.... Did you have any trouble getting away?... That's fine.... Borg got to worrying about giving all that dough back so he ducked over to MacAlmon's place and climbed in a window.... Uh huh. The crazy bastard damn near got me the works, but if he hadn't been there I wouldn't be here—so what? I don't know whether to give him a punch in the nose or a bonus... I have an idea Crotti would've tried to smack me down whether Borg had been there to put the cash on the line or not, I don't think he liked me very well... So long, Shep, and good luck—I'll send you a postcard."

He hung up and went out and got into the cab with Granquist and Borg.

The driver turned around, asked: "Where to?"

"How'd you like to make a long haul?" Kells glanced at Granquist, smiled at the driver. The driver said: "Sure. The longer the better." Kells said: "San Bernardino." He leaned back and closed his eyes.

Chapter Eight

THE ROOM WAS about thirty by fifteen. There were six booths along each long side. At one end there was a door leading to a kind of kitchen and at the other end there was a door that led to steps down to the alley. There was a small radio on a table beside the door that led to the kitchen and there was a clock on the wall above the table. It was five minutes past nine. Kells and Granquist and Borg sat in the third booth on the right, coming in. There was no one in any of the other booths.

The cab driver went back to the door to the kitchen and called: "Jake." Then he bent over the radio, snapped it on.

A man came out of the kitchen, said "Hi" to the driver, came up to the booth. He was a tall man, about fifty-five, with a long crooked nose, a three or four-day growth of gray beard. He wiped his hands on his dirty gray-white apron.

Kells asked: "Do you know how to make a whiskey sour?" The man grinned with one side of his mouth, nodded. "Oke—and put some whiskey in it." Granquist was rubbing powder onto her nose, holding her head back and looking into a small mirror which she held in one hand, a little higher than her head.

She said: "Me too—an' ham and eggs."

Borg had slid low in the seat. His chin was on his chest

and his eyes were closed. He asked, "Got any buttermilk?" without moving or opening his eyes.

The man shook his head.

Kells said: "Give him a whiskey sour, too—and give all of us ham and eggs. Fresh eggs."

He raised his head, called to the driver: "Is that all right for you?"

A dance orchestra blared suddenly out of the radio. The driver turned his head, smiled, nodded.

Jake went back into the kitchen.

Granquist called to the driver: "See if you can get Louie Armstrong."

Jake stuck his head through the door, said: "He don't come on till eleven." His head disappeared.

Kells grinned at Granquist.

She said: "Let's dance."

"Don't be silly." He glanced down at his leg.

"Oh, I'm sorry, darling." Her face was suddenly serious, concerned. "How is it?"

He shook his head without looking at her, was silent; after a minute or so he watched Jake come in with four tall glasses on a scarred tin tray.

Jake put the tray on the table, spoke over his shoulder to the driver: "Turn 'er down to ten—that's KGPL, the police reports to the radio cars." He went back toward the kitchen. "Last night they held up the gas station down on the corner an' we knew it here, right away. I went downstairs an' saw the bandit car go by—sixty miles an hour." He jerked his head violently up and to the left, an unspoken "By Crackey!"

The driver turned the dial, then came to the booth and took one of the tall glasses. He sat down on the table directly across the narrow room, said, "Here's mud in your eye," drank.

It was quiet a little while, except for the hiss of frying eggs in the kitchen.

Then the radio hummed slowly, buzzed to words: "KGPL—Los Angeles Police Department.... Calling car number one thirty-two—car number one three two.... At Berkeley and Gaines streets—an ambulance follow-up.... That is all..... Gordon"

Granquist held her glass in both hands, her elbows on the table. She tipped the glass, drank, said: "Not bad. Not good, but not bad."

Kells raised his head, called: "Bring out the bottle, Jake."

Borg opened his eyes, stared gloomily at his drink.

The radio sputtered to sound: "KGPL... Attention all cars—attention all cars.... Repeat as of eight-fifteen on Crotti killing.... Persons wanted are: Number One—Gerard A Kells. Description: six foot one—a hundred an' sixty pounds—about thirty-five—red hair—sallow complexion—wearing a dark blue suit, black soft hat—walks with a limp, recent leg wound...."

Jake came out of the kitchen carrying a bottle of whiskey by the neck. He put it on the table and Kells took out the cork and tipped the bottle, sweetened Granquist's, Borg's and his own drink. He waved the bottle at the driver. The driver slid off the table and came over and held out his glass and Kells poured whiskey into it. The driver went back and sat down on the table and Jake went back into the kitchen.

He said, "Ham an' eggs coming up," over his shoulder as he went through the door.

The radio droned on: "Number Two—a woman, thought to be Miss Granquist—first name unknown—also wanted in connection with Bellmann murder. Description: five eight—a hundred an' twenty pounds—twenty-seven—blonde—high color.... Number Three—Borg—Otto J. Description: five six—a hundred an' ninety pounds—forty—sandy complexion.... Particular attention cars on roads out of Los Angeles: these people are probably trying to get out of town.... Don't take any chances—they're dangerous.... That is all.... Gordon."

The driver put his glass down, slid off the table. He said, "I forgot to turn off my lights," started toward the door.

Borg said: "Sit down." He had not raised his head or straightened up in his feet. The heavy snub-nosed revolver glittered in his left hand.

Kells stood up slowly, squeezed out of the booth and limped back to the kitchen door. He stood in the doorway and said: "You can put that phone down and bring out our ham and eggs now."

He continued to stand in the doorway until Jake came out past him with four orders of ham and eggs on a big tray. Jake's nose and forehead were shiny with sweat. He put the tray on the table and stood wiping his hands on his apron.

The driver turned and went back and sat down on the table. He was very pale and there was a weak smile on his face. He picked up his drink.

Borg gestured with his head and Jake went over and sat down in the booth with the driver. Kells went into the kitchen.

Granquist's eyes were hard, opaque. She took one of the plates of ham and eggs off the tray, sat staring down at it.

Kells's voice came from the kitchen: "Madison two four five six.... Hello—Chronicle?... City desk, please.... Hello—is Shep Beery there? ..." Then he lowered his voice and they could not hear. He called another indistinguishable number, talked a long time in a low voice.

Granquist ate mechanically. Borg finished his drink, got up and handed the driver's plate across to him. The driver sat down beside Jake, sliced the fried ham into thin strips.

After a while Kells came in and sat down. He pushed his plate away, poured whiskey into the glasses on the table. He said quietly: "They've picked up Shep."

No one said anything. Granquist tipped her glass and Borg stared expressionlessly at Kells.

"And they've been tipped to our reservations on the Chief tomorrow night—they're watching all trains, all roads—they'll ride that train to Albuquerque." Kells drank. He looked at Granquist, then slowly turned his head and looked at Borg. "And they've tied us up with Abner here—or his bus." He moved his head slightly toward the cab driver.

Borg said: "Beery's talked."

"No." Kells shook his head slowly. "No. I don't think so."

Granquist put down her glass. "Don't be a sap, Gerry," she said—"he has."

Kells leaned across the table and slapped her very sharply across the mouth.

She stared at him out of wide, startled eyes and put her hands up to her face, slowly. Kells looked at her mouth, and his face was very white, his eyes were almost closed.

Borg was sitting up very straight.

Kells's hand was lying palm-up on the table. Granquist put out one hand slowly and touched his and then she said, "I'm sorry," very softly.

Kells shook his head sharply, closed his eyes for a moment, then opened them and looked down at the table. He said: "I'm sorry too, baby." He patted the back of her hand.

He stood up and leaned against the back of the booth, stared a long minute at Jake and the driver.

The driver looked up from his plate, said: "Ain't we goin' on to San Berdoo?"

Kells didn't show that he had heard. His eyes were blank, empty. He spoke sidewise to Borg: "I'm going back into town and find out what it's all about."

Granquist stood up swiftly. Her eyes were very bright and her face was set and determined. She said: "So am I."

Kells bent his head a little to one side. "You're going to stay here—and Fat is going to stay here. If I don't make out, I'll get a steer to you over the radio—or some way." He moved his eyes to Borg. "You snag a car and take her to Las Vegas or some station on the UP where you can get a train."

Borg nodded.

"I'm going to find out what happened to the immunity we were promised by Beery's pal, the captain," Kells went on. "He's supposed to have the chief of police in his pocket—and the DA is his brother-in-law." He poured a drink. "Now he puts the screws on us for knocking over Crotti. Public Enemy Number One." He drank, smiled without mirth. "God! That's a laugh."

Kells glanced at Granquist, moved his head and shoulders slightly, turned and went out into the kitchen. She followed him. He was half sitting on a big table and she went to him and put one arm around his shoulders, one hand on his chest. She moved her head close to his.

He spoke very quietly, almost whispered: "I've got to go by myself, baby. It's taking enough of a chance being spotted that way—it'd be a cinch if we were together."

"Can't we wait here till it cools off, or take a chance on getting away now?" Her eyes were hot and dry; her voice trembled a little.

Kells said: "No. That'd mean getting clear out of the country—and it'd mean being on the run wherever we were. I had that once before and I don't want any more of it."

He took a small package wrapped in brown paper out of his inside breast pocket and handed it to her. "There's somewhere a hundred and ninety grand here," he said. "Don't let Borg know you've got it. I think he's okay but that's a lot of money."

She took the package and put it in one of the big pockets of her long tweed topcoat.

Kells asked: "Have you got a gun?"

She nodded, patted her handbag. "I picked up the spick's—the guy who was with Crotti."

Kells kissed her. He said: "I'll get word to you some way, or be back by tomorrow noon. Watch yourself."

He limped to the door, through it into the other room.

Granquist followed him to the door, stood leaning against the frame; her face was dead white and she held her deep red lower lip between her teeth.

Kells spoke over his shoulder to the driver: "Come on." The driver jumped up and followed him to the outer door. Kells turned at the door, said, "Be seeing you," to Borg. He did not look at Granquist. He went out and the driver went out after him and closed the door.

* * * * *

ON KENMORE NEAR Beverly Boulevard Kells leaned forward and tapped on the glass. The cab swung to the curb and the driver slid the glass. Kells asked: "Are you married?"

The driver looked blank for a moment, then said: "Uh huh—only we don't get along very well."

Kells smiled faintly in the darkness. "Maybe you'd get along better if you took her for a little vacation down to Caliente—or Catalina." He held out four crumpled bills and the driver reached back and took them. He held them in the dim light of the taxi meter and whistled, and then he stuck the bills hurriedly in his pocket and said: "Yes, sir."

Kells said: "I want you to remember that you took us up to Lankershim and that we transferred to another car there and headed for Frisco. Is your memory that good?"

"Yes, sir." The driver nodded emphatically.

"If it isn't," Kells went on—"I give you two days. My friends here would be awfully mad if anything happened to me on account of your memory slipping up." He lowered his voice, spoke each word very distinctly: "Do you understand what I mean?"

The driver said: "Yes, sir—I understand."

Kells got out and stood at the curb until the cab had turned down Beverly, disappeared. Then he went to the drugstore on the corner and called the taxi stand at the Ambassador, asked if Number Fifty-eight was in. He was on a short trip, was expected back soon. Kells left word for Fifty-eight to pick him up on Beverly near Normandie, went out of the drugstore, west.

His leg didn't hurt so badly now. He wasn't quite sure whether it was a great deal better or only momentarily numb. Anyway, it felt a lot better—he could walk fairly comfortably.

The cab detached itself from northbound traffic at the corner of Normandie, pulled into the curb. Fifty-eight stuck his head out and grinned at Kells.

Kells climbed into the cab, asked: "How are ya?"

Fifty-eight said: "Swell—an' yourself? Where to?"

"Let's go out to the apartment house on the corner of Yucca and Cahuenga first." Kells leaned back.

They went over Normandie to Franklin, west on Franklin to Argyle, down the curve of Argyle and west two more blocks to Cahuenga. Kells got out, said, "I won't be long," and went into the apartment house on the corner. He asked at the desk for the number of Mister Beery's apartment, went into the elevator and pressed the third-floor button.

Florence Beery was tall—almost as tall as Kells—slim. Her hair was very dark and her eyes were big, heavily shadowed. She stood in the doorway and looked at Kells, and her face was a hard, brittle mask.

She said slowly: "Well—what do you want?" Her voice was icy, bitter.

Kells put up one arm and leaned against the doorframe.

He asked: "May I come in?"

She looked at him steadily for a moment, then she turned and went through the short hallway into the living room. He closed the door and followed her into the living room, sat down. She stood in the center of the room, staring at the wall, waiting.

Kells took off his hat and put it on the divan beside him. He said: "I'm sorry about Shep–"

"Sorry!" She turned her head toward him slowly. Her eyes were long upward-slanted slits. "Sorry! This is a hell of a time to be sorry!" She swayed a little forward.

Kells said: "Wait, Florence. Shep wouldn't be in the can if he hadn't thrown in with me. He wouldn't be ten or twelve grand ahead, either. The dough hasn't been so hard to take, has it?"

She stood staring at him with blank unseeing eyes, swaying a little. Then she sobbed and the sound was a dry, burnt rattle in her throat, took two steps toward him, blindly. She spoke and it was as if she were trying to scream—but her throat was too tight, her words were low, harsh, like coarse cloth tearing:

"God damn you! Don't you know Shep is dead—dead!"

The word seemed to release some spring inside her—sight came to her eyes, swift motion to her body—she sprang at Kells, her clawed hands outstretched.

He half rose to meet her, caught one of her wrists, swung her down beside him. The nails of her free hand caught the flesh of his cheek, ripped downward. He threw his right arm around her shoulders, imprisoned her wrists in his two hands, then he took her wrists tightly in his right hand, pressed her head down on her breast with his left. She was panting sharply, raggedly. Then she relaxed suddenly, went limp against his arm—her shoulders went back and forth rhythmically, limply—she was sobbing and there was no sound except sharp intake of breath.

Kells released her gradually, gently, stood up. He walked once to the other side of the room, back. His eyes were wide open and his mouth hung a little open, black against the green pallor of his face. He sank down beside her, put his arm again around her shoulders, spoke very quietly: "Florence. For the love of Mary! — when?—how?"

After a little while she whispered without raising her head: "When they were taking him to the Station—from a car—they don't know who it was...."

Kells was staring over her shoulder at a flashing electric sign through the window. His eyes were glazed, cold—his mouth twitched a little. He sat like that a little while and then he took his arm from around her shoulders, picked up his hat and put it on, stood up. He stood looking down at her for perhaps a minute, motionlessly. Then he turned and went out of the room.

* * * * *

IT WAS TEN-FIFTY when the cab swung in to the curb in front of a bungalow on South Gramercy.

Fifty-eight turned around, said: "You'd better be wiping the blood off your face before you go in, Mister Kells."

Kells mechanically put the fingers of his left hand up to his cheek, took them away wet, sticky. He took out a handkerchief and pressed it against his cheek, got out of the cab and went toward the dark house.

After he had rung the bell four or five times, a light was switched on upstairs, he heard someone coming down. The lower part of the house remained dark, but a light above him—in the ceiling of the porch—snapped on. He stood with his chin on his chest, his hat pulled down over his eyes, watching the bottom of the door.

It opened and Captain Larson's voice said: "Come in," out of the darkness. Kells went in.

The light on the porch snapped off, the light in the room snapped on. The door was closed.

It was a rather large living room which, with the smaller dining room, ran across all the front of the house. The furniture was mostly Mission, mostly built-in. The wall paper was bright, bad.

Larson stood with his back to the door in a nightshirt, big, fleece-lined slippers. He held a Colt .38 revolver steadily in his right hand. He said: "Take a chair."

Kells sat down in the most comfortable-looking chair, leaned back. Larson pulled another chair around and sat down on its edge, facing Kells. He leaned forward, put his elbows on his knees—he held the revolver in his right hand hanging down between his legs, said: "What's on your mind?"

Kells tipped his hat back a little and stared at Larson sleepily.

"You gave me a free bill this afternoon," he said, "in exchange for some stuff that would have split your administration—your whole political outfit—wide open." He paused, changed his position slightly. "Now you clamp down on me because somebody gets the dumb idea I had something to do with the Crotti chill. What's the answer?"

"Crotti's the answer." Larson spat far and accurately into the fireplace, wiped his mouth on his sleeve. He leaned back and crossed his legs and held the revolver loosely in his lap. "There's a lot of water been under the bridge since I seen you this afternoon," he went on. "In the first place I didn't give you no free bill, as you call it—I told you that you and your gal would probably be wanted for questioning in connection with a lot of things. An' I hinted that if you wasn't around when question time came we wouldn't look too far for you." He took a crumpled handkerchief from the pocket of his nightshirt, blew his nose gustily. "Crotti's something else again."

Kells smiled slowly. "Crotti was your Number One Gangster," he said. "If I had something to do with his killing I ought to be getting a medal for it—not a rap."

A woman's cracked querulous voice came down the stairs: "What is it, Gus?"

Larson spat again into the fireplace, looked at the stairs. "Nothin". Go back to bed."

He turned back toward Kells and his big loose mouth split to a wide grin. "You're way behind the times," he said. "Crotti hooked up with my people this morning. They were tickled to death to get an organization like his behind them and they were plumb disappointed when you bumped him off. That's one of the reasons there's a tag out for you...."

Kells held his handkerchief to his bleeding cheek. He said: "What are the other reasons?"

"Jack Rose moved into Crotti's place."

Kells laughed soundlessly. "You're kidding."

"No." Larson spun the revolver once around his big forefinger. "Rose made a deal with Crotti a couple of days ago. When Crotti was shot this evening, Rose didn't lose any time putting the pressure on my people and they didn't lose any time putting it on me. You're it."

"But Rose is wanted for the O'Donnell–"

"Not any more." Larson chuckled. "I told you you wasn't keeping in touch with things. For one thing, Lee Fenner shot himself about eight o'clock tonight. He was the only one there was to testify against Rose on the O'Donnell angle—so that's out. And Rose says you killed O'Donnell, says he'll swear to it—an' he's got another witness."

Kells said wearily: "Is that all—I'm only wanted on two counts of murder?"

"That's all for tonight. Matheson called me up a couple hours ago an' said the Perry woman had phoned in, drunk, an' said she wanted to repudiate her confession that Perry killed Doc Haardt." Larson grinned broadly, stood up. "Maybe we can tie you up to that in the morning."

He took two sidewise steps to a small stand and picked up the telephone receiver with one hand, squatted down until his mouth was near the transmitter. He held the revolver in his right hand, watched Kells closely while he spoke into the phone:

"Gimme Michigan six one one one, sister. Uh huh... Hello, Mike—this is Gus... Kells is out here—out at my house... Come on out an' get him... Uh huh."

He hung up the receiver, stood up and went back to the chair and sat down.

"You been mixed up in damn near every killing we had the past week," he said. "It looks to me like you been our Number One Gunman—not Crotti."

Kells leaned forward slowly.

Larson said: "Sit still."

Kells asked: "What do you think my chances are of getting to the Station on my feet?"

"Wha' d'you mean?" Larson was blowing his nose.

"I mean they got Beery on the way in after he'd been pinched tonight. I mean your desk sergeant has tipped Rose that I'm out here by now—he'll be here by the time your coppers are-will be waiting outside. They'll take me in to a slab."

Larson said: "Aw, don't talk that way." He squinted his eyes as if he were trying to remember something, then said proudly: "You got a prosecution complex, that's what you got—a prosecution complex."

Kells stood up.

Larson jerked his head emphatically at the chair, snapped: "Sit down."

Kells said slowly: "I work pretty fast, Gus. I'll bet you can shoot me through the heart an' I'll have my gun out an' have a couple slugs in your belly before I hit the floor." He smiled a little. "Let's try it."

Larson said, "Sit down," loudly.

"I'll bet you can't even hit my heart—I'll bet you're a lousy shot." Kells took a short step forward, balanced himself evenly on both feet.

Larson was white. His big mouth hung a little open.

Kells said: "Let's go." His hand went swiftly to his side.

Larson's shoulders moved convulsively, his right hand went forward, up, with the revolver. At the same time he threw his head forward and down, fell forward out of the chair. The revolver clattered on the floor.

Kells was standing on the balls of his feet, an automatic held crosswise against his chest. He stared down at Larson and his eyes were wide, surprised.

He said, "Well, I'll be god-damned," under his breath.

Larson was on his hands and knees; his big shoulders and thick neck were pulled in tightly, rigidly.

Kells stooped and picked up the revolver, stuck it into his overcoat pocket. Then he laughed quietly, said: "Copper yellow. That's the first time my reputation ever did me any good."

He went to the door swiftly, turned once to glance hurriedly at Larson. Larson had risen to his knees. He did not look at Kells; he looked at the wall—he was breathing heavily.

Kells opened the door and went out and closed it behind him.

* * * * *

FIFTY-EIGHT SAID: "There it is."

They were parked in the deep shadow between two street lights in the next block to the one Larson's house was in. A big touring car had come up quietly, without lights, stopped across the street from Larson's.

Kells didn't say anything. He sat huddled in a corner of the cab and although the night was fairly warm he shivered a little.

After a few minutes another car swung around the corner, pulled up in front of Larson's. Kells leaned forward and watched through the glass. Three men got out and went into the house. In a little while they came out; one of them went across the street and stood beside the car that had come up first, the others got into the other car and drove away.

Then the man got into the second car, its lights were switched on and it too drove away.

Kells said: "Give 'em enough room."

Fifty-eight waited until the other car was more than halfway down the long block, let the clutch in slowly. Kells felt in his pockets until he found the tin box of aspirin tablets, took two. The other car turned left on Third Street. Fifty-eight stepped on it, swung into Third; there were two taillights about a block and a half ahead. He followed the faster one north on Rossmore, got close enough to see that he'd guessed right, fell back.

They turned west again on Beverly, to La Brea.

Kells was sitting sideways on the seat looking through the rear window. He leaned forward suddenly, spoke rapidly to Fifty-eight: "Keep that car in sight—an' you'll have to do it by yourself. I've got something else to watch. We're being tailed.

They turned off La Brea, west on Santa Monica Boulevard.

Then Kells was sure they were being followed. The car was a big blue or black coupe—shiny, powerful.

On Santa Monica, a little way beyond Gardner, Fifty-eight said over his shoulder: "They're stopping."

"Go on past 'em—slow."

Kells squeezed back into the corner, saw four men get out

of the touring car and start across the street. He thought one of them was Detective Lieutenant Reilly; wasn't sure. He didn't recognize any of the others.

Fifty-eight asked: "What'll I do?"

"Go on—slow." Kells took the automatic from its shoulder holster, balanced it across his hand. He watched the big coupe come up slowly.

It overtook them in the second block, stayed alongside.

Kells said: "Turn off right, at the next side street." He was deep in the dark corner of the cab, watching the coupe narrowly. Then the driver of the coupe put up his hand and Kells saw that it was Borg. They turned together into the side street, drove up about a hundred yards to comparative darkness. Borg parked a little way ahead of the cab.

Kells got out and went up to the coupe. He said. "That's the way people have accidents," unpleasantly.

Borg was silent.

Granquist was sitting very low in the seat beside Borg. She straightened, said: "Your other driver spilled his guts an' the tip went out on the joint we were at—"

Borg interrupted her: "That's a swell invention, the radio. I don't know what we would've done without it."

"Then while we were getting out," Granquist went on, "the call went out to the car in Larson's neighborhood to go and pick you up—we got the address from that. Fat couldn't find a car so we hired this one at a garage–"

"An' damn' near busted our necks getting to Larson's," Borg finished.

Kells asked: "Where did you pick me up?"

"We were turning off Third onto Gramercy when you turned into Third." Borg lighted his stump of cigar. He bent his head toward Granquist. "Miss Eagle-eye here thought she spotted you in the cab—an' I thought she was nuts. She wasn't."

"Did you know I was following another car?"

Granquist said: "Sure."

"That was one of Rose's cars." Kells put one foot on the running board, leaned on the door. "It was planted across from Larson's to smack me down when the cops brought me out." He hesitated a moment. "That's what happened to Shep when they were taking him in."

Borg swallowed, started to speak: "They..."

Granquist said: "Gerry—for God's sake get in and let's get out of here." Her voice was low; she spoke very rapidly. "Please, Gerry, let's go now—we can make the Border by three o'clock."

"Sure. In a little while." Kells was looking at the black and yellow sky.

It began to rain a little.

Borg said: "So what?"

"That car stopped at Ansel's." Kells jerked his head back toward Santa Monica Boulevard. "Ansel runs a cheap crap game that's backed by Rose—I've been there. It's a pretty safe bet that Rose is there, and his carload of rods went back there to report to him."

Borg said: "Uh huh. So, what?"

Kells stared at Borg vacantly. "So I'm going up an' tell Rose about Beery—about Beery's wife."

Granquist opened the door suddenly, got out on the sidewalk on the other side of the car. She held her arms stiff at her sides and her hands were clenched; she was trembling violently. She walked up the sidewalk about thirty feet—walked as if she were making a tremendous effort to walk slowly. Then she turned and leaned against a telephone pole and looked back at the car.

Kells watched her; he could not see her face in the darkness, only the dim outline of her body. He turned slowly to Borg.

"You can wait here," he said. "Or maybe you'd better wait down at the first corner this side of Ansel's. And stay with the car—both of you."

Borg said: "All right."

Kells walked up to Granquist. He stood looking down at her a little while, asked: "What's the matter, baby?"

Her voice, when she finally answered, was elaborately sarcastic. "What's the matter? What's the matter?" Then her tone changed abruptly—she put one trembling hand on his arm. "Gerry—don't do this," she said. "Let it go—please this time...."

He was smiling a little. He shook his head slightly.

She took her hand from his arm and her voice was suddenly acid, metallic. "You—and your pride! Your long chances—your little tin-horn revenge!" She laughed shrilly, hysterically. "You've seen too many gangster pictures—that's what's wrong with you...."

Kells was staring at her expressionlessly. He turned abruptly, strode back toward the car.

She was behind him, sobbing, trying to hold his arm.

"Gerry!" Her words, were blurred, broken. "Gerry—can't you think of me a little—can't you let this one thing go—for me? For us?"

He shook her hand off, spoke briefly to Borg: "An' stay with the car this time—I'll be wanting it in a hurry, when I want it."

Borg said: "Oke. First corner this side of the joint."

Kells went back to the, cab, got in, said: "Take me down to Gardner, about a half-block the other side of the Boulevard.

Fifty-eight grunted affirmatively and swung the cab around in the narrow street.

Kells glanced back through the rear window. Granquist was standing motionlessly in the middle of' the street, silhouetted against the glow of a street light on the far corner.

It began raining harder, pounded on the roof of the cab.

Fifty-eight started the windshield wiper and it swished rhythmically in a wide arc across the glass.

They stopped in the shelter of a big palm on Gardner and Kells got out.

Fifty-eight asked: "Can I help, Mister Kells?"

Kells shook his head. "I'll make out." He peeled two bills off the roll in his pocket, handed them to the little Irishman. He turned swiftly and went into the darkness between two houses, heard Fifty-eight's "Thank you, sir," behind him.

The driveway ended in a small garage; there was a gate at one side leading to a kind of narrow alley. Kells crossed the alley and walked north along a five-foot board fence for about a hundred feet. Then he climbed over the fence and went across a vacant weed-grown lot toward the rear end of the building that housed Ansel's.

Its three stories were dark and forbidding in the rain; no light came from the rear, and the side that Kells could see seemed entirely windowless. It was raining hard by now—he rolled his coat collar up, pulled the brim of his soft hat down.

He slipped once in the mud, almost fell. In righting himself he remembered his wounded leg suddenly, sharply. It was throbbing steadily, swollen and hot with pain.

He went close to the building. It was very dark there, but looking up he could see the vague outline of a fire escape against the yellow glow of the sky. He smiled to himself in the darkness, put the back of his hand against his forehead. It was hot, dry.

He felt his way along the wall of the building until he was under the free-swinging end of the fire escape. It was almost four feet beyond his reach. He went back the way he had come to the fence, went along it until, in the corner the fence made with a squat outbuilding, he found a fairly large packing case. He stood on it and found that it would hold his weight; he balanced it on his shoulder and carried it back into the shadow of the building.

Standing on the box, he could just reach the end of the fire escape; he put his weight on it, slowly. It creaked a little, came slowly down.

When the bottom step was resting on the packing case he crawled slowly, carefully up to the first landing. He lay on his side, held the free-swinging part so that it would come up quietly. Then he stood up.

Two windows gave on the second landing. One was boarded up snugly, no light came through. Kells put his ear to it, could hear only a confused hum of voices. The other window had been painted black on the inside but a long scratch ran diagonally across one of the panes. He took off his hat, put his eye close to the scratch.

He was looking into the office that ran almost the width of the building, was partitioned off from the big upstairs room by a wall of rough, unpainted pine boards.

The first person he saw was a woman whom he had never seen before. She-was sitting on a broad desk, talking to two men. One of the men, in ill-fitting dinner clothes, was unfamiliar—the other man turned as he watched, and Kells recognized Lieutenant Reilly.

Reilly was heavy, shapeless. A cast in one eye gave his bloated, florid face a shrewdly evil quality. He was holding a tall glass of beer in-one hand; he lifted it, drank deeply.

There were two large washtubs full of bottled beer and ice on the floor near the desk.

Another woman, in a bright orange evening gown, crossed Kells's line of vision, stooped and took two bottles from one of the tubs, disappeared.

Kells's lips framed the word. "Party." He was grinning.

Then he saw Ruth Perry. She was sitting on a dilapidated couch at one side of the room, swaying drunkenly back and forth, talking loudly to the man beside her. Kells put his ear to the pane but couldn't quite make out the words.

The man beside her was MacAlmon.

Then the rough pine door in the middle of the far wall opened and two men came in. In the moment the door was open, Kells saw a swirl of people around one of the crap tables in the big gambling room. Then the door closed; Kells looked at the two men.

One of them was a short-bodied, long-armed man whom Kells remembered vaguely from somewhere. His face was broad and bland and child-like.

The other was Jack Rose.

Kells slid the big automatic out of its holster.

Rose's long, tanned, good-looking face was cheerful; his thin red mouth was curved to a smile. He crossed the room and sat down beside Ruth Perry, spoke across her to MacAlmon.

Kells looked thoughtfully down at the dark slippery steps beneath him. Looking down made him suddenly dizzy—he blinked, shook his head sharply, put one hand on the railing for support. He thought he was going to be sick for a moment, but the feeling passed. He was hot and the rain felt terribly cold on his head.

Then he looked up again, at the door. There was a big, planed two-by-four up and down its middle that could be swung sideways into two iron slots—one on each side of the door.

As he watched, the woman and Reilly and the other man whom he had seen first took up their glasses, went out of the room. That left—as nearly as he could judge—six or seven people. Rose, Ruth Perry, MacAlmon, the short man who had come in with Rose, the woman in the orange dress; perhaps two or three more whom he hadn't seen.

He looked at the crosspieces between the four panes of the window, felt their thickness with his fingers. Then he stood up and braced himself against the railing, released the safety on the automatic, put one foot against the crosspieces and pushed suddenly with all his weight. They gave way with a small splintering noise, glass tinkled on the floor. Kells stumbled on the lower part of the window frame, almost fell. He saved himself; by grabbing the upper edge, felt a long sharp splinter of glass sink into the flesh of his hand. He held the automatic low, put one foot slowly down to the floor.

The woman in the orange dress looked as if she were going to scream; the man beside her took her arm suddenly, roughly—she put her free hand up to her mouth, was silent.

Rose had stood up; one hand was behind him. Kells jerked the automatic up in a savage gesture—Rose put his hands up slowly. Ruth Perry and MacAlmon were still sitting on the couch, and the short man was standing near them with his back to Kells, looking at Kells over his shoulder. The short man and MacAlmon put their hands up slowly.

Kells went swiftly sideways to the door, swung the bar. A great deal of noise came through the wall from the outer room and it occurred to him that perhaps the crashing of the window hadn't been heard outside.

Ruth Perry was staring blearily at Kells. She said: "Shay—whatch ish all about?"

MacAlmon put down one hand and put it over her mouth, said: "Shut up." MacAlmon was dead white.

Kells looked at the other man—the one he hadn't seen before, the one with the woman in the orange dress. He, too, put his hands up, rather more rapidly than the others had.

Someone pounded on the door, a voice shouted: "What's the matter in there?"

Kells looked at Rose. The automatic was rigid in his hand, focused squarely on Rose's chest. Rose looked at the gun, swallowed.

MacAlmon said: "Nothing...."

Rose swallowed again. He smiled weakly, licked his lips. "We're playing games." There was laughter outside the door—a man's laughter and a woman's. The voice asked: "Post office?"

The woman in the orange dress giggled. Then her eyes rolled back in her head and she slumped down softly to the floor.

Ruth Perry pushed MacAlmon's hand away, stood up. She swayed, stared drunkenly at Kells; she shook her head sharply and staggered forward, said: "Well, 'm a dirty name—ish Gerry—good ol' son of a bitch, Gerry. Lesh have a drink." She stooped over one of the tubs, almost fell.

Kells was standing with his back to the door. His face was bloody and blood dripped from his cut left hand. He took a handkerchief out of his overcoat, held it to his face.

He said: "We'll take a walk, Jakie."

Rose moved his shoulders a little, half nodded. Ruth Perry lost her balance, sprawled down on the floor. She sat up slowly and leaned against the wall. Kells was staring at Rose. His eyes were bright and cold and his mouth curved upward at the corners, ever so little. He said: "Come here."

Rose came across the room slowly. When he was close enough, Kells put his left hand on his shoulder suddenly, spun him around, slid his hand down to jerk a small caliber automatic out of Rose's hip pocket.

Kells said: "We're going out of here now. You're going to walk a little ahead of me, on my right. If we have any trouble, or if any of these gentlemen"—he jerked his head toward MacAlmon and the short man and the other man—"forget to sit still, I'm going to let your insides out on the floor."

He swung the bar up straight, took the key out of the door. "Do you understand?"

Rose nodded.

Ruth Perry staggered clumsily to her feet. She had

picked up an ice pick that was laying by one of the tubs; she waved it at' Kells. She said: "Don' go, Gerry—'s a swell party." She weaved unsteadily toward him.

Kells dropped Rose's gun into his left coat pocket, shifted his own gun to his left hand and shoved Ruth Perry away gently with his right.

She ducked suddenly under his outstretched arm, straightened up and brought her right hand around in a long arc hard against his back. The ice pick went in deep between his shoulder blades.

* * * * *

KELLS STOOD VERY still for perhaps five seconds. Then he moved his head down slowly, looked at her.

Rose half turned and Kells straightened the automatic suddenly, viciously against his side. Rose put his hands a little higher, slowly lowered his head.

Ruth Perry was clinging to Kells with both arms. She had taken her hand away from the handle of the ice pick and her arms were around his waist, her face was pressed against his shoulder.

He moved the fingers of his right hand up into her hair and jerked her head back. She opened her eyes and looked up into his face; she was pale, white-lipped. Then she opened her mouth and threw her head back against his hand and laughed.

He smiled a little and took his hand from her hair, took his arm slowly from around her shoulder. He put his hand against her breast, pushed her gently away. She staggered back against the wall and slid slowly down to the floor; she lay there laughing and there was no sound but the sound of her laughter and the low buzz of voices outside.

Kells reached back with his right hand, pulled the ice pick halfway out. He swayed, leaned against the door a moment, jerked it the rest of the way out. It fell and stuck in the floor, the handle quivering.

He straightened then, swung the door partly open, stuck the automatic in his big overcoat pocket and said: "Let's go."

Rose put his hands down. He opened the door the rest of the way and went out of the room; Kells went out behind him and closed the door, said: "Wait a second."

Rose half turned, looked down at Kells's overcoat pocket. The muzzle of the automatic bulged the cloth.

Kells watched Rose, locked the door quickly with his left hand. They started down the long room together; Rose a pace to the right, a pace ahead.

There were perhaps thirty or thirty-five people—mostly men—in the room; most of them around the two crap tables, several at two small green-covered tables, drinking.

The lighting was as Kells remembered it: Two powerful shaded globes over the big tables lighting all the rear end of the room. Toward the front of the room—the street—the light faded to partial darkness, black in the far corners.

Kells said, "Talk to me, Jakie," out of the side of his mouth.

Rose turned his head and twisted his mouth to a terribly forced grin. His eyes were wide, frightened. "What'll I talk about?"

Several people turned to look at them.

Kells said: "The weather—an' walk faster."

Then someone crashed against the locked door behind them.

In the same moment Kells saw Reilly. He had risen from one of the smaller tables, was staring at Rose. He said: "Jack—what the hell? ..." Then he looked at Kells, his hand dipped toward his hip. Kells shot from his pocket—twice.

Reilly put his two hands against the middle of his chest, slowly. He sat down on the edge of the table, slid slowly down—as his knees buckled, fell backward, half under the table.

Another gun roared and Kells felt the shoulder of his coat lift, tear; felt a hot stab in the muscle of his upper arm.

Rose was running toward the other end of the room, zigzagging a little, swiftly.

Kells started after him, stumbled, almost fell. He jerked the big automatic out of his pocket, swung it toward Rose. Then the door beyond Rose opened and someone came in. Kells couldn't see who it was; he staggered on after Rose, stopped suddenly as Rose stopped.

Borg said, "Cinch," out of the darkness.

Kells's gun roared and almost simultaneously another roared, flashed yellow out of the darkness near the door.

Rose's hands were together high in the air. He spun as though suspended by his hands from the ceiling, fell down to his knees, bent slowly forward.

Kells went to him swiftly and put the muzzle of the automatic against the back of his head and fired three times. He grunted, "Compliments Flo Beery," straightened and watched Rose topple forward, crush his dead face against the floor.

He turned to look toward the rear of the room and in that instant the two big lights went out, it was entirely black.

Borg's voice whispered beside him: "Oh, boy! Did I have a swell hunch when I turned off the lights in the little room outside—they could pick us off going out if I hadn't."

Borg led him to the door and they went across the little room in the darkness. Kells stumbled over something soft—Borg said: "I had to sap the doorman—he wasn't going to let me in."

Borg swung the heavy outer door wide and they went through to the stairs.

About halfway down Kells put his hand out suddenly and groped for the banister—his body pivoted slowly on one foot, crashed against the wall. He slid to his knees, still holding the banister tightly.

Borg put his hands under Kells's arms and locked them on his chest, tried to lift him.

Kells muttered something that sounded like, "Wait—minute," coughed.

Borg pried his hand off the banister, half dragged; half carried him the rest of the way downstairs.

It was raining very hard.

* * * * *

KELLS STRAIGHTENED SUDDENLY and pushed Borg away, said: "I'm all right." Then he leaned against the building and coughed, and the cough was a harsh, tearing sound deep inside him. He stood there coughing terribly until Borg dragged him away, shoved him into the car that had come swiftly to the curb.

Granquist was at the wheel. She said, "Well—hero!" sarcastically, as if she had been wanting to say that, thinking about saying that for a long time.

Kells's head sagged to her shoulder. There was blood on his mouth and his eyes were closed.

Borg climbed in behind him, closed the door. "Granquist threw her arms around Kells suddenly and pressed his head close against her shoulder. Her eyes were wide, stricken; her lower lip was caught between her teeth—she almost screamed: "Gerry—darling—for God's sake, say something!"

Borg was looking back through the side window at the dark archway that led to the stairs.

He said: "Let's get going."

Kells raised his head and opened his eyes. He waved an

arm in the general direction of the car across the street—the car they had followed from Larson's.

Borg said: "We ain't got time to jim it up—besides, they got a flock of cars." He reached in front of Kells, shook Granquist, shouted: "Let's go."

She looked up blankly, then mechanically took her left arm from around Kells and grasped the wheel. She let the clutch in and the big coupe slid away from the curb.

"Duck down Gardner." Borg snapped on the dashlight, pulled Kells's overcoat and suit coat off his shoulder, ripped his shirt open and looked at the wound on the outer muscle of his left arm. "Crease," he said. Then he glanced through the rear window, went on: "Turn right, here—no—the next one. This one's full of holes."

Granquist was bent over the wheel, staring intently through the dripping windshield. She jerked her head at Kells, asked: "Why's he coughing blood?" She spoke in a small, harsh, breathless voice.

Borg shrugged, went on examining Kells. He glanced again through the rear window, said: "Here they come—give it everything."

They swung around a corner and the car leaped ahead, the engine throbbed, thundered. When Borg looked back again the headlights that marked the pursuing car were almost three blocks behind them.

He had bent Kells forward, was examining his back. He said: "He's bleeding like a stuck pig from a little hole in his back. Wha' d' ya suppose done that?"

Kells straightened suddenly, sat up, struggled into his coat. He looked at Granquist, smiled faintly and put up one hand and rubbed it down his face. He said: "I guess I passed out—where we going?"

"Doctor's."

Kells said: "Don't be silly. We're going north—fast." He started coughing again, took out a handkerchief and held it to his mouth.

Borg said slowly: "I thought south—I guess I'm a lousy guesser."

"I told the cab driver who turned us in, north—they'll probably figure us for south—the Border." Kells spoke hoarsely, with a curious halting lisp. He leaned forward and began coughing again.

Granquist swung the car right, around another corner. Borg was looking back. After a couple of blocks, he said: "I think we've lost 'em."

Kells sat up again as Granquist turned east on Sunset Boulevard. He said: "The other way, baby—the other way."

"We're going to a doctor's." She was almost crying. Kells put his two hands forward and pulled the emergency brake back hard. The car skidded, turned half around, stopped.

Kells said, "Drive, Fat," wearily. He looked down at Granquist, went on patiently: "Listen. We've got one chance in a hundred of getting away. Every police car and highway patrol in the county is looking for us by now...."

Borg had opened the door, jumped-out. He ran around the car and opened the other door and climbed in. Granquist and Kells moved over to make room for him.

Then, before Borg could close the door, a car bore down on them on Borg's side—a car without lights. Yellow-orange flame spurted from its side as it swerved sharply to avoid hitting them—Borg sank slowly forward over the wheel, sank slowly sideways, fell outline door into the street. The car was going too fast to stop suddenly—it went on toward the next corner, slowing. Flame spurted from its rear window; the windshield shattered, showered Kells and Granquist with glass.

Kells moved very swiftly. He crawled across Granquist, slammed the door shut, had flipped off the emergency and was headed west, in second, before the other car had turned around. He shifted to high, pressed the throttle to the floor. Granquist was slumped low in the seat. Kells glanced at her, asked: "You all right, baby?"

"Uh huh." She pressed close against him.

They went out Sunset at around seventy miles an hour, went on through Beverly Hills, on. At the ocean they turned north. The road was being repaired for a half-mile or so; Kells slowed to thirty-five.

Granquist had been watching through the rear window, had seen no sign of the other car. She was close against Kells and her arm was around his shoulders. Her eyes were wide, excited. She kept saying: "Maybe we'll make it, darling—maybe we'll make it."

Kells started coughing again—Granquist held the wheel while he leaned against the door, coughed terribly, as if his lungs were being torn apart. Rain swept in through the broken windshield. Kells took the wheel again, said in a choked whisper: "I'll get a doctor in Ventura—if we get through." He stepped on the throttle until the needle of the speedometer quivered around seventy again.

There were very few cars on the road. A little way beyond Topanga Canyon, Kells threw the car out of gear, jerked back the brake. He said: "I guess you'd better drive...." Granquist helped him slide over in the seat, crawled across him to the wheel—they started again. Kells leaned back in the corner, was silent. As they neared the bridge south of Malibu, Granquist slowed a little. There was someone swinging a red lantern in the middle of the road. Then she pressed the throttle far down, veered sharply to the left past a car that was parked across the road.

She glanced back in a little while and saw its lights behind her, pressed the throttle to the floor.

The road curved a great deal. Granquist was bent forward over the wheel—the rain beat against her face; her eyes were narrowed to slits against the wind and the rain.

There was the faint sound of a shot, two, behind them, a metallic thud as a bullet buried itself somewhere in the body of the car. Kells opened his eyes, turned to look back. He grinned at Granquist and his face was whiter than anything she had ever seen. He glanced ahead, said: "Give it hell, baby."

Then he groped in his pocket, pulled out the big automatic. He smashed the glass of the rear window with the muzzle and rested the barrel on his forearm, sighted, fired.

He said, "Missed," swore softly.

He fired again, and as the car behind them swerved crazily off the road and stopped, said, "Bull's-eye," laughed soundlessly.

They passed two cars going the other way. Kells, looking back, saw one of them stop and start to turn around. Then they went around a curve and he couldn't see the car any more.

He glanced at the speedometer. "You'll have to do a little better. I think there's a fast one on our tail now."

She said: "The curves...."

"I know, baby—you're doing beautifully. Only a little faster." He smiled.

Granquist asked: "How's the cough?"

"Swell—I can't feel it any more." He patted his chest. "I feel a lot better."

She braced herself and used the brake hard as they went around a sharp curve.

"There's a pint of Bourbon in the side pocket. We got it from Jake back at the trick speakeasy...."

Kells said: "My God! Why didn't you tell me about it before?" He reached for the bottle.

"I forgot–"

She jerked the wheel suddenly, hard, screamed between clenched teeth.

Kells felt the beginning of the skid; he looked outward, forward into blackness. They were in space, falling sidewise into blackness; there was grinding, tearing, crashing sound. Falling.

Black.

* * * * *

THERE WAS A light somewhere. There was a voice.

Kells moved his arm an inch or so, dug his fingers deep in mud. The rain beat hard, cold on his face.

The voice come from somewhere above him, kept talking about light.

"I can't get down any farther," it said. "We got to have more light."

Kells tried to roll over on his side. There was something heavy on his legs, he couldn't move them, couldn't feel them. But he twisted his body a little and opened his eyes. It was entirely dark.

He twisted his body the other way and saw the narrow beam of a flashlight high above him in the darkness. The rain looked like snow in the light.

He pushed himself up slowly, leaned on one elbow, saw something white a little distance away. He got his legs, somehow, out of the dark sharp metal that imprisoned them and crawled slowly, painfully toward the whiteness.

The whiteness was Granquist. She was dead.

Kells lay there awhile in the mud, on his belly, with his face close to Granquist's face.

He could not think. He could feel the awful, barbed pain in his body; after a while, fear. He looked up at the light and a wave of panic swept suddenly over him, twisted his heart. He wanted to go into the darkness, away from the light. He wanted the darkness very much.

He kissed Granquist's cold mouth and turned and

crawled through the mud away from the light, away from the voices.

He wanted to be alone in the darkness; he wanted the light to please go away.

He whispered, "Please go away," to himself, over and over.

The ground was rough; great rocks jutted out of the mud, and there were little gullies that the rain had made.

After a while he stopped and turned and looked back and he could not see the light any more. Still he crawled on, dragged his torn body over the broken earth.

In the partial shelter of a steep sloping rock he stopped, sank forward, down.

There, after a little while, life went away from him.

Seven Slayers (1946)

Table of Contents

Black

THE MAN SAID: "McCary."

"No." I shook my head and started to push past him, and he said: "McCary," again thickly, and then he crumpled into a heap on the wet sidewalk.

It was dark there, there wasn't anyone on the street—I could have walked away. I started to walk away and then the sucker instinct got the best of me and I went back and bent over him.

I shook him and said: "Come on, chump—get up out of the puddle."

A cab came around the corner and its headlights shone on me—and there I was, stooping over a drunk whom I'd never seen before, who thought my name was McCary. Any big-town driver would have pegged it for a stick-up, would have shoved off or sat still. That wasn't a big town—the cab slid alongside the curb and a fresh-faced kid stuck his face into the light from the meter and said: "Where to?"

I said: "No place." I ducked my head at the man on the sidewalk. "Maybe this one'll ride—he's paralyzed."

The kid clucked: "Tch, tch."

He opened the door and I stooped over and took hold of the drunk under his armpits and jerked him up and across the sidewalk and into the cab. He was heavy in a funny limp way. There was a hard bulge on his left side, under the arm.

I had an idea. I asked the kid: "Who's McCary?"

He looked self-consciously blank for a minute and then he said: "There's two—Luke and Ben. Luke's the old man-owns a lot of real estate. Ben runs a pool-hall."

"Let's go see Ben," I said. I got into the cab.

We went several blocks down the dark street and then I tapped on the glass and motioned to the kid to pull over to the curb. He stopped and slid the glass and I said: "Who's McCary?"

"I told you."

I said: "What about him?"

The kid made the kind of movement with his shoulders that would pass for a shrug in the sticks. "I told you—he runs a pool-hall."

I said: "Listen. This guy came up to me a few minutes ago and said 'McCary'—this guy is very dead."

The kid looked like he was going to jump out of the cab. His eyes were hanging out.

I waited.

The kid swallowed. He said: "Let's dump him."

I shook my head slightly and waited.

"Ben and the old man don't get along—they've been raising hell the last couple of weeks. This is the fourth." He jerked his head towards the corpse beside me.

"Know him?"

He shook his head and then—to be sure—took a flashlight out of the side-pocket and stuck it back through the opening and looked at the man's dead face. He shook his head again.

I said: "Let's go see Ben."

"You're crazy, Mister. If this is one of Ben's boys he'll tie you up to it, and if it ain't..."

"Let's go see Ben."

Ben McCary was a blond fat man, about forty—he smiled a great deal.

We sat in a little office above his pool-hall and he smiled heartily across all his face and said: "Well, sir—what can I do for you?"

"My name is Black. I came over from St. Paul—got in about a half hour ago."

He nodded, still with the wide hearty smile; stared at me cordially out of his wide-set blue eyes.

I went on: "I heard there was a lot of noise over here and I thought I might make a connection—pick up some change."

McCary juggled his big facial muscles into something resembling innocence.

"I don't know just what you mean, Buddy," he said. "What's your best game?"

"What's yours?"

He grinned again. "Well," he said, "you can get plenty of action up in the front room."

I said: "Don't kid me, Mister McCary. I didn't come over here to play marbles."

He looked pleasantly blank.

"I used to work for Dickie Johnson down in K C," I went on.

"Who sent you to me?"

"Man named Lowry—that's the name on the label of his coat. He's dead."

McCary moved a little in his chair but didn't change his expression.

"I came in on the nine-fifty train," I went on, "and started walking uptown to a hotel. Lowry came up to me over on Dell Street and said 'McCary!' and fell down. He's outside in a cab—stiff."

McCary looked up at the ceiling and then down at the desk. He said: "Well, well"—and took a skinny little cigar out of a box in one of the desk-drawers and lighted it. He finally got around to looking at me again and said: "Well,

well," again.

I didn't say anything.

After he'd got the cigar going, he turned another of his big smiles on and said: "How am I supposed to know you're on the level?"

I said: "I'll bite. What do you think?"

He laughed. "I like you," he said. "By—! I like you."

I said I thought that was fine and, "Now let's try to do some business."

"Listen," he said. "Luke McCary has run this town for thirty years. He ain't my old man—he married my mother and insisted on my taking his name."

He puffed slowly at his cigar. "I guess I was a pretty ornery kid"—he smiled boyishly—"when I came home from school I got into a jam—you know—kid stuff. The old man kicked me out."

I lighted a cigarette and leaned back.

"I went down to South America for about ten years, and then I went to Europe. I came back here two years ago and everything was all right for a while and then the old man and I got to scrapping again."

I nodded.

"He'd had everything his own way too long. I opened this place about three months ago and took a lot of his gambling business away—a lot of the shipyard men and miners..."

McCary paused, sucked noisily at his cigar.

"Luke went clean off his nut," he went on. "He thought I was going to take it all away from him..." McCary brought his big fist down hard on the desk. "And by the—! I am. Lowry's the third man of mine in two weeks. It's plenty in the open now."

I said: "How about Luke's side?"

"We got one of the–" he said. "A runner."

"It isn't entirely over the gambling concession?"

"Hell, no. That's all it was at first. All I wanted was to make a living. Now I've got two notch-joints at the other end of town. I've got a swell protection in with the law and I'm building up a liquor business that would knock your eye out."

I asked: "Is Luke in it by himself?"

McCary shook his head slowly. "He don't show anywhere. There's a fellah named Stokes runs the works for him—a young fellah. They been partners nearly eight years. It's all in Stokes's name..."

"What does Stokes look like?"

"Tall—about your build. Shiny black hair, and a couple of big gold teeth"—McCary tapped his upper front teeth with a fat finger—"here."

I said: "How much is he worth to you?"

McCary stood up. He leaned across the desk and grinned down at me and said: "Not a nickel." His eyes were wide and clear like a baby's. He said slowly: "The old man is worth twenty-five hundred smackers to you."

I didn't say anything and McCary sat down and opened another drawer and took out a bottle of whiskey. He poured a couple of drinks.

"I think the best angle for you," he said, "is to go to Stokes and give him the same proposition you gave me. Nobody saw you come in here. It's the only way you can get near the old man."

I nodded. We drank.

"By—! I like your style," he said. "I've been trying to get along with an outfit of yokels."

We smiled at one another. I was glad he said he liked me because I knew he didn't like me at all. I was one up on him, I didn't like him very well either.

Stokes sat on a corner of the big library-table, his long legs dangling.

He said: "You're airing Ben—how do we know you'll play ball with us?" His eyes were stony.

I looked at the old man. I said: "I don't like that fat—son of yours—and I never double-cross the best offer."

Luke McCary was a thin little man with a pinched red face, bushy white hair. He sat in a big armchair on the other side of the table, his head and neck and wild white hair sticking up out of the folds of a heavy blue bathrobe.

He looked at me sharply. He said: "I don't want any part of it."

"Then I'll have to act on the best offer."

Stokes grinned.

The old man stood up. He said: "Why—damn you and your guts..." He opened a humidor on the table and took out a small automatic. "I can shoot the buttons off your vest, young fella... I can shoot you for a yegg right now, and no one'll ever know the difference..."

I said: "You'll know the difference—for not having taken advantage of talent, when you had the chance."

He put the automatic back in the box and sat down and smiled gently at Stokes.

Stokes was looking at the floor. He said: "Five grand if you wipe out the whole outfit. Run 'em out of town, stick 'em in jail, poison 'em... Anything."

"Wouldn't you like a new railroad station too?"

They didn't say anything for a minute. They looked at me.

I went on: "No sale. I'll take care of Ben for that—but busting up the organization would mean sending for a few friends—would cost a hell of a lot more than five..."

The old man looked the least bit scared for a second then he said: "Ben'll do."

"How about laying something on the line?"

Stokes said: "Don't be silly."

The old man cackled. "Well I never saw such guts," he

said.

I said: "All right, gentlemen. Maybe I'll call you later."

Stokes went downstairs with me. He smiled in a strange way. "I never knew the old man to go for anything that look's as tricky as this. I guess it looks good because Ben thinks you're working for him."

I nodded. I said: "Uh huh—Ben's a swell guy. He'll probably blast me on sight."

"I don't think you'll find him at his joint."

I waited and Stokes leaned against the door, said: "There's a big outfit downstate that's been running twelve trucks a week through here from the Border. They've paid off for this division of the highway for years—to the old man. The last two convoys have been hi-jacked at Four-mile Creek, north of town—a couple drivers were killed..."

He paused, looked wise a minute, went on: "That was Ben. There was a convoy due through last night—they run in bunches of four, or six—it didn't show up. It's a cinch for tonight—and that's where Ben'll be."

I said: "That's fine. How do I get there?"

Stokes told me to follow the main highway north, and where to take the cutoff that crossed Four-mile. I thanked him and went out.

I walked down to a drugstore on the corner and called a cab. When it came, I got in and had the driver jockey around until he was parked in a spot where I could watch the front door of the McCary house.

After a while, Stokes came out and got into a roadster and snorted up past us and turned down the side street. I told the driver to follow him. I don't think the driver knew who it was. It didn't matter a hell of a lot anyway.

I got out and told the driver to wait and walked on down Dell Street, keeping close to the fence. It was raining pretty hard again. I passed the place where Lowry had come up to me, and I went on to the corner; and then went back the same way until I came to the narrow gate I had missed in the darkness.

It was more a door than a gate, set flush with the high fence. I finagled with the latch for a while and then pushed the gate open slowly and went into a yard. It was a big yard, full of old lumber and old box-car trucks—stuff like that. There was a long shed along one side, and a small two-story building on the far side.

I stumbled along as quietly as I could towards the building and then I went around the corner of a big pile of ties, and Stokes's roadster was sitting there very dark and quiet in the rain. I went past it and up to the building and along the wall until I saw the lighted window.

I had to rustle around quietly and find a box and stand on it to see through the little square window. The panes were dirty; the inside looked like a time-office. Stokes and Ben McCary and another man were there. They were arguing about something. McCary was walking around waving his arms; Stokes and the other man were sitting down. I couldn't hear a word they said. The rain was roaring on the tin-roof of the shed and all I could hear was a buzz of voices.

I didn't stay there very long. It didn't mean anything. I got down and put the box back and wandered around until I found McCary's car. Anyway, I guessed it was his car. It was a big touring-car and it was parked near the gate on the opposite side of the block from Dell Street, where Stokes had come in.

I got in and sat in the back seat. The side-curtains were drawn and it was nice to get out of the rain for a while.

In about ten minutes, the light went out and I could hear voices coming towards the car. I sat down on the floor. The three of them stood outside for a minute talking about "a call from Harry"—then Stokes and the other man went off towards Stokes's car, and McCary squeezed into the front seat and stepped on thc starter.

I waited till we had burned through the gate and were halfway up the block, and then I put a gun against the back of McCary's neck. He straightened out in the seat and eased the brake on. I told him to go on to the old man's house.

We sat in the big room upstairs. The old man sat in the big armchair by the table, and Ben sat across from him. I was half lying down in another chair out of the circle of light and I had the gun on my lap.

The old man was fit to be tied. He was green with hate and he kept glaring at Ben out of his little red-rimmed eyes.

I said: "Well, gran'pa—if you'll make out that check now, we'll finish this business." The old man swallowed.

"You can give me your twenty-five hundred in cash," I went on to Ben. "Then I'll put the chill on both of you—and everybody'll be happy."

They must have thought I meant it. Ben got rigid, and the old man cleared his throat and made a slow pass at the humidor.

I fiddled with the gun. I threw a pack of cigarettes on the table and said: "Smoke?"

The old man looked at the cigarettes and at the gun in my hand, and relaxed.

I said: "Still and all—it don't quite square with my weakness for efficiency, yet. Maybe you boys'll get together and make me an offer for Stokes. He's the star—he's been framing both of you."

I don't think Ben was very surprised—but the old man looked like he'd swallowed a mouse.

"He's been in with Ben on the truck heistings," I went on. "He's been waiting for a good spot to dump you—working on your connections."

The old man said: "That's a—damned lie."

"Suit yourself."

I went on to Ben: "He made the five-grand offer for your hide, in Luke's name, tonight—and he gave me the Fourmile steer..." I hesitated a moment. "Only you wouldn't try three in the same spot, would you?"

Ben finally got his smile working. He started to say something but I interrupted him:

"Stokes told me you rubbed the two boys on the trucks, too."

Ben's smile went out like a light. He said: "Stokes shot both those men himself—and there wasn't any need for it. They were lined up alongside the road..."

Something in the soft way he said it made it sound good.

I said: "He'll be around your place—no?"

"He went home."

Ben gave me the number and I called up, but there wasn't any answer.

We sat there without saying anything for several minutes, and then the door downstairs opened and closed and somebody came up.

I said to Ben: "What'll you bet?"

The door opened and Stokes came in. He had a long gray raincoat on and it made him look even taller and thinner than he was. He stood in the doorway looking mostly at the old man; then he came in and sat down on a corner of the table.

I said: "Now that the class is all here, you can start bidding."

The old man laughed deep in his throat. Stokes was watching me expressionlessly, and Ben sat smiling stupidly at his hands.

"I'm auctioning off the best little town in the state, gentlemen," I went on. "Best schools, sewage system, postoffice... Best street-lighting, water supply..."

I was having a swell time.

The old man was staring malevolently at Stokes. "I'll give you twenty-five thousand dollars," he said to me, "to give me that pistol and get out of here."

If I'd thought there was any chance of collecting, I might have talked to him. Things happen that way sometimes.

I looked at my watch and put the gun down on the arm of the chair where it looked best and picked up the phone.

I asked Ben: "Where's the business going to be pulled off tonight?"

Ben wanted to be nice. He said: "A coffee joint about six miles north of town." He glanced at Stokes. "This—tried to swing it back to Four-mile when he thought you'd be there sniping for me."

"The boys are there now?"

He nodded. "The trucks have been stopping there to eat lately."

I asked the operator for long-distance, and asked for the Bristol Hotel in Talley, the first town north. The connection went right through. I asked for Mister Cobb.

When he answered, I told him about the coffee place, and that I wasn't sure about it; and told him he'd find the stuff that had been heisted in the sheds of the yard on Dell Street. I wasn't sure of that either, but I watched Ben and Stokes when I said it and it looked all right. Cobb told me that he'd gotten into Talley with the convoy about midnight and had been waiting for my call since then. I hung up. "There'll be some swell fireworks out there," I said. "There's a sub-machine-gun on every truck—double crews. And it don't matter much," I went on to Ben, "how good your steer is. They'll be watching out all the way."

Stokes stood up.

I picked up the gun. "Don't move so far, Skinny," I said. "It makes me nervous."

He stood there staring at the gun. The water was running off his raincoat and it had formed into a little dark pool at his feet.

He said: "What the hell do you want?"

"I wanted you to know that one of the kids you shot up last week at Four-mile was my boss's brother. He went along for the ride."

I don't think Stokes could move. I think he tried to move sidewise or get his hand into his pocket, or something, but all he could do was take a deep breath. Then I shot him in the middle of the body where he shot the kid, and he sank down on the floor with his legs crossed under him, like a tailor.

The old man didn't get up. He sat a little deeper in his chair and stared at Stokes.

Ben moved very fast for a fat man. He was up and out the door like a bat out of hell. That was OK with me—he couldn't get to the coffee place before the trucks got there. I had the keys to his car, and it was too far anyway.

I got up and put the rod away and went over to the table and picked up my cigarettes. I looked down at the old man, said: "Things'll be a little quieter now, maybe. You'll get the dough for haulage through your territory, as usual. See that it gets through."

He didn't answer.

I started for the door and then there was a shot out in front of the house. I ran on down to the front door. It was open and Ben was flat on the threshold—had fallen smack on his face, half through the door.

I ducked back through the hall and tried a couple locked doors. When I came up through the hall again, the old man was on his knees beside Ben, and was rocking back and forth, moaning a little.

I went through another room and into the kitchen and on through, out the back door. I crossed the backyard and jumped a low fence and walked through another yard to a gate that led into an alley. I sloshed along through the mud until I came to a cross-street, and went on down to the corner that was diagonally across the block from the McCary house.

A cab came down the street and I waited until it was almost to the corner, stepped out in front of it. The driver swerved and stepped on the gas, but he had slowed enough to give me time to jump on the running-board.

I stuck my head in to the light from the meter. That turned out to be my best hunch of the evening because in another second, the driver would have opened up my chest with one of the dirtiest looking .45s I ever saw, at about two feet. It was the kid who had picked Lowry and me up. He hesitated just long enough when he saw who I was.

We nearly ran into a tree and I had time to reach in and knock that cannon out of his hand. He stepped on the brake, and reached for the gun, but I beat him to it by a hair and stuck it in my overcoat pocket and got in beside him.

I said: "Shame on you—almost crashing an old pal like me."

He sat tight in the seat and got a weak grin working and said: "Where to?"

"Just away."

We went on through the mud and rain, and turned into a slightly better lighted street.

I said: "How did you know Ben shot Lowry?"

The kid kept his head down, his eyes ahead. "Lowry and me have lived together for two years," he said. "He used to be in the hack racket too, till he got mixed up with McCary...

"Lowry won a lot of jack in one of Ben's crap games a couple day ago, and Ben wanted him to kick back with it—said everybody that worked for him was automatically a shill, and couldn't play for keeps. But Lowry's been dropping every nickel he made in the same game, for months. That was okay with Ben. It was all right to lose, but you mustn't win."

I nodded, lighted a cigarette.

"Ben shot Lowry tonight at the joint on Dell Street. I know it was him because Lowry's been afraid of it—and that's why he said 'McCary.'"

"Did you know it was Lowry when you picked us up?"

"Not until I used the light. Then, when we got to Ben's I saw him get out of his car and go in just ahead of you—then I was sure. I took Lowry up to his pa's after you went in."

The kid drove me to the next town south. I forget the name. I got a break on a train—I only had to wait about ten minutes.

Red 71

SHANE PRESSED THE button beneath the neat red 71. Then he leaned close against the building and tilted his head a little and looked up at the thick yellow-black sky. Rain swept in great uneven and diagonal sheets across the dark street, churned the dark puddle at his feet. The street-light at the corner swung, creaked in the wind.

Light came suddenly through a slit in the door, the door was opened. Shane went into a narrow heavily carpeted hallway. He took off his dark soft hat, shook it back and forth, handed it to the man who had opened the door.

He said: "Hi, Nick. How is it?"

Nick said: "It is very bad weather—and business is very bad."

Nick was short, very broad. It was not fat broadness, but muscled, powerful. His shoulders sloped heavily to long curving arms, big white hands. His neck was thick and white and his face was broad and so white that his long black hair looked like a cap. He hung Shane's hat on one of a long row of numbered pegs, helped him with his coat, hung it beside the hat.

He stared at Shane reproachfully. "He has been waiting for you a long time," he said.

Shane said: "Uh-huh," absently, went back along the hallway and up a flight of narrow stairs. At the top he turned into another hallway, crossed it diagonally to an open double doorway.

The room was large, dimly lighted. Perhaps fifteen or eighteen people, mostly in twos or threes, sat at certain of the little round white covered tables. Three more, a woman and two men, stood at the aluminum bar that ran across one corner.

Shane stood in the doorway a moment, then crossed the room to where Rigas sat waiting for him at a table against the far wall. Several people looked up, nodded or spoke as he passed; he sat down across the table from Rigas, said: "Bacardi," to the hovering waiter.

Rigas folded his paper, leaned forward with his elbows on the table and smiled.

"You are late, my friend." He put up one hand and rubbed one side of his pale blue jaw. Shane nodded slightly. He said: "I've been pretty busy." Rigas was Greek. His long rectangular face was deeply lined; his eyes were small, dark, wide-set; his mouth was a pale upward-curved gash. He was in dinner clothes. He said: "Things are good with you—Yes?" Shane shrugged. "Fair."

"Things are very bad here." Rigas picked up his cocktail, sipped it, leaned back. Shane waited.

"Very bad," Rigas went on. "They have raised our protection overhead more than fifty per cent."

The waiter lifted Shane's cocktail from the tray with a broad flourish, put it on the table in front of him. Shane looked at it, then up at Rigas, said: "Well..."

Rigas was silent. He stared at the tablecloth, with his thin lips stuck out in an expression of deep concentration.

Shane tasted his cocktail, laughed a little. "You know damned well," he said, "that I'm not going to put another dime into this place." He put down his glass and stared morosely at Rigas. "And you know that I can't do anything about your protection arrangement. That's your business."

Rigas nodded sadly without looking up. "I know—I

know."

Shane sipped his drink, waited.

Rigas finally looked up, spoke hesitantly: "Lorain—Lorain is going to get a divorce."

Shane smiled, said: "That's a break."

Rigas nodded slowly. "Yes." He spoke very slowly, deliberately: "Yes—that is a break for all of us."

Shane leaned forward, put his elbows on the table, put one hand down slowly, palm up. He stared at Rigas and his face was hard, his eyes were very cold. He said: "You made that kind of a crack once before—remember?"

Rigas didn't speak. He gazed wide-eyed, expressionlessly at Shane's tie.

"Remember what happened?" Shane went on.

Rigas didn't speak, or move.

Shane relaxed suddenly. He leaned back, glanced around, smiled faintly.

"I back this joint," he said, "because I thought you might make it go. I don't like you—never have—but I like Lorain, have liked her ever since we were kids together. I thought she was an awful chump when she married you and I told her so."

He sipped his cocktail, widened his smile. "She told me what a great guy you were," he went on, "an' she stuck to it, even after you'd dropped all your dough, and hers. Then she told me you wanted to take over this place, an' I came in on it, laid fifteen grand on the line."

Rigas moved uncomfortably in his chair, glanced swiftly around the room.

"Since then," Shane went on, "I've chunked in somewhere around five more..."

Rigas interrupted: "We've got nearly twelve thousand dollars' worth of stock." He made a wide gesture.

"What for?" Shane curved his mouth to a pleasant sneer. "So you can be knocked over, and keep the enforcement boys in vintage wines for a couple of months."

Rigas shrugged elaborately, turned half away. "I cannot talk to you," he said. "You fly off the handle..."

"No." Shane smiled. "You can talk to me all you like, Charley—and I don't fly off the handle—and I'm not squawking. But don't make any more cracks about Lorain and me. Whatever I've done for you I've done for her—because I like her. Like her. Can you get that through that thick spick skull of yours? I wouldn't want her if she was a dime a dozen—an' I don't like that raised eyebrow stuff. It sounds like pimp."

Rigas's face turned dull red. His eyes were very sharp and bright. He stood up, spoke very softly, breathlessly, as if it was hard for him to get all the words out: "Let's go upstairs, Dick."

Shane got up and they crossed the room together, went out through the double door.

On the third floor they crossed an identical hallway, Rigas unlocked a tall gray door and they went into another large room. There were two large round tables, each with a green-shaded drop-light over it. There were eight men at one of the tables, seven at the other; Rigas and Shane crossed the room to another tall gray door.

The stud dealer and two players looked up from the nearest table, one of the players said: "H' are yah, Charley?" Then Rigas opened the tall door and they went into a little room that was furnished as an office.

Rigas pressed the light switch, closed the door and stood with his back to it for a moment. His hands were in his coat pockets.

Shane sat down on the edge of the desk. Rigas crossed to the desk slowly and when he was near Shane he jerked his right hand out of his pocket suddenly and swung a thin-bladed knife up at Shane's throat.

Shane moved a little to one side, grabbed Rigas's arm

near the elbow with one open hand; the knife ripped up crosswise across the lapel of his coat. At the same time he brought his right knee up hard against Rigas's stomach. Rigas grunted and one of his knees gave way and he slumped down slowly, sidewise to the floor. The knife clattered on the glass desk-top.

As Shane slid off the desk, stood over Rigas, the door opened and a very tall, very spare man came a little way into the room.

Shane glanced at the man and then he looked down at Rigas and his eyes were almost closed, his mouth was a thin hard line. Rigas groaned and held his hands tight against his stomach, his chin tight against his chest.

Shane looked up at the tall man, said: "You'd better not let this brother of yours play with knives. He's liable to put somebody's eye out." He spoke with his teeth together. The tall man stared blandly at Rigas. Shane went past the tall man, to the door, went out and across the big room. All of the men at the tables were looking at him; all of them were very quiet. Two men were standing up at the nearest table.

Shane went out and closed the door behind him, went swiftly down two flights. He found his hat and coat and put them on. Nick came up from the basement as he was knotting his scarf.

Nick said: "Shall I get you a cab, Mister Shane?" Shane shook his head. He slid the big bolt and opened the door and went out into the driving rain. He walked to Madison Avenue, got into a cab and said: "Valmouth—on Forty-Ninth." It was five minutes after eight.

Shane's rooms at the Valmouth were on the eighteenth floor. He stood at one of the wide windows and looked down through the swirling, beating rain to Fiftieth Street.

After a little while he went into the bathroom, turned off the water that was roaring into the tub, slipped off his robe.

Someone knocked at the outer door and he called: "Come in," looked into the long mirror in the bathroom door that reflected part of the living room. A waiter with a wide oval tray opened the door, came in and put the tray down on a low table.

Shane said: "There's some change on the telephone stand." He kicked off his slippers and stepped into the tub.

In five minutes he was out, had put on a long dark-green robe, slippers, and was sitting at the low table cutting a thick T-bone steak into dark pink squares.

As he poured coffee the phone buzzed; he leaned sidewise, picked it up, said: "Hello." Then he said: "Mister Shane is not in... She's on the way up!... What the hell did you let her start up for?..."

He slammed the phone down, went swiftly to the door and turned the bolt. He stood near the door a moment, then shrugged slightly, turned the bolt back and went slowly back and sat down.

Lorain Rigas was slender, dark. Her black eyes slanted upward a little at the corners, her mouth was full, deeply red, generous. She wore a dark close-fitting raincoat, a small suede hat. She closed the door and stood with her back to it.

Shane said: "Coffee?"

She shook her head. She said: "Charley called me up this afternoon and said he was going to give me the divorce—that he wouldn't fight it."

"That's fine." Shane put two lumps of sugar in a spoon, held it in the coffee and intently watched the sugar crumble, disappear. "So what?"

She came over and sat down near him. She unbuttoned her coat, crossed her slim silken legs, took a cigarette out of a tiny silver case and lighted it.

She said: "So you've got to help me locate Del before he gets to Charley."

Shane sipped his coffee, waited.

"Del started drinking last night," she went on, "an' he kept it up this morning. He went out about eleven, and some time around one, Jack Kenny called up an' told me that Del was over at his joint—roaring drunk, and howling for Charley's blood. He gets that way every time he gets boiled—crazy jealous about Charley and me."

She leaned back and blew a thin cone of smoke at the ceiling. "I told Jack to let him drink himself under the table, or lock him up, or something—an' in a little while Jack called back and said everything was all right—that Del had passed out."

Shane was smiling a little. He got up and went to the central table and took a long green-black cigar from a humidor, clipped it, lighted it. Then he went back and sat down.

The girl leaned forward. "About three o'clock," she said, "the Eastman Agency—that's the outfit I've had tailing Charley for evidence—called up and said they'd located the apartment house up on the West Side where Charley's been living with the McLean woman..."

Shane said: "How long have they been on the case?"

"Three days—an' Charley's ducked them until today—they traced a phone call or something."

Shane nodded, poured more coffee into the little cup.

Lorain Rigas mashed out her cigarette. "I told Eastman to keep his boys on the apartment until they spotted Charley going in—then I figured on going over tonight and crashing in with a load of witnesses—but in a little while Charley calls me and says everything's okay, that he'll give me the divorce any time, any place, and so on."

Shane said: "You've had a busy day."

"Uh-huh." She reached over and picked up the cup of coffee, sipped a little. "I didn't call Eastman back—I figure on going through with it the way I intended to—get the evidence an' the affidavits an' what not. Then if Charley changes his mind..." She put the cup back on the tray, leaned back and lighted another cigarette. "But we've got to find Del."

Shane said: "I thought he was cold at Kenny's."

She shook her head, smiled. "I called Kenny to see how Del was, and Del was gone. He came to and started where he left off—stole a gun out of Jack's trunk, and went out the back way. I don't think he'd really go through with it, but he goes nuts when he gets enough red-eye under his belt..."

Shane was leaning far back in the deep chair, staring vacantly at the ceiling. He said: "If you think Del would really make a pass at Charley–" He puffed at the cigar, finished slowly: "You don't seem quite as excited about it as you should be."

"What the hell's the use getting excited?" She stood up. "It's a cinch they won't let Del into 71—an' he wouldn't wait outside for Charley—not when he's drunk. He gets big ideas about face to face and man to man when he's drunk. I know Del."

"Then what are you worrying about?" Shane looked up at her, smiled gently. "He's probably at home waiting for you."

"No—I just called up." She went over to the window.

Shane looked at her back. He said: "You're pretty crazy about Del—aren't you?"

She nodded without turning.

Shane put his cigar down, reached for the phone. "Where do you think we ought to start?"

She turned, cocked her head a little to one side and looked at him sleepily. "If I knew where we ought to start, Dick," she said, "I wouldn't have had to bother you. You've known Del for years—you know the screwy way his mind works as well as I do—and you know the places. Where would he go, do you think, looking for Charley—besides 71?"

Shane picked up the phone, stared at it a little while, put it down. He got up, said: "I'm going to put on some clothes," and went into the bedroom.

Lorain Rigas sat down near the window. She pushed the small suede hat back off her forehead, leaned back and closed her eyes.

When Shane came in, knotting his tie, she was lying very still. He stood over her a moment, looking out the window. Then he finished his tie and looked down at her and put one hand out tentatively, touched her forehead with his fingers. She opened her eyes and looked up at him expressionlessly for a little while; he turned and went to the chair where he had thrown his coat, put it on.

The phone buzzed a second after Shane had closed and locked the door. He swore under his breath, fished in his pockets. The girl leaned against the wall of the corridor, smiled at his futile efforts to find the key.

The phone buzzed insistently.

He finally found the key, unlocked the door hurriedly, and went to the phone. Lorain Rigas leaned against the frame of the open door.

Shane said: "Hello... Put him on..." He stood, holding the phone, looking at the girl; spoke again into the phone: "Hello, Bill—Yeah—Yeah—What the hell for...?" Then he was silent a while with the receiver at his ear. Finally he said: "Okay, Bill—thanks." Hung up slowly.

He sat down, gestured with his head for the girl to come in and close the door. She closed the door and stood with her back to it, staring at him questioningly.

He said: "Charley was shot to death in the Montecito Apartments on West Eighty-Second, some time around eight-thirty tonight."

Lorain Rigas put her hand out slowly, blindly a little way.

Her eyes were entirely blank. She went slowly, unsteadily to a chair, sank into it.

Shane said: "They're holding the McLean gal—an' they've found out that Charley and I had an argument this evening—they want to talk to me. They're on the way over to pick me up."

He glanced at his watch. It was nine-forty. He got up and went to the table, took a cigar from the humidor, lighted it. Then he went to the window and stared out into the darkness.

"One—base of brain. One—slightly lower—shattered cervical." The autopsy surgeon straightened, tossed the glittering instrument into a sterilizer and skinned off his rubber gloves. He glanced at Shane, turned and started towards the door.

Sergeant Gill and an intern turned the body over.

Gill said: "Rigas?" looked up at Shane.

Shane nodded.

Gill spread a partially filled-out form on the examining table near Rigas's feet, took a stub of pencil from his pocket and added several lines to the form. Then he folded it and put it in his pocket and said: "Let's go back upstairs."

Shane followed him out of the room that smelled of ether and of death; they went down a long corridor to an elevator.

On the third floor they left the elevator and crossed the hall diagonally to the open door of a large office, went in. A tall, paunched man with a bony, purplish face turned from the window, went to a swivel chair behind the broad desk and sat down.

He said: "How come you stopped by tonight, Dick?" He leaned back, squinted across the desk at Shane.

Shane shrugged, sat down sidewise on the edge of the desk. "Wanted to say hello to all my buddies."

"You're a damned liar!" The tall man spoke quietly, impersonally. "A couple of my men were on the way over to pick you up when you showed up, here. You were tipped, an' I want to know who it was—it don't make so much difference about you, but that kind of thing is bad for the department."

Shane was smiling at Gill. He turned his head to look down at the tall man silently. Finally he said: "What are you going to do, Ed—hold me?"

The tall man said: "Who tipped you to the pinch?"

Shane stood up, faced the tall man squarely. He said: "So it's a pinch?" He turned and started towards the door, spoke over his shoulder to Gill: "Come on, Sarge."

"Come here, you—!"

Shane turned. His expression was not pleasant. He took two short, slow steps back towards the desk.

The tall man was grinning. He drawled: "You're hard to get along with—ain't you!"

Shane didn't answer. He stood with one foot a little in advance of the other and stared at the tall man from under the brim of his dark soft hat. The flesh around his eyes and mouth was very tightly drawn.

The tall man moved his grin from Shane to Gill. He said: "See if you can find that Eastman Op."

Gill went out of the room hurriedly.

The tall man swung a little in the chair, turned his head to look out the window. His manner when he spoke was casual, forced:

"The McLean girl killed Rigas."

Shane did not move or speak.

"What did you and him fight about tonight?" The tall man turned to look at Shane. His hands were folded over his broad stomach and he clicked his thumbnails nervously.

Shane cleared his throat. He said huskily: "Am I under arrest?"

"No. But we've got enough to held you on suspicion. You've sunk a lot of dough in Rigas's joint and so far as we know you ain't taken much out. Tonight you had an argument..."

The tall man unclasped his hands and leaned forward, put his arms on the desk. "Why don't you help us get this thing right instead of being so damned fidgety?" He twisted his darkly florid face to a wry smile.

Shane said: "Rigas and I had an argument about money—I left his place at eight o'clock and I was in my hotel at a quarter after. I was there until I came here." He went forward again to the desk. "I can get a half-dozen people at the hotel to swear to that."

The tall man made a wide and elaborate gesture of deprecation. "Hell, Dick, we know you didn't do it—and it's almost a natural for McLean. Only we thought you might help us clean up the loose ends."

Shane shook his head slowly, emphatically.

Sergeant Gill came in with an undersized blond youth in a shiny blue-serge suit.

The young man went to the desk, nodded at Shane, said: "H' are you, Cap?" to the tall man.

The tall man was looking at Shane. He said: "This man"—he jerked his head at the youth—"works for Eastman. He was on an evidence job for Mrs. Rigas and went in with the patrolman when Rigas was shot..."

"Yes, sir," the youth interrupted. "The telephone operator come running out screaming bloody murder an' the copper come running down from the corner an' we both went upstairs"—he paused, caught his breath—"an' there was this guy Rigas, half in the bedroom and half out-, an' dead as a doornail... The gun was on the floor, and this dame, McLean, was in pyjamas, yelling that she didn't do it."

The tall man said: "Yes—you told us all that before."

"I know—only I'm telling him." The youth smiled at Shane.

Shane sat down again on the edge of the desk. He looked from the youth to the tall man, asked: "What does McLean say?"

"She's got a whole raft of stories."

The tall man spat carefully into a big brass cuspidor beside the desk. "The best one is that she was asleep and didn't wake up till she heard the shots—and then she turned on the lights an' there he was, on the floor in the doorway. The outer door to the apartment was unlocked-had been unlocked all evening. She says she always left it that way when he was out because he was always losing his key, an' then he could come in without waking her up."

Shane said: "What was she doing in bed at eight-thirty?"

"Bad headache."

Sergeant Gill took a .38 automatic from the drawer of a steel cabinet, handed it to Shane. "No fingerprints," he said—"clean as a whistle."

Shane looked at the gun, put it down on the desk.

The tall man looked at the youth and at Gill, then bobbed his head meaningly towards the door. They both went out. The youth said: "So long, Cap—so long, Mister Shane." Gill closed the door behind him.

Shane was smiling.

The tall man said: "Rigas's wife had these Eastman dicks on his tail—she got anything to do with this?"

"Why?" Shane shrugged. "She wanted a divorce."

"How long they been having trouble?"

"Don't know."

The tall man stood up, stuck his hands in his pockets and went to the window. He spoke over his shoulder: "Didn't you and her used to be pretty good friends?"

Shane didn't answer. His face was entirely

expressionless.

The tall man turned and looked at him and then he said: "Well—I guess that's all."

They went out together.

In the corridor Shane made a vague motion with his hand, said: "Be seeing you," went down two flights of stairs and out the door to the street. He stood in the wide arch of the entrance, out of the rain, looked up and down the street for a cab. There was one in front of a drugstore six or seven doors up from the Police Station; he whistled, finally walked swiftly up to it through the blinding rain.

As he got in, the youth in the shiny blue-serge suit came out of the drugstore, scuttled across the sidewalk and climbed in beside him, sat down.

The driver turned around and said: "Where to?"

Shane said: "Wait a minute."

The youth leaned back, put his hand confidentially on Shane's shoulder. He said: "Tell him to drive around the block. I got something to tell you."

The driver looked at Shane, Shane nodded. They swung out from the curb.

The youth said: "I seen Mrs. Rigas about a half a block from the place uptown where Rigas was killed, about ten minutes before we found him."

Shane didn't say anything. He rubbed the side of his face with one hand, glanced at his watch, nodded.

"I was coming back from the delicatessen on the corner, where I got a bite to eat. She was going the same way, on the other side of the street. I wasn't sure it was her at first—I only seen her once when she came in to see Mister Eastman—but there was a car coming down the street and its headlights were pretty bright and I was pretty sure it was her."

Shane said: "Pretty sure."

"Aw hell—it was her." The youth took a soggy cigarette

out of his pocket, lighted it.

"Where did she go?"

"That's what I can't figure out. It was raining so damned hard—and the wind was blowing—when I got to our car, that was parked across the street from the Montecito, she'd disappeared." The youth shook his head slowly. "I told my partner about it. He said I was probably wrong, because if it was her she would have called up the office and found out how to spot us, because she would be wanting us to go in with her. He went on down to the corner to get something to eat, an' I sat in the car an' figured that I probably had been wrong, an' then in a few minutes I heard the shots an' the telephone operator come running out."

Shane said: "Did you see Rigas go in?"

The youth shook his head. "No—an' my partner swears he didn't go in while he was on watch. He must've gone in the back way."

Shane took a cigar out of a blue leather case, bit off the end, lighted it. "And you say you were figuring you were wrong about thinking you'd seen her?"

The youth laughed. "Yeah—that's what I figured then. But that ain't what I figure now."

"Why not?"

"Because I pride myself, Mister Shane, on being able to look at a dame what is supposed to have just bumped a guy off, an' knowing whether she did it or not. That's why I'm in the business." He turned his head and looked very seriously at Shane.

Shane smiled faintly in the darkness.

The youth said: "It wasn't McLean." He said it very positively.

Shane said: "Why didn't you tell the Captain about this?"

"Christ! We got to protect our clients."

The cab stopped in front of the drugstore, the driver

turned around and looked at Shane questioningly.

Shane blew out a great cloud of gray-blue smoke, glanced at the youth, said: "Where do you want to go?"

"This is oke for me." The youth leaned forward, put his hand on the inside handle of the door. Then he paused, turned his head slightly towards Shane.

"I'm in a spot, Mister Shane. My wife's sick—an' I took an awful beating on the races the other day, trying to get enough jack for an operation..."

Shane said: "Does anybody besides your partner know about Mrs. Rigas?"

The youth shook his head.

Shane tipped his hat back on his head, drew two fingers across his forehead, said: "I'll see what I can do about it. Where do you live?"

The youth took a card out of his pocket, took out a thin silver pencil and wrote something on it. He handed the card to Shane, said, "So long," and got out of the cab and ran across the sidewalk to the drugstore.

Shane said: "Downtown."

On Twelfth Street, a little way off Sixth Avenue, Shane rapped on the glass, the cab swung to the curb. He told the driver to wait, got out and went down a narrow passageway between two buildings to a green wooden door with a dim electric light above it. He opened the door, knocked on another heavier door set at an angle to the first. It was opened after a little while and he went down four wide steps to a long and narrow room with a bar along one side.

There were seven or eight men at the bar, two white-aproned men behind it: a squat and swarthy Italian and a heavily built Irishman.

Shane went to the far end of the room, leaned on the bar and spoke to the Italian: "What've you got that's best?"

The Italian put a bottle of brandy and a glass on the bar in front of him: Shane took a handkerchief out of his breast pocket, held the glass up to the light, wiped it carefully. He poured a drink, tasted it.

He said: "That's lousy—give me a glass of beer."

The Italian picked up the glass of brandy, drank it, put the bottle away and drew a glass of beer. He skimmed off the foam, put the tall glass on the bar.

He said: "Seventy-five cents."

Shane put a dollar bill on the bar, asked: "Kenny around?"

The Italian shook his head.

Shane said: "Where's the phone?"

The Italian inclined his head towards a narrow door back of Shane. Shane went into the booth and called the Valmouth, asked for Miss Johnson. When the connection had been made, he said: "Hello, Lorain—what room are you in?... All right, stay there until I get back—don't go out for anything—anybody... I'm down at Jack Kenny's... Tell you when I see you... Uh-huh... G'bye..." He hung up and went back to the bar.

The Italian and the Irishman were talking together. The Irishman came down to Shane and said: "Jack's upstairs, asleep. Wha'd you want to see him about?"

"You'd better wake him up—I want to tell him how to keep out of the can." Shane tasted the beer, said: "That's lousy—give me a glass of water."

The Irishman looked at him suspiciously for a minute, put a glass of water on the bar, went to the door at the end of the room. He said: "Who'll I say it is?"

"Shane."

The Irishman disappeared through the door.

He was back in a little while, said: "You can go on up—it's the open door at the top of the stairs."

Shane went back and through the door, across a dark, airless hallway. He lighted a match and found the bottom of the stair, went up. There was a door ajar at the top of the stair through which faint light came, he shoved it open, went in.

Jack Kenny was big and round and bald. He was sitting deep in a worn and battered wicker armchair. He was very drunk.

There was another man, lying face down across the dirty, unmade bed. He was snoring loudly, occasionally exhaled in a long sighing whistle.

Kenny lifted his chin from his chest, lifted bleary eyes to Shane. He said: "Hi, boy?"

Shane asked: "What kind of a rod did you give Del Corey?"

Kenny opened his eyes wide, grinned. He leaned heavily forward, then back, stretched luxuriously.

"I didn't give him any—the louse stole it."

Shane waited.

Kenny was suddenly serious. He said: "What the hell you talking about?"

Shane said: "Charley Rigas was killed tonight with a .38 Smith & Wesson automatic—the safety was knocked off, an' the number on the barrel started with four six six two. ."

Kenny stood up suddenly, unsteadily.

Shane said: "I thought you might like to know." He turned and started towards the door.

Kenny said: "Wait a minute."

Shane stopped in the doorway, turned.

All the color had gone out of Kenny's bloated, florid face, leaving it pasty, yellow-white.

He said: "You sure?" He went unsteadily to a little table in the room, picked up an empty bottle, held it up to the light, threw it into a corner.

Shane nodded, said: "Pretty damned dumb for Del to get so steamed up about Lorain an' Charley that he killed Charley—huh? Lorain's been washed up with Charley for months—an' Del ought to've known about it if anybody did..."

Kenny said: "He wasn't worrying about Lorain. It was that little cigarette gal—Thelma, or Selma, or something—that works for Charley. Del's been two-timing Lorain with her for the last couple weeks. That's what he was shooting off his mouth about this afternoon—he had some kind of office on her an' Charley."

Kenny went to a dresser and opened a drawer and took out a bottle of whiskey.

Shane said: "Oh."

He went out and down the dark stair, out to the bar. The glass of beer and the glass of water were on the bar where he had left them. He picked up the glass of water, tasted it, said: "That's lousy," and went out through the front door and the passageway to the cab.

It was a few minutes before eleven when Shane got out of the cab, paid off the driver and went into the Valmouth. The clerk gave him a note that a Mister Arthur had telephoned, would call again in the morning.

Shane went up to his rooms, sat down with his coat and hat on and picked up the telephone.

He said: "Listen, baby—tell the girl that relieves you in the morning that when Mister Arthur calls, I'm out of the city—won't be back for a couple months. He wants to sell me some insurance."

He hung up, looked up the number of 71 in his little black book, called it. A strange voice answered. Shane said: "Is Nick there?... Is Pedro there?... Never mind—what I want to know is what's Thelma's last name? Thelma, the cigarette girl?... Uh-huh—Never mind who I am—I'm one of your best customers... Uh-huh... How do you spell it?... B-u-r-r... You haven't got her telephone number, have you?"... The receiver clicked, Shane smiled, hung up.

He found Thelma Burr's address in the telephone

directory: a number on West Seventy-Fourth, off Riverside Drive. He got up and went to the table and took several cigars from the humidor, put all but one of them in the blue leather case. He lighted the cigar and stood a little while at one of the windows, staring at the tiny lights in the buildings uptown. Gusts of rain beat against the window and he shuddered suddenly, involuntarily.

He went to a cabinet and took out a square brown bottle, a glass, poured himself a stiff drink. Then he went out, downstairs to the sixteenth floor. He knocked several times at the door of 1611, but there was no answer. He went to the elevator, down to the lobby.

The night clerk said: "That's right, sir—1611, but I think Miss Johnson went out shortly before you came in."

Shane went to the house phone, spoke to the operator: "Did Miss Johnson get any calls after I talked to her around ten-thirty?... Right after I called—huh?... Thanks."

He went out to a cab, gave the driver the number on Seventy-Fourth Street.

It turned out to be a narrow, five-story apartment house on the north side of the street. Shane told the driver to wait and went up steps, through a heavy door into a dark hall. There were mailboxes on each side of the hall; he lighted a match and started on the left side. The second from the last box on the left bore a name scrawled in pencil that interested him: N. Manos—the apartment number was 414. He went on to the right side of the hall, found the name and the number he was looking for, went up narrow creaking steps to the third floor.

There was no answer at 312.

After a little while, Shane went back downstairs. He stood in the darkness of the hall for several minutes. Then he went back up to the fourth floor, knocked at 414. There was no answer there either. He tried the door, found it to be locked, went back down to 312.

He stood in the dim light of the hallway a while with his ear close to the door. He heard the outside door downstairs open and close, voices. He went halfway down the stair, waited until the voices had gone away down the corridor on the first floor, went back to the door of 312 and tried several keys in the lock. The sixth key he tried turned almost all the way; he took held of the knob, lifted and pushed, forcing the key at the same time. The lock clicked, gave way, the door swung open.

Shane went into the darkness, closed the door and lighted a match. He found the light switch, pressed it. A floor lamp with a colorful and tasteless batik shade; a smaller table lamp with a black silk handkerchief thrown over it, lighted. The globes were deep amber; the light of the two lamps was barely sufficient to see the brightly papered walls, the mass of furniture in the room. Shane picked his way to the table, jerked the black handkerchief off the table lamp; then there was a little more light.

There was a man on his knees on the floor, against a couch at one end of the little room. The upper part of his body was belly down on the couch and his arms hung limply, ridiculously to the floor; the back of his skull was caved in and the white brightly flowered couch-cover beneath his head and shoulders was dark red, shiny.

Shane went to him and squatted down and looked at the gashed and bloody side of his face. It was Del Corey.

Shane stood up and crossed the room to an ajar door, pushed it open with his foot. The light over the wash basin was on, covered with several layers of pink silk; the light was very dim.

Thelma Burr was lying on her back on the floor. Her green crepe de chine nightgown was torn, stained. There were black marks on her throat, her breast; her face was puffy, a bruised discolored mask, and her mouth and one cheek were brown-black with iodine. There was a heavy pewter candlestick a little way from one outstretched hand.

Shane knelt, braced his elbow on the edge of the bathtub and held his ear close to her chest. Her heart was beating faintly.

He stood up swiftly, went out of the bathroom, went to the door. He took out his handkerchief, wiped off the light switch carefully, snapped the lights out. Then he went out and locked the door, wiped the knob, put the key in his pocket and went downstairs, out and across the street to the cab.

The driver jerked his head towards another lone cab halfway down the block. "That hack come up right after we got here," he said. "Nobody got out or nothing. Maybe it's a tail." He stared sharply at Shane.

Shane said: "Probably."... He glanced carelessly at the other cab. "You can make yourself a fin if you can get me to the nearest telephone, and then over to 71 East Fifty—in five minutes."

The driver pointed across the street, said: "Garage over there—they ought to have a phone."

Shane ran across to the garage, found a phone and called Central Station, asked for Bill Hayworth. When Hayworth answered, he said: "There's a stiff and a prospective in apartment 312 at—West Seventy-Fourth. Hurry up—the girl's not quite gone. Call you later." He ran out to the waiting cab, climbed in, leaned back and clipped and lighted a cigar, watched the other cab through the rear window. They went over to the Drive, down two blocks, turned east. Shane thought for a while that the other cab wasn't following, but after they'd gone several blocks on Seventy-Second he saw it again. They cut down Broadway to Columbus Circle, across Fifty-Ninth.

In front of 71, Shane jumped out of the cab, said: "That's swell—wait," went swiftly across the sidewalk and pressed the button beneath the red number.

The slit opened, a voice that Shane did not know whispered: "What is it you want?"

Shane said: "In." He stuck his face in the thin shaft of light that came through the slit.

The door was opened and Shane went into the narrow hallway. The man who had let him in was about fifty-five—a slight, thin-faced man with white hair combed straight back from high forehead. He closed the door, bolted it.

Nick was standing behind and a little to one side of the slight man. He held a blunt blue automatic steadily in his right hand. His chin was on his chest and he stared at Shane narrowly through thick, bushy brows. He jerked his head up suddenly, sharply, said: "Put your hands up, you—!"

Shane smiled slowly, raised his hands slowly as high as his shoulders.

A bell tinkled faintly above the door, the slight white-haired man opened the slit and looked out, closed the slit and opened the door. Another man whom Shane recognized as one of the stud dealers came in. The slight man closed the door.

Nick jerked his head up again, said: "Upstairs." He put the automatic in the pocket of his dinner coat, the muzzle held the cloth out stiff.

Shane turned and went slowly up the stairs, and Nick and the man who followed him in came up behind him. The slight man stayed at the door.

On the second floor, Shane put his hands down as he passed the double-door into the big room, glanced in. There were three people, a man and two women, in earnest and drunken conversation at one of the corner tables. There was a couple at a table against the far wall. With the exception of these and a waiter and the man behind the bar, the room was deserted.

Shane spoke over his shoulder to Nick: "Swell crowd."

Nick took two or three rapid steps, took the automatic out of his pocket and jabbed it against Shane's back, hard. Shane put his hands up again and went up the second flight to the third floor. Nick and the other man followed him. He stopped at the top of the stair, leaned against the balustrade. Nick went past him and knocked at the tall gray door. It was opened in a little while and the three of them went into the room.

Pedro Rigas, Charley's brother, was sitting on one of the big round tables, swinging his feet back and forth. He was very tall and spare and his face was dark, handsome, his features sharply cut.

There was a plump young man with rosy cheeks, bright blue eyes, shingled sand-colored hair, on a straight cane-bottomed chair near Pedro. His legs were crossed and he leaned on one elbow on the table. There was a heavy nickeled revolver on the table near his elbow. He stared at Shane with interest.

Lorain Rigas was sitting on a worn imitation-leather couch against one wall. She was leaning forward with her elbows on her knees, her hands over her eyes. She had taken off the small suede hat, her dull black hair curved in damp arabesques over her white forehead and throat and hands.

The little Eastman operative was half sitting, half lying on the floor against the wall near the couch. His face was a pulpy mass of bruised, beaten flesh; one arm was up, half covering the lower part of his face, the other was propped in the angle of the floor and wall. He was sobbing quietly, his body shook.

Pedro Rigas looked at the dealer who had come in with Shane and Nick, nodded towards Shane, asked: "You bring him in?"

Nick said: "He came in—by himself." He grinned mirthlessly at Shane.

Shane was staring sleepily at Lorain Rigas.

She lifted her face, looked at him helplessly. “Somebody called up a little while after I talked to you,” she said—“said it was the night clerk—said you were waiting for me out in front of the hotel. I went down and they smacked me into a cab, brought me over here.”

Shane nodded slightly.

She turned her eyes towards the Eastman man on the floor. “He was here,” she went on, “an’ they were beating hell out of him. I don’t know where they picked him up.”

Shane said: “Probably at the Station, after he talked to me. They’ve been tailing me all night—since I left the hotel to go over an’ talk to the captain. That’s how they knew you were at the hotel—they saw you come in around nine—an’ they got the fake Johnson name from the register.”

Pedro Rigas was smiling coldly at Shane, swinging his feet back and forth nervously.

He said: “One of you two,”—he jerked his head towards the girl—“killed Charley. I find out pretty soon which one—or by God I kill you both.”

Shane had put his hands down. He held them in front of him and looked down at them, stroked the back of one with the palm of the other. Then he looked up at the rosy-cheeked young man, questioned Rigas: “Executioner?” He smiled slightly, sarcastically.

Lorain Rigas stood up suddenly, faced Pedro. She said: “You fool! Can’t you get it through that nut of yours that Del killed Charley? Dear God!”—she made a hopeless gesture. “Read the papers—the gun they found was the one Del swiped from Jack Kenny this afternoon. Jack’ll verify that.”

Pedro’s face was cold and hard and expressionless when he looked at her. “What were you doing up there?”

“I told you!” she almost screamed. “I went to warn Charley that Del was after him! I heard the shots when I was halfway upstairs—got out.”

Shane was looking at Lorain Rigas and there was a dim mocking glitter in his eyes.

She glanced at him, said: "I didn't tell you about that, Dick, because I was afraid you'd get ideas. You wouldn't trust your own mother across the street, you know."

Shane nodded gently, slowly.

He turned to Pedro. "Where do I come in?" he said. "I went from here to the hotel—an' I was there till about a quarter of ten..."

The dealer, who was still standing near the door, spoke for the first time: "No. After you left here, you didn't get to the hotel till about ten minutes of nine. I found that out from a friend of mine—a bellhop."

Lorain Rigas looked from the dealer to Shane. Her eyes were wide, surprised. She said: "My God!"

Pedro stopped swinging his feet suddenly. He said: "Where did you go after you left here?" He was staring at Shane and his eyes were thin heavily fringed slits.

Shane was silent a moment. Then he reached slowly, deliberately towards his inside pocket, smiled at Lorain Rigas, said: "May I smoke?"

Pedro stood up suddenly.

The rosy-cheeked youth stood up, too. The revolver glistened in his hand and he went swiftly to Shane, patted his pockets, his hips, felt under his arms. He finished, stepped back a pace.

Shane took out the blue case, took out a cigar and lighted it.

It was silent except for the choked sobbing of the little Eastman man.

Nick came suddenly forward, took Shane by the shoulder, shook him. Nick said: "You answer Pedro when he asks you a question."

Shane turned slowly and frowned at Nick. He looked down at Nick's hand on his shoulder, said slowly: "Take your hand off me, you—!" He looked back at Pedro. "Ask Nick where he went tonight."

Pedro jerked his head impatiently.

Shane took the cigar out of his mouth, said: "Did you know that Thelma—downstairs—is Nick's gal?" He hesitated a moment, glanced swiftly at Nick. "An' did you know that Charley's been playing around with her?"

Pedro was staring at Nick. His mouth was a little open.

Shane went on: "Nick knew it..."

He whirled suddenly and smashed his left fist down hard on Nick's broad forearm, grabbed for the automatic with his right hand. The automatic fell, clattered on the floor. Shane and Nick and the rosy-cheeked young man all dived for it, but the young man was a little faster; he stood up grinning widely, murderously—a gun in each hand.

Pedro said: "Go on."

Shane didn't say anything. He was looking at Nick and his eyes were bright, interested—he was smiling a little.

Pedro snapped at the dealer: "Go downstairs an' send Mario up—you stay at the door."

The dealer went out and closed the door.

They were all very quiet. Nick was staring at the automatic in the young man's hand and there was a very silly, far-away expression on his face. Shane was watching Nick like a vivisectionist about to make the crucial incision. Lorain Rigas was sitting down again on the couch with her hands over her eyes.

Pedro only waited, looked at the floor.

The door opened and the slight, white-haired man came in.

Pedro said: "What time did Nick go out tonight?"

The slight man looked at Nick bewilderedly. He cleared his throat, said: "Nick went out right after Charley went home. He said there wasn't any business anyway, an' he wanted to go to a picture-show, an' would I take the door for a while. He came back some time around nine..."

Pedro said: "All right—go on back downstairs."

The slight man gestured with one hand. "You seen me on the door when you went out right after we heard about Charley," he said. "Wasn't it all right for me to be on the door?"

"Sure." Pedro was looking at Nick. "Sure—only I thought Nick was down in the basement or something—I didn't know he'd gone out."

The slight man shrugged and went out and closed the door.

Shane said evenly: "Nick had a hunch that Charley was going to Thelma's. He didn't follow Charley, but he jumped in a cab, probably, an went to her place. He didn't find Charley—but he found Del Corey."

Lorain Rigas put her hands down and looked up at Shane. Her face was drawn, white.

"That's what Del went there for," Shane went on—"expecting to find Charley. Del's been making a big play for Thelma—an' he knew about Charley and her—was cockeyed an' burnt up an' aimed to rub Charley." Shane was watching Nick narrowly. "Thelma must've calmed Del down—Nick found them there..." Shane turned his eyes towards Lorain Rigas. "... And caved in Del's head."

Lorain Rigas stood up, screamed.

Pedro crossed to her swiftly, put one hand over her mouth, the other on her back, pushed her back down on the couch gently.

Shane said: "Then Nick beat the hell out of Thelma, made her admit that Charley had been in the woodpile, too, damn' near killed her."

He was looking at Nick again.

"He dragged what was left of her into the bathroom and poured some iodine on her mouth, an' put the candlestick that he'd smacked Del with in her hands so it would look like she'd killed Del an' then committed suicide."

Nick turned to stare at Shane vacantly.

Shane was puffing out great clouds of blue-gray smoke, seemed to be enjoying himself hugely.

"She wasn't quite dead, though," he went on. He glanced at his watch. "The law ought to be over there by now—getting her testimony."

Pedro said: "Hurry up."

Shane shrugged. "Nick took the gun that Del got from Jack Kenny, jumped up to Charley's. He knew he was in a good spot to let Charley have it because Charley and I had that argument tonight—an' it'd look like me—or he could make it look like me. Charley evidently stopped some place on the way home—Nick got there first and either stuck Charley up in the corridor and took him into the apartment to kill him, or sneaked in—the door was unlocked—and waited in the dark. Then he went out the back way—the way Charley came in—and came back down here."

Pedro went to the door, turned to Shane, said: "You and the lady go."

Shane gestured towards the Eastman man. "What about him?"

"We'll fix him up—give him some money. It is too bad." Pedro smiled, opened the door.

Shane looked at Nick. Nick's face was pasty, yellow, still wore the silly, far-away expression.

Lorain Rigas stood up and took up her hat and went to Shane.

They went together to the door, out into the hallway. Pedro leaned over the balustrade, called down to the little man at the outside door: "Okay."

Shane and the girl went downstairs, past the doors of the dark and empty barroom, down to the street floor.

The slight, white-haired man and the dealer were whispering together. The slight man opened the door for them, said: "Good night—come again."

They went out and got into the cab.

Shane said: "Valmouth."

It had stopped raining for the moment, but the streets were still black and glistening and slippery.

He tossed the cigar out through the narrow space of open window, leaned back, said: "Am I a swell dick?—or am I a swell dick?"

Lorain Rigas didn't answer. Her elbow was on the armrest, her chin in her hand. She stared out the window blankly.

"You're not very appreciative." Shane smiled to himself, was silent a little while.

The light held them up at Fifth Avenue. Theater traffic was heavy in spite of the weather.

Shane said: "The only thing I'm not quite sure about is whether you went to Charley's to warn him—or whether you'd heard about Del and Thelma—thought that the day Del was yelping about shooting Charley, in front of witnesses, was a swell time for you to shoot Charley yourself."

She did not answer.

As the cab curved into Sixth Avenue, she said: "Where did you go after you left 71—before you went back to the hotel?"

Shane laughed. "That lousy alibi held up with the captain," he said. "He didn't question it." He unbuttoned the top button of his topcoat, took something wrapped in tissue paper out of his inside pocket. "You know what a sucker I am for auction sales?"

She nodded.

He unfolded the tissue paper and took out a platinum-mounted diamond ring. The stone was large, pure white, very beautiful.

He said: "Pip?"

She nodded again.

He put the ring back in the tissue paper, folded it, put it back in his pocket.

The cab slid to the curb in front of the Valmouth.

Shane said: “Where you going?”

She shook her head.

He said: “You keep the cab.” He pressed a bill into her hand, said: “This’ll take care of it—why don’t you take a nice long ride?”

He brushed her forehead lightly with his lips and got out of the cab and went into the hotel.

Parlor Trick

I KNOCKED ON the door at the end of the hall. It was cold in the hall, almost dark. I knocked again, and Bella's voice said: "Come in," faintly; then she said: "Oh—it's locked." The key scratched in the lock and the door opened and I went into the room.

It was very hot in there. It was dark, with only a little light from a gas heater. There was a little more light that came through a short corridor from the kitchen, but it was pretty dark.

Bella closed the door and went over to the davenport and sat down. She was near the heater, and the yellow light flickered over the lower part of her face.

I took off my coat and put it on a chair. Bella kept scraping her teeth lightly over her lower lip. Her teeth were like a little animal's and she ran them over her soft lower lip rapidly, like an animal. The light from the heater was bright on the lower part of her face.

I went through the short corridor to the kitchen. The bathroom door was open; I glanced in as I passed and Gus Schaeffer turned his head and looked over his shoulder at me. He was standing at the basin with his back to the door and when he turned his head to look at me his face was awful. His skin was damp and gray and his eyes had something leaden and dying in them.

I said: "Hi, Gus," and went in to the kitchen.

There was a man sitting on one of the benches at one side of the narrow breakfast table. The table was set lengthwise into a niche, with a bench at each side, and the man on one of the benches was sitting with his back in the corner of the niche, his knees drawn up, his feet on the outside end of the bench. His head was back against the wall and his eyes and mouth were open. There was a thin knife handle sticking out of one side of his throat.

Gus came out of the bathroom and stood behind me in the doorway.

There were several nearly empty glasses on the table. One had fallen to the floor, broken into many glittering pieces.

I looked at the glass and I looked up at the man again. I think I said: "–" very softly.

"I did it. I did it and I didn't know it. I was blind..." Gus was clawing at my arm.

Bella came through the corridor and stood behind him. She looked very scared, very beautiful.

She said huskily: "Gus was terribly drunk. Frank said something out of turn and Gus picked up the knife and stuck it into his neck. He choked—I guess–"

She looked at the dead man, and then her eyes turned up white in their sockets and she fainted.

Gus turned around and almost fell down trying to catch her. He said: "Oh, baby—baby!" He took her up in his arms and carried her back into the living-room.

I followed him in and switched on the lights. He put Bella on the davenport. I watched him bend over her and flick ice water across her face with his fingers, from a pitcher; he rubbed her hands and wrists, and tried to force a little whiskey between her clenched pale lips. He kept saying: "Oh, baby—baby," over and over. I sat down.

He sat on the edge of the davenport and looked at me while he rubbed and patted Bella's hands.

"You better telephone," he said. Then he looked at Bella a long time. "I did it—see—I did it; only I didn't know about it. I was cockeyed–"

I nodded. I said: "Sure, Gus," and I leaned forward and picked up the telephone.

Gus was looking at Bella's white beautiful face. He bobbed his head up and down mechanically.

I said: "What's the best play—self-defense?"

He turned suddenly. "I don't care—no play at all." He dropped her hand and stood up. "Only I did it myself. She didn't have anything to do with it. She was in here..." He came towards me, shaking his finger at me, speaking very earnestly.

I said: "Maybe I can get Neilan. The longer we let it go, the worse it'll be." I dialed a number.

Neilan was a short chubby man with a strangely long face, a high bony forehead. He and Frank had been partners in a string of distilleries for almost five years. He said: "When did you get here, Red?"

"Bella called me up and told me something had happened—I live around the corner."

I was sitting near the door that led in to the kitchen. Bella was sitting in the middle of the davenport, leaning forward with her elbows on her knees, staring vacantly into the brightness of the heater. Gus was sitting in a straight-backed chair in the middle of the room.

Neilan had been walking around looking at the pictures on the walls. He sat down straddling an arm of the davenport.

"So you were so drunk you don't remember?" Neilan was looking at Gus.

Gus nodded. Bella looked up at him for a moment and nodded a little and then looked back into the fire.

There was a light tap at the door and it opened and a big man came in quietly and closed the door behind him. He wore glasses and his soft black hat was tilted over the back of his head. I think his name was McNulty, or McNutt—something like that. He said: "Ed's downstairs with a couple of the boys."

"They can wait downstairs." Neilan turned his head a little and looked at Bella out of the corners of his eyes. "So Gus was so drunk he don't remember?"

Gus stood up. He said: "—damn it! Pat—I was so drunk I didn't know any better, but I wasn't so drunk I don't know it was me. Lay off Bella—she was in here..."

"She didn't say so."

Bella said: "I was nearly asleep and I could hear Gus and Frank talking in the kitchen and then they didn't talk any more. After a while I got up and went out in the kitchen-Frank was like he is now, and Gus was out—with his head on the table."

Her chin was in her hands, and her head bobbed up and down when she talked. Gus was sitting down again, on the edge of the chair.

Neilan grinned at McNulty. He said: "What do you think, Mac?"

McNulty went over to Bella and reached down and put one big finger under her chin and jerked her head back.

"I think she's a liar," he said.

Gus stood up.

McNulty turned as if that had been what he wanted. He hit Gus very hard in the face, twice. Gus fell down and rolled over on his side. He pulled his knees up and moaned a little.

McNulty took off his coat and folded it carefully and put it on a chair. He went to Gus and kicked him hard in the chest and then kicked his head several times. Gus tried to protect himself with his arms. He didn't make any more noise but put his arms up and tried to protect himself. He tried to get up once and McNulty kicked him in the stomach and he fell down and lay quietly. In a little while, McNulty stopped kicking him and sat down. He was panting. He took off his hat and took a handkerchief out of his pocket and wiped his face.

I looked at Neilan. "I called you," I said, "because I thought you'd give Gus a break..."

He said: "You ought to of called the police. They'd be after giving Gus a break, and your lady friend here"—he jerked his head at Bella—"with a length of hose."

Bella was leaning back on the davenport with her hands up to her face. She stared at Gus and tried to look at McNulty.

McNulty smiled, said: "Sure—why don't you call a cop? Frankie had everybody from the Chief down on his payroll—they'll have to go back to working for the city." He was out of breath, spoke unevenly.

Bella stood up and started to go towards the door, and Neilan stood up too, and put one hand over her mouth and one on her back. He held her like that for a minute and then he pushed her back down on the davenport.

McNulty got up then and stooped over and took hold of the back of Gus' shirt collar and pulled him up a little way.

McNulty said: "Come on, boy—we'll get some air."

Gus' shirt collar started to tear and McNulty cupped his other hand around the back of Gus' neck and jerked him up on his feet. Gus couldn't stand by himself; McNulty stood there holding him with his arm around his shoulders. Gus' face was in pretty bad shape.

McNulty said: "Come on, boy," again and started guiding Gus towards the door.

Neilan said: "Wait a minute, Mac."

McNulty turned and stared vacantly at Neilan for a minute and then pushed Gus down in a big chair. He sat down on the arm of the chair and took out his handkerchief and wiped Gus' face.

Neilan went out into the kitchen. He was out there two or three minutes without making any noise, then he snapped off the light and came back. He turned off the lights in the living room too, and it was dark except for the faint yellow light from the heater.

Neilan went back and sat down at the end of the davenport, out of the light. The light rippled over Bella's face, and after a while, when my eyes were used to the darkness, I could make out dark shapes where McNulty and Gus sat—and Neilan.

It was so dark and quiet except for the sharp sound of Gus' breathing. There wasn't anything to look at except Bella and she was leaning back with her eyes closed and her face very still.

It got on my nerves after several minutes and I said: "What's it all about, Pat?"

Neilan didn't answer, so I leaned forward in my chair, but I didn't get up. I sat there with all my muscles tight.

Then I heard something moving out in the kitchen. I don't know whether anybody else heard it, but I know there was a sound out there like something moving across the floor.

I stood up and I couldn't speak. I didn't hear the sound again but I stood there without moving, and then Bella started talking. She talked in a conversational tone, with her head back, her eyes closed:

"Frank came here to see me. He's been coming to see me every night for four nights. He brought along a lot of lousy whiskey and got Gus drunk, and he got drunk too. He got Gus drunk once before and tried to sell me an idea. He wouldn't give up."

She stopped talking a moment and the light beat up and down on her face. She was very beautiful then.

"He made a crack tonight while Gus was in the bathroom about telling Gus about Red and me..."

She opened her eyes and looked towards me in the darkness a minute, and then closed her eyes and went on:

"I was scared. I called Red while they were raising hell in the kitchen and he came over and I let him in. We listened to them for a few minutes from in here in the dark, and then when Frank got to talking about what a great guy Red was, and started getting dirty about it, Red went in there very quickly and killed him. I guess Gus was too far gone to see it or know anything about it."

She stopped talking again and it was quiet.

"Then Red beat it and I stayed in here a while and then I went out like I told you and woke up Gus. He thought I did it, I guess. I called Red again..."

Neilan got up and went over and switched on the lights.

McNulty got up too and stood there blinking, staring stupidly at Bella.

I went over and got my hat and coat and put them on. I stood looking at Bella for a while after I had put on my coat. She was still leaning back with her eyes closed. She was one of the most beautiful women I have ever seen.

Neilan opened the door and McNulty and I went out into the hall. It was very cold there after the intense heat of the room. Then Neilan closed the door and the three of us went downstairs.

There was a small touring car at the curb, with the side-curtains on. There were two men whom I had never seen before in the front seat, and another man standing on the sidewalk. The engine was running.

McNulty opened the door and got in the back seat, and then I got in, and then Neilan. There wasn't anything else to do. I sat between them, and Neilan said: "Let's go."

We went down the street slowly. The man who had been standing on the sidewalk didn't get into the car; he stood there looking after us. I turned around a little and looked at him through the rear window; as we turned the corner, he went on back up the street, the other way.

When we got out of town a ways we went faster. It was very cold.

I said: “Hurry up.”

Neilan turned and grinned at me. I could see his face a little as we passed a street light. He said: “Hurry up—what?”

“Hurry up.” The cold was beginning to get in to the pit of my stomach, and my legs. I wanted to be able to stand up. I wanted it standing up, if I could.

Neilan glanced out the rear window. He said: “I think our tail light’s out.”

The car slowed, stopped. We were pretty well out in the country by that time and the road was dark.

Neilan said: “See if we’ve got a tail light, Mac.”

McNulty grunted and reached up and opened the door and heaved himself up into the door. He stooped and put one foot out on the running board, and then Neilan reached in front of me very quickly. There was a gun in his hand and he put it close to McNulty’s back and shot him three times. The explosions were very close together. McNulty’s knees crumpled up and he fell out of the car on his face.

The car started again and the man who sat next to the driver reached back and slammed the door shut hard.

Neilan cleared his throat. He said: “Frank’s number has been up a long time. He’s been tipping our big deliveries, South; we haven’t got a truck through for two months.”

I could feel the blood getting back into my arms and legs. I wasn’t so cold and I could breathe without pain.

“McNulty was in it with him. McNulty was in the outfit downstate. We found out about that last night.”

We rode on for a little while and nobody said anything.

“If the dame sticks to her beef,” Neilan went on, “the scarcer you are, the better. If she doesn’t, Gus’ll stand it.

You can't do yourself any good around here any more anyway."

Pretty soon we stopped at a little interurban station where I could get a car in to the city.

I had to wait a while. I sat in the station where it was warm, and thought about Bella. After a while the car came.

One, Two, Three

I'D BEEN IN Los Angeles waiting for this Healey to show for nearly a week. According to my steer, he'd taken a railroad company in Quebec for somewhere in the neighborhood of a hundred and fifty grand on a swarm of juggled options or something. That's a nice neighborhood.

My information said further that he was headed west and that he dearly loved to play cards. I do, too.

I'll take three off the top, please.

I missed him by about two hours in Chicago and spent the day going around to all the ticket offices, getting chummy with agents, finally found out Healey had bought a ticket to L A, so I fanned on out there and cooled.

Pass.

Sunday afternoon I ran into an op for Eastern Investigators, Inc., named Card, in the lobby of the Roosevelt. We had a couple drinks and talked about this and that. He was on the Coast looking for a gent named Healey. He was cagey about who the client was, but Eastern handles mostly missing persons, divorces, stuff like that.

Monday morning Card called me and said the Salt Lake branch of his outfit had located Healey in Caliente, Nevada. He said he thought I might like to know. I told him I wasn't interested and thanked him and then I rented a car in a U Drive place and drove up to Caliente.

I got there about four in the afternoon and spotted

Healey in the second joint I went into. He was sitting in a stud game with five of the home boys and if they were a fair sample of local talent I figured I had plenty of time.

Healey was a big man with a round cheery face, smooth pink skin. His mouth was loose and wet and his eyes were light blue. I think his eyes were the smallest I've ever seen. They were set very wide apart.

He won and lost pretty evenly, but the game wasn't worth a nickel. The home boys were old-timers and played close to their vests and Healey's luck was the only thing that kept him even. He finally scared two of them out of a seventy- or eighty-dollar pot and that made him feel so good that he got up and came over to the bar and ordered drinks for the boys at the table. He ordered lemonade for himself.

I said: "Excuse me, but haven't I seen you around Lonnie Thompson's in Detroit?" Lonnie makes a book and I had most of my dope on Healey from him.

He smiled and said: "Maybe," and asked me what I drank.

I ordered whiskey.

He asked me if I'd been in town long and I said I'd just driven up from LA to look things over and that things didn't look so hot and that I would probably drive back to LA that night or the next morning.

I bought him another lemonade and had another whiskey and we talked about Detroit. In a little while he went back to the table and sat down.

That was enough for a beginning. I had registered myself with him as one of the boys. I went out and drove a couple of blocks to the Pine Hotel and took a room. The Pine was practically the only hotel in town, but I flipped the register back a day or so and found Healey's name to make sure. Then I went up and washed and lay down to smoke a cigarette and figure out the details.

According to Lonnie Thompson, Healey was a cash boy—carried his dough in paper and traveler's cheques. I couldn't be sure of that but it was enough. The point was to get him to LA and in to one or two or three places where I could work on him.

I guess I must have slept almost an hour because it was dark when I woke up. Somebody was knocking at the door and I got up and stumbled over and switched on the light and opened the door. I was too sleepy to take Healey big—I mumbled something about coming in and sitting down, and I went over to the basin and put some cold water on my face.

When I turned around he was sitting on the bed looking scared. I offered him a cigarette and he took it and his hand was shaking.

He said: "Sorry I woke you up like that."

I said: "That's all right," and then he leaned forward and spoke in a very low voice:

"I've got to get out of here right away. I want to know how much it's worth to you to take me down to Los Angeles."

I almost fell off the chair. My first impulse was to yell, "Sure," and drag him down to the car; but he was scared of something and when a man's scared is a swell time to find out what it's all about.

I stalled. I said: "Oh, that's all right," sort of hesitantly.

He said: "Listen... I got here Saturday morning. I was going to stay here long enough to establish residence and then apply for one of those quick divorces, under the Nevada law.

"My wife has been on my tail six weeks with a blackmail gag," he went on. "She's here. When I got back to the hotel a little while ago she came into my room and put on an act."

I thought then I knew who Card's client was.

"She came in this afternoon. She's got the room next to

mine."

He was silent so long that I laughed a little and said: "So what?'"

"I've got to duck, quick," he went on. "She's a bad actor. She came into my room and put on an act. She's got a guy with her that's supposed to be her brother and he's a bad actor, too. You said you were going to drive back to LA. I saw your name on the register when I came in and I thought you might take me along. I can't rent a car here and there isn't a train till midnight."

He pulled the biggest roll I ever saw out of his pocket and skimmed off a couple notes. "If it's a question of money..."

I shook my head with what I hoped was a suggestion of dignity. I said: "I'd decided to go back myself tonight. It will be a pleasure to take you, Mister Healey," and I got up and put on my coat. "How about your stuff?"

He looked blank until I said: "Luggage," and then he said: "That's all right—I'll leave it." He smiled again. "I travel light."

At the top of the stairs he whispered: "This is sure a big lift." Then he remembered that he had to sneak up to his room to get something and said he'd meet me at the car. I told him where it was. He said he'd paid his hotel bill.

I went on downstairs and checked out.

My car was wedged in between a Ford truck and a light-blue Chrysler roadster. There was plenty of room ahead of the roadster, so I went up and snapped off the hand-brake and pushed it ahead about eight feet. Then I got into my car and leaned back and waited.

The whole layout looked pretty bad, what with him scared to death of a deal he admitted was blackmail and all. He said he didn't want his luggage and then, right on top of it, he had to go up to his room to get something. That would be taking a chance on running into the wife again. I wondered if she was his wife.

I couldn't figure out how a wife could blackmail a husband while she was jumping from state to state with a man who was "supposed" to be her brother; but then almost anything is possible in Nevada.

After about five minutes I began to get nervous. I opened the door of the car and stepped out on the sidewalk, and as I closed the door there were five shots close together some place upstairs in the hotel.

I can take trouble or leave it alone; only I always take it. Like a sap, I went into the hotel.

The clerk was a big blond kid with glasses. He came out from behind the counter as I went in the door; we went upstairs together, two or three at a time.

There was a man in long woolly underwear standing in the corridor on the third floor and he pointed to a door and we went in. Healey was lying flat on his face in the middle of the room, and beyond him, close to the wall, was the body of a woman, also face downward.

The clerk turned a beautiful shade of green; he stood there staring at Healey. I went over and rolled the woman over on her back. She couldn't have been much over twenty-two or three; little, gray-eyed, blonde. There was a knife in her side, under the arm. There was a .38 automatic near her outstretched hand. She was very dead.

The man in the woolly underwear peeked in and then hurried across the hall and into another room. I could hear him yelling the news to somebody there.

I went over and tapped the clerk on the shoulder and pointed at the girl. The clerk swallowed a couple of times, said: "Miss Mackay," and looked back at Healey. He was hypnotized by the way Healey's back looked. Hamburger.

Then about two dozen people came into the room all at once.

The sheriff had been in the pool-hall across the street. He rolled Healey over and said: "This is Mister Healey," as if he'd made a great discovery.

I said: "Uh-huh. He's been shot."

I guess the sheriff didn't like the way I said it very well. He glanced at the clerk and then asked me who I was. I told him my name and the clerk nodded and the sheriff scratched his head and went over and looked at the girl. I wanted to say that she'd been knifed, but I restrained myself.

Shaggy underwear was back with his pants on. He said he hadn't heard anything except somebody swearing and then, suddenly, the shots.

I asked him how long after the shots it had been when he came into the corridor and he said he wasn't sure, but it was somewhere around half a minute.

The first interesting thing that turned up was that it wasn't Healey's room—it was Miss Mackay's room. His was next door. That probably meant that Healey had deliberately gone into her room; that she hadn't surprised him in his room while he was getting something he'd forgotten.

Number two was that the knife was Healey's. Half a dozen people had seen him with it. It was an oversize jack-knife with a seven-inch blade—one of the kind that snaps open when you press a spring. Somebody said Healey had a habit of playing mumblety-peg with it when he was trying to out-sit a raise or scare somebody into splitting a pot.

Number three was the topper. The dough was gone. The sheriff and a couple of deputies searched Healey and went through both rooms with a fine-tooth comb. They weren't looking for big money because they didn't know about it; they were looking for evidence.

All they found on Healey were four hundred-dollar bills tucked into his watch pocket, and the usual keys, cigarettes, whatnot. There were no letters or papers of any kind. There was one big suitcase in his room and it was full of dirty clothes. The roll he'd flashed on me was gone.

In the next half-hour I found out a lot of things. The girl had come to the hotel alone. No one else had checked in that day, except myself. The door to the girl's room was about twenty feet from the top of the back stairs and there was a side-door to the hotel that they didn't lock until ten o'clock.

It looked like a cinch for the man Healey had told me about, the one who was supposed to be Miss Mackay's brother.

Healey had probably gone upstairs to take care of the girl. I knew that his being scared of her was on the level because I know bona-fide fear when I see it. She evidently had plenty on him. He'd arranged his getaway with me and then gone up to carve the girl, shut her up forever.

The alleged brother had come in the side-door and had walked in on the knife act and opened up Healey's back with the automatic at about six feet.

Then he'd grabbed the roll and whatever else Healey had in his pocket that was of any value—maybe a book of traveler's cheques—had tossed the gun on the floor and screwed back down the back stairway and out the side-door. Something like that. It wasn't entirely plausible, but it was all I could figure right then.

By the time I'd figured that much out the sheriff had it all settled that Healey had knifed the girl and then she'd plugged him five times, in a ten-inch square in his back. With about three inches of steel in her heart.

That was what the sheriff said so I let it go. They didn't know about the brother and I didn't want to complicate their case for them. And I did want a chance to look for that roll without interference.

When I got out to the car the blue Chrysler was gone. That wasn't important except that I wondered who had been going away from the hotel when it looked like everybody in town was there or on the way there.

I didn't get much information at the station. The agent said he'd just come on duty; the telegraph operator had been there all afternoon but he was out to supper. I found him in a lunch-room across the street and he said there'd been a half-dozen or so people get off the afternoon train from Salt Lake; but the girl had been alone and he wasn't sure who the other people had been except three of four home-towners. That was no good.

I tried to find somebody else who had been in the station when the train came in but didn't have any luck. They couldn't remember.

I went back to the car and that made me think about the blue Chrysler again. It was just possible that the Mackay girl had come down from Salt Lake by rail, and the boy-friend or brother or whatever he was had driven down. It didn't look particularly sensible but it was an idea. Maybe they didn't want to appear to be traveling together or something.

I stopped at all the garages and gas-stations I could find but I couldn't get a line on the Chrysler. I went back to the hotel and looked at the register and found out that Miss Mackay had put down Chicago as her home, and I finagled around for a half hour and talked to the sheriff and the clerk and everybody who looked like they wanted to talk but I didn't get any more angles.

The sheriff said he'd wired Chicago because it looked like Healey and Miss Mackay were both from Chicago, and that he'd found a letter in one of Healey's old coats from a Chicago attorney. The letter was about a divorce, and the sheriff had a hunch that Miss Mackay was Mrs. Healey.

I had a sandwich and a piece of pie in the hotel restaurant and bundled up and went out and got in the car and started for LA.

I didn't get up till around eleven o'clock Tuesday

morning. I had breakfast in my room and wired a connection in Chi to send me all he could get on Miss Mackay and her brother. I called the desk and got the number of Card's room and on the way down stopped in to see him.

He was sitting in his nightshirt by the window, reading the morning papers. I sat down and asked him how he was enjoying his vacation and he said swell, and then he said: "I see by the papers that our friend Healey had an accident."

I nodded.

Card chuckled: "Tch, tch, tch. His wife will sure be cut up."

I smiled a little and said, "Uh-huh," and Card looked up and said: "What the hell are you grinning about and what do you mean: Uh-huh?"

I told him that according to my paper Mrs. Healey was the lady who had rubbed Healey—the lady who was on her way back East in a box.

Card shook his head intelligently and said: "Wrong. That one was an extra. Mrs. Healey is alive and kicking and one of the sweetest dishes God ever made."

I could see that he was going to get romantic so I waited and he told me that Mrs. Healey had been the agency's client in the East and that she'd come in from Chicago Monday morning by plane and that he'd met her in the agency office, and then he went on for five or ten minutes about the color of her eyes and the way she wore her hair, and everything.

Card was pretty much of a ladies' man. He told it with gestures.

Along with the poetry he worked in the information that Mrs. Healey, as he figured it, had had some trouble with Healey and that they'd split up and that she wanted to straighten it all out. That was the reason she'd wired the Salt Lake office of his agency to locate Healey. And almost as soon as they'd found Healey he'd shoved off for LA and the agency had wired her in Chicago to that effect. She'd arrived the morning Healey had been spotted in Caliente and had decided to wait in LA for him.

Card said he had helped her find an apartment. He supposed the agency had called her up and told her the bad news about Healey. He acted like he was thinking a little while and then asked me if I didn't think he ought to go over and see if he could help her in any way. "Comfort her in her bereavement," was the way he put it.

I said: "Sure—we'll both go."

Card didn't go for that very big, but I told him that my having been such a pal of Healey's made it all right.

We went.

Mrs. Healey turned out a great deal better than I had expected from Card's glowing description. As a matter of fact she was swell. She was very dark, with dark blue eyes and blue-black hair; her clothes were very well done and her voice was cultivated, deep. When she acknowledged Card's half-stammered introduction, inclined her head towards me and asked us to sit down, I saw that she had been crying.

Card had done pretty well in the way of helping her find an apartment. It was a big luxurious duplex in the Garden Court on Kenmore.

She smiled at Card. "It's very nice of you gentlemen to call," she said.

I said we wanted her to know how sorry we were about it all and that I had known Healey in Detroit, and if there was anything we could do—that sort of thing.

There wasn't much else to say. There wasn't much else said.

She asked Card to forgive her for bothering him so much the previous evening with her calls, but that she'd been nervous and worried and kept thinking that maybe Healey had arrived in LA after the agency was closed and that she hadn't been notified. They'd been watching the trains of course.

Card said that was all right and got red and stammered some more. He was stunned by the lady. So was I. She was a pip.

She said she thought she'd stay in California and she told us delicately that she'd made arrangements for Healey's body to be shipped to his folks in Detroit.

Finally I said we'd better go and Card nodded and we got up. She thanked us again for corning and a maid helped us with our coats and we left.

Card said he had to go downtown so I took a cab and went back to the hotel. There was a wire from Chicago:

> JEWELMACKAYTWOCONVICTIONS EXTORTION STOP WORKS WITH HUSBAND ARTHUR RAINES ALIAS J L MAXWELL STOP LEFT CHICAGO WEDNESDAY FOR LOS ANGELES WITH RAINES STOP DESCRIPTION MACKAY FOUR ELEVEN ONE HUNDREDTWOBLONDEGRAYEYES RAINES FIVE SIX ONE HUNDRED TWENTY-FIVE RED BROWN EYES STOP MAY LOCATE THROUGH BROTHER WILLIAM RAINES REAL ESTATE SOUTH LABREA REGARDS ED.

I got the number of Raines's real estate office from the telephone book and took a cab and went down and looked it over. I didn't go in. Then I told the driver to take me to the Selwyn Apartments on Beverly Boulevard. That was the place the telephone book had listed as Raines's residence.

It took a half-hour of jabbering about spark plugs with the Bohunk in the Selwyn garage to find out that Mister

Raines had gone out about ten o'clock with another gentleman, and what Mister Raines looked like and what kind of a car he drove. The gentleman who had been with him was tailor maybe he was short. Or maybe it had been a lady. The Bohunk wasn't sure.

I jockeyed the cab around to a good spot in the cross street and went into the drug-store on the opposite corner and drank Coca-Colas. Along about the fifth Coca-Cola the car I was looking for pulled up in front of the Selwyn. A medium-sized middle-aged man who I figured to be the brother got out of the driver's seat and went into the apartment house. The other man in the car moved over into the driver's seat and started west on Beverly. By that time I was back in the cab and after him.

Of course I couldn't he sure it was Raines. It looked like a little man. I had to take that chance.

We followed the car out Beverly to Western, up Western. I wondered what had become of the blue Chrysler. Then we drew up close behind Raines's car at an intersection and I nearly fell out the window. The man in the car ahead turned around and looked back; we looked smack at one another for five seconds.

I'd seen him before! I'd seen him the night before in Miss Mackay's room at the Pine Hotel in Caliente! He'd been one of the raft of people who'd busted in with the Sheriff and stood around ah-ing and oh-ing. The man had guts. He'd come in while Healey and the girl were still warm to see what a neat job he'd done.

The traffic bell rang and I knew he'd recognized me, too. He went across that intersection like a bat out of hell, up Western to Fountain.

He lost us on Fountain. I talked to my driver like a father. I got down on my knees and begged him to keep that car in sight. I called him all the Portuguese pet-names I could think of and made up a few new ones, but Raines ran away from us on Fountain.

On the way back to the hotel I stopped at the Hollywood Branch of the Automobile Club and had a friend of mine look up the license number of the car. Of course it was the brother's car, in the brother's name. That didn't get me anywhere. I was pretty sure Raines wouldn't go back to his brother's place now that he knew I'd spotted him; and it was a cinch he wouldn't use that car very long.

He didn't know what I wanted. He might figure me for a dick and scram out of LA—out of the country. I sat in my room at the hotel and thought soft thoughts about what a chump I'd been not to go to him directly when he'd stopped with his brother in front of the Selwyn, and the speed of taxi-cabs as compared to automobiles—things like that. It looked like the Healey case was all washed up as far as I was concerned.

I went out about five o'clock and walked. I walked down one side of Hollywood Boulevard to Bronson and back up the other side to Vine and went into the U Drive joint and rented the car again. I was nervous and jumpy and disgusted, and the best way for me to get over feeling that way is to drive it off.

I drove out through Cahuenga Pass a ways and then I had an idea and drove back to the Selwyn Apartments. The idea wasn't any good. William Raines told the clerk to send me up and he asked me what he could do for me and smiled and offered me a drink.

I said I wanted to get in touch with his brother on a deal that would do us both a lot of good. He said his brother was in Chicago and that he hadn't seen him for two years. I didn't tell him he was a liar. It wouldn't have done any good. I thanked him and went back down to the car.

I drove down to LA and had dinner in a Chinese place. Then I went back by the Santa Fe and found out about trains—I figured on going back to New York the next day.

On the way back to Hollywood I drove by the Garden Court. Not for any particular reason—I thought about Mrs. Healey and it wasn't much out of the way.

The blue Chrysler was sitting squarely across the street from the entrance.

I parked up the street a little way and got out and went back to be sure. I lit a match and looked at the card on the steering column; the car was registered to another U Drive place, downtown, on South Hope.

I went across the street and walked by the desk with my nose in the air. The Spick elevator boy didn't even look at the folded bill I slipped him; he grinned self-consciously and said that a little red-haired man had gone up to four just a couple minutes ago. Mrs. Healey was on four and there were only three apartments on a floor.

I listened at the door but could only hear a confused buzz that sounded like fast conversation. I turned the knob very slowly and put a little weight against the door. It was locked. I went down to the end of the hall and went out as quietly as possible through a double door to a fire-escape platform. By standing outside the railing and holding on with one hand and leaning far out I could see into the dining-room of Mrs. Healey's apartment, could see a couple inches of the door that led, as well as I could remember, into the drawing-room. It was closed.

There is nothing that makes you feel quite so simple as hanging on a fire-escape, trying to look into a window. Particularly when you can't see anything through the window. After a few minutes I gave it up and climbed back over the railing.

I half sat on the railing and tried to figure things out. What business would the guy who shot Healey have with Mrs. Healey? Did the blackmail angle that Raines and Mackay had hold over Healey cover Mrs. Healey, too? Was Raines milking his lowdown for all it was worth? It was too deep for me.

I went back into the hall and listened at the door again. They were a little louder but not loud enough to do me any good. I went around a bend in the hall to what I figured to be the kitchen-door and gave it the slow turn and it opened. I mentally kicked myself for wasting time on the fire-escape, tiptoed into the dark kitchen and closed the door.

It suddenly occurred to me that I was in a quaint spot if somebody should come in. What the hell business did I have there! I fixed that, to myself, with some kind of vague slant about protecting Mrs. Healey and edged over to the door, through to the room I'd been looking into from the fire-escape.

The door into the drawing-room was one of those pasteboard arrangements that might just as well not be there. The first thing I heard was a small, suppressed scream like somebody had smacked a hand over somebody else's mouth, and then something like a piece of furniture being tipped over. It was a cinch someone was fighting in there, quietly—or as quietly as possible.

There wasn't much time to think about whether I was doing the right thing or not. If I'd thought about it I'd probably have been wrong, anyway. I turned the knob, swung the door open.

Mrs. Healey was standing against the far wall. She was standing flat against the wall with one hand up to her mouth. Her eyes were very wide.

There were two men locked together on the floor near the central table and as I came in they rolled over a turn or so and one broke away and scrambled to his feet. It was Raines. He dived after a nickel-plated revolver that was lying on the floor on the far side of the table, and the other man, who had risen to his knees, dived after it, too. The other man was Card.

He beat Raines by a hair but Raines was on his feet; he kicked the gun out of Card's hand, halfway across the room. Card grabbed his leg and pulled him down and they went round and round again. They fought very quietly; all you could hear was the sound of heavy breathing and an occasional bump.

I went over and picked up the gun and stooped over the mess of arms and legs and picked out Raines's red head and took hold of the barrel of the gun. I took dead aim and let Raines have it back of the ear. He relaxed.

Card got up slowly. He ran his fingers through his hair and jiggled his shoulders around to straighten his coat and grinned foolishly.

I said: "Fancy, meeting you here."

I turned around and looked at Mrs. Healey. She was still standing against the wall with her hand across her mouth. Then the ceiling fell down on top of my head and everything got dark very suddenly.

Darkness was around me when I opened my eyes, but I could see the outlines of a window and I could hear someone breathing somewhere near me. I don't know how long I was out. I sat up and my head felt like it was going to explode; I lay down again and closed my eyes.

After a while I tried it again and it was a little better. I crawled towards what I figured to be a door and ran into the wall and I got up on my feet and felt along the wall until I found the light switch.

Raines was lying in the same place I'd smacked him, but his hands and feet were tied with a length of clothes-line and there was a red, white and blue silk handkerchief jammed into his mouth. His eyes were open and he looked at me with an expression that I can only describe as bitter amusement.

Card was lying belly-down on the floor near the door into the dining-room. He was the hard breather I'd heard in the darkness. He was still out.

I ungagged Raines and sat down. I kept having the feeling that my head was going to blow up. It was a very unpleasant feeling.

In a little while Raines got his jaws limbered up and started talking. The first thing he said was: "What a bright boy you turned out to be!" I was too sick to know very much about what that meant—or care.

He went on like that for some time, talking in a high, squeaky voice, and the idea gradually filtered through the large balloon-shaped ache that my head had turned into.

It seems that Raines and the Mackay gal had juggled Healey into a swell spot. One of their angles was that Healey, in an expansive moment, had entirely forgotten about Mrs. Healey and married Miss Mackay. They had a lot of material besides; everything from the Mann Act to mayhem. When he'd made the hundred and fifty grand lick in Quebec they'd jumped him in Chicago.

Healey had ducked out of Chi and they'd tailed him, first to Salt Lake, then to Caliente. Monday night, Raines had helped Mackay put on the act in the hotel that Healey had told me about.

Raines hadn't got off the train with her or checked into the hotel with her because they didn't want to be seen together in case anything went wrong, but he ducked up that handy back stairway and they'd given Healey the act, showing him exactly the color and size of the spot they had him on.

Then, when Healey came down to my room, Raines had gone down and planted across the street in case Healey tried to powder.

Raines hadn't been there five minutes before Mrs. Healey and a man rolled up in the blue Chrysler. Raines recognized Mrs. Healey because she'd spotted Healey with Miss Mackay and Raines in a cabaret in Chicago once and crowned Miss Mackay with a beer bottle. It seems Mrs. Healey was a nice quiet girl.

They parked in front of the hotel and the man went in a minute, probably to buy a cigar and get a peek at the register. Then he came out and talked to Mrs. Healey a little while and went back in the little alleyway that led to the side door. He was only there a minute; he probably found out that it was practical to go into the hotel that way and came back and told her.

Along about that time in Raines's yarn I woke up to the fact that he was referring to the man who was with Mrs. Healey as "this guy." I opened my eyes and looked at him and he was looking at Card.

Card had stayed in the car while Mrs. Healey went back through the alleyway and into the hotel. After a couple minutes he got nervous and got out and walked up the street a little ways, and Raines went across the street and went upstairs to find out what it was all about. That must have been about the time I was checking out.

Card must have been coming back down the other side of the street and he saw me come out and finagle with his car and get into mine, and he stayed away until hell started popping upstairs and I went into the hotel.

Raines stopped a minute. I got up and went over and rolled Card over on his back. He groaned and opened his eyes and blinked up at me and then he sat up slowly and leaned against the wall.

Raines said Mrs. Healey must have tried Healey's door and then waited till Healey came up the front stairway after he left me, and she ducked around a corner and watched Healey go into Mackay's room. By that time Raines was at the top of the back stairway and he watched Mrs. Healey take a gun out of her bag and go down and listen at Miss Mackay's door. When Healey opened the door after whittling Mackay, she backed him into the room and closed the door. Raines said she probably told him a few pertinent truths about himself and relieved him of what was left of the hundred and fifty and then opened him up with the .38.

It was a swell spot for her, with the Mackay gal there with a knife in her heart. Raines said he figured she'd intended to rub Healey from the start, before he could divorce her—Healey had said she'd sworn to kill him, before he left Chicago. A nice quiet girl—Mrs. Healey. A lady.

She'd dodged Raines on the stairs and he'd chased her down to the car, but by that time Card was back in the car with the engine running and they'd shoved off fast. Then Raines had come back up with the sheriff and his gang to look things over. That's where I'd seen him.

He'd taken the midnight train for LA and it had taken him all day Tuesday to locate Mrs. Healey. He'd been putting the screws on her and Card for a split of the important money and Card had gone into a wrestling number with him just before I arrived.

By the time Raines had got all that out of his system Card was sitting up straight with his mouth open and his hands moving around fast and that dumb, thoughtful look on his face as if he wanted to say something. When Raines stopped to breathe, Card said that the lady had talked him into driving her up to Caliente because she said she was too nervous to wait for Healey in LA—she said she had to see Healey and try to make their scrap up right away, or she'd have a nervous breakdown or something and Card—the big chump—fell for it.

He said he was the most surprised man in the world when the shooting started, and that when she came galloping down and they scrammed for LA she'd told him that she'd walked in on Mackay ventilating Healey, just like the sheriff said, and that Mackay had shot at her as she ran away. Card had fallen for that, too. She had the poor sap hypnotized.

Card knew I'd been up at Caliente, of course—he'd seen me; so when I walked into his place in the morning he'd figured I had some kind of slant on what it was all about and he'd taken me over to her place so they could put on their "comfort her in her bereavement" turn for my benefit. Then, Tuesday night, when I'd walked in on the shakedown and knocked Raines out, Card, who had had a load of what

Raines had to say to Mrs. Healey and who half believed it, calculated that his best play was to take the air with her. He was too much-mixed up in it to beat an accessory rap anyway, so he'd sapped me with a bookend and they'd tied Raines, who was coming to, and he'd helped her pack her things. They were going to light out for New Zealand or some quiet place like that; only she'd sneaked up behind him and smacked him down at the last minute. A lovely lady.

We all stopped talking about that time—Raines and Card and me—and looked at one another.

Card laughed. He squinted at me and said: "You looked silly when I clipped you with the bookend!"

Raines said: "You didn't look particularly intelligent when our girl-friend let you have it."

Card snickered on the wrong side of his face and got up and went out into the kitchen for a drink of water. He found a bottle out there—almost a full fifth of White Horse. He brought it in, I untied Raines and we all had a snort.

I was thinking about what suckers we'd been. I'd popped Raines and Card had popped me and Mrs. Healey had popped Card—all of us. One, two, three. Tinker to Evers to Chance—only more so.

I think we were all pretty washed up with La Belle Healey. It was a cinch Card wouldn't want any more of her. I don't know about Raines, but I know I didn't.

We finished the bottle and Raines snooped around and found a full one and we did a little business with that.

I didn't find out I had a concussion till next morning. I was a week and two days in the hospital at twenty dollars a day, and the doctor nicked me two-fifty. He'll get the rest of it when he catches me.

The whole Healey play, what with one thing and another, cost somewhere in the neighborhood of a grand. I got a lame skull and about two-bits' worth of fun out of it. I pass.

Murder In Blue

COLEMAN SAID: "Eight ball in the corner." There was soft click of ball against ball and then sharper click as the black ball dropped into the pocket Coleman had called.

Coleman put his cue in the rack. He rolled down the sleeves of his vividly striped silk shirt and put on his coat and a pearl gray velour hat. He went to the pale fat man who slouched against a neighboring table and took two crisp hundred dollar notes from the fat man's outstretched hand, glanced at the slim, pimpled youth who had been his opponent, smiled thinly, said: "So long," went to the door, out into the street.

There was sudden roar from a black, curtained roadster on the other side of the street; the sudden ragged roar of four or five shots close together, a white pulsing finger of flame in the dusk, and Coleman sank to his knees. He swayed backwards once, fell forward onto his face hard; his gray hat rolled slowly across the sidewalk. The roadster was moving, had disappeared before Coleman was entirely still. It became very quiet in the street.

Mazie Decker curved her orange mouth to its best "Customer" smile. She took the little green ticket that the dark-haired boy held out to her and tore off one corner and dropped the rest into the slot. He took her tightly in his arms and as the violins melted to sound and the lights dimmed they swung out across the crowded floor.

Her head was tilted back, her bright mouth near the blue smoothness of his jaw.

She whispered: “Gee—I didn’t think you was coming.”

He twisted his head down a little, smiled at her.

She spoke again without looking at him: “I waited till one o’clock for you last night” She hesitated a moment then went on rapidly: “Gee—I act like I’d known you for years, an’ it’s only two days. What a sap I turned out to be!” She giggled mirthlessly.

He didn’t answer.

The music swelled to brassy crescendo, stopped. They stood with a hundred other couples and applauded mechanically.

She said: “Gee—I love a waltz! Don’t you?”

He nodded briefly and as the orchestra bellowed to a moaning foxtrot he took her again in his arms and they circled towards the far end of the floor.

“Let’s get out of here, kid.” He smiled to a thin line against the whiteness of his skin, his large eyes half closed.

She said: “All right—only let’s try to get out without the manager seeing me. I’m supposed to work till eleven.”

They parted at one of the little turnstiles; he got his hat and coat from the check-room, went downstairs and got his car from a parking station across the street.

When she came down he had double-parked near the entrance. He honked his horn and held the door open for her as she trotted breathlessly out and climbed in beside him. Her eyes were very bright and she laughed a little hysterically.

“The manager saw me,” she said. “But I said I was sick—an’ it worked.” She snuggled up close to him as he swung the car into Sixth Street. “Gee—what a swell car!”

He grunted affirmatively and they went out Sixth a block or so in silence.

As they turned north on Figueroa she said: “What’ve you

got the side curtains on for? It's such a beautiful night."

He offered her a cigarette and lighted one for himself and leaned back comfortably in the seat.

He said: "I think it's going to rain."

It was very dark at the side of the road. A great pepper tree screened the roadster from whatever light there was in the sky.

Mazie Decker spoke softly: "Angelo. Angelo—that's a beautiful name. It sounds like angel."

The dark youth's face was hard in the narrow glow of the dashlight. He had taken off his hat and his shiny black hair looked like a metal skullcap. He stroked the heel of his hand back over one ear, over the oily blackness and then he took his hand down and wriggled it under his coat. His other arm was around the girl.

He took his hand out of the darkness of his coat and there was brief flash of bright metal; the girl said: "My God!" slowly and put her hands up to her breast...

He leaned in front of her and pressed the door open and as her body sank into itself he pushed her gently and her body slanted, toppled through the door, fell softly on the leaves beside the road. Her sharp breath and a far quavering "Ah!" were blotted out as he pressed the starter and the motor roared; he swung the door closed and put on his hat carefully, shifted gears and let the clutch in slowly.

As he came out of the darkness of the dirt road on to the highway he thrust one hand through a slit in the side-curtain, took it in and leaned forward over the wheel.

It was raining, a little.

R. F. Winfield stretched one long leg out and planted his foot on a nearby leather chair. The blonde woman got up and walked unsteadily to the phonograph. This latter looked like a grandfather clock, had cost well into four figures, would probably have collapsed at the appellation "phonograph"—but it was.

The blonde woman snapped the little tin brake; she lifted the record, stared empty-eyed at the other side.

She said: "'s Minnie th' Moocher. Wanna hear it?"

Mr. Winfield said: "Uh-huh." He tilted an ice and amber filled glass to his mouth, drained it. He stood up and gathered his very blue dressing-gown about his lean shanks. He lifted his head and walked through a short corridor to the bathroom, opened the door, entered.

Water splashed noisily in the big blue porcelain tub. He braced himself with one hand on the shower-tap, turned off the water, slipped out of the dressing-gown and into the tub.

The blonde woman's voice clanged like cold metal through the partially open door.

"Took 'er down to Chinatown; showed 'er how to kick the gongaroun'."

Mr. Winfield reached up into the pocket of the dressing-gown, fished out a cigarette, matches. He lighted the cigarette, leaned back in the water, sighed. His face was a long tan oblong of contentment. He flexed his jaw, then mechanically put up one hand and removed an upper plate, put the little semi-circle of shining teeth on the basin beside the tub, ran his tongue over thick, sharply etched lips, sighed again. The warm water was soft, caressing; he was very comfortable.

He heard the buzzer and he heard the blonde woman stagger along the corridor past the bathroom to the outer door of the apartment. He listened but could hear no word of anything said there; only the sound of the door opening and closing, and silence broken faintly by the phonograph's "Hi-de-ho-oh, Minnie."

Then the bathroom door swung slowly open and a man stood outlined against the darkness of the corridor. He was bareheaded and the electric light was reflected in a thin line across his hair, shone dully on the moist pallor of his skin. He wore a tightly belted raincoat and his hands were thrust deep into his pockets.

Winfield sat up straight in the tub, spoke tentatively "Hello!" He said "hello" with an incredulous rising inflection, blinked incredulously upward. The cigarette dangled loosely from one corner of his mouth.

The man leaned against the frame of the door and took a short thick automatic out of his coat pocket and held it steadily, waist high.

Winfield put his hands on the sides of the tub and started to get up.

The automatic barked twice.

Winfield half stood, with one hand and one leg braced against the side of the tub for perhaps five seconds. His eyes were wide, blank. Then he sank down slowly, his head fell back against the smooth blue porcelain, slid slowly under the water. The cigarette still hung in the corner of his clenched mouth and as his head went under the water it hissed briefly, was gone.

The man in the doorway turned, disappeared.

The water reddened. Faintly, the phonograph lisped: "Hi de ho..."

Doolin grinned up at the waiter. "An' see the eggs are four minutes, an' don't put any cream in my coffee."

The waiter bobbed his head sullenly and disappeared through swinging doors.

Doolin unfolded his paper and turned to the comic page. He read it carefully, chuckling audibly, from top to bottom. Then he spread pages two and three across the counter and began at the top of page two. Halfway across he read the headline: Winfield, Motion Picture Executive, Slain by Sweetheart: Story continued from page one.

He turned to the front page and stared at a two-column

cut of Winfield, read the accompanying account, turned back to page two and finished it. There was another cut of Winfield, and a woman. The caption under the woman's picture read: "Elma O'Shea Darmond, well-known screen actress and friend of Winfield, who was found unconscious in his apartment with the automatic in her hand."

Doolin yawned and shoved the paper aside to make room for the eggs and toast and coffee that the sour-faced waiter carried. He devoured the eggs and had half-finished his coffee before he saw something that interested him on page three. He put his cup down, leaned over the paper, read: "Man shot in Glendale Mystery. H J (Jake) Coleman, alleged gambler, was shot and killed as he came out of the Lyric Billiard Parlors in Glendale yesterday evening. The shots were fired from a mysterious black roadster which the police are attempting to trace."

Doolin read the rest of the story, finished his coffee. He sat several minutes staring expressionlessly at his reflection in the mirror behind the counter, got up, paid his check and went out into the bright morning.

He walked briskly down Hill Street to First, over First, to the Los Angeles Bulletin Building. He was whistling as the elevator carried him up.

In the back files of the Bulletin he found what he was looking for, a front-page spread in the Home Edition of December 10th:

MASSACRE IN NIGHTCLUB

SCREEN-STARS DUCK FOR COVER AS

MACHINE-GUNS BELCH DEATH

Early this morning The Hotspot, famous

> cabaret near Culver City, was the scene of the bloodiest battle the local gang war has afforded to date. Two men who police believe to be Frank Riccio and Edward (Whitey) Conroy of the Purple Gang in Detroit were instantly killed when a private room in the club was invaded by four men with sub-machine guns. A third man, a companion of Riccio and Conroy, was seriously wounded and is not expected to live.

Doolin skimmed down the column, read:

> R. F. Winfield, prominent motion-picture executive, who was one of the party in the private room, said that he could not identify any of the killers. He said it all happened too quickly to be sure of any of them, and explained his presence in the company of the notorious gangsters as the result of his desire for first-hand information about the underworld in connection with a picture of that type which he is supervising. The names of others in the party are being withheld...

Under a sub-head Doolin read:

> H. J. Coleman and his companion, Miss Mazie Decker, were in the corridor leading to the private room when the killers entered. Miss Decker said she could positively identify two of them. Coleman, who is nearsighted, was equally positive that he could not...

An hour and a half later, Doolin left the Bulletin Building. He had gone carefully through the December file, and up to the middle of January. He had called into service the

City Directory, telephone book, Dun & Bradstreet, and the telephone, and he had wheedled all the inside dope he could out of a police-reporter whom he knew casually.

He stood on the wide stone steps and looked at the sheet of paper on which he had scrawled notes. It read:

> People in private room and corridor who might be able to identify killers of Riccio and Conroy:
>
> Winfield. Dead.
>
> Coleman. Dead.
>
> Martha Grainger. Actress. In show, in N. Y.
>
> Betty Crane. Hustler. Died of pneumonia January 4th.
>
> Isabel Dolly. Hustler and extra-girl. Was paralyzed drunk during shooting; probably not important. Can't locate.
>
> Mazie Decker. Taxi-dancer. Works at Dreamland on Sixth and Hill. Failed to identify killers from rogues-gallery photographs.
>
> Nelson Halloran. Man-about-town. Money. Friend of Win-field's. Lives at Fontenoy, same apartment-house as Winfield.

Doolin folded and creased the sheet of paper. He wound it abstractedly around his forefinger and walked down the steps, across the sidewalk to a cab. He got into the cab and sat down and leaned back.

The driver slid the glass, asked: "Where to?"

Doolin stared at him blankly, then laughed. He said: "Wait a minute," spread the sheet of paper across his knee. He took a stub of pencil out of his pocket and slowly, thoughtfully, drew a line through the first five names; that left Mazie Decker and Nelson Halloran.

Doolin leaned forward and spoke to the driver: "Is that Dreamland joint at Sixth an' Hill open in the afternoon?"

The driver thought a moment, shook his head.

Doolin said: "All right, then—Fontenoy Apartments—on Whitley in Hollywood."

Nelson Halloran looked like Death. His white face was extremely long, narrow; his sharp chin tapered upward in unbroken lines to high sharp cheek-bones, great deep-sunken eyes; continued to a high, almost degenerately narrow, forehead. His mouth was wide, thin, dark against the whiteness of his skin. His hair was the color of water. He was six-feet-three inches tall, weighed a hundred and eighty.

He half lay in a deeply upholstered chair in the living room of his apartment and watched a round spot of sunlight move across the wall. The shades were drawn and the apartment was in semi-darkness. It was a chaos of modern furniture, books, magazines, papers, bottles; there were several good but badly hung reproductions on the pale walls.

Halloran occasionally lifted one long white hand languidly to his mouth, inhaled smoke deeply and blew it upward into the ray of sunlight.

When the phone buzzed he shuddered involuntarily, leaned side wise and took it up from a low table.

He listened a moment, said: "Send him up." His voice was very low. There was softness in it; and there was coldness and something very far-away.

He moved slightly in the chair so that one hand was near his side, in the folds of his dressing gown. There was a Luger there in the darkness of the chair. He was facing the door.

With the whirl of the buzzer he called: "Come in."

The door opened and Doolin came a little way into the room, closed the door behind him.

Halloran did not speak.

Doolin stood blinking in the half-light, and Halloran

watched him and was silent.

Doolin was around thirty; of medium height, inclined to thickness through all the upper part of his body. His face was round and on the florid side and his eyes were wide-set, blue. His clothes didn't fit him very well.

He stood with his hat in his hand, his face expressionless, until Halloran said coldly: "I didn't get the name."

"Doolin. D—double o-l-i-n." Doolin spoke without moving his mouth very much. His voice was pleasant; his vowels colored slightly by brogue.

Halloran waited.

Doolin said: "I read a couple of things in the paper this morning that gave me an idea. I went over to the Bulletin an' worked on the idea, an' it pans out you're in a very bad spot."

Halloran took a drag of his cigarette, stared blankly at Doolin, waited. Doolin waited, too. They were both silent, looking at one another for more than a minute. Doolin's eyes were bright, pleased.

Halloran finally said: "This is a little embarrassing." He hesitated a moment. "Sit down."

Doolin sat on the edge of a wide steel and canvas chair against the wall. He dropped his hat on the floor and leaned forward, put his elbows on his knees. The little circle of sunlight moved slowly across the wall above him.

Halloran mashed his cigarette out, changed his position a little, said: "Go on."

"Have you read the papers?" Doolin took a cellophane-wrapped cigar out of his pocket and ripped off the wrapper, clamped the cigar between his teeth.

Halloran nodded, if moving his head the merest fraction of an inch could be called a nod.

Doolin spoke around the cigar: "Who rubbed Riccio and Conroy?"

Halloran laughed.

Doolin took the cigar out of his mouth. He said very earnestly: "Listen. Last night Winfield was murdered—an' Coleman. You're next. I don't know why the people who did it waited so long—maybe because the trial of a couple of the boys they've been holding comes up next week..."

Halloran's face was a blank white mask.

Doolin leaned back and crossed his legs. "Anyway—they got Winfield an' Coleman. That leaves the Decker broad—the one who was with Coleman—an' you. The rest of them don't count—one's in New York an' one died of pneumonia an, one was cockeyed..."

He paused to chew his cigar, Halloran rubbed his left hand down over one side of his face, slowly.

Doolin went on: "I used to be a stunt-man in pictures. For the last year all the breaks have been bad. I haven't worked for five months." He leaned forward, emphasized his words with the cigar held like a pencil: "I want to work for you."

There was thin amusement in Halloran's voice: "What are your qualifications?"

"I can shoot straight, an' fast, an' I ain't afraid to take a chance—any kind of a chance! I'd make a hell of a swell bodyguard."

Doolin stood up in the excitement of his sales-talk, took two steps towards Halloran.

Halloran said: "Sit down." His voice was icy. The Luger glistened in his hand.

Doolin looked at the gun and smiled a little, stuck the cigar in his mouth and backed up and sat down.

Halloran said: "How am I supposed to know you're on the level?"

Doolin slid his lower lip up over the upper. He scratched his nose with the nail of his thumb and shook his head slowly, grinning.

"Anyway—it sounds like a pipe dream to me," Halloran

went on. "The paper says Miss Darmond killed Winfield." He smiled. "And Coleman was a gambler—any one of a half dozen suckers is liable to have shot him."

Doolin shrugged elaborately. He leaned forward and picked up his hat and put it on, stood up.

Halloran laughed again. His laugh was not a particularly pleasing one.

"Don't be in a hurry," he said.

They were silent a while and then Halloran lighted a cigarette and stood up. He was so tall and spare that Doolin stared involuntarily as he crossed, holding the Luger loosely at his side, patted Doolin's pockets, felt under his arms with his free hand. Then Halloran went to a table across a corner of the room and dropped the Luger into a drawer.

He turned and smiled warmly at Doolin, said: "What will you drink?"

"Gin."

"No gin."

Doolin grinned.

Halloran went on: "Scotch, rye, bourbon, brandy, rum, Kirsch, champagne. No gin."

Doolin said: "Rye."

Halloran took two bottles from a tall cabinet, poured two drinks. "Why don't you go to the Decker girl? She's the one who said she could identify the men who killed Riccio and Conroy. She's the one who needs a bodyguard."

Doolin went over to the table and picked up his drink. "I ain't had a chance," he said. "She works at Dreamland downtown, an' it ain't open in the afternoon." They drank.

Halloran's mouth was curved to a small smile. He picked up a folded newspaper, pointed to a headline, handed it to Doolin.

Doolin took the paper, a late edition of the Morning Bulletin, read:

MURDERED GIRL IDENTIFIED AS TAXI-DANCER

> The body of the girl who was found stabbed to death on the road near Lankershim early this morning, has been identified as Mazie Decker of 305 S. Lake Street, an employee of the Dreamland Dancing Studio.
>
> The identification was made by Peggy Galbraith, the murdered girl's room-mate. Miss Decker did not return home last night, and upon reading an account of the tragedy in the early editions, Miss Galbraith went to the morgue and positively identified Miss Decker. The police are...

Doolin put the paper down, said: "Well, well... Like I said..." There was a knock at the door, rather a curious rhythmic tapping of fingernails.

Halloran called: "Come in."

The door opened and a woman came in slowly, closed the door. She went to Halloran and put her arms around him and tilted her head back.

Halloran kissed her lightly. He smiled at Doolin, said: "This is Mrs. Sare." He turned his smile to the woman. "Lola—meet Mr. Doolin—my bodyguard."

Lola Sare had no single feature, except her hair, that was beautiful; yet she was very beautiful.

Her hair was red, so dark that it was black in certain lights. Her eyes slanted; were so dark a green they were usually black. Her nose was straight but the nostrils flared the least bit too much; her mouth red and full; too wide and curved. Her skin was smooth, very dark. Her figure was good, on the slender side. She was ageless; perhaps twenty-six, perhaps thirty-six.

She wore a dark green robe of heavy silk, black mules;

her hair was gathered in a large roll at the nape of her neck.

She inclined her head sharply towards Doolin, without expression.

Doolin said: "Very happy to know you, Mrs. Sare."

She went to one of the wide windows and jerked the drape aside a little; a broad flat beam of sunshine yellowed the darkness.

She said: "Sorry to desecrate the tomb." Her voice was deep, husky.

Halloran poured three drinks and went back to his chair and sat down. Mrs. Sare leaned against the table, and Doolin, after a hesitant glance at her, sat down on the chair against the wall.

Halloran sipped his drink. "The strange part of it all," he said, "is that I couldn't identify any of the four men who came in that night if my life depended upon it—and I'm almost sure Winfield couldn't. We'd been on a bender together for three days—and my memory for faces is bad, at best..."

He put his glass on the floor beside the chair, lighted a cigarette. "Who else did you mention, besides the Decker girl and Coleman and Winfield and myself, who might...?"

Doolin took the folded sheet of paper out of his pocket, got up and handed it to Halloran. Halloran studied it a while, said: "You missed one." Mrs. Sare picked up the two bottles and went to Doolin, refilled his glass.

Doolin stared questioningly at Halloran, his eyebrows raised to a wide inverted V.

"The man who was with Riccio and Conroy," Halloran went on. "The third man, who was shot..."

Doolin said: "I didn't see any more about him in the files—the paper said he wasn't expected to live..."

Halloran clicked the nail of his forefinger against his teeth, said: "I wonder."

Mrs. Sare had paused to listen. She went to Halloran and refilled his glass and put the bottles on the floor, sat down on the arm of Halloran's chair.

"Winfield and I went to The Hotspot alone," Halloran went on. "We had some business to talk over with a couple girls in the show." He grinned faintly, crookedly at Mrs. Sare. "Riccio and Conroy and this third man—I think his name was Martini or something dry like that—and the three girls on your list, passed our table on their way to the private-room..."

Doolin was leaning forward, chewing his cigar, his eyes bright with interest.

Halloran blew smoke up into the wedge of sun. "Winfield knew Conroy casually—had met him in the East. They fell on one another's necks, and Conroy invited us to join their party. Winfield went for that—he was doing a gangster picture and Conroy was a big shot in the East—Winfield figured he could get a lot of angles..."

Doolin said: "That was on the level, then?"

"Yes," Halloran nodded emphatically. "Winfield even talked of making Conroy technical expert on the picture-before the fireworks started."

"What did this third man—this Martini, look like?"

Halloran looked a little annoyed. He said: "I'll get to that. There were eight of us in the private room—the three men and the three girls and Winfield and I. Riccio was pretty drunk, and one of the girls was practically under the table. We were all pretty high."

Halloran picked up his glass, leaned forward. "Riccio and Martini were all tangled up in some kind of drunken argument and I got the idea it had something to do with drugs—morphine. Riccio was pretty loud. Winfield and I were talking to Conroy, and the girls were amusing themselves gargling champagne, when the four men—I guess there were four-crashed in and opened up on Riccio and Conroy..."

"What about Martini?" Doolin's unlighted cigar was growing rapidly shorter.

Halloran looked annoyed again. "That's the point," he said. "They didn't pay any attention to Martini—they wanted Riccio and Conroy. And it wasn't machine-guns—that was newspaper color. It was automatics..."

Doolin said: "What about Martini?"

"For Christ's sake—shut up!" Halloran grinned cheerlessly, finished his drink. "Riccio shot Martini."

Doolin stood up slowly, said: "Can I use the phone?"

Halloran smiled at Mrs. Sare, nodded.

Doolin called several numbers, asked questions, said "Yes" and "No" monotonously.

Halloran and Mrs. Sare talked quietly. Between two calls, Halloran spoke to Doolin: "You've connections—haven't you." It was an observation, not a question.

Doolin said: "If I had as much money as I have connections, I'd retire."

He finished after a while, hung up and put the phone back on the low round-table.

"Martinelli," he said, "not Martini. Supposed to have been Riccio and Conroy's partner in the East. They had the drug business pretty well cornered. He showed up out here around the last of November, and Riccio and Conroy came in December tenth, were killed the night they got in..."

Halloran said: "I remember that—they were talking about the trip."

Doolin took the cigar out of his mouth long enough to take a drink. "Martinelli was discharged from St. Vincent's Hospital January sixteenth—day before yesterday. He's plenty bad—beat four or five murder raps in the East and was figured for a half dozen others. They called him The Executioner. Angelo Martinelli—The Executioner."

Mrs. Sare said: "Come and get it."

Doolin and Halloran got up and went into the little dining room. They sat down at the table and Mrs. Sare brought in a steaming platter of bacon and scrambled eggs, a huge double-globe of bubbling coffee.

Doolin said: "Here's the way it looks to me: If Martinelli figured you an' Winfield an' whoever else was in the private room had seen Riccio shoot him, he'd want to shut you up; it was a cinch he'd double-crossed Riccio and if it came out at the trial, the Detroit boys would be on his tail."

Halloran nodded, poured a large rosette of chili-sauce on the plate beside his scrambled eggs.

"But what did he want to rub Coleman an' Decker for?"

Halloran started to speak with his mouth full, but Doolin interrupted him: "The answer to that is that Martinelli had hooked up with the outfit out here, the outfit that Riccio and Conroy figured on moving in on..."

Halloran said: "Martinelli probably came out to organize things for a narcotic combination between here and Detroit, in opposition to our local talent. He liked the combination here the way it was and threw in with them—and when Riccio and Conroy arrived Martinelli put the finger on them, for the local boys..."

Doolin swallowed a huge mouthful of bacon and eggs, said: "Swell," out of the corner of his mouth to Mrs. Sare.

He picked up his cigar and pointed it at Halloran. "That's the reason he wanted all of you—you an' Winfield because you'd get the Detroit outfit on his neck if you testified; Decker an' Coleman because they could spot the LA boys. He didn't try to proposition any of you—he's the kind of guy who would figure killing was simpler."

Halloran said: "He's got to protect himself against the two men who are in jail too. They're liable to spill their guts. If everybody who was in on it was bumped there wouldn't be a chance of those two guys being identified—everything would be rosy."

They finished their bacon and eggs in silence.

With the coffee, Doolin said: "Funny he didn't make a pass at you last night—before or after he got Winfield. The same building an' all..."

"Maybe he did." Halloran put his arm around Mrs. Sare who was standing beside his chair. "I didn't get home till around three—he was probably here, missed me."

Doolin said: "We better go downtown an' talk to the DA. That poor gal of Winfield's is probably on the grill. We can clear that up an' have Martinelli picked up..."

Halloran said: "No." He said it very emphatically.

Doolin opened his eyes wide, slowly. He finished his coffee, waited.

Halloran smiled faintly, said: "In the first place, I hate coppers." He tightened his arm around Mrs. Sare. "In the second place I don't particularly care for Miss Darmond—she can God damned well fry on the griddle from now on, so far as I'm concerned. In the third place—I like it..."

Doolin glanced at Mrs. Sare, turned his head slowly back towards Halloran.

"I've got three months to live," Halloran went on—"at the outside." His voice was cold, entirely unemotional. "I was shell-shocked and gassed and kicked around pretty generally in France in 'eighteen. They stuck me together and sent me back and I've lasted rather well. But my heart is shot, and my lungs are bad, and so on—the doctors are getting pretty sore because I'm still on my feet..."

He grinned widely. "I'm going to have all the fun I can in whatever time is left. We're not going to call copper, and we're going to play this for everything we can get out of it. You're my bodyguard and your salary is five hundred a week, but your job isn't to guard me—it's to see that there's plenty of excitement. And instead of waiting for Martinelli to come to us, we're going to Martinelli."

Doolin looked blankly at Mrs. Sare. She was smiling in a

very curious way. Halloran said: "Are you working?" Doolin smiled slowly with all his face. He said: "Sure."

Doolin dried his hands and smoothed his hair, whistling tunelessly, went through the small cheaply furnished living room of his apartment to the door of the kitchenette. He picked up a newspaper from a table near the door, unfolded it and glanced at the headlines, said: "They're calling the Winfield kill 'Murder in Blue' because it happened in a blue bathtub. Is that a laugh!"

A rather pretty fresh-faced girl was stirring something in a white sauce-pan on the little gas stove. She looked up and smiled and said: "Dinner'll be ready in a minute," wiped her hands on her apron and began setting the table.

Doolin leaned against the wall and skimmed through the rest of the paper. The Coleman case was limited to a quarter column—the police had been unable to trace the car. There was even less about Mazie Decker. The police were "working on a theory..."

The police were working on a theory, too, on the Winfield killing. Miss Darmond had been found near the door of Winfield's apartment with a great bruise on her head, the night of the murder; she said the last she remembered was opening the door and struggling with someone. The "Best Minds" of the Force believed her story up to that point; they were working on the angle that she had an accomplice.

Doolin rolled up the paper and threw it on a chair. He said: "Five hundred a week—an' expenses! Gee!—is that swell!" He was grinning broadly.

The girl said: "I'm awfully glad about the money, darling—if you're sure you'll be safe. God knows it's about time we had a break." She hesitated a moment. "I hope it's all right..."

She was twenty-three or four, a honey-blonde pink-cheeked girl with wide gray eyes, a slender well-curved figure.

Doolin went to her and kissed the back of her neck. "Sure, it's all right, Mollie," he said. "Anything is all right when you get paid enough for it. The point is to make it last—five hundred is a lot of money, but a thousand will buy twice as many lamb chops."

She became very interested in a tiny speck on one of the cheap white plates, rubbed it industriously with a towel. She spoke without looking up: "I keep thinking about that Darmond girl—in jail. What do you suppose Halloran has against her?"

"I don't know." Doolin sat down at the table. "Anyway—she's okay. We can spring her any time, only we can't do it now because we'd have to let the Law in on the Martinelli angle an' they'd pick him up—an' Halloran couldn't have his fun."

"It's a funny kind of fun." The girl smiled with her mouth.

Doolin said: "He's a funny guy. Used to be a police reporter in Chi—maybe that has something to do with it. Anyway, the poor bastard's only got a little while to go—let him have any kind of fun he wants. He can afford it..."

They were silent while the girl cut bread and got the butter out of the Frigidaire and finished setting the table.

Doolin was leaning forward with his elbows on the table, his chin in his hands. "As far as the Darmond gal is concerned, a little of that beef stew they dish up at the County will be good for her. These broads need a little of that—to give them perspective."

The girl was heaping mashed potatoes into a big bowl. She did not speak.

"The way I figure it," Doolin went on—"Halloran hasn't got the guts to bump himself off. He's all washed up, an' he knows it—an' the idea has made him a little batty. Then along comes Martinelli—a chance for him to go out dramatically—the way he's lived—an' he goes for it. Jesus! so would I if I was as near the edge as he is. He doesn't give a god-damn about anything—he doesn't have to..."

The girl finished putting food on the table, sat down. Doolin heaped their plates with chops and potatoes and cauliflower while she served salad. They began to eat.

Doolin got up and filled two glasses with water and put them on the table.

The girl said: "I'm sorry I forgot the water..."

Doolin bent over and kissed her, sat down.

"As far as Halloran is concerned," he went on—"I'm just another actor in his show. Instead of sitting and waiting for Martinelli to come to get him—we go after Martinelli. That's Halloran's idea of fun—that's the kind of sense of humor he's got. What the hell!—he's got nothing to lose..."

The girl said: "Eat your dinner before it gets cold."

They were silent a while.

Finally she said: "What if Martinelli shoots first?"

Doolin laughed. "Martinelli isn't going to shoot at all. Neither am I—an' neither is Mr. Halloran."

The girl lighted a cigarette, sipped her coffee. She stared expressionlessly at Doolin, waited.

"Halloran is having dinner with Mrs. Sare," Doolin went on. "Then they're going to a show an' I'm picking them up afterwards—at the theatre. Then Halloran an' I are going to have a look around for Martinelli."

He finished his coffee, refilled both their cups. "In the meantime I'm supposed to be finding out where we're most likely to find him—Halloran is a great believer in my 'connections.'"

Doolin grinned, went on with a softly satisfied expression, as if he were taking a rabbit out of a hat: "I've already found Martinelli—not only where he hangs out, but where he lives. It was a cinch. He hasn't any reason to think he's pegged for anything—he's not hiding out."

The girl said: "So what?"

He stood up, stretched luxuriously. "So I'm going to Martinelli right now." He paused dramatically. "An' I'm going to tell him what kind of a spot he's in—with half a dozen murder raps hanging over his head, and all. I'm going to tell him that plenty people besides myself know about it an' that the stuff's on the way to the DA's office an' that he'd better scram toot sweet..."

The girl said: "You're crazy."

Doolin laughed extravagantly. "Like a fox," he said. "Like a fox. I'm doing Martinelli a big favor—so I'm set with him. I'm keeping Halloran from running a chance of being killed—an' he'll think he's still running the chance, an' get his throb out of it. I'm keeping five hundred smackers coming into the cash register every week as long as Halloran lives, or as long as I can give him a good show. An' everybody's happy. What more do you want?"

"Sense." The girl mashed her cigarette out, stood up. "I never heard such a crazy idea in all my life!..."

Doolin looked disgusted. He walked into the living room, came back to the doorway. "Sure, it's crazy," he said. "Sure, it's crazy. So is Halloran—an' you—an' me. So is Martinelli—probably. It's the crazy ideas that work—an' this one is going to work like a charm."

The girl said: "What about Darmond? If Martinelli gets away she'll be holding the bag for Winfield's murder."

"Oh, no, she won't! As soon as the Halloran angle washes up I'll turn my evidence over to the DA an' tell him it took a few weeks to get it together—an' be sure about it. It's as plain as the nose on your face that Martinelli killed all three of them. Those chumps downtown are too sappy to see it now but they won't be when I point it out to them. It's a set-up case against Martinelli!"

The girl smiled coldly. She said: "You're the most

conceited, bull-headed Mick that ever lived. You've been in one jam after another ever since we were married. This is one time I'm not going to let you make a fool of yourself—an' probably get killed..."

Doolin's expression was stubborn, annoyed. He turned and strode across the living room, squirmed into his coat, put on his hat and jerked it down over his eyes.

She stood in the doorway. Her face was very white and her eyes were wide, round.

She said: "Please. Johnny..."

He didn't look at her. He went to the desk against one wall and opened a drawer, took a nickel-plated revolver out of the drawer and dropped it into his coat pocket.

She said: "If you do this insane thing—I'm leaving." Her voice was cold, brittle.

Doolin went to the outer-door, went out, slammed the door.

She stood there a little while looking at the door.

Angelo Martinelli stuck two fingers of his left hand into the little jar, took them out pale, green, sticky with Smoothcomb Hair Dressing. He dabbed it on his head, held his hands stiff with the fingers bent backwards and rubbed it vigorously into his hair. Then he wiped his hands and picked up a comb, bent towards the mirror.

Martinelli was very young—perhaps twenty-four or—five. His face was pale, unlined; pallor shading to blue towards his long angular jaw; his eyes red-brown, his nose straight and delicately cut. He was of medium height but the high padded shoulders of his coat made him appear taller.

The room was small, garishly furnished. A low bed and two or three chairs in the worst modern manner were made a little more objectionable by orange and pink batik throws; there was an elaborately wrought iron floor lamp, its shade made of whiskey labels pasted on imitation parchment.

Martinelli finished combing his hair, spoke over his shoulder to a woman who lounged across the foot of the bed: "Tonight does it..."

Lola Sare said: "Tonight does it—if you're careful..." Martinelli glanced at his wrist-watch. "I better get going—it's nearly eight. He said he'd be there at eight."

Lola Sare leaned forward and dropped her cigarette into a half-full glass on the floor.

"I'll be home from about eight-thirty on," she said. "Call as soon as you can."

Martinelli nodded. He put on a lightweight black felt hat, tilted it to the required angle in front of the mirror. He helped her into her coat, and then he put his arms around her, kissed her mouth lingeringly.

She clung to him, whispered: "Make it as fast as you can, darling." They went to the door and Martinelli snapped off the light and they went out.

Martinelli said: "Turn right at the next corner." The cab driver nodded; they turned off North Broadway into a dimly lighted street, went several blocks over bad pavement.

Martinelli pounded on the glass, said: "Oke." The cab slid to an abrupt stop and Martinelli got out and paid the driver, stood at the curb until the cab had turned around in the narrow street, disappeared. He went to a door above which one pale electric globe glittered, felt in the darkness for the button, pressed it. The door clicked open; Martinelli went in and slammed it shut behind him.

There were a half dozen or so men strung out along the bar in the long dim room. A few more sat at tables against the wall.

Martinelli walked to the far end of the bar, leaned across it to speak quietly to a chunky bald-headed man who sat on a high stool near the cash register:

"Chief here?"

The bald man bobbed his head, jerked it towards a door behind Martinelli.

Martinelli looked surprised, said mildly: "He's on time for once in his life!"

The man bobbed his head. His face was blank.

Martinelli went through the door, up two short flights of stairs to a narrow hallway. At the end of the hallway he knocked at a heavy steel-sheathed fire-door.

After a little while the door opened and a voice said: "Come in."

Doolin stood on his toes and tried to make out the number above the door but the figures were too faded by weather, time; the electric light was too dim.

He walked down the dark street a half block and then walked back and pressed the button beside the door; the door clicked open and he went through the short passageway into the long barroom.

A bartender wiped off the stained wood in front of him, questioned with his eyes.

Doolin said: "Rye."

He glanced idly at the men at the bar, at the tables, at the heavily built bald man who sat on a stool at the far end of the bar. The little bald man was stooped over a wide-spread newspaper.

The bartender put a glass on the bar in front of Doolin, put a flat brightly labeled flask beside it.

Doolin said: "Seen Martinelli tonight?"

The bartender watched Doolin pour his drink, picked up the bottle and put it under the bar, said: "Yeah. He came in a little while ago. He's upstairs."

Doolin nodded, tasted the rye. It wasn't too bad. He finished it and put a quarter on the bar, sauntered towards the door at the back of the room.

The little bald man looked up from his paper.

Doolin said: "Martinelli's expecting me. He's upstairs—ain't he?"

The little man looked at Doolin. He began at his face and went down to his feet and then back up, slowly. "He didn't say anything about you." He spat with the admirable precision of age and confidence into a cuspidor in the corner.

Doolin said: "He forgot." He put his hand on the doorknob.

The little man looked at him, through him, blankly.

Doolin turned the knob and opened the door, went through, closed the door behind him.

The stairs were dimly lighted by a sputtering gas-jet. He went up slowly. There was one door at the top of the first flight; it was dark; there was no light under it, no sound beyond it. Doolin went up another flight very quietly. He put his ear against the steel-sheathed door; he could hear no sound, but a little light filtered through under the door. He doubled up his fist, knocked with the heel of his hand.

Martinelli opened the door. He stood a moment staring questioningly at Doolin and then he glanced over his shoulder, smiled, said: "Come in."

Doolin put his hands in his overcoat pockets, his right hand holding the revolver tightly, went forward into the room.

Martinelli closed the door behind him, slid the heavy bolt.

The room was large, bare; somewhere around thirty-five by forty. It was lighted by a single green-shaded droplight over a very large round table in the center; there were other tables and chairs stacked in the dusk of the corner. There were no windows, no other doors.

Halloran sat in one of the four chairs at the table. He was leaning slightly forward with his elbows on the table, his long waxen hands framing his face. His face was entirely cold, white, expressionless.

Martinelli stood with his back against the door, his hands behind him.

Doolin glanced over his shoulder at Martinelli, looked back at Halloran. His eyebrows were lifted to the wide V, his mouth hung a little open.

Halloran said: "Well, well—this is a surprise."

He moved his eyes to Martinelli, said: "Angelo. Meet Mr. Doolin—my bodyguard..." For an instant his wide thin mouth flickered a fraction of an inch upward; then his face became a blank, white mask again. "Mr. Doolin—Mr. Martinelli..."

Martinelli had silently come up behind Doolin, suddenly thrust his hands into Doolin's pockets, hard, grabbed Doolin's hands. Doolin bent sharply forward. They struggled for possibly half a minute, silently except for the tearing sound of their breath; then Martinelli brought his knee up suddenly, savagely; Doolin groaned, sank to his knees, the nickel-plated revolver clattered to the floor, slid halfway across the room.

Martinelli darted after it.

Halloran had not appeared to move. He said: "Wait a minute, baby..." The blunt Luger that Doolin had experienced in the afternoon glittered on the table between his two hands.

Martinelli made an impatient gesture, stooped to pick up Doolin's gun.

"Wait a minute, baby." Halloran's voice was like a cold swift scythe.

Martinelli stood up very straight.

Doolin got to his feet slowly. He bent over and held the middle of his body, rolled his head toward Martinelli, his eyes narrow, malevolent. He said very quietly, as if to himself: "Dirty son of a bitch—dirty, dirty son of a bitch!"

Martinelli grinned, stood very straight. His hands,

cupped close to his thighs, trembled rigidly.

Halloran said slowly: "Don't do it, baby. I'll shoot both your eyes out before you get that shiv of yours into the air—and never touch your nose."

Martinelli looked like a clothing store dummy. He was balanced on the balls of his feet, his hands trembling at his sides; his grin artificial, empty.

Doolin laughed suddenly. He stood up straight and looked at Martinelli and laughed.

Halloran moved his eyes to Doolin, smiled faintly. He said: "Gentlemen—sit down." Martinelli tottered forward, sank into one of the chairs. Halloran said: "Put your hands on the table, please." Martinelli obediently put his hands on the table. The empty grin seemed to have congealed on his face.

Halloran turned his eyes towards Doolin. Doolin smiled, walked gingerly to the other chair and sat down.

Halloran said: "Now..." He put one hand up to his face; the other held the Luger loosely on the table.

Doolin cleared his throat, said: "What's it all about, Mr. Halloran?"

Martinelli laughed suddenly. The empty grin exploded into loud high-pitched mirth. "What's it all about! Dear God—what's it all about!..."

Halloran was watching Doolin, his shadowed sunken eyes half closed.

Martinelli leaned forward, lifted his hands and pointed two fingers at Doolin. "Listen—wise guy... You've got minutes to live—if you're lucky. That's what it's all about!" Doolin regarded Martinelli with faint amusement. Martinelli laughed again. He moved his hand slowly until the two fingers pointed at Halloran. "He killed Coleman," he said. "He shot Coleman an' I drove the car. An' he killed Winfield himself. An' his outfit killed Riccio an' Conroy..."

Doolin glanced at Halloran, turned back to smile dimly,

dumbly at Martinelli.

"He propositioned me into killing the dance-hall dame," Martinelli went on—"an' now he's going to kill you an' me..."

Doolin grinned broadly but it was all done with his mouth. He didn't look like he felt it very much. He looked at Halloran. Halloran's face was white and immovable as plaster.

"Listen—wise-guy!" Martinelli leaned forward, moved his hand back to point at Doolin. He was suddenly very intense; his dark eyes burned into Doolin's. "I came out here for Riccio to make connections to peddle M—a lot of it—an' I met Mr. Halloran." Martinelli moved his head an eighth of an inch towards Halloran. "Mr. Halloran runs the drug racket out here—did you know that?"

Doolin glanced swiftly at Halloran, looked back at Martinelli's tense face.

"Mr. Halloran aced me into double-crossing Frankie Riccio an' Conroy," Martinelli went on. "Mr. Halloran's men rubbed Riccio an' Conroy, an' would've taken care of me if Riccio hadn't almost beat 'em to it..."

Halloran said coldly, amusedly: "Oh—come, come, Angelo..."

Martinelli did not look at Halloran. He said: "I met Riccio an' Conroy at the train that night an' took them to that joint in Culver City to talk business to Mr. Halloran—only I didn't know the kind of business Mr. Halloran was going to talk..."

"Is it quite necessary to go into all this?" Halloran spoke sidewise to Martinelli, smiled at Doolin. It was his first definite change of expression since Doolin had come into the room.

Martinelli said: "Yes," emphatically. He scowled at Halloran, his eyes thin black slits. "Bright-boy here"—he indicated Doolin with his hand—"wants to know what it's all about. I'd like to have somebody know—besides me. One of us might leave here alive—if I get this all out of my system it's a cinch it won't be Bright-boy."

Halloran's smile was very cheerful. He said: "Go on."

"One of the men the Law picked up for the Hotspot shooting was a good guess—he's on Mr. Halloran's payroll," Martinelli went on. He was accenting the "Mr." a little unnecessarily, a little too much. "When I got out of the hospital Mr. Halloran suggested we clean things up—move Coleman an' Decker an' Winfield—anybody who might identify his man or testify that Riccio shot me—out of the way. He hated Winfield anyway, for beating his time with the Darmond gal—an' he hated her..."

Halloran was beaming at Doolin, his hand tight and steady on the Luger. Doolin thought about the distance across the big table to Halloran, the distance to the light.

Martinelli was leaning forward, talking swiftly, eagerly: "I brought eighty-five grand worth of morphine out with me, an' I turned it over to his nibs here when we threw in together. I ain't had a nickel out of it. That's the reason I went for all this finagling—I wanted my dough. I was supposed to get it tonight, but I found out about ten minutes ago I ain't going to get it at all..."

Martinelli smiled at Halloran, finished: "Mr. Halloran says it was hi-jacked." He stood up slowly.

Halloran asked: "All through, baby?"

Martinelli was standing very stiff and straight, his hands cupped at his sides.

Doolin ducked suddenly, exerted all his strength to upset the table. For a moment he was protected by the edge, could see neither Martinelli nor Halloran; then the big round table-top slid off its metal base, crashed to the floor.

Halloran was holding Martinelli very much in the way a great ape would hold a smaller animal. One long arm was out stiff, the long white hand at Martinelli's throat, almost encircling it. Halloran's other hand held Martinelli's wrist, waved it back and forth slowly. The blade of a short curved knife glistened in Martinelli's hand. Except for the slow waving of their two hands they were as if frozen, entirely still. There was nothing human in their position, nothing human in their faces.

Doolin felt in that instant that Halloran was not human. He was mad, insane; but it was not the madness of a man, it was the cold murderous lust of an animal.

The Luger and Doolin's revolver were on the floor near their feet. Doolin circled until he was behind Halloran, moved slowly towards them.

As he dived for one of the guns Halloran swung Martinelli around swiftly, kicked viciously at Doolin's head. He missed once, but the second caught Doolin's hand as it closed over the Luger, sent the Luger spinning to a corner.

As Doolin half rose, Halloran's long leg lashed out again, his heavy shoe struck the side of Doolin's head. Doolin grunted, fell sidewise to the floor.

Doolin lay on his back and the room went around him. Later, in remembering what followed, it was like short strips of motion-picture film, separated by strips of darkness.

Halloran backed Martinelli slowly to the wall. It was as if they were performing some strange ritualistic dance; their steps were measured; Halloran's face was composed, his expression almost tender. Martinelli's face was darkening from the pressure on his throat. Halloran waved the hand holding the knife slowly back and forth.

The next time the darkness in Doolin's head cleared, they were against the wall, his head high, at a curious twisted angle above Halloran's white relentless hand, his face purpling. Halloran's other hand had slipped down over Martinelli's chest.

Martinelli's eyes bulged. His face was the face of a man who saw death coming, and was afraid. Doolin could no longer see Halloran's face. He watched the knife near Martinelli's chest, slowly.

Martinelli, some way, made a high piercing sound in his throat as the knife went into him. And again as Halloran withdrew the knife, pressed it in again slowly. Halloran did not stab mercifully on the left side, but on the right, puncturing the lung again and again, slowly.

Doolin rolled over on his side. The revolver lay on the floor midway between him and Halloran. He shook his head sharply, crawled towards it.

Halloran suddenly released Martinelli, stepped back a pace. Martinelli's knees buckled, he sank slowly down, sat on the floor with his back against the wall, his legs out straight. He sucked in air in great rattling gasps, held both hands tightly against his chest, tightly against the shaft of the knife.

He lifted his head and there was blood on his mouth. He laughed; and Doolin forgot the gun, stopped, stared fascinated at Martinelli. Martinelli laughed and the sound was as if everything inside him was breaking. His head rolled back and he grinned upward with glazing eyes at Halloran, held his hands tightly against his chest, spoke:

"Tell Lola we can't go away now..." He paused, sucked in air. "She's waiting for me... Tell her Angelo sends his regrets..." His voice was thick, high-pitched, but his words were telling, deadly, took deadly effect.

Halloran seemed to grow taller, his great shoulders seemed to widen as Doolin watched.

Martinelli laughed again. He said: "So long—sucker..."

Halloran kicked him savagely in the chest. He drew his long leg back and as Martinelli slumped sidewise he kicked his face, hard, repeatedly.

Doolin scrambled swiftly, forward, picked up the revolver, raised it.

Halloran turned slowly.

Doolin held the revolver unsteadily in his right hand, aimed at Halloran's chest while the muzzle described little circles, pulled the trigger twice.

Halloran came towards him. Doolin made a harsh sound in his throat, scuttled backwards a few feet, held the revolver out limply and fired again.

Halloran's face was cold, impassive; his eyes were great black holes in his skull. He came towards Doolin slowly.

Doolin tried to say something but the words stuck in his throat, and then Halloran was above him and there was a terribly crushing weight against Doolin's forehead and it was suddenly dark.

Slowly, Doolin came to, lay a little while with his eyes closed. There were sharp twisting wires of pain in his head; he put his hand up, took it away wet, sticky.

He opened his eyes. It was entirely dark, a cold penetrating darkness; entirely still.

Suddenly he laughed, a curious hysterical sound in the quiet room; and as suddenly, panic seized him. He struggled to his knees, almost fell down again as the pain in his head throbbed to the swift movement. He got to his feet slowly, fumbled in his pockets and found a match, lighted it.

Martinelli's body was slumped in the angle of floor and wall at one side of the room. There was no one else. Doolin's revolver shone dimly on the floor in the flare of the match. The door was ajar.

Doolin lighted another match and picked up his revolver, his hat. He took out a handkerchief and wiped his face and the handkerchief was wet, dark. He walked, unsteadily to the door, down the dark stairs.

One faint globe burned above the deserted bar. Doolin felt his way along the wall, lifted the heavy bar across the outside door and went out, closed the door behind him. It was raining lightly, a thin cold drizzle.

He took air into his lungs in great gulps, soaked the

handkerchief in a little puddle of rainwater and tried to clean his face. Then he went down the dark street swiftly towards Broadway.

The druggist looked at him through thick spectacles, gestured towards the back of the store.

Doolin said: "Fix me up some peroxide an' bandages an' stuff—I had an accident." He went back to the telephone booth, found the number of the Fontenoy, called it, asked for Mrs. Sare.

The operator said Mrs. Sare didn't answer.

Doolin hung up and went out and cleaned the blood from his face in front of a mirror. A little girl stared at him wide-eyed from the soda fountain; the druggist said: "Automobile...?"

Doolin nodded.

The druggist asked: "How much bandage do you want?"

Doolin said: "Let it go—it's not as bad as I thought it was."

He put his hat on the back of his head and went out and got into a cab, said: "Fontenoy Apartments—Hollywood. An' make it snappy."

Lola Sare's voice said: "Yes," with rising inflection.

Doolin opened the door, went in.

She was sitting in a long low chair beneath a crimson-shaded bridge lamp. It was the only light in the room. Her arms were bare, straight on the arms of the chair, her hands hanging limply downward. Her dark head was against the back of the chair and her face was taut, her eyes wide, vacant.

Doolin took off his hat, said: "Why the hell don't you answer your phone?"

She did not speak, nor move.

"You'd better get out of here—quick." Doolin went

towards her. "Halloran killed Martinelli—an' Martinelli opened up about you before he died. Halloran will be coming to see you..."

Her blank eyes moved slowly from his face to some place in the dusk behind him. He followed her gaze, turned slowly.

Halloran was standing against the wall near the door. The door had covered him when Doolin entered; he put out one hand and pushed it gently, it swung closed with a sharp dick.

As Doolin's eyes became used to the dimness of the room he saw Halloran clearly. He was leaning against the wall and the right shoulder and breast of his light gray suit was dark, sodden. He held the short blunt Luger in his left hand.

He said: "You're a little late..."

The Luger roared.

Lola Sare put her hands up to the middle of her breast, low; her head came forward slowly. She started to get up and the Luger leaped in Halloran's hand, roared again.

At the same instant Doolin shot, holding the revolver low. The two explosions were simultaneous, thundered in the dark and narrow room.

Halloran fell as a tree falls; slowly, stiffly, his arm stiff at his sides; crashed to the floor.

Doolin dropped the revolver, walked unsteadily towards Lola Sare. His knees buckled suddenly and he sank forward, down.

There was someone pounding at the door.

Doolin finished dabbing iodine on his head, washed his hands and went into the little living room of his apartment. A first dull streak of morning grayed the windows. He pulled down the shades and went into the kitchenette, lighted the gas under the percolator.

When the coffee was hot he poured a cup, dropped four lumps of sugar into it absently, carried it into the living room. He sat down on the davenport and put the coffee on an end-table, picked up the phone and dialed a number.

He said: "Hello, Grace? Is Mollie there?..." He listened a moment, went on: "Oh—I thought she might be there. Sorry I woke you up..." He hung up, sipped his steaming coffee.

After a few minutes he picked up the phone, dialed again, said. "Listen, Grace—please put Mollie on... Aw nuts! I know she's there—please make her talk to me..."

Then he smiled, waited a moment, said: "Hello darling... Listen—please come on home—will you?... Aw listen, Honey—I did what you said—everything's all right... Uh-huh... Halloran's dead—an' Martinelli... Uh-huh... The Sare dame is shot up pretty bad, but not too much to give evidence an' clean it all up... Uh-huh..."

He reached over and picked up the cup and took a long drink of coffee, smiled into the phone, said: "Sure—I'm all right—I got a little scratch on my head but I'm all right... Sure. .—Sure—we were right... All right, Honey—I'll be waiting for you. Hurry up... G'bye..."

He hung up, curved his mouth to a wide grin, finished his coffee, lit a cigarette and waited.

Pigeon Blood

THE WOMAN WAS bent far forward over the steering-wheel of the open roadster. Her eyes, narrowed to long black-fringed slits, moved regularly down and up, from the glistening road ahead, to the small rear-view mirror above the windshield. The two circles of white light in the mirror grew steadily larger. She pressed the throttle slowly, steadily downward; there was no sound but the roar of the wind and the deep purr of the powerful engine.

There was a sudden sharp crack; a little frosted circle appeared on the windshield. The woman pressed the throttle to the floor. She was pale; her eyes were suddenly large and dark and afraid, her lips were pressed tightly together. The tires screeched on the wet pavement as the car roared around a long, shallow curve. The headlights of the pursuing car grew larger.

The second and third shots were wild, or buried themselves harmlessly in the body of the car; the fourth struck the left rear tire and the car swerved crazily, skidded halfway across the road. Very suddenly there was bright yellow light right ahead, at the side of the road. The woman jammed on the brakes, jerked the wheel hard over; the tires slid, screamed raggedly over the gravel in front of the gas station, the car stopped. The other car went by at seventy-five miles an hour. One last shot thudded into the back of the seat beside the woman and then the other car had disappeared into the darkness.

Two men ran out of the gas station. Another man stood in the doorway. The woman was leaning back straight in the seat and her eyes were very wide; she was breathing hard, unevenly.

One of the men put his hand on her shoulder, asked: "Are you all right, lady?"

She nodded.

The other man asked: "Hold-ups?" He was a short, middle-aged man and his eyes were bright, interested.

The woman opened her bag and took out a cigarette. She said shakily: "I guess so." She pulled out the dashboard lighter, waited until it glowed red and held it to her cigarette.

The younger man was inspecting the back of the car. He said: "They punctured the tank. It's a good thing you stopped—you couldn't have gone much farther."

"Yes—I guess it's a very good thing I stopped," she said, mechanically. She took a deep drag of her cigarette.

The other man said: "That's the third hold-up out here this week."

The woman spoke to the younger man. "Can you get me a cab?"

He said: "Sure." Then he knelt beside the blown-out tire, said: "Look, Ed—they almost cut it in two."

The man in the doorway called to her: "You want a cab, lady?"

She smiled, nodded, and the man disappeared into the gas station; he came back to the doorway in a minute, over to the car. "There'll be a cab here in a little while, lady," he said.

She thanked him.

"This is one of the worst stretches of road on Long Island—for highwaymen." He leaned on the door of the car. "Did they try to nudge you off the road—or did they just start shooting?"

"They just started shooting."

He said: "We got a repair service here—do you want us to fix up your car?"

She nodded. "How long will it take?"

"Couple days. We'll have to get a new windshield from the branch factory in Queens—an' take off that tank..."

She took a card out of her bag and gave it to him, said: "Call me up when it's finished."

After a little while, a cab came out of the darkness of a side street, turned into the station. The woman got out of the car and went over to the cab, spoke to the driver: "Do you know any shortcuts into Manhattan? Somebody tried to hold me up on the main road a little while ago, and maybe they're still laying for me. I don't want any more of it—I want to go home." She was very emphatic.

The driver was a big red-faced Irishman. He grinned, said: "Lady—I know a million of 'em. You'll be as safe with me as you'd be in your own home."

She raised her hand in a gesture of farewell to the three men around her car and got into the cab. After the cab had disappeared, the man to whom she had given the card took it out of his pocket and squinted at it, read aloud: "Mrs. Dale Hanan—Five-eighty Park Avenue."

The short, middle-aged man bobbed his head knowingly. "Sure," he said—"I knew she was class. She's Hanan's wife—the millionaire. Made his dough in oil—Oklahoma. His chauffeur told me how he got his start—didn't have a shoestring or a place to put it, so he shot off his big toe and collected ten grand on an accident policy—grubstake on his first well. Bright boy. He's got a big estate down at Roslyn."

The man with the card nodded. He said: "That's swell. We can soak him plenty." He put the card back into his pocket.

When the cab stopped near the corner of Sixty-third and Park Avenue the woman got out, paid the driver and hurried into the apartment house. In her apartment, she put in a long-distance call to Roslyn, Long Island; when the connection had been made, she said: "Dale—it's in the open, now. I was followed, driving back to town—shot at—the car was nearly wrecked... I don't know what to do. Even if I call Crandall, now, and tell him I won't go through with it—won't go to the police—he'll probably have me killed, just to make sure... Yes, I'm going to stay in—I'm scared... All right, dear. 'Bye."

She hung up, went to a wide center table and poured whiskey into a tall glass, sat down and stared vacantly at the glass—her hand was shaking a little. She smiled suddenly, crookedly, lifted the glass to her mouth and drained it. Then she put the glass on the floor and leaned back and glanced at the tiny watch at her wrist. It was ten minutes after nine.

At a few minutes after ten a black Packard town-car stopped in front of a narrow building of gray stone on East Fifty-fourth Street; a tall man got out, crossed the sidewalk and rang the bell. The car went on. When the door swung open, the tall man went into a long, brightly lighted hallway, gave his hat and stick to the checkroom attendant, went swiftly up two flights of narrow stairs to the third floor. He glanced around the big, crowded room, then crossed to one corner near a window on the Fifty-fourth Street side and sat down at a small table, smiled wanly at the man across from him, said: "Mister Druse, I believe."

The other man was about fifty, well set up, well-groomed in the way of good living. His thick gray hair was combed sharply, evenly back. He lowered his folded newspaper to the table, stared thoughtfully at the tall man.

He said: "Mister Hanan," and his voice was very deep, metallic.

The tall man nodded shortly, leaned back and folded his arms across his narrow chest. He was ageless, perhaps thirty-five, forty-five; his thin, colorless hair was close-clipped, his long, bony face deeply tanned, a sharp and angular setting for large seal-brown eyes. His mouth was curved, mobile.

He asked: "Do you know Jeffrey Crandall?"

Druse regarded him evenly, expressionlessly for a moment, raised his head and beckoned a waiter. Hanan ordered a whiskey sour.

Druse said: "I know Mister Crandall casually. Why?"

"A little more than an hour ago Crandall, or Crandall's men, tried to murder Mrs. Hanan, as she was driving back from my place at Roslyn." Hanan leaned forward: his eyes were wide, worried.

The waiter served Hanan's whiskey sour, set a small bottle of Perrier and a small glass on the table in front of Druse.

Druse poured the water into the glass slowly. "So what?"

Hanan tasted his drink. He said: "This is not a matter for the police, Mister Druse. I understand that you interest yourself in things of this nature, so I took the liberty of calling you and making this appointment. Is that right?" He was nervous, obviously ill at ease.

Druse shrugged. "What nature? I don't know what you're talking about."

"I'm sorry—I guess I'm a little upset." Hanan smiled.

"What I mean is that I can rely on your discretion?"

Druse frowned. "I think so," he said slowly. He drank half of the Perrier, squinted down at the glass as if it tasted very badly.

Hanan smiled vacantly. "You do not know Mrs. Hanan?"

Druse shook his head slowly, turned his glass around

and around on the table.

"We have been living apart for several years," Hanan went on. "We are still very fond of one another, we are very good friends, but we do not get along—together. Do you understand?"

Druse nodded.

Hanan sipped his drink, went on swiftly: "Catherine has—has always had—a decided weakness for gambling. She went through most of her own inheritance—a considerable inheritance—before we were married. Since our separation she has lost somewhere in the neighborhood of a hundred and fifteen thousand dollars. I have, of course, taken care of her debts." Hanan coughed slightly. "Early this evening she called me at Roslyn, said she had to see me immediately—that it was very important. I offered to come into town but she said she'd rather come out. She came out about seven."

Hanan paused, closed his eyes and rubbed two fingers of one hand slowly up and down his forehead. "She's in a very bad jam with Crandall." He opened his eyes and put his hand down on the table.

Druse finished his Perrier, put down the glass and regarded Hanan attentively.

"About three weeks ago," Hanan went on, "Catherine's debt to Crandall amounted to sixty-eight thousand dollars—she had been playing very heavily under the usual gambler's delusion of getting even. She was afraid to come to me—she knew I'd taken several bad beatings on the market—she kept putting it off and trying to make good her losses, until Crandall demanded the money. She told him she couldn't pay—together, they hatched out a scheme to get it. Catherine had a set of rubies—pigeon blood—been in her family five or six generations. They're worth, perhaps, a hundred and seventy-five thousand—her father insured them for a hundred and thirty-five, forty years ago and the insurance premiums have always been paid..."

Hanan finished his whiskey sour, leaned back in his chair.

Druse said: "I assume the idea was that the rubies disappear; that Mrs. Hanan claim the insurance, pay off Crandall, have sixty-seven thousand left and live happily forever after."

Hanan coughed; his face was faintly flushed. "Exactly."

"I assume further," Druse went on, "that the insurance company did not question the integrity of the claim; that they paid, and that Mrs. Hanan, in turn, paid Crandall."

Hanan nodded. He took a tortoise-shell case out of his pocket, offered Druse a cigarette.

Druse shook his head, asked: "Are the insurance company detectives warm—are they making Crandall or whoever he had do the actual job, uncomfortable?"

"No. The theft was well engineered. I don't think Crandall is worrying about that." Hanan lighted a cigarette. "But Catherine wanted her rubies back—as had, of course, been agreed upon." He leaned forward, put his elbows on the table. "Crandall returned paste imitations to her—she only discovered they weren't genuine a few days ago."

Druse smiled, said slowly: "In that case, I should think it was Crandall who was in a jam with Mrs. Hanan, instead of Mrs. Hanan who was in a jam with Crandall."

Hanan wagged his long chin back and forth. "This is New York. Men like Crandall do as they please. Catherine went to him and he laughed at her; said the rubies he had returned were the rubies that had been stolen. She had no recourse, other than to admit her complicity in defrauding the insurance company. That's the trouble—she threatened to do exactly that."

Druse widened his eyes, stared at Hanan.

"Catherine is a very impulsive woman," Hanan went on. "She was so angry at losing the rubies and being made so completely a fool, that she threatened Crandall. She told him that if the rubies were not returned within three days she would tell what he had done; that he had stolen the rubies—take her chances on her part in it coming out. Of course she wouldn't do it, but she was desperate and she thought that was her only chance of scaring Crandall into returning the rubies—and she made him believe it. Since she talked to him, Wednesday, she has been followed. Tomorrow is Saturday, the third day. Tonight, driving back to town, she was followed, shot at—almost killed."

"Has she tried to get in touch with Crandall again?"

Hanan shook his head. "She's been stubbornly waiting for him to give the rubies back—until this business tonight. Now she's frightened—says it wouldn't do any good for her to talk to Crandall now because he wouldn't believe her—and it's too easy for him to put her out of the way."

Druse beckoned the waiter, asked him to bring the check. "Where is she now?"

"At her apartment—Sixty-third and Park."

"What do you intend doing about it?"

Hanan shrugged. "That's what I came to you for. I don't know what to do. I've heard of you and your work from friends..."

Druse hesitated, said slowly: "I must make my position clear."

Hanan nodded, lighted a fresh cigarette.

"I am one of the few people left," Druse went on, "who actually believes that honesty is the best policy. Honesty is my business—I am primarily a business man—I've made it pay."

Hanan smiled broadly.

Druse leaned forward. "I am not a fixer," he said. "My acquaintance is wide and varied—I am fortunate in being able to wield certain influences. But above all I seek to further justice—I mean real justice as opposed to book justice—I was on the Bench for many years and I realize the distinction keenly." His big face wrinkled to an expansive grin. “And I get paid for it—well paid.”

Hanan said: “Does my case interest you?”

“It does.”

“Will five thousand be satisfactory—as a retaining fee?”

Druse moved his broad shoulders in something like a shrug. “You value the rubies at a hundred and seventy-five thousand,” he said. “I am undertaking to get the rubies back, and protect Mrs. Hanan’s life.” He stared at Hanan intently. “What value do you put on Mrs. Hanan’s life?”

Hanan frowned self-consciously, twisted his mouth down at the corners. “That is, of course, impossible to–”

“Say another hundred and seventy-five.” Druse smiled easily. “That makes three hundred and fifty thousand. I work on a ten per cent basis—thirty-five thousand—one-third in advance.” He leaned back, still smiling easily. “Ten thousand will be sufficient as a retainer.”

Hanan was still frowning self-consciously. He said: “Done,” took a checkbook and fountain pen out of his pocket.

Druse went on: “If I fail in either purpose, I shall, of course, return your check.”

Hanan bobbed his head, made out the check in a minute, illegible scrawl and handed it across the table. Druse paid for the drinks, jotted down Hanan’s telephone number and the address of Mrs. Hanan’s apartment. They got up and went downstairs and out of the place; Druse told Hanan he would call him within an hour, got into a cab. Hanan watched the cab disappear in east-bound traffic, lighted a cigarette nervously and walked towards Madison Avenue.

Druse said: “Tell her I’ve come from Mister Hanan.”

The telephone operator spoke into the transmitter, turned to Druse. “You may go up—Apartment Three D.”

When, in answer to a drawled, “Come in,” he pushed open the door and went into the apartment, Catherine

Hanan was standing near the center table, with one hand on the table to steady herself, the other in the pocket of her long blue robe. She was beautiful in the mature way that women who have lived too hard, too swiftly, are sometimes beautiful. She was very dark; her eyes were large, liquid, black and dominated her rather small, sharply sculptured face. Her mouth was large, deeply red, not particularly strong.

Druse bowed slightly, said: "How do you do."

She smiled, and her eyes were heavy, nearly closed. "Swell—and you?"

He came slowly into the room, put his hat on the table, asked: "May we sit down?"

"Sure." She jerked her head towards a chair, stayed where she was.

Druse said: "You're drunk."

"Right."

He smiled, sighed gently. "A commendable condition. I regret exceedingly that my stomach does not permit it." He glanced casually about the room. In the comparative darkness of a corner, near a heavily draped window, there was a man lying on his back on the floor. His arms were stretched out and back, and his legs were bent under him in a curious broken way, and there was blood on his face.

Druse raised his thick white eyebrows, spoke without looking at Mrs. Hanan: "Is he drunk, too?"

She laughed shortly. "Uh-huh—in a different way." She nodded towards a golf-stick on the floor near the man. "He had a little too much niblick."

"Friend of yours?"

She said: "I rather doubt it. He came in from the fire-escape with a gun in his hand. I happened to see him before he saw me."

"Where's the gun?"

"I've got it." She drew a small black automatic half out

of the pocket of her robe.

Druse went over and knelt beside the man, picked up one of his hands. He said slowly: "This man is decidedly dead."

Mrs. Hanan stood, staring silently at the man on the floor for perhaps thirty seconds. Her face was white, blank. Then she walked unsteadily to a desk against one wall and picked up a whiskey bottle, poured a stiff drink. She said: "I know it." Her voice was choked, almost a whisper. She drank the whiskey, turned and leaned against the desk, stared at Druse with wide unseeing eyes. "So what?"

"So pull yourself together, and forget about it—we've got more important things to think about for a little while." Druse stood up. "How long ago?..."

She shuddered. "About a half-hour—I didn't know what to do..."

"Have you tried to reach Crandall? I mean before this happened—right after you came in tonight?"

"Yes—I couldn't get him."

Druse went to a chair and sat down. He said: "Mister Hanan has turned this case over to me. Won't you sit down, and answer a few questions?..."

She sank into a low chair near the desk. "Are you a detective?" Her voice was still very low, strained.

Druse smiled. "I'm an attorney—a sort of extra-legal attorney." He regarded her thoughtfully. "If we can get your rubies back, and assure your safety, and"—he coughed slightly—"induce Mister Hanan to reimburse the insurance company, you will be entirely satisfied, will you not?"

She nodded, started to speak.

Druse interrupted her: "Are the rubies themselves—I mean intrinsically, as stones—awfully important to you? Or was this grandstand play of yours—this business of threatening Crandall—motivated by rather less tangible factors-such as self-respect, things like that?"

She smiled faintly, nodded. "God knows how I happen to have any self-respect left—I've been an awful ass—but I have. It was the idea of being made such a fool—after I've lost over a hundred thousand dollars to Crandall—that made me do it."

Druse smiled. "The rubies themselves," he said—"I mean the rubies as stones—entirely apart from any extraneous consideration such as self-respect—would more seriously concern Mister Hanan, would they not?"

She said: "Sure. He's always been crazy about stones."

Druse scratched the tip of his long nose pensively. His eyes were wide and vacant, his thick lips compressed to a long downward curved line. "You are sure you were followed when you left Crandall's Wednesday?"

"As sure as one can be without actually knowing—it was more of a followed feeling than anything else. After the idea was planted I could have sworn I saw a dozen men, of course."

He said: "Have you ever had that feeling before—I mean before you threatened Crandall?"

"No."

"It may have been simply imagination, because you expected to be followed—there was reason for you to be followed?"

She nodded. "But it's a cinch it wasn't imagination this evening."

Druse was leaning forward, his elbows on his knees. He looked intently at her, said very seriously: "I'm going to get your rubies back, and I can assure you of your safety—and I think I can promise that the matter of reimbursement to the insurance company will be taken care of. I didn't speak to Mister Hanan about that, but I'm sure he'll see the justice of it."

She smiled faintly.

Druse went on: "I promise you these things—and in

return I want you to do exactly as I tell you until tomorrow morning."

Her smile melted to a quick, rather drunken, laugh. "Do I have to poison any babies?" She stood up, poured a drink.

Druse said: "That's one of the things I don't want you to do."

She picked up the glass, frowned at him with mock seriousness. "You're a moralist," she said. "That's one of the things I will do."

He shrugged slightly. "I shall have some very important, very delicate work for you a little later in the evening. I thought it might be best."

She looked at him, half smiling, a little while, and then she laughed and put down the glass and went into the bathroom. He leaned back comfortably in the chair and stared at the ceiling; his hands were on the arms of the chair and he ran imaginary scales with his big blunt fingers.

She came back into the room in a little while, dressed, drawing on gloves. She gestured with her head towards the man on the floor, and for a moment her more or less alcoholic poise forsook her—she shuddered again—her face was white, twisted.

Druse stood up, said: "He'll have to stay where he is for a little while." He went to the heavily draped window, to the fire-escape, moved the drape aside and locked the window. "How many doors are there to the apartment?"

"Two." She was standing near the table. She took the black automatic from a pocket of her suit, took up a gray suede bag from the table and put the automatic into it.

He watched her without expression. "How many keys?"

"Two." She smiled, took two keys out of the bag and held them up. "The only other key is the pass-key—the manager's."

He said: "That's fine," went to the table and picked up his hat and put it on. They went out into the hall and closed and locked the door. "Is there a side entrance to the building?"

She nodded.

"Let's go out that way."

She led the way down the corridor, down three flights of stairs to a door leading to Sixty-third Street. They went out and walked over Sixty-third to Lexington and got into a cab; he told the driver to take them to the corner of Fortieth and Madison, leaned back and looked out the window. "How long have you and Mister Hanan been divorced?"

She was quick to answer: "Did he say we were divorced?"

"No." Druse turned to her slowly, smiled slowly.

"Then what makes you think we are?"

"I don't. I just wanted to be sure."

"We are not." She was very emphatic.

He waited, without speaking.

She glanced at him sidewise and saw that he expected her to go on. She laughed softly. "He wants a divorce. He asked me to divorce him several months ago." She sighed, moved her hands nervously on her lap. "That's another of the things I'm not very proud of—I wouldn't do it. I don't quite know why—we were never in love—we haven't been married, really, for a long time—but I've waited, hoping we might be able to make something out of it..."

Druse said quietly: "I think I understand—I'm sorry I had to ask you about that."

She did not answer.

In a little while the cab stopped; they got out and Druse paid the driver and they cut diagonally across the street, entered an office building halfway down the block. Druse spoke familiarly to the Negro elevator boy; they got off at the forty-fifth floor and went up two flights of narrow stairs, through a heavy steel fire-door to a narrow bridge and across it to a rambling two-story penthouse that covered all one side of the roof. Druse rang the bell and a thin-faced Filipino boy let them in.

Druse led the way into a very big, high-ceilinged room that ran the length and almost the width of the house. It was beautifully and brightly furnished, opened on one side onto a wide terrace. They went through to the terrace; there were steamer-chairs there and canvas swings and low round tables, a great many potted plants and small trees. The tiled floor was partially covered with strips of coco-matting. There was a very wide, vividly striped awning stretched across all one side. At the far side, where the light from the living room faded into darkness, the floor came to an abrupt end—there was no railing or parapet—the nearest building of the same height was several blocks away.

Mrs. Hanan sat down and stared at the twinkling distant lights of Upper Manhattan. The roar of the city came up to them faintly, like surf very far away. She said: "It is very beautiful."

"I am glad you find it so." Druse went to the edge, glanced down. "I have never put a railing here," he said, "because I am interested in Death. Whenever I'm depressed I look at my jumping-off place, only a few feet away, and am reminded that life is very sweet." He stared at the edge, stroked the side of his jaw with his fingers. "Nothing to climb over, no windows to raise—just walk."

She smiled wryly. "A moralist—and morbid. Did you bring me here to suggest a suicide pact?"

"I brought you here to sit still and be decorative."

"And you?"

"I'm going hunting." Druse went over and stood frowning down at her. "I'll try not to be long. The boy will bring you anything you want—even good whiskey, if you can't get along without it. The view will grow on you—you'll find one of the finest collections of books on satanism, demonology, witchcraft, in the world inside." He gestured with his head and eyes. "Don't telephone anyone—and, above all, stay here, even if I'm late."

She nodded vaguely.

He went to the wide doors that led into the living room, turned, said: "One thing more—who are Mister Hanan's attorneys?"

She looked at him curiously. "Mahlon and Stiles."

He raised one hand in salute. "So long."

She smiled, said: "So long—good hunting."

He went into the living room and talked to the Filipino boy a minute, went out.

In the drugstore across the street from the entrance to the building, he went into a telephone booth, called the number Hanan had given him. When Hanan answered, he said: "I have very bad news. We were too late. When I reached Mrs. Hanan's apartment, she did not answer the phone—I bribed my way in and found her—found her dead... I'm terribly sorry, old man—you've got to take it standing up... Yes—strangled."

Druse smiled grimly to himself. "No, I haven't informed the police—I want things left as they are for the present—I'm going to see Crandall and I have a way of working it so he won't have a single out. I'm going to pin it on him so that it will stay pinned—and I'm going to get the rubies back, too... I know they don't mean much to you now, but the least I can do is get them back—and see that Crandall is stuck so he can't wriggle out of it." He said the last very emphatically, was silent a little while, except for an occasionally interjected "Yes" or "No."

Finally he asked: "Can you be in around three-thirty or four?... I'll want to get in touch with you then... Right, I know how you must feel—I'm terribly sorry... Right. Good-bye." He hung up and went out into Fortieth Street.

Jeffrey Crandall was a medium-sized man with a close-cropped mustache, wide-set greenish gray eyes. He was conservatively dressed, looked very much like a prosperous real estate man, or broker.

He said: "Long time no see."

Druse nodded abstractedly. He was sitting in a deep red leather chair in Crandall's very modern office, adjoining the large room in a midtown apartment building that was Crandall's "Place" for the moment. He raised his head and looked attentively at the pictures on the walls, one after the other.

"Anything special?" Crandall lighted a short stub of green cigar.

Druse said: "Very special," over his shoulder. He came to the last picture, a very ordinary Degas pastel, shook his head slightly, disapprovingly, and turned back to Crandall. He took a short-barrelled derringer out of his inside coat-pocket, held it on the arm of his chair, the muzzle focused steadily on Crandall's chest.

Crandall's eyes widened slowly; his mouth hung a little open. He put one hand up very slowly and took the stub of a cigar out of his mouth.

Druse repeated: "Very special." His full lips were curved to a thin, cold smile.

Crandall stared at the gun. He spoke as if making a tremendous effort to frame his words casually, calmly: "What's it all about?"

"It's all about Mrs. Hanan." Druse tipped his hat to the back of his head. "It's all about you gypping her out of her rubies—and her threatening to take it to the police—and you having her murdered at about a quarter after ten tonight, because you were afraid she'd go through with it."

Crandall's tense face relaxed slowly; he tried very hard to smile. He said: "You're crazy," and there was fear in his eyes, fear in the harsh, hollow sound of his voice.

Druse did not speak. He waited, his cold eyes boring into Crandall's.

Crandall cleared his throat, moved a little forward in his

chair and put his elbows on the wide desk.

"Don't ring." Druse glanced at the little row of ivory push buttons on the desk, shook his head.

Crandall laughed soundlessly as if the thought of ringing had never entered his mind. "In the first place," he said, "I gave her back the stones that were stolen. In the second place, I never believed her gag about telling about it." He leaned back slowly, spoke very slowly and distinctly as confidence came back to him. "In the third place, I couldn't be chump enough to bump her off with that kind of a case against me."

Druse said: "Your third place is the one that interests me. The switched rubies, her threat to tell the story—it all makes a pip of a case against you, doesn't it?"

Crandall nodded slowly.

"That's the reason," Druse went on, "that if I shoot you through the heart right now, I'll get a vote of thanks for avenging the lady you made a sucker of, and finally murdered because you thought she was going to squawk."

All the fear came back into Crandall's face suddenly. He started to speak.

Druse interrupted him, went on: "I'm going to let you have it when you reach for your gun, of course—that'll take care of any technicalities about taking the law into my own hands—anything like that."

Crandall's face was white, drained. He said: "How come I'm elected? What the hell have you got against me?"

Druse shrugged. "You shouldn't jockey ladies into trying to nick insurance companies..."

"It was her idea."

"Then you should have been on the level about the rubies."

Crandall said: "So help me God! I gave her back the stuff I took!" He said it very vehemently, very earnestly.

"How do you know? How do you know the man you had

do the actual job didn't make the switch?"

Crandall leaned forward. "Because I took them. She gave me her key and I went in the side way, while she was out, and took them myself. They were never out of my hands." He took up a lighter from the desk and relighted the stump of cigar with shaking hands. "That's the reason I didn't take her threat seriously. I thought it was some kind of extortion gag she'd doped out to get some of her dough back. She got back the stones I took—and if they weren't genuine they were switched before I took them, or after I gave them back."

Druse stared at him silently for perhaps a minute, finally smiled, said: "Before."

Crandall sucked noisily at his cigar. "Then, if you believe me"—he glanced at the derringer—"what's the point?"

"The point is that if I didn't believe you, you'd be in an awfully bad spot."

Crandall nodded, grinned weakly.

"The point," Druse went on, "is that you're still in an awfully bad spot because no one else will believe you."

Crandall nodded again. He leaned back and took a handkerchief out of his breast pocket and dabbed at his face.

"I know a way out of it." Druse moved his hand, let the derringer hang by the trigger-guard from his forefinger. "Not because I like you particularly, nor because I think you particularly deserve it—but because it's right. I can turn up the man who really murdered her—if we can get back the rubies—the real rubies. And I think I know where they are."

Crandall was leaning far forward, his face very alive and interested.

"I want you to locate the best peterman we can get." Druse spoke in a very low voice, watched Crandall intently. "We've got to open a safe—I think it'll be a safe—out on

Long Island. Nothing very difficult—there'll probably be servants to handle but nothing more serious than that."

Crandall said: "Why can't I do it?" He smiled a little. "I used to be in the box business, you know—before I straightened up and got myself a joint. That's the reason I took the fake rubies myself—not to let anyone else in on it."

Druse said: "That'll be fine."

"When?" Crandall stood up.

Druse put the derringer back in his pocket. "Right now—where's your car?"

Crandall jerked his head towards the street. They went out through the crowded gambling room, downstairs, got into Crandall's car. Crossing Queensborough Bridge Druse glanced at his watch. It was twenty minutes past twelve.

At three thirty-five Druse pushed the bell of the penthouse, after searching, vainly as usual, for his key. The Filipino boy opened the door, said: "It's a very hot night, sir."

Druse threw his hat on a chair, smiled sadly at Mrs. Hanan, who had come into the little entrance-hall. "I've been trying to teach him English for three months," he said, "and all he can say is 'Yes sir,' and 'No, sir,' and tell me about the heat." He turned to the broadly grinning boy. "Yes, Tony, it is a very hot night."

They went through the living room, out onto the terrace. It was cool there, and dim; a little light came out through the wide doors, from the living room.

Mrs. Hanan said: "I'd about given you up."

Druse sat down, sighed wearily. "I've had a very strenuous evening—sorry I'm so late." He looked up at her. "Hungry?"

"Starved."

"Why didn't you have Tony fix you something?"

"I wanted to wait." She had taken off her suit-coat, hat;

in her smartly cut tweed skirt, white mannish shirt, she looked very beautiful.

Druse said: "Supper, or breakfast, or something will be ready in a few minutes—I ordered it for four." He stood up. "Which reminds me—we're having a guest. I must telephone."

He went through the living room, up four broad, shallow steps to the little corner room that he used as an office. He sat down at the broad desk, drew the telephone towards him, dialed a number.

Hanan answered the phone. Druse said: "I want you to come to my place, on top of the Pell Building, at once. It is very important. Ring the bell downstairs—I've told the elevator boy I'm expecting you... I can't tell you over the phone—please come alone, and right away." He hung up and sat staring vacantly at his hands a little while, and then got up and went back to the terrace, sat down.

"What did you do with yourself?"

Mrs. Hanan was lying in one of the low chairs. She laughed nervously. "The radio—tried to improve my Spanish and Tony's English—chewed my fingernails—almost frightened myself to death with one of your damned demon books." She lighted a cigarette. "And you?"

He smiled in the darkness. "I earned thirty-five thousand dollars."

She sat up, said eagerly: "Did you get the rubies?"

He nodded.

"Did Crandall raise much hell?"

"Enough."

She laughed exultantly. "Where are they?"

Druse tapped his pocket, watched her face in the pale orange glow of her cigarette.

She got up, held out her hand. "May I see them?"

Druse said: "Certainly." He took a long flat jewel-case of black velvet out of his inside coat-pocket and handed it to her.

She opened the case and went to the door to the living room, looked at its contents by the light there, said: "They are awfully beautiful, aren't they?"

"They are."

She snapped the case closed, came back and sat down.

Druse said: "I think I'd better take care of them a little while longer."

She leaned forward and put the case on his lap; he took it up and put it back in his pocket. They sat silently, watching the lights in buildings over towards the East River. After awhile the Filipino boy came out and said that they were served.

"Our guest is late." Druse stood up. "I make a rule of never waiting breakfast—anything but breakfast."

They went together through the living room, into the simply furnished dining room. There were three places set at the glittering white and silver table. They sat down and the Filipino boy brought in tall and spindly cocktail glasses of iced fruit; they were just beginning when the doorbell rang. The Filipino boy glanced at Druse, Druse nodded, said: "Ask the gentleman to come in here." The Filipino boy went out and there were voices in the entrance-hall, and then Hanan came into the doorway.

Druse stood up. He said: "You must forgive us for beginning—you are a little late." He raised one hand and gestured towards the empty chair.

Hanan was standing in the doorway with his feet wide apart, his arms stiff at his sides, as if he had been suddenly frozen in that position. He stared at Mrs. Hanan and his eyes were wide, blank—his thin mouth was compressed to a hard, straight line. Very suddenly his right hand went towards his left armpit.

Druse said sharply: "Please sit down." Though he seemed scarcely to have moved, the blunt derringer glittered in his hand.

Mrs. Hanan half rose. She was very pale; her hands were clenched convulsively on the white tablecloth.

Hanan dropped his hand very slowly. He stared at the derringer and twisted his mouth into a terribly forced smile, came slowly forward to the empty chair and sat down.

Druse raised his eyes to the Filipino boy who had followed Hanan into the doorway, said: "Take the gentleman's gun, Tony—and serve his cocktail." He sat down, held the derringer rigidly on the table in front of him.

The Filipino boy went to Hanan, felt gingerly under his coat, drew out a small black automatic and took it to Druse. Then he went out through the swinging-door to the kitchen. Druse put the automatic in his pocket. He turned his eyes to Mrs. Hanan, said: "I'm going to tell you a story. After I've finished, you can both talk all you like—but please don't interrupt."

He smiled with his mouth—the rest of his face remained stonily impassive. His eyes were fixed and expressionless, on Hanan. He said: "Your husband has wanted a divorce for some time. His principal reason is a lady—her name doesn't matter—who wants to marry him—and whom he wants to marry. He hasn't told you about her because he has felt, perhaps justifiably, that your knowing about her would retard, rather than hasten, an agreement..."

The Filipino boy came in from the kitchen with a cocktail, set it before Hanan. Hanan did not move, or look up. He stared intently at the flowers in the center of the table. The Filipino boy smiled self-consciously at Druse and Mrs. Hanan, disappeared into the kitchen.

Druse relaxed a little, leaned back; the derringer was still focused unwaveringly on Hanan.

"In the hope of uncovering some adequate grounds for bringing suit," Druse went on, "he has had you followed for a month or more—unsuccessfully, need I add? After you threatened Crandall, you discovered suddenly that you were being followed and, of course, ascribed it to Crandall."

He paused. It was entirely silent for a moment, except for the faint, faraway buzz of the city and the sharp, measured sound of Hanan's breathing.

Druse turned his head towards Mrs. Hanan. "After you left Mister Hanan at Roslyn, last night, it suddenly occurred to him that this was his golden opportunity to dispose of you, without any danger to himself. You wouldn't give him a divorce—and it didn't look as if he'd be able to force it by discovering some dereliction on your part. And now, you had threatened Crandall—Crandall would be logically suspected if anything happened to you. Mister Hanan sent his men—the men who had been following you—after you when you left the place at Roslyn. They weren't very lucky."

Druse was smiling slightly. Mrs. Hanan had put her elbows on the table, her chin in her hands; she regarded Hanan steadily.

"He couldn't go to the police," Druse went on—"they would arrest Crandall, or watch him, and that would ruin the whole plan. And the business about the rubies would come out. That was the last thing he wanted"—Druse widened his smile—"because he switched the rubies himself—some time ago."

Mrs. Hanan turned to look at Druse; very slowly she matched his smile.

"You never discovered that your rubies were fake," he said, "because that possibility didn't occur to you. It was only after they'd been given back by Crandall that you became suspicious and found out they weren't genuine." He glanced at Hanan and the smile went from his face, leaving it hard and expressionless again. "Mister Hanan is indeed 'crazy about stones.'"

Hanan's thin mouth twitched slightly; he stared steadily

at the flowers.

Druse sighed. "And so—we find Mister Hanan, last night, with several reasons for wishing your—shall we say, disappearance? We find him with the circumstance of being able to direct suspicion at Crandall, ready to his hand. His only serious problem lay in finding a third, responsible party before whom to lay the whole thing—or enough of it to serve his purpose."

Mrs. Hanan had turned to face Hanan. Her eyes were half closed and her smile was very hard, very strange.

Druse stood up slowly, went on: "He had the happy thought of calling me—or perhaps the suggestion. I was an ideal instrument, functioning as I do, midway between the law and the underworld. He made an appointment, and arranged for one of his men to call on you by way of the fire-escape, while we were discussing the matter. The logical implication was that I would come to you when I left him, find you murdered, and act immediately on the information he had given me about Crandall. My influence and testimony would have speedily convicted Crandall. Mister Hanan would have better than a divorce. He'd have the rubies, without any danger of his having switched them ever being discovered—and he'd have"—Druse grinned sourly—"the check he had given me as an advance. Failing in the two things I had contracted to do, I would of course return it to him."

Hanan laughed suddenly; a terribly forced, high-pitched laugh.

"It is very funny," Druse said. "It would all have worked very beautifully if you"—he moved his eyes to Mrs. Hanan—"hadn't happened to see the man who came up the fire-escape to call on you, before he saw you. The man whose return Mister Hanan has been impatiently waiting. The man"—he dropped one eyelid in a swift wink—"who confessed to the whole thing a little less than an hour ago."

Druse put his hand into his inside pocket and took out the black velvet jewel-case, snapped it open and put it on the table. "I found them in the safe at your place at Roslyn," he said. "Your servants there objected very strenuously—so strenuously that I was forced to tie them up and lock them in the wine cellar. They must be awfully uncomfortable by now—I shall have to attend to that."

He lowered his voice to a discreet drone. "And your lady was there, too. She, too, objected very strenuously, until I had had a long talk with her and convinced her of the error of her—shall we say, affection, for a gentleman of your instincts. She seemed very frightened at the idea of becoming involved in this case—I'm afraid she will be rather hard to find."

Druse sighed, lowered his eyes slowly to the rubies, touched the largest of them delicately with one finger. "And so," he said, "to end this vicious and regrettable business—I give you your rubies"—he lifted his hand and made a sweeping gesture towards Mrs. Hanan—"and your wife—and now I would like your check for twenty-five thousand dollars."

Hanan moved very swiftly. He tipped the edge of the table upward, lunged up and forward in the same movement; there was a sharp, shattering crash of chinaware and silver. The derringer roared, but the bullet thudded into the table. Hanan bent over suddenly—his eyes were dull, and his upper lip was drawn back over his teeth—then he straightened and whirled and ran out through the door to the living room.

Mrs. Hanan was standing against the big buffet; her hands were at her mouth, and her eyes were very wide. She made no sound.

Druse went after Hanan, stopped suddenly at the door. Hanan was crouched in the middle of the living room. The Filipino boy stood beyond him, framed against the darkness of the entrance-hall; a curved knife glittered in his hand and his thin yellow face was hard, menacing. Hanan ran out on the terrace and Druse went swiftly after him. By the dim light from the living room he saw Hanan dart to the left, encounter the wall there, zigzag crazily towards the darkness of the outer terrace, the edge.

Druse yelled: "Look out!" ran forward, Hanan was silhouetted a moment against the mauve glow of the sky; then with a hoarse, cracked scream he fell outward, down.

Druse stood a moment, staring blindly down. He took out a handkerchief and mopped his forehead, then turned and went into the living room and tossed the derringer down on the big center table. The Filipino boy was still standing in the doorway. Druse nodded at him and he turned and went through the dark entrance-hall into the kitchen. Druse went to the door to the dining room; Mrs. Hanan was still standing with her back to the buffet, her hands still at her mouth, her eyes wide, unseeing. He turned and went swiftly up the broad steps to the office, took up the telephone and dialed a number. When the connection had been made, he asked for MacCrae.

In a minute or so MacCrae answered; Druse said: "You'll find a stiff in Mrs. Dale Hanan's apartment on the corner of Sixty-third and Park, Mac. She killed him—self-defense. You might find his partner downstairs at my place—waiting for his boss to come out... Yeah, his boss was Hanan—he just went down—the other way... I'll file charges of attempted murder against Hanan, and straighten it all out when you get over here... Yeah—hurry."

He hung up and went down to the dining room. He tipped the table back on its legs and picked up the rubies, put them back into the case. He said: "I called up a friend of mine who works for Mahlon and Stiles. As you probably know, Mister Hanan has never made a will." He smiled. "He so hated the thought of death that the idea of a will was extremely repugnant to him."

He picked up her chair and she came slowly across and sank into it.

"As soon as the estate is settled," he went on. "I shall expect your check for a hundred and thirty-five thousand dollars, made out to the insurance company."

She nodded abstractedly.

"I think these"—he indicated the jewel-case—"will be safer with me, until then."

She nodded again.

He smiled. "I shall also look forward with a great deal of pleasure to receiving your check for twenty-five thousand—the balance on the figure I quoted for my services."

She turned her head slowly, looked up at him. "A moralist," she said—"morbid—and mercenary."

"Mercenary as hell!" He bobbed his big head up and down violently.

She looked at the tiny watch at her wrist, said: "It isn't morning yet, strictly speaking—but I'd rather have a drink than anything I can think of."

Druse laughed. He went to the buffet and took out a squat bottle, glasses, poured two big drinks. He took one to her, raised the other and squinted through it at the light. "Here's to crime."

They drank.

Pineapple

THE MAN IN the dark-brown camel's-hair coat turned east against the icy wind. Near First Avenue he cut diagonally across the deserted street towards an electric sign: Tony Maschio's Day and Night Tonsorial Parlor.

A step or so beyond the sign, just outside the circle of warm yellow light from the shop, he stopped and put down the suitcase he was carrying, produced a cigarette and a lighter. He stood close to the building with his back to the wind, flicked the lighter several times without producing a flame, then turned back into the wind and went on towards First Avenue.

He forgot his suitcase. It sat in the darkness just under the corner of Tony's plate-glass window and if anyone had been close enough to it they might have heard it ticking between screaming gusts of wind—merrily, or ominously, depending upon whether one took it for the ticking of a cheap alarm clock or the vastly more intricate and alarming tick of a time-bomb.

The man walked up First Avenue to Thirteenth. He got into a cab on the northwest corner, said, "Grand Central," and leaned back and looked at his watch.

It was nine minutes after one.

At sixteen minutes after one Tony Maschio came out of the backroom, washed his hands, whistling a curiously individual version of "O Sole Mio," and turned to grin cheerily at the big bald man who sat reading a paper with his feet propped up on the fender of the stove.

"You are next, Mister Maccunn," he chirped brightly.

Tony Maschio looked like a bird, a white-faced bird with a bushy halo of black feathers on his head; he spoke with an odd twittering lilt, like a bird.

Maccunn folded his paper carefully and unfolded his big body as careful from the chair, stood up. He was about fifty-five, a very heavily built, heavily jowled Scot with glistening shoe-button eyes, a snow-white walrus mustache.

He lumbered over and sat down in Number One Chair, observed in a squeaky voice that contrasted strangely with his bulk:

"It's a cold, cold night."

For eight years Maccunn had come to Tony's every Friday night at around this time; for eight years his greeting, upon being invited into Tony's chair, had been: "It's a cold night," or "It's a hot night," or "It's a wet night," or whatever the night might be. When it was any of these things to an extreme degree he would repeat the adjectives in honor of the occasion. Tony agreed that it was a "cold, cold night" and asked his traditional question in turn, with a glittering smile:

"Haircut?"

Maccunn did not have so much as a pin-feather hair on his broad and shining head. He shook it soberly, as was his eight-year habit, closed his eyes, and Tony took up his shears and began trimming the enormous mustache with deft and graceful gusto.

Angelo, who presided over Number Two Chair, was industriously shaving the slack chin of a slight gray-faced youth in overalls. Giuseppe, Number Three, had gone out for something to eat. Giorgio, Number Four, was sitting in his chair, nodding over an ancient number of "The New Art Models Weekly." There were no other customers in the shop.

At nineteen minutes after one the telephone rang.

Maschio put down his shears and comb and started to answer it.

Angelo said: "If that's for me, boss—tell her to wait a minute."

Maschio nodded and put his hand out towards the receiver, and the telephone and wall came out to meet him, the whole side of the shop twisted and curled and was a smothering sheet of white flame, and pain. He felt his body torn apart as if it were being torn slowly and he thought "God!—please stop it!"—and then he didn't feel any more, or think any more.

Maccunn raised his head once and looked down at the right side of his chest and it seemed curiously flat, curiously distant; he lowered his head and was still. Angelo moaned.

The wind was like an icy wall.

In the reporters' room of the Ninth Precinct Police Station, Nick Green was playing cooncan with Blondie Kessler, when the Desk Sergeant yelled from the next room:

"Blondie! Pineapple at Tony Maschio's Barber Shop on Seventh—nothin' left but a grease-spot!"

Kessler put his cards face down on the table and stood up slowly.

He said very simply: "Dear, sweet Jesus!"

Green looked up at him with elaborately skeptical disdain. "Every time I get a swell hand," he muttered plaintively, "something happens so you have an excuse to run out on me."

Kessler, moving towards the door, yipped: "Come on."

Nicholas, sometimes "St. Nick," Green was thirty-six—with the smooth tanned skin, bright China-blue eyes of twenty, the snowy white hair of sixty. He was tall and slim and angular, and his more or less severe taste in clothes was violently relieved by a predilection for flaming-red neckties.

His nickname derived from his rather odd ideas about philanthropy. He had been at one time or another a tent-show actor, a newspaperman, gambler, gun-runner, private detective and a few more ill-assorted what-nots, and that wide experience had given him decidedly revolutionary convictions as to who was deserving and who was not.

A stroke of luck combined with one of his occasional flashes of precise intuition had enabled him to snatch a fortune from a falling stock-market and for three years he had used his money and the power it carried to do most of the things young millionaires don't do. He numbered legmen, Park Avenue debutantes, pickpockets, touts, bank robbers and bank presidents, wardheelers and international confidence-men among his wide and varied circle of friends, and he had played Santa Claus to more than a few of them at one time or another. He found the devious twistings and turnings of politics, the complicated intrigues of the New York underworld exciting, spent more, of his time in night courts than in night-clubs and was a great deal prouder of his accuracy with a Colt .45 than he was of his polo.

He got up and followed Blondie Kessler out of the Reporters' Room and down the corridor. In his car—a black and shiny and powerful coupe—they careened around the corner and roared north. Green swerved to miss a sleepily meandering cab by inches, asked:

"Now, about this Maschio?"

Blondie was a police-reporter on the Star-Telegram. His hair was as black as St. Nick's was white. He was a squat stocky Dutchman almost as broad as he was long and he had a habit of staccato, almost breathless expression, particularly when he was a little excited.

"Tony Maschio is—or was—Gino's brother. He's run a barber shop where a lot of the town's big shots go to have their fringes trimmed for eleven or twelve years, an' he's been partners with Gino an' Lew Costain in a high-powered gambling syndicate on the side. His shop was a little bit of a two-by-four joint, but Tony an' his hand-picked barbers were artists and it was usually full of names from Wall Street or Park Row."

Kessler was silent a moment; and Green invited: "And..."

"And—Bruce Maccunn, my Managing Editor, has been dropping in at Tony's for a mustache trim an' a mudpack every Friday night for as long as I can remember. I've located him there a half-dozen times in the last two or three years—late Friday nights."

Green whistled softly. "And..."

Kessler had no time to answer; the car slid to the curb across the street from the pile of smoking ruins that had been Maschio's Barber Shop. In spite of the hour, the glacial wind, the usual gallery of morbidly curious had gathered. Several firemen, policemen, and an ambulance squad from the Emergency Hospital were industriously combing the debris of bricks and steel and charred wood.

Kessler was the first reporter on the scene; he scurried about from one to another after information. Green strolled over to join two men who were standing a little way down the street in earnest conversation. One of them was Doyle, a plainclothesman whom he knew slightly, and the other was a wild-eyed Italian who was explaining with extravagant gestures that if he hadn't lingered in the corner lunchroom for a second cup of coffee he, too, would have been blown to bits. He, it appeared, was Giuseppe Picelli, Tony's Number Three Barber, and he'd been on his way back to the shop when the explosion occurred.

Green jerked his head towards the heap of wreckage. "How many have they found?"

"Don't know." Doyle chewed his unlighted cigar noisily.

"Most of 'em are in pieces—little pieces. We've identified Tony an' one of his barbers, but there's a lot of pieces left over. This guy"—he nodded at Picelli—"says Bruce Maccunn was there—came in jus' before he left."

Picelli bobbed his head up and down, jabbered excitedly: "Sure, Mister Maccunn came in as I went out—an' there was another fellow—I don't know him... An' Tony an' Angelo an' Giorgio..."

"That all?" Green was blowing hard in his bare hands to warm them.

"That's all were there when I left—but Gino an' Mister Costain were coming over. Tony was expecting them..."

Green and Doyle looked at each other.

Doyle grunted: "If Lew Costain got there for the blow-off it makes my job about eight hundred percent harder. I don't guess there are more than eight hundred people in New York that'd like to see him in little pieces."

Kessler galloped over. He was a little green around the mouth and eyes.

"Mac g-got it!" he stuttered. "They just dug him out—or wh—what's left of him..."

Doyle tried to light his cigar in the screaming wind. "Why did Gino Maschio an' Costain get it," he growled. "Maybe there's not enough left of them to find out, but if Picelli here knows his potatoes they were in the shop or on their way to the shop—an' if they were on their way they would've showed up by now."

Kessler gurgled: "Where's a telephone?"

"There's one in the lunchroom around the corner on Second Avenue." Picelli waved his arm dramatically.

A police car, its siren moaning shrilly, pulled up and a half dozen assorted detectives piled out.

Kessler grabbed Green's arm, shouted, "Come on, Nick—I gotta telephone an' I wanna talk to you." They hurried towards Second Avenue.

Green grinned down at the tugging, puffing reporter.

"You look like a crazed bloodhound," he said. "Don't tell me you've got another one of those red-hot Kessler theories."

"Theory my eye! I've got the whole business—the whole bloody shebang!"

"Uh-huh." Green's grunt was elaborately incredulous.

Kessler snorted. "Listen, John Sallust was released from Atlanta three days ago!"

"So what?"

Kessler's mouth made an amazed O. "So what! So Bruce Maccunn was the man who rode Sallust—in the paper—an' finally stuck him for the Arbor Day Parade bombing nearly five years ago. So Sallust swore by the beards of Marx and Lenin he'd get Maccunn. So, after a half-dozen appeals and new trials and whatnot he finally got a commutation and what does he do but make good and plant a pineapple under the man who put him behind the bars!"

They turned the corner.

Green murmured softly: "Blondie, my child—you're just as dippy as a bedbug—an especially dippy bedbug."

Kessler stopped suddenly, stood with his arms expressively outstretched and said:

"For the love of God—do you mean to tell me you don't get it? Maccunn, more than anyone else, or all the rest of 'em put together, hung that rap on Sallust. The Government wanted to drop the case on insufficient evidence, but Maccunn hated radicals like poison an' wouldn't let 'em. His editorials yelled about corruption and anarchy and it finally worked. What's more natural than Sallust wanting to wipe Maccunn as soon as he got out?"

Green shook his head slowly. "Nothing's more natural," he admitted. "Only I happen to know Sallust a little and he's much too bright a guy to do anything like this three days after he's sprung—or any other time."

Kessler's mouth flattened to a thin, sarcastic line.

"I followed his case very closely," Green went on, "and he was railroaded if anybody ever was. He's really a swell guy who has his own ideas about the way the country should be run. I'll bet he never saw a bomb in his life."

"Nuts." Kessler half turned. "It all fits like a glove. He's an anarchist an' those boys say it with dynamite. He couldn't blow up the whole paper—that was too big an order—and Maccunn never lit long enough at his home for that to be practical, but he went to Tony Maschio's every Friday night between twelve-thirty and one-thirty. It's open and shut."

Green smiled sadly, shook his head, murmured: "Mostly shut."

"That's my story an' I'll stick to it." Kessler turned and went into the lunchroom.

Green walked slowly back towards his car, whispered into the wind:

"An especially dippy bedbug."

The hands of the big clock over the information desk pointed to one forty-one. The great concourse of Grand Central Station was speckled with the usual scattered crowd.

On the wide balcony above the west side of the concourse, the man in the dark-brown camel's-hair coat who had forgotten his suitcase in front of Tony Maschio's walked slowly back and forth. The collar of his coat was turned up and his hands were thrust deep in his pockets; his large dark eyes were fixed on Gate Twenty-seven, which led to the one-forty-five Boston train, and his head turned slowly as he walked back and forth.

He was a powerfully built man of uncertain age and as much of his face as could be seen above the heavy coat collar was unnaturally flushed.

Suddenly he stopped pacing and leaned forward against the marble balustrade. He had caught sight of a man of about his own build and coloring—moving swiftly across the concourse. The man's most striking features were the grace with which he moved and his bright yellowish-green velour hat. He flashed a ticket in front of the conductor and disappeared through Gate Twenty-seven.

The man in the dark-brown coat hurried down the great stairway, across to one of the ticket windows. When he turned away he held a little piece of pasteboard and he strode with it through Gate Twenty-seven. He walked the length of the train to the first coach back of the baggage car and swung aboard.

He found the man he was looking for in the smoking car of the third Pullman back. There was no one else in the smoking room; the porter was making up a berth at the other end of the car.

The man in the dark-brown coat held the curtain aside with one arm and leaned against the side of the narrow doorway.

He said: "Hello."

The other swarthy man was sitting next to the window, reading a paper. He put the paper down and looked up and his color changed slowly, curiously, until his face was almost as yellow and as green as his jauntily cocked hat. He did not speak.

From outside, the conductor's voice came in to them: "All aboard..."

The man in the dark-brown coat smiled a little; he whispered:

"Let's walk back and look at the lights."

The train began to move, slowly.

The other man's empty eyes were on one of the big pockets of the brown coat where something besides the big man's hand bulged the material. He did not move, seemed incapable of moving.

The man in the brown coat repeated: "Let's walk back..."

Then he crossed swiftly and grabbed the other's coat-collar with his free hand and jerked him to his feet, shoved him to the door and out into the narrow corridor; they went towards the rear of the train.

They went through four cars, most of them with the berths made up and curtains drawn, encountered only a heavily breathing drunk in pajamas who had mislaid something, and two sleepy porters. The last car was partly compartments, partly observation car. As they entered it, a red-haired brakeman passed them without looking at them and went forward. They went to the observation rear end and the man in the green hat said: "This is far enough, Lew, if you want to talk."

The man in the brown coat smiled. His right hand moved the coat pocket suggestively. He nodded his head sidewise, erupted, "Out on the platform, Gino. Then no one will hear us."

Gino took one glance at the bulged coat pocket, and opened the door to the observation platform.

The train was just coming out of the tunnel to the elevated tracks and the rosy glow of midtown Manhattan was reflected by the gray wind-driven clouds. The wind slashed like an icy knife and green-hat mechanically turned up his collar, shivered violently

Following him, the man in the brown coat pulled the door shade down—both window shades were drawn—and closed the door tightly. He jerked his hand from his pocket. There was a momentary flash of something bright and glittering as he swung his hand up and down in a short arch against the other's skull. The hat went whirling away into the wind and darkness and the man sank to his knees, toppled forward to crush his face against the floor.

The man in the brown coat knelt beside him and went through his pockets swiftly, carefully. In the inside pocket of his suitcoat he found a thick packet of currency, slipped it into his own inside pocket.

A new sound, the faint stutter of an incoming train on the adjoining track, grew above the roar of the wind. The man glanced ahead, around the corner of the car, seemed for a moment to be calculating the distance away of the approaching headlight, then stooped again, swiftly.

Hurriedly he stripped off the man's overcoat, then his own. He struggled into the former—a rather tight-fitting tweed Chesterfield—and somehow forced the other man's arms and shoulders into his own big dark-brown camel's hair; then he finished transferring the contents of his own inside pockets—several letters, a monogrammed cigarette case and other odds and ends—to the inside pockets of the unconscious man.

The stutter of the approaching train grew to a hoarse scream. He boosted the limp body onto his shoulder, stood up, and when the blinding headlight of the train on the adjoining track was about twenty-five or thirty feet away, he dumped his burden over the side-rail of the observation platform down onto the track in front of the onrushing locomotive.

Then he turned swiftly and went back through the observation car. As he reached the third car forward the train slowed and he heard a far-off voice shout:

"Hundred an' Twenty-fifth Street."

When the train stopped and a porter opened the doors of the vestibule between the third and fourth car, the man, now in a tight-fitting tweed Chesterfield, swung off and sauntered down the stairs that led from the station to the street.

As he crossed the street towards a cab he heard the conductor's thin far off wail above the wind: "All aboard..."

He climbed into the cab, snapped: "Three thirty-two West Ninetieth—and make it fast."

Green lit a match and examined the mailboxes carefully. The second one on the left rewarded him with a dingy label upon which:

JOHN DARRELL SALLUST PAULA SALLUST

had been typewritten in bright-blue ink.

He rang the bell under the label and after a minute the lock of the outside door buzzed; he went in and climbed two flights of narrow stairs to Apartment B5. The door was ajar; he knocked and a man's high-pitched voice called:

"Come in."

Green went into a very large and bare studio, dimly lighted by two floor-lamps in opposite corners and a small but very bright desk lamp on a wide central table.

The high-pitched voice: "Well, Mister Green—this is an unexpected pleasure."

Green took off his hat and went to the wide table. He bowed slightly.

"Might you, by any chance," he inquired blandly, "have been out this evening—since, say eleven o'clock?"

John Sallust was a thin, consumptive-looking Englishman with a high bulging forehead, stringy mouse-colored hair, and cold gray eyes, so light in color that they appeared almost white. He sat straddling a chair, his chin resting on his clasped hands on the back of the chair.

"I not only might have," he said evenly—"I was. I only got home about a quarter of an hour ago."

Green glanced at the square heavy watch on the inside of his left wrist; it was fifty-two minutes after one.

Sallust turned his head. "This is Paula, my sister. This is Nick Green. You've probably heard me speak of him."

She was half sitting, half lying on a low couch against one of the long walls of the room, a very dark, very diminutive girl with porcelain-white skin, a deep-red mouth and large oddly opaque eyes.

She nodded and Green bowed again slightly.

"We went to a theater." She sat up slowly. "We went to a theater and John brought me home afterwards—it must have been about ten-thirty—and then he went for a walk."

Green smiled. "That's simply dandy. Now, if you two can jump into your hats and coats and the three of us can get out of here in about one minute flat"—he raised one snowy eyebrow and grinned at Sallust—"you won't have to take another of those very unpleasant trips to jail."

Paula leapt to her feet, almost screamed: "Jail!"

Sallust's thin face twisted to a wry smile. "You choose a rather bizarre time to joke, Mister Green," he said softly.

Green was looking at his watch. "Maybe in two minutes," he whispered as if to himself.

Paula crossed to him swiftly.

"What are you talking about?" she gulped. "What is it?"

"I haven't time to tell you about it, now. Take my word for it that the Law will be here in a split-jiffy to arrest your brother for the murder of Bruce Maccunn and a half-dozen or so innocent bystanders. Let's go first and talk about it afterwards..."

Sallust did not move. His eyes moved swiftly to his sister once, then back to Green.

He muttered: "No."

Green stared at him blankly. "No? No what?"

Sallust shook his head a little. "I returned three days ago," he said gently, "from the better part of five years in prison, I was as I believe you call it, framed. I was accused by lies, tried by lies, convicted by lies..."

He cleared his throat and straightened in the chair, gazed very intently at Green.

"I know you very slightly, Mister Green. I have been led to believe at one time or another that you are in some way sympathetic to our cause, but I have just returned from a painful five-year lesson in misplaced trust. I do not know what you are talking about, now, but I know that I have done no wrong and I shall stay exactly where I am."

It was entirely silent for a moment and then Paula's voice rang softly, tremulously: "Perhaps you're making a mistake, John. Mister Green is–" She stopped.

Green put his hand up and rubbed the heel of it slowly down the left side of his face. His eyes were fixed more or less vacantly on a small turkey-red cigarette box on the table. Very suddenly he went forward and as Sallust sprang to his feet, Green's arm moved in a long looping arc, his knuckles smacked sharply against Sallust's chin; Sallust crumpled and fell to his knees, clutched blindly at the chair, went limp.

Paula was too surprised to scream, or move; she stood with her hands to her mouth, her great eyes fixed on Green in startled amazement.

Green mumbled, "Sorry," shortly, stooped and swept Sallust's slight figure up into his arms and moved towards the door. "Come on," he grunted over his shoulder, "and make it snappy."

She followed in stunned silence; at the door he turned and jerked his head at her coat and she took it up from a chair and put it on like a somnambulist motivated and moved by something unknown, something irresistible.

The bleak Greenwich Village street was deserted; Green carried Sallust across the glistening sidewalk and put him in the car, hurried around to climb in behind the wheel. Paula stood hesitantly on the sidewalk; the cold air had brought back her momentarily dimmed senses and she reflected that it was not too late to scream, reflected further, after glancing up and down the street, that it was more or less useless. She got into the car and closed the door, put her arm around Sallust and waited.

Just east of Eighth Avenue, Green slowed and pulled over to the curb to allow two speeding police-cars to pass, then turned and watched them skid to the curb outside the building where the Sallusts lived.

He grinned at Paula. "My timing wasn't so hot," he observed. "The Law was about three minutes less efficient than I figured."

She turned from watching the men swarm out of the cars and run into the house. Her inclination to scream was definitely gone; she tried to return his smile.

"What is it all about?" she whispered. "I don't understand..."

"Neither do I yet." He let the clutch in and the car rounded the corner, whirred north on Eighth Avenue. "I'm sorry I had to resort to that to get your brother out, but I thought he got a raw deal before and I want to do what I can to prevent his getting another one. After five years on the inside he shouldn't mind a sock on the jaw if it saves him even one night in the cooler."

Green's apartment was on East Sixty-first; the elevator boy helped him with Sallust, who was beginning to stir and moan feebly; Green explained that he was very drunk and when they reached his apartment on the top floor they put Sallust on one of the divans in the huge living room. The elevator boy went away.

Green turned to Paula. "He'll be all right in a little while," he said. "The main thing is that he's not to show up outside of this place until certain matters—I'm not quite sure what, yet, so I can't tell you about them—are straightened out. Do you trust me enough to help, and to see to it that he stays here?"

She nodded.

Green smiled slightly. "Your word?"

She nodded again, returned the faint shadow of a smile.

He went towards the door. "I'll be back or give you a

ring as soon as I can. Make yourself at home. If you get hungry or thirsty try the icebox."

He went out and closed the door.

Downstairs, he admonished the night clerk. "There're a man and woman in my apartment and I want them to stay there. I think they will, but if they get tough call Mike and let him handle them."

The clerk nodded; he was accustomed to more or less curious orders from Mister Green. Mike was the janitor, a husky Norwegian who had performed odd jobs of a strong-arm nature for Green upon more than one occasion.

Green turned in the doorway. "And if they make any telephone calls, keep a record of who they call and what they have to say."

The clerk nodded again. Green went out into Sixty-first Street and walked to a drugstore.

At eighteen minutes after two the phone on Blondie Kessler's desk jingled cheerily for the tenth time in twenty-five minutes.

He whirled from his typewriter, picked up the receiver and yelped: "Hello."

Green's voice hummed silkily over the wire: "How many more identifiable pieces have they dug out of Tony's? And how's that red-hot Kessler theory coming along?"

Kessler scowled sourly into the transmitter.

"That Kessler theory is holding its head up and taking nourishment very nicely, thank you!" he barked with elaborate irony. "We found a chunk of the fuse with a foundry label on it, a place in Jersey–"

Green interrupted: "Don't tell me. Let me guess... Sallust used to work there, or anyway, he used to live in Jersey, or maybe he went to Jersey once to visit his aunt."

Kessler snorted: "All right, all right. I say Sallust is a cinch for this job, you say not. I'll bet—I'll bet you fifty dollars."

Green snapped: “Bet.”

Kessler cackled shrilly. “The clincher is that Sallust and his sister took a powder about a minute and a half before the boys in blue swept in. Their next-door neighbors heard them go out and from the timing it looks like it was a tip.”

Green sighed. “Maybe I’m the bedbug, after all,” he murmured. “And how about my first and most important question—what else have they dug up?”

“Nothing more that they could make sense of. They’ve got a lot of arms and legs that might have been Gino or Costain or who-have-you.” Green’s voice droned on: “I’m still curious about whether Gino and Costain got to Tony’s before the fireworks. Has anybody tried to locate them?”

“Uh-huh. Gino was supposed to leave for Boston on a late train, after he went to Tony’s. A business trip according to his wife. She don’t know whether he reached Tony’s or whether he made the train or not. She’s going nuts. Then I reached Costain’s girl and she said Lew started for Tony’s about midnight, said he was going to stop by a couple places first. She hasn’t heard from him since. She’s jumping up and down and yelling and screaming, too, and calling me back every two minutes.”

There was silence for several seconds, then Green’s voice concluded dreamily:

“Don’t forget, Blondie, that Lew Costain has, or had, more enemies than any other picked dozen highbinders in this town. Maccunn had one, or at least you’re trying to hang his chill on one. Whether Costain reached Tony’s or not, he was headed there, and in some strange way that seems more important to me than the fact that Sallust wanted Maccunn’s blood. With all due respect to the Kessler theory, of course... And don’t forget the fifty...”

The phone clicked, an electric period.

Kessler looked like he was going to take a large bite out of the transmitter for a minute, then he hung up slowly and turned back to his typewriter with enormous disgust.

Haley, the City Editor, was working feverishly, trying very hard not to whistle. He, for one, had hated Maccunn as a slave driver, and now it looked like he'd be moving into the big oak-paneled office on the seventh floor and be writing M.E. after his name.

He looked up as Kessler hung up the receiver, yelled: "Anything new?"

Kessler shook his head. "Nothing new, only that guy Green is losing his mind."

Solly Allenberg, short and fat, was sitting in his cab near the corner of Forty-ninth and Broadway, when Green crossed the street to him.

Allenberg stopped short in the middle of a yawn and his face lit up like a chubby Christmas tree.

"Hello, Mister Green," he croaked heartily. "Where you been keeping yourself?"

Green leaned on the door.

"I've been around," he said. "How've you been doing Solly? How are the kids?"

"Swell, Mister Green, just swell. The wife was asking about you just the other night. I told her–"

Green interrupted quietly: "Lew Costain's been murdered."

Solly's thick mouth fell open slowly. "Murdered? What the hell you talking about?"

Green's head bobbed up and down.

"He was at Tony Maschio's tonight when the firecracker went off—he and Gino..."

Solly said: "I was just reading about it in the paper, but it didn't say nothing about Mister Costain."

"They hadn't identified him when they snapped that Extra out."

Green reached past Solly and clicked down the taximeter flag. "Let's take a ride," he suggested—"only let's take it inside, where it's warm and where we can get a drink."

Solly tumbled out of the cab and they crossed the slippery sidewalk and went into the Rialto Bar. They both ordered rye. Green studied Solly's reflection in the big mirror behind the bar.

"How long have you been working for Lew?" he began. Solly hesitated and Green went on swiftly: "Listen. I knew him pretty well, liked him. I intend to find who rubbed him out and you can help me, if you will..."

Solly gulped his drink. "Sure," he blurted—"I wanta help." He glanced at his empty glass and Green nodded to the bartender to fill it up.

"I never really worked for him," Solly went on. "He was scared of cars—scared to drive his own car in town. He got the batty idea two, three years ago I was a swell, careful driver, so he's been riding in my cab most of the time since. Whenever he'd light anywhere for awhile or go home an' go to bed or anything like that, he'd tell me an' I'd pick up what I could on the side. He paid me a flat rate of a saw-buck a day no matter what the meter read an' some days he wouldn't use me at all, so it worked out swell."

"Did you take him anywhere tonight?"

"Uh-huh." Solly drank, nodded. "I picked him up at his apartment a little after midnight an' took him to the corner of Bleecker an' Thompson Street. He said he wouldn't need me any more tonight." Green tasted his rye, made a face and put a twenty-dollar bill on the bar.

Solly said, "Don't you like it, Mister Green?"

Green shook his head and edged the glass along the bar with the side of his hand until it was in front of Solly.

Solly regarded it meditatively. "I'll be damned," he said, "a swell guy like Mister Costain getting the works like that..." He picked up the glass.

Green was lighting a cigarette. "Who did it?"

Solly shrugged. "There is a lot of guys who never liked him, because they didn't understand him. He was—uh—ec–" Solly stopped, tasted his fresh drink and tried again: "He was ec–"

"Eccentric?"

Solly bobbed his head.

Green persisted: "But who hated him enough and had guts enough to tip him over?"

Solly drained his glass, then closed one eye and looked immeasurably wise. "Well, if you ask me," he said quickly, "the guy who had plenty of reason to, an' maybe enough guts to, was plenty close to home... Did'ja ever meet a fella named Demetrios—something Demetrios? A Greek-tall shiny-haired sheik with a big smile?"

Green shook his head.

Solly leaned closer. "He worked as a kind of bodyguard an' all-around handy-man for Mister Costain. Mister Costain liked him..." Solly's voice dissolved to a hoarse stage-whisper. "I happen to know that Demetrios an' June Neilan, Costain's girl, was like that"—he held up two grimy fingers pressed close together—"right under Costain's nose."

Green's brows ascended to twin inverted v's. "That's a good reason for Costain to hang it on the Greek," he objected, "but not the other way around."

"Wait a minute. You don't get it." Solly's face split to a wide grin. "I happen to know this Demetrios has tried to let Costain have it in the back a couple times, only it went wrong, an' Costain didn't even tumble to who it was. I happened to be in the right place at the right time."

"Why didn't you tell Costain?"

Solly stared hard at his empty glass.

Green smiled faintly. "Did Demetrios pay off?"

Solly nodded sheepishly. Green rapped on the bar and the bartender filled both glasses.

"It's just like it always is," Solly croaked philosophically.

"Costain was crazy jealous of everybody except the right guy, an' distrusted everybody except the guy who was holding the knife."

"Where did Costain live? Some place on West Ninetieth, wasn't it?"

"Uh-huh. Three thirty-one."

Green picked up his change and Solly gulped both drinks and they went out and started across the slippery sidewalk towards the cab.

A slight, white-faced man with his coat collar turned up and the brim of his soft black hat turned down as much as possible to cover his face came up to them and said, "Hello, Solly. Hello, Mister Green," in a soft muffled voice. He took a short snub-nosed revolver out of his overcoat pocket and shot Solly in the stomach twice. Solly slipped and fell sidewise against Green and they both fell; Solly took two more slugs that were intended for Green. The cold magnified the roar of the gun to thunder. The wind whipped around the corner and the brim of the white-faced man's hat blew up and Green recognized Giuseppe Picelli, Number Three Barber.

Then Green and Solly were a tangled mass of threshing arms and legs on the icy sidewalk and Picelli turned and ran east on Forty-ninth Street.

On the third floor of the rooming house at Three Thirty-two West Ninetieth, directly across the street from Three Thirty-one, a man sat motionlessly at the window of the large dimly lighted front room. He had taken off the tweed Chesterfield he had worn when he left the Boston train at One Hundred and Twenty-fifth Street, and his suit coat; he sat in his deep-pink silk shirt-sleeves on the edge of a heavily upholstered chair, leaning forward to peer steadily through the slit under the drawn window shade.

From time to time he lighted a fresh cigarette from the

butt of the last, glanced at his watch; these were the sole disturbances to his rigid immobility, his entirely silent vigil.

At two thirty-six the phone rang. He picked it up from the floor with his eyes on the slit, grunted: "Yeah."

He listened silently for perhaps a minute, then said: "What the hell difference does it make whether Green recognized you or not if he's dead?... Oh, you're not sure. They both fell, but you're not sure"—his tone dripped sarcasm—"Well, you'd better make sure. I don't care how you do it, you've had your orders. Check on it some way and then come on up here, and be careful when you come in."

He put the phone on the floor, lighted a fresh cigarette.

Demetrios said: "I don't know nothing about it."

Doyle glanced swiftly at the detective lieutenant who had accompanied him. "Well, we figured you'd want to know," he mumbled.

Demetrios pulled his bright yellow dressing-gown more closely around his shoulders, shivered slightly, nodded.

They were in Demetrios' small apartment on Seventy-sixth Street. He'd been in bed, asleep; Doyle and the lieutenant had pounded on the door for three or four minutes before they'd succeeded in waking him.

The detective lieutenant stood up, stretched, yawned extravagantly.

Someone knocked at the door.

Doyle opened it and Green came in. He nodded to Doyle and the lieutenant, jerked his head at Demetrios.

"I don't know this gent, but I want to have a little talk with him," he said. "Will somebody please introduce me?"

Demetrios stared at him unpleasantly. "Is this guy a dick?"

Doyle grinned, shook his head. "Huh-uh. This is St. Nick Green. He's a nice fella. You two ought to know each other."

Demetrios stood up angrily. "What the hell you mean coming into my house like this?" He whirled on Doyle and the lieutenant. "You, too. You got a warrant? I don't know nothing about Costain–"

Doyle clucked: "Tch, tch, such a temper!" He smiled at Green. "Don't mind him. We woke him up an' he's pouting."

Green sat down on the arm of a chair.

"Speaking of Costain," he said softly, "has he turned up yet?" He turned to Doyle. "Something tells me he wasn't at Tony's and that he's still in one piece."

They were all looking at Green; Demetrios and the lieutenant with more or less puzzled expressions, Doyle with a broad grin.

Doyle laughed. "You're a little behind the times, Nicky," he boomed. "They found what was left of Costain on the New York Central tracks at a Hundred an' Twenty-first Street a little while ago. No mistake about it this time. He was identified by a lot of papers an' stuff in his pockets."

The lieutenant said: "That's why we woke up his nibs, here. We thought he might know something about it."

Demetrios turned and closed the window savagely. "I don't know nothing about it," he snarled. "I told Lew I didn't want no part of it.. I been in bed since ten o'clock an' got a witness to prove it. There's been three phone calls through the switchboard, so the operator knows I was in."

Green asked gently: "Told Lew you didn't want any part of what?"

"Any part of nothing! Me an' him was washed up. He's been screwy for the last week. He thought everybody was trying to double-cross him."

Green purred: "Everybody probably was."

Doyle repeated: "Any part of what, Demetrios?"

Demetrios sat down. "He was tipped off yesterday that

Gino an' Tony were juggling the books. One of Tony's barbers called him an' said instead of the syndicate going into the red like it's supposed to been going the last few weeks, it's been cleaning up important money. Costain never paid any attention to the business. He didn't have no head for figures. He furnished the original bankroll an' trusted Gino an' Tony to take care of the business."

The lieutenant muttered: "Christ! what a character shark! Trusting Gino and Tony!"

"They were going to take a powder, according to Lew's info," Demetrios went on. "Gino was going to shag a boat out of Boston for Havana an' Tony was going to Florida by rail an' meet him there. Between them they were supposed to have about four hundred grand. Lew told me about it an' said he'd made a date to meet both of them at Tony's at a quarter after one tonight. He wanted me to go along, but I couldn't see it. It looked like a dumb play. Anyway, me an' him was washed up and I been in bed since ten o'clock."

The lieutenant snapped: "You're good enough for us, Demetrios, as a material witness. Get on your clothes."

"That's what I get for trying to help you dumb bastards," Demetrios bleated. He got up and went into the bathroom.

Green stood up, crossed quietly to Doyle and the lieutenant, whispered: "Don't pick him up. Tell him to stand by for a call in the morning and let him go. I'll lay six, two, and even he doesn't go back to bed, but goes out. We can wait outside and if he doesn't lead us somewhere I'm a Tasmanian watchmaker."

Doyle looked doubtful, but the lieutenant seemed to like the idea.

He called: "Let it go, Demetrios. But stick around for a call in the morning."

Demetrios appeared in the bathroom doorway in his pajamas. He looked a little bewildered.

"Can I go back to bed?"

Doyle said: "Sure. Get some sleep. You'll probably need it. After all, we wouldn't be getting nowhere in figuring out what this's all about if it wasn't for you."

Demetrios nodded glumly, went over and sat down on the edge of the bed.

Doyle grunted, "G'night," and he and Green and the lieutenant filed out.

Demetrios sat silent for two or three minutes and then got up and went to the door, opened it and looked up and down the hall. Then he closed the door and crossed to the private telephone that stood on the stand beside the bed, beside the regular house phone. He sat down on the bed again and dialed a Schuyler number, said:

"Hello, honey. Listen. The big news just came through. They found 'im on the New York Central tracks, uptown. Uh-huh. I guess he left the pinwheel at Tony's an' picked up Gino on the Boston train. Only Gino saw him first... A couple coppers just stopped by an' told me. They thought I might like to know."

He laughed quietly. "Sure, I gave 'em enough so they know he blasted Tony's. They can figure the rest of it out for themselves. Now, listen. They're probably waiting for me outside, but I'm going to duck out through the basement." He glanced at the alarm clock on the dresser. "It's a quarter of three. I'll be over there in half an hour at the outside unless they tail me an' then I'll have to lose 'em. You throw some things in a bag an' be ready to leave. We'll take a little trip. Some place where it's cool... Okay, baby—'Bye."

He hung up, dressed swiftly and took a traveling-bag out of a closet, began stuffing clothes into it.

Green's car was parked on the other side of Broadway, on Seventy-sixth. He went into an all-night drugstore on the corner and called the Star-Telegram, asked for Kessler.

Kessler grunted, "Hello," wearily, snapped out of it when

he recognized Green's voice.

"Hey, Nick! I just heard somebody took a shot at you," he yelped. "You all right?"

"I'm okay. I'll tell you all about it when I see you."

"That's swell!" Kessler whooped. "Everything's swell! I just put the Star-Telegram exclusive on Sallust to bed. What a story! It oughta be on the streets in an hour."

Green said softly: "Blondie, if you want to keep your job, and keep the Star out of an awful jam, kill it." Then, before Kessler could answer, he went on: "I just left Demetrios' apartment. He's the tall good-looking Greek that worked for Costain. Doyle and his partner are waiting for him to show, to tail him, but I'm afraid he'll get past them and I have a very merry hunch where he's going."

Kessler interrupted: "But listen, Nick–"

"You listen." Green's tone was ominous. "Hold that story for at least an hour, and leap up to Three Thirty-one West Ninetieth with some Law, fast. I'll be outside, or if I'm not, I'll be upstairs in Costain's apartment. Come up, and come quick. This is going to be the payoff on everything that's happened tonight and it'll make your Sallust story look like a want ad."

"But listen..." Kessler sounded like he was about to cry.

Green snapped: "I'm depending on you. Make it fast and make it quiet. And don't forget to bring along that fifty skins."

He hung up the receiver and went out and got into his car drove to Amsterdam Avenue, up Amsterdam to Eighty-ninth, turned west. He parked just off Riverside Drive on Ninetieth, about a hundred and fifty feet west of the entrance to Three Thirty-one.

Then he lighted a cigarette and sat still and waited.

The man in the third-floor-front room at Three Thirty-two didn't smoke any more; he simply waited, his eyes at the slit under the window shade. Occasionally he leaned back in the big chair, but for only a few seconds at a time and only after ten minutes or so of rigid, wary immobility.

At four minutes after three someone knocked at the door. He got up and opened it swiftly. Giuseppe Picelli came in; the man went back to the window.

Picelli sat down, said dully: "Got Solly. Green got away. There was ice..."

"There was ice," the man at the window repeated slowly. "All right, there was ice. How long were they together?"

"Green came up to Solly—Solly was in his cab. They went into the bar and I called you. Two or three minutes after I came out of the booth, they came out. I went up to them on the sidewalk..."

"And there was ice."

The man at the window stiffened suddenly, shaded his eyes from the dim light in the room. He peered intently through the slit for perhaps ten or fifteen seconds, then stood up and picked up his suit-coat and put it on.

"Come on, Joe. We're going places," he said.

He took a big blue automatic out of the pocket of the tweed Chesterfield and stuck it against his stomach, under the belt, pulled the points of his vest down over it.

The two men went together out of the room and down two flights of stairs, out of the rooming house and across the street to Three Thirty-one.

The elevator boy stared wide-eyed at the man who had been sitting at the window.

"Jeeze, Mister Costain," he stuttered. "I thought—Miss Neilan has been going crazy—calling up the newspapers every few minutes..."

Costain did not answer.

They got off at the fourth floor, went to the door of the front apartment on the right. Costain took a bunch of keys out of his pocket and unlocked it, opened it. They went in and closed the door.

June Neilan was a very pretty platinum blonde with wide blue eyes, orange lips that looked as if they had been put on to stay. She turned and stared at Costain and her creamy skin went gray.

Demetrios' hand moved swiftly upward across his chest and then he looked at the snub-nosed revolver in Picelli's hand, changed his mind and dropped his hands to his side, slowly.

Costain said: "Sit down."

June Neilan walked unsteadily to the nearest chair, sat down. Demetrios stood still.

Costain went to Demetrios and reached inside his coat, jerked a .35 automatic out of a shoulder holster and handed it back to Picelli. Then he doubled up his right fist and swung hard at Demetrios' jaw. Demetrios moved backward a little and Costain's fist cut his cheek; two tiny drops of blood started out on the white skin just beneath the cheekbone.

Costain drew his fist back and swung again; this time his timing was better, there was a soft splat as his fist struck Demetrios' jaw, Demetrios reeled backward against the wall. Costain went after him, cocked his right again. June Neilan said, "Please don't, Lew," dully. Costain's right fist ripped into Demetrios' throat, his left smashed his nose. Demetrios made a curious strangling sound and slid sidewise down the wall to the floor.

Costain was panting, his heavy florid face was purple. He drew his foot back and kicked Demetrios' face, hard, again and again; it made a soft, smacking sound like someone snapping their fingers in water and Demetrios' face darkened with glistening deep-red blood. Someone pounded on the door.

Costain did not seem to hear; he raised his foot and stamped on Demetrios' face so hard that the bones of the nose and cheek crunched like crumpled paper. Picelli whimpered: "Boss—there's somebody outside..."

Costain did not turn his head; he panted: "Okay—let 'em be outside. I'm busy..."

The pounding came on the door again.

June Neilan was staring at Costain and Demetrios blindly; she jumped up suddenly and ran to the door. Picelli was a split-second too late. She turned the lock, the door swung open and Nick Green stood in the opening.

Costain turned from Demetrios and jerked the big automatic out of his belt, shot twice. June Neilan spun around as if a heavy unseen hand were on her shoulder, twisting her slight body.

Green felt the sleeve of his coat lift, tear, a hot stab of pain in the outer muscle of his left arm. He shot once from a little above the hip. Costain bent forward slowly as if in an extravagant bow; then he sank to one knee and raised his head, stared vacantly at June Neilan.

She was holding on to the edge of the door with her two hands. Her eyes went back in her head suddenly and her body folded; she fell.

Green came forward into the room.

Picelli was shivering violently and his face looked very pinched and small; his revolver fell to the floor and he raised his hands slowly.

Costain's mouth twisted upward a little to a kind of grin, he toppled sidewise and as he struck the floor he straightened his right arm until the muzzle of the big automatic was jammed into Demetrios' stomach.

The dark doorway was suddenly crowded with faces, men. Doyle and Kessler and two detectives from the Ninth Precinct Station came into the room. One of the detectives picked up Picelli's and Demetrios' guns, the other knelt beside June Neilan.

Doyle went past Green and stood looking down at

Costain. Costain had emptied the big automatic into Demetrios' stomach; he rolled over and raised his head a little, grinned up at Doyle, then at Green.

"That was a good job," he whispered. "That was the best job I've ever done..."

His head fell back. Doyle stooped over him.

"He'll be all right, I think," Green said slowly. "I tried to shoot him in the leg and in the shoulder..." He turned to Kessler with a very faraway expression on his face. "I wonder why."

The detective kneeling beside June Neilan looked up. "The gal hasn't got a scratch," he mumbled. "She bumped her head on the door when she fell but that's all."

Green said: "I guess she fainted. Costain's a lousy shot."

He peeled off his overcoat and his suit coat, sat down and rolled up his shirtsleeve. The wound on the arm was slight, a crease; one of the detectives wrapped a clean handkerchief around it and tied it.

Kessler was staring blankly at Costain. "I still don't get it," he stuttered. "How many times can you kill one guy? Who was the guy they—they found on the tracks?"

Doyle was at the phone.

Green smiled at Kessler. "That'd be Gino," he said. "Picelli tipped Costain that Gino and Tony were running out on him with all the syndicate's dough. Costain left the ticker at Tony's and then caught up with Gino on the late Boston train. He probably got the bright idea that if he made it look like he'd been killed he could sneak back to a spot where he could watch the apartment, he might catch Demetrios and his girl friend in the act."

Doyle hung up the receiver and turned to listen.

"He's probably been suspicious of them for a week or so," Green went on. "That was his reason for keeping away from her until Demetrios showed. He planted his things on Gino and tossed him under the train; he wasn't sure it'd work or how long it'd take for 'em to find what was left of Gino, so he called Picelli and told him to check on it. Picelli checked and sure enough, the report had gone out that Costain's body had been found. Then all Costain had to do was wait for Demetrios to turn up to break the big news to the girl."

Green rolled his shirtsleeve down and got up and put on his coat.

"Picelli shot Solly Allenberg tonight because Solly drove Costain to the corner of Bleecker and Thompson. That's about a half-block from where Maxie Sillmann lives and Maxie's the boy who specializes in plain and fancy pineapples. Costain wanted to be sure no one got to Solly because Solly knew a little bit too much about the whole business, and he probably had Picelli watching him. My guess is that Picelli called him back and told him Solly and I were in the bar and that I'd been at Tony's after the blast, so Costain told Picelli to let both of us have it."

Green was looking at Picelli. Picelli nodded slightly.

Kessler had perked up amazingly; he suddenly dashed for the telephone.

Green said: "Wait a minute, Blondie. I've get a couple of important calls to make."

He crossed to the telephone and sat down and called the Receiving Hospital, asked about Solly Allenberg. He waited a minute, then shook his head and whispered, "That's too bad," hung up the receiver and looked at Kessler. "I'll take that fifty, now," he said softly.

Printed in the United States
208799BV00002B/26/A